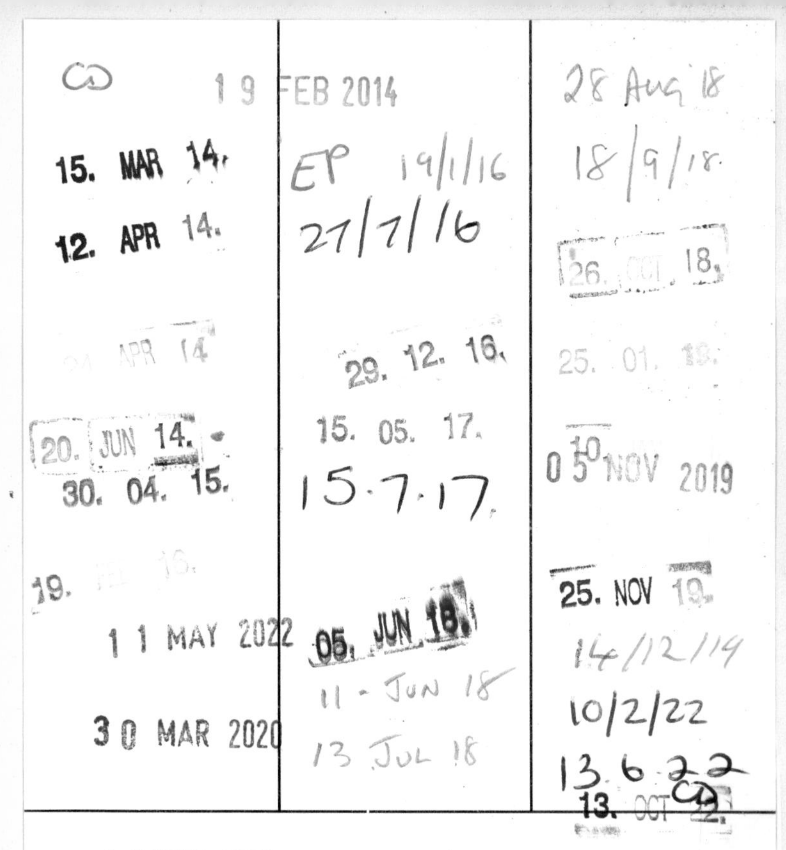

By James S. A. Corey

The Expanse
Leviathan Wakes
Caliban's War
Abaddon's Gate
Cibola Burn

ABADDON'S GATE

BOOK THREE OF THE EXPANSE

JAMES S. A. COREY

www.orbitbooks.net

ORBIT

First published in Great Britain in 2013 by Orbit
Reprinted 2013 (three times)

All characters and events in this publication, other than those clearly in the public domain, are fictitious and any resemblance to real persons, living or dead, is purely coincidental.

A CIP catalogue record for this book is available from the British Library.

ISBN 978-1-84149-992-5

Printed and bound by CPI Group (UK) Ltd, Croydon, CR0 4YY

Papers used by Orbit are from well-managed forests and other responsible sources.

MIX
Paper from responsible sources
FSC® C104740

Orbit
An imprint of
Little, Brown Book Group
100 Victoria Embankment
London EC4Y 0DY

An Hachette UK Company
www.hachette.co.uk

www.orbitbooks.net

For Walter Jon Williams, who showed us how to do it, and for Carrie Vaughn, who made sure we didn't screw it up too badly

Prologue: Manéo

Manéo Jung-Espinoza—Néo to his friends back on Ceres Station—huddled in the cockpit of the little ship he'd christened the *Y Que*. After almost three months, there were maybe fifty hours left before he made history. The food had run out two days before. The only water that was left to drink was half a liter of recycled piss that had already gone through him more times than he could count. Everything he could turn off, he'd turned off. The reactor was shut down. He still had passive monitors, but no active sensors. The only light in the cockpit came from the backsplash of the display terminals. The blanket he'd wrapped himself in, corners tucked into his restraints so it wouldn't float away, wasn't even powered. His broadcast and tightbeam transmitters were both shut off, and he'd slagged the transponder even before he'd painted the name on her hull. He hadn't flown this far just to have some kind of accidental blip alert the flotillas that he was coming.

Fifty hours—less than that—and the only thing he had to do was not be seen. And not run into anything, but that part was in *las manos de Dios.*

His cousin Evita had been the one who introduced him to the underground society of slingshots. That was three years ago, just before his fifteenth birthday. He'd been hanging at his family hole, his mother gone to work at the water treatment plant, his father at a meeting with the grid maintenance group that he oversaw, and Néo had stayed home, cutting school for the fourth time in a month. When the system announced someone waiting at the door, he'd figured it was school security busting him for being truant. Instead, Evita was there.

She was two years older, and his mother's sister's kid. A real Belter. They had the same long, thin bodies, but she was *from* there. He'd had a thing for Evita since the first time he saw her. He'd had dreams about what she'd look like with her clothes off. What it would feel like to kiss her. Now here she was, and the place to himself. His heart was going three times standard before he opened the door.

"Esá, unokabátya," she said, smiling and shrugging with one hand.

"Hoy," he'd said, trying to act cool and calm. He'd grown up in the massive city in space that was Ceres Station just the way she had, but his father had the low, squat frame that marked him as an Earther. He had as much right to the cosmopolitan slang of the Belt as she had, but it sounded natural on her. When he said it, it was like he was putting on someone else's jacket.

"Some coyos meeting down portside. Silvestari Campos back," she said, her hip cocked, her mouth soft as a pillow, and her lips shining. "Mit?"

"Que no?" he'd said. "Got nothing better."

He'd figured out afterward that she'd brought him because Mila Sana, a horse-faced Martian girl a little younger than him, had a thing, and they all thought it was funny to watch the ugly inner girl padding around after the half-breed, but by then he didn't care. He'd met Silvestari Campos and he'd heard of slingshotting.

Went like this: Some coyo put together a boat. Maybe it was salvage. Maybe it was fabbed. Probably at least some of it was stolen. Didn't need to be much more than a torch drive, a crash couch, and enough air and water to get the job done. Then it was all about plotting the trajectory. Without an Epstein, torch drive burned pellets too fast to get anyone anywhere. At least not without help. The trick was to plot it so that the burn—and the best only ever used one burn—would put the ship through a gravity assist, suck up the velocity of a planet or moon, and head out as deep as the push would take them. Then figure out how to get back without getting dead. Whole thing got tracked by a double-encrypted black net as hard to break as anything that the Loca Greiga or Golden Bough had on offer. Maybe they ran it. It was illegal as hell, and somebody was taking the bets. Dangerous, which was the point. And then when you got back, everyone knew who you were. You could lounge around in the warehouse party and drink whatever you wanted and talk however you wanted and drape your hand on Evita Jung's right tit and she wouldn't even move it off.

And just like that, Néo, who hadn't ever cared about anything very much, developed an ambition.

"The thing people have to remember is that the Ring isn't magical," the Martian woman said. Néo had spent a lot of time in the past months watching the newsfeeds about the Ring, and so far he liked her the best. Pretty face. Nice accent. She wasn't as thick as an Earther, but she didn't belong to the Belt either. Like him. "We don't understand it yet, and we may not for decades. But the last two years have given us some of the most interesting and exciting breakthroughs in materials technology since the wheel. Within the next ten or fifteen years, we're going to start seeing the applications of what we've learned from watching the protomolecule, and it will—"

"Fruit. Of. A poisoned. Tree," the old, leathery-looking coyo beside her said. "We cannot allow ourselves to forget that this was built from mass murder. The criminals and monsters at Protogen and Mao-Kwik released this weapon on a population of innocents. That slaughter began all of this, and profiting from it makes us all complicit."

The feed cut to the moderator, who smiled and shook his head at the leathery one.

"Rabbi Kimble," the moderator said, "we've had contact with an undisputed alien artifact that took over Eros Station, spent a little over a year preparing itself in the vicious pressure cooker of Venus, then launched a massive complex of structures just outside the orbit of Uranus and built a thousand-kilometer-wide ring. You can't be suggesting that we are morally required to ignore those facts."

"Himmler's hypothermia experiments at Dachau—" the leathery coyo began, wagging his finger in the air, but now it was the pretty Martian's turn to interrupt.

"Can we move past the 1940s, please?" she said, smiling in a way that said, *I'm being friendly but shut the fuck up.* "We're not talking about space Nazis here. This is the single most important event in human history. Protogen's role in it was terrible, and they've been punished for it. But now we have to—"

"Not *space* Nazis!" the old coyo yelled. "The Nazis aren't from *space*. They are right here among us. They are the beasts of our worst nature. By profiting from these discoveries, we *legitimize* the path by which we came to them."

The pretty one rolled her eyes and looked at the moderator like she wanted help. The moderator shrugged at her, which only made the old one angrier.

"The Ring is a temptation to sin," the old coyo shouted. There were little flecks of white at the corners of his mouth that the video editor had chosen to leave visible.

"We don't know what it is," the pretty one said. "Given that it was intended to do its work on primordial Earth with single-celled organisms and wound up on Venus with an infinitely more complex substrate, it probably doesn't work at all, but I can say that temptation and sin have nothing to do with it."

"They are victims. Your 'complex substrate'? It is the corrupted bodies of the innocent!"

Néo turned down the feed volume and just watched them gesture at each other for a while.

It had taken him months to plan out the trajectory of the *Y Que*, finding the time when Jupiter, Europa, and Saturn were all in the right positions. The window was so narrow it had been like throwing a dart from a half klick away and pinning a fruit fly's wing with it. Europa had been the trick. A close pass on the Jovian moon, then down so close to the gas giant that there was almost drag. Then out again for the long trip past Saturn, sucking more juice out of its orbital velocity, and then farther out into the black, not accelerating again, but going faster than anyone would imagine a little converted rock hopper could manage. Through millions of klicks of vacuum to hit a bull's-eye smaller than a mosquito's asshole.

Néo imagined the expressions of all the science and military ships parked around the Ring when a little ship, no transponder and flying ballistic, appeared out of nowhere and shot straight through the Ring at a hundred and fifty thousand kilometers per hour. After that, he'd have to move fast. He didn't have enough fuel left to kill all his velocity, but he'd slow down enough that they could get a rescue ship to him.

He'd do some time in slam, that was sure. Maybe two years, if the magistrates were being pissy. It was worth it, though. Just the messages from the black net where all his friends were tracking him with the constant and rising chorus of *holy shit it's going to work* made it worth it. He was going down in history. In a hundred years, people were still going to be talking about the biggest-balled slingshot ever. He'd lost months building the *Y Que*, more than that in transit, then jail time after. It was worth it. He was going to live forever.

Twenty hours.

The biggest danger was the flotilla surrounding the Ring. Earth and Mars had kicked each other's navies into creaky old men months ago, but what was left was mostly around the Ring. Or else down in the inner planets, but Néo didn't care about them. There were maybe twenty or thirty big military ships watching each other while every science vessel in the system peeked and listened and floated gently a couple thousand klicks from the Ring. All the navy muscle there to make sure no one touched. Scared, all of them. Even with all that metal and ceramic crammed into the same little corner of space, even with the relatively tiny thousand klicks across what was the inner face of the Ring, the chances that he'd run into anything were trivial. There was a lot more nothing than something. And if he did hit one of the flotilla ships, he wasn't going to be around to worry about it, so he just gave it up to the Virgin and started setting up the high-speed camera. When it finally happened, it would be so fast, he wouldn't even know whether he'd made the mark until he analyzed the data. And he was making sure there was going to be a record. He turned his transmitters back on.

"Hoy," he said into the camera, "Néo here. Néo solo. Captain and crew of souverän Belt-racer *Y Que*. Mielista me. Got six hours until biggest slipper since God made man. Es pa mi mama, the sweet Sophia Brun, and Jesus our Lord and Savior. Watch close. Blink it and miss, que sa?"

He watched the file. He looked like crap. He probably had time; he could shave the ratty little beard off and at least tie back his hair. He wished now he'd kept up with his daily exercises so he wouldn't look so chicken-shouldered. Too late now. Still, he could mess with the camera angle. He was ballistic. Wasn't like there was any thrust gravity to worry about.

He tried again from two other angles until his vanity was satisfied, then switched to the external cameras. His introduction was a little over ten seconds long. He'd start the broadcast twenty seconds out, then switch to the exterior cameras. More than a thousand frames per second, and it still might miss the Ring between images. He had to hope for the best. Wasn't like he could get another camera now, even if a better one existed.

He drank the rest of his water and wished that he'd packed just a little more food. A tube of protein slush would have gone down really well. It'd be done soon. He'd be in some Earther or Martian brig where there would be a decent toilet and water to drink and prisoner's rations. He was almost looking forward to it.

His sleeping comm array woke up and squawked about a tightbeam. He opened the connection. The encryption meant it was from the black net, and sent long enough ago that it would reach him here. Someone besides him was showing off.

Evita was still beautiful, but more like a woman now than she'd been when he'd started getting money and salvage to build the *Y Que*. Another five years, she'd be plain. He'd still have a thing for her, though.

"Esá, unokabátya," she said. "Eyes of the world. Toda auge. Mine too."

She smiled, and just for a second, he thought maybe she'd lift her shirt. For good luck. The tightbeam dropped.

Two hours.

"I repeat, this is Martian frigate *Lucien* to the unidentified ship approaching the Ring. Respond immediately or we will open fire."

Three minutes. They'd seen him too soon. The Ring was still three minutes away, and they weren't supposed to see him until he had less than one.

Néo cleared his throat.

"No need, que sa? No need. This is the *Y Que*, racer out sa Ceres Station."

"Your transponder isn't on, *Y Que*."

"Busted, yeah? Need some help with that."

"Your radio's working just fine, but I'm not hearing a distress beacon."

"Not distressed," he said, pulling the syllables out for every extra second. He could keep them talking. "Ballistic is all. Can fire up the reactor, but it's going to take a couple minutes. Maybe you can come give a hand, eh?"

"You are in restricted space, *Y Que*," the Martian said, and Néo felt the grin growing on his face.

"No harm," he said. "No harm. Surrender. Just got to get slowed down a little. Firing it up in a few seconds. Hold your piss."

"You have ten seconds to change trajectory away from the Ring or we will open fire."

The fear felt like victory. He was doing it. He was on target for the Ring and it was freaking them out. One minute. He started warming up the reactor. At this point, he wasn't even lying anymore. The full suite of sensors started their boot sequence.

"Don't fire," he said, as he made a private jacking-off motion. "Please, sir, please don't shoot me. I'm slowing down as fast as I can."

"You have five seconds, *Y Que*."

He had thirty seconds. The friend-or-foe screens popped up as soon as the full ship system was on. The *Lucien* was going to pass close by. Maybe seven hundred klicks. No wonder they'd seen him. At that distance, the *Y Que* would light up the threat boards like it was Christmas. Just bad luck, that.

"You can shoot if you want, but I'm stopping as fast as I can," he said.

The status alarm sounded. Two new dots appeared on the display. *Hijo de puta* had actually launched torpedoes.

Fifteen seconds. He was going to make it. He started broadcast and the exterior camera. The Ring was out there somewhere, its thousand-kilometer span still too small and dark to make out with the naked eye. There was only the vast spill of stars.

"Hold fire!" he shouted at the Martian frigate. "Hold fire!"

Three seconds. The torpedoes were gaining fast.

One second.

As one, the stars all blinked out.

Néo tapped the monitor. Nothing. Friend-or-foe didn't show anything. No frigate. No torpedoes. Nothing.

"Now that," he said to no one and nothing, "is weird."

On the monitor, something glimmered blue and he pulled himself closer, as if being a few inches closer to the screen would make it all make sense.

The sensors that triggered the high-g alert took five hundredths of a second to trip. The alert, hardwired, took another three hundredths of a second to react, pushing power to the red LED and the emergency Klaxon. The little console telltale that pegged out with a ninety-nine-g deceleration warning took a glacial half second to excite its light-emitting diodes. But by that time Néo was already a red smear inside the cockpit, the ship's deceleration throwing him forward through the screen and into the far bulkhead in less time than it took a synapse to fire. For five long seconds, the ship creaked and strained, not just stopping, but being stopped.

In the unbroken darkness, the exterior high-speed camera kept up its broadcast, sending out a thousand frames per second of nothing.

And then, of something else.

Chapter One: Holden

When he'd been a boy back on Earth, living under the open blue of sky, one of his mothers had spent three years suffering uncontrolled migraines. Seeing her pale and sweating with pain had been hard, but the halo symptoms that led into it had almost been worse. She'd be cleaning the house or working through contracts for her law practice and then her left hand would start to clench, curling against itself until the veins and tendons seemed to creak with the strain. Next her eyes lost their focus, pupils dilating until her blue eyes had gone black. It was like watching someone having a seizure, and he always thought *this* time, she'd die from it.

He'd been six at the time, and he'd never told any of his parents how much the migraines unnerved him, or how much he dreaded them, even when things seemed good. The fear had become familiar. Almost expected. It should have taken the edge off the terror, and maybe it did, but what replaced it was a sense of being trapped. The assault could come at any time, and it could not be avoided.

It poisoned everything, even if it was only a little bit.

It felt like being haunted.

"The house always wins," Holden shouted.

He and the crew—Alex, Amos, Naomi—sat at a private table in the VIP lounge of Ceres' most expensive hotel. Even there, the bells, whistles, and digitized voices of the slot machines were loud enough to drown out most casual conversation. The few frequencies they weren't dominating were neatly filled in by the high-pitched clatter of the pachinko machines and the low bass rumble of a band playing on one of the casino's three stages. All of it added up to a wall of sound that left Holden's guts vibrating and his ears ringing.

"What?" Amos yelled back at him.

"In the end, the house always wins!"

Amos stared down at an enormous pile of chips in front of him. He and Alex were counting and dividing them in preparation for their next foray out to the gaming tables. At a glance, Holden guessed they'd won something like fifteen thousand Ceres new yen in just the last hour. It made an impressive stack. If they could quit now, they'd be ahead. But, of course, they wouldn't quit now.

"Okay," Amos said. "What?"

Holden smiled and shrugged. "Nothing."

If his crew wanted to lose a few thousand bucks blowing off steam at the blackjack tables, who was he to interfere? The truth was it wouldn't even put a dent in the payout from their most recent contract, and that was only one of three contracts they'd completed in the last four months. It was going to be a very flush year.

Holden had made a lot of mistakes over the last three years. Deciding to quit his job as the OPA's bagman and become an independent contractor wasn't one of them. In the months since he'd put up his shingle as a freelance courier and escort ship, the *Rocinante* had taken seven jobs, and all of them had been profitable. They'd spent money refitting the ship bow to stern. She'd had a tough couple of years, and she'd needed some love.

When that was done and they still had more money in their general account than they knew what to do with, Holden had asked for a crew wish list. Naomi had paid to have a bulkhead in their quarters cut out to join the two rooms. They now had a bed large enough for two people and plenty of room to walk around it. Alex had pointed out the difficulty in buying new military-grade torpedoes for the ship, and had requested a keel-mounted rail gun for the *Roci*. It would give them more punch than the point defense cannons, and its only ammunition requirements were two-pound tungsten slugs. Amos had spent thirty grand during a stopover on Callisto, buying them some after-market engine upgrades. When Holden pointed out that the *Roci* was already capable of accelerating fast enough to kill her crew and asked why they'd need to upgrade her, Amos had replied, "Because this shit is awesome." Holden had just nodded and smiled and paid the bill.

Even after the initial giddy rush of spending, they had enough to pay themselves salaries that were five times what they'd made on the *Canterbury* and keep the ship in water, air, and fuel pellets for the next decade.

Probably, it was temporary. There would be dry times too when no work came their way and they'd have to economize and make do. That just wasn't today.

Amos and Alex had finished counting their chips and were shouting to Naomi about the finer points of blackjack, trying to get her to join them at the tables. Holden waved at the waiter, who darted over to take his order. No ordering from a table screen here in the VIP lounge.

"What do you have in a scotch that came from actual grain?" Holden asked.

"We have several Ganymede distillations," the waiter said. He'd learned the trick of being heard over the racket without straining.

He smiled at Holden. "But for the discriminating gentleman from Earth, we also have a few bottles of sixteen-year Lagavulin we keep aside."

"You mean, like, actual scotch from Scotland?"

"From the island of Islay, to be precise," the waiter replied. "It's twelve hundred a bottle."

"I want that."

"Yes sir, and four glasses." The waiter tipped his head and headed off to the bar.

"We're going to play blackjack now," Naomi said, laughing. Amos was pulling a stack of chips out of his tray and pushing them across the table to her. "Want to come?"

The band in the next room stopped playing, and the background noise dropped to an almost tolerable level for a few seconds before someone started piping Muzak across the casino PA.

"Guys, wait a few minutes," Holden said. "I've bought a bottle of something nice, and I want to have one last toast before we go our separate ways for the night."

Amos looked impatient right up until the bottle arrived, and then spent several seconds cooing over the label. "Yeah, okay, this was worth waiting for."

Holden poured out a shot for each of them, then held his glass up. "To the best ship and crew anyone has ever had the privilege of serving with, and to getting paid."

"To getting paid!" Amos echoed, and then the shots disappeared.

"God damn, Cap," Alex said, then picked up the bottle to look it over. "Can we put some of this on the *Roci*? You can take it out of my salary."

"Seconded," Naomi said, then took the bottle and poured out four more shots.

For a few minutes, the stacks of chips and the lure of the card tables were forgotten. Which was all Holden had wanted. Just to keep these people together for a few moments longer. On every other ship he'd ever served on, hitting port was a chance to get away from the same faces for a few days. Not anymore. Not with this crew. He stifled an urge to say a maudlin, *I love you guys!* by drinking another shot of scotch.

"One last hit for the road," Amos said, picking up the bottle.

"Gonna hit the head," Holden replied, and pushed away from the table. He weaved a bit more than he expected on his walk to the restroom. The scotch had gone to his brain fast.

The restrooms in the VIP lounge were lush. No rows of urinals and sinks here. Instead, half a dozen doors that led to private facilities with their own toilet and sink. Holden pushed his way into one and latched it behind him. The noise level dropped almost to nothing as soon as the door closed. A little like stepping outside the world. It was probably designed that way. He was glad whoever built the casino had allowed for a place of relative calm. He wouldn't have been shocked to see a slot machine over the sink.

He put one hand on the wall to steady himself while he did his business. He was mid-stream when the room brightened for a moment and the chrome handle on the toilet reflected a faint blue light. The fear hit him in the gut.

Again.

"I swear to God," Holden said, pausing to finish and then zip up. "Miller, you better not be there when I turn around."

He turned around.

Miller was there.

"Hey," the dead man started.

" 'We need to talk,' " Holden finished for him, then walked to the sink to wash his hands. A tiny blue firefly followed him and landed on the counter. Holden smashed it with his palm, but when he lifted his hand nothing was there.

In the mirror, Miller's reflection shrugged. When he moved, it was with a sickening jerkiness, like a clockwork ticking through its motions. Human and inhuman both.

"Everyone's here at once," the dead man said. "I don't want to talk about what happened to Julie."

Holden pulled a towel out of the basket next to the sink, then leaned against the counter facing Miller and slowly dried his hands. He was trembling, the same as he always did. The sense of threat and evil was crawling up his spine, just the same way it always did. Holden hated it.

Detective Miller smiled, distracted by something Holden couldn't see.

The man had worked security on Ceres, been fired, and gone off hunting on his own, searching for a missing girl. He'd saved Holden's life once. Holden had watched when the asteroid station Miller and thousands of victims of the alien protomolecule had been trapped on crashed into Venus. Including Julie Mao, the girl Miller had searched for and then found too late. For a year, the alien artifact had suffered and worked its incomprehensible design under the clouds of Venus. When it rose, hauling massive structures up from the depths and flying out past the orbit of Neptune like some titanic sea creature translated to the void, Miller rose with it.

And now everything he said was madness.

"Holden," Miller said, not talking to him. Describing him. "Yeah, that makes sense. You're not one of them. Hey, you have to listen to me."

"Then you have to say something. This shit is out of hand. You've been doing your random appearing act for almost a year now, and you've never said even one thing that made sense. Not one."

Miller waved the comment away. The old man was starting to breathe faster, panting like he'd run a race. Beads of sweat glistened on his pale, gray-tinged skin.

"So there was this unlicensed brothel down in sector eighteen. We went in thinking we'd have fifteen, twenty in the box. More, maybe. Got there, and the place was stripped to the stone. I'm supposed to think about that. It means something."

"What do you want from me?" Holden said. "Just tell me what you *want*, all right?"

"I'm not crazy," Miller said. "When I'm crazy, they kill me.

God, did they kill me?" Miller's mouth formed a small O, and he began to suck air in. His lips were darkening, the blood under the skin turning black. He put a hand on Holden's shoulder, and it felt too heavy. Too solid. Like Miller had been remade with iron instead of bones. "It's all gone pear-shaped. We got there, but it's empty. The whole sky's empty."

"I don't know what that means."

Miller leaned close. His breath smelled like acetate fumes. His eyes locked on Holden, eyebrows raised, asking him if he understood.

"You've got to help me," Miller said. The blood vessels in his eyes were almost black. "They know I find things. They know you help me."

"You're dead," Holden said, the words coming out of him without consideration or planning.

"Everyone's dead," Miller said. He took his hand from Holden's shoulder and turned away. Confusion troubled his brow. "Almost. Almost."

Holden's terminal buzzed at him, and he took it out of his pocket. Naomi had sent DID YOU FALL IN? Holden began typing out a reply, then stopped when he realized he'd have no idea what to say.

When Miller spoke, his voice was small, almost childlike with wonder and amazement.

"Fuck. It *happened*," Miller said.

"What happened?" Holden said.

A door banged as someone else went into a neighboring stall, and Miller was gone. The smell of ozone and some rich organic volatiles like a spice shop gone rancid were all the evidence that he had been there. And that might only have been in Holden's imagination.

Holden stood for a moment, waiting for the coppery taste to leave his mouth. Waiting for his heartbeat to slow back down to normal. Doing what he always did in the aftermath. When the worst had passed, he rinsed his face with cold water and dried it with a soft towel. The distant, muffled sound of the gambling decks rose to a frenzy. A jackpot.

He wouldn't tell them. Naomi, Alex, Amos. They deserved to have their pleasure without the thing that had been Miller intruding on it. Holden recognized that the impulse to keep it from them was irrational, but it felt so powerfully like protecting them that he didn't question it much. Whatever Miller had become, Holden was going to stand between it and the *Roci.*

He studied his reflection until it was perfect. The carefree, slightly drunk captain of a successful independent ship on shore leave. Easy. Happy. He went back out to the pandemonium of the casino.

For a moment, it was like stepping back in time. The casinos on Eros. The death box. The lights felt a little too bright, the noises sounded a little too loud. Holden made his way back to the table and poured himself another shot. He could nurse this one for a while. He'd enjoy the flavor and the night. Someone behind him shrieked their laughter. Only laughter.

A few minutes later, Naomi appeared, stepping out of the bustle and chaos like serenity in a female form. The half-drunken, expansive love he'd felt earlier came back as he watched her make her way toward him. They'd shipped together on the *Canterbury* for years before he'd found himself falling in love with her. Looking back, every morning he'd woken up with someone else had been a lost opportunity to breathe Naomi's air. He couldn't imagine what he'd been thinking. He shifted to the side, making room for her.

"They cleaned you out?" he asked.

"Alex," she said. "They cleaned Alex out. I gave him my chips."

"You are a woman of tremendous generosity," he said with a grin.

Naomi's dark eyes softened into a sympathetic expression.

"Miller showed up again?" she asked, leaning close to be heard over the noise.

"It's a little unsettling how easily you see through me."

"You're pretty legible. And this wouldn't be Miller's first bathroom ambush. Did he make any more sense this time?"

"No," Holden said. "He's like talking to an electrical problem. Half the time I'm not sure he even knows I'm there."

"It can't really be Miller, can it?"

"If it's the protomolecule wearing a Miller suit, I think that's actually creepier."

"Fair point," Naomi said. "Did he say anything new, at least?"

"A little bit, maybe. He said something happened."

"What?"

"I don't know. He just said, 'It happened,' and blinked out."

They sat together for a few minutes, a private silence within the riot, her fingers interlaced with his. She leaned over, kissing his right eyebrow, and then pulled him up off the chair.

"Come on," she said.

"Where are we going?"

"I'm going to teach you how to play poker," she said.

"I know how to play poker."

"You think you do," she said.

"Are you calling me a fish?"

She smiled and tugged at him.

Holden shook his head. "If you want to, let's go back to the ship. We can get a few people together and have a private game. It doesn't make sense to do it here. The house always wins."

"We aren't here to win," Naomi said, and the seriousness in her voice made the words carry more than the obvious meaning. "We're here to play."

The news came two days later.

Holden was in the galley, eating takeout from one of the dock-side restaurants: garlic sauce over rice, three kinds of legumes, and something so similar to chicken, it might as well have been the real thing. Amos and Naomi were overseeing the loading of nutrients and filters for the air recycling systems. Alex, in the pilot's seat, was asleep. On the other ships Holden had served aboard, having the full crew back on ship before departure required it was almost unheard of, and they'd all spent a couple of nights in dockside hotels before they'd come home. But they were home now.

Holden ran through the local feeds on his hand terminal, sipping news and entertainment from throughout the system. A security flaw in the new Bandao Solice game meant that financial and personal information from six million people had been captured on a pirate server orbiting Titan. Martian military experts were calling for increased spending to address the losses suffered in the battle around Ganymede. On Earth, an African farming coalition was defying the ban on a nitrogen-fixing strain of bacteria. Protesters on both sides of the issue were taking to the streets in Cairo.

Holden was flipping back and forth, letting his mind float on the surface of the information, when a red band appeared on one of the newsfeeds. And then another. And then another. The image above the article chilled his blood. The Ring, they called it. The gigantic alien structure that had left Venus and traveled to a point a little less than 2 AU outside Uranus' orbit, then stopped and assembled itself.

Holden read the news carefully as dread pulled at his gut. When he looked up, Naomi and Amos were in the doorway. Amos had his own hand terminal out. Holden saw the same red bands on that display.

"You seen this, Cap'n?" Amos asked.

"Yeah," Holden said.

"Some mad bastard tried to shoot the Ring."

"Yeah."

Even with the distance between Ceres and the Ring, the vast empty ocean of space, the news that some idiot's cheapjack ship had gone in one side of the alien structure and hadn't come out the other should have only taken about five hours. It had happened two days before. That's how long the various governments watching the Ring had been able to cover it up.

"This is it, isn't it?" Naomi said. "This is what happened."

Chapter Two: Bull

Carlos c de Baca—Bull to his friends—didn't like Captain Ashford. Never had.

The captain was one of those guys who'd sneer without moving his mouth. Before Ashford joined up with the OPA full-time, he'd gotten a degree in math from the Lunar Campus of Boston University, and he never let anyone forget it. It was like because he had a degree from an Earth university, he was better than other Belters. Not that he wouldn't be happy to bad-mouth guys like Bull or Fred who really had grown up down the well. Ashford wasn't one thing or another. The way he latched on to whatever seemed like it made him the big man—education, association with Earth, growing up in the Belt—made it hard not to tease him.

And Ashford was going to be in command of the mission.

"There's a time element too," Fred Johnson said.

Fred looked like crap. Too thin. Everyone looked too thin

these days, but Fred's dark skin had taken on an ashy overtone that left Bull thinking about things like autoimmune disorders or untreated cancer. Probably it was just stress, years, and malnutrition. Same thing that got everyone if nothing else did. Point of fact, Bull was looking a little gray around the temples too, and he didn't like the crap LEDs that were supposed to mimic sunlight. That he was still darker than an eggshell had more to do with a nut-brown Mexican mother than anything ultraviolet.

He'd been out in the dark since he was twenty-two. He was over forty now. And Fred, his superior officer under two different governments, was older than he was.

The construction gantry sloped out ahead of them, the flexible walls shining like snake scales. There was a constant low-level whine, the vibrations of the construction equipment carried along the flesh of the station. The spin gravity here was a little less than the standard one-third g on Tycho Station proper, and Ashford was making a little show of speeding up and then slowing down for the Earthers. Bull slowed his own steps down just a little to make the man wait longer.

"Time element? What's that look like, Colonel?" Ashford asked.

"Not as bad as it could be," Fred said. "The Ring hasn't made any apparent changes since the big one during the incident. No one else has gone through, and nothing's come out. People have backed down from filling their pants to just high alert. Mars is approaching this as a strictly military and scientific issue. They've got half a dozen science vessels on high burn already."

"How much escort?" Bull asked.

"One destroyer, three frigates," Fred said. "Earth is moving slower, but larger. They've got elections coming up next year, and the secretary-general's been catching hell about turning a blind eye to rogue corporate entities."

"Wonder why," Bull said dryly. Even Ashford smiled. Between Protogen and Mao-Kwikowski, the order and stability of the solar system had pretty much been dropped in a blender. Eros

Station was gone, taken over by an alien technology and crashed into Venus. Ganymede was producing less than a quarter of its previous food output, leaving every population center in the outer planets relying on backup agricultural sources. The Earth-Mars alliance was the kind of quaint memory someone's grandpa might talk about after too much beer. The good old days, before it all went to hell.

"He's putting on a show," Fred went on. "Media. Religious leaders. Poets. Artists. They're hauling them all out to the Ring so that every feed he can reach is pointed away from him."

"Typical," Ashford said, then didn't elaborate. Typical for a politician. Typical for an Earther. "What are we looking at out there?"

The gantry sang for a moment, an accident of harmonics setting it ringing and shaking until industrial dampers kicked in and killed the vibration before it reached the point of doing damage.

"All we've confirmed is that some idiot flew through the Ring at high ballistic speeds and didn't come out the other side," Fred said, moving his hands in the physical shrug of a Belter. "Now there's some kind of physical anomaly in the Ring. Could be that the idiot kid's ship got eaten by the Ring and converted into something. The ring sprayed a lot of gamma and X-rays, but not enough to account for the mass of the ship. Could be that he broke it. Could be that it opened a gate, and there's a bunch of little green men in saucers about to roll through and make the solar system into a truck stop."

"What—" Bull began, but Ashford talked over him.

"Any response from Venus?"

"Nothing," Fred said.

Venus was dead. For years after a corrupted Eros Station fell through its clouds, all human eyes had turned to that planet, watching as the alien protomolecule struggled in the violence and heat. Crystal towers kilometers high rose and fell away. Networks of carbon fibers laced the planet and degraded to nothing. The weapon had been meant to hijack simple life on Earth, billions of years before. Instead, it had the complex ecosystem of human bodies and the structures to sustain them in the toxic oven of Venus. Maybe it had taken longer to carry out its plan. Maybe having complex life to work with had made things easier. Everything pointed to it being finished with Venus. And all that really mattered was it had launched a self-assembling ring in the emptiness outside the orbit of Uranus that sat there dead as a stone.

Until now.

"What are we supposed to do about it?" Bull asked. "No offense, but we don't got the best science vessels. And Earth and Mars blew the crap out of each other over Ganymede."

"Be there," Fred said. "If Earth and Mars send their ships, we send ours. If they put out a statement, we put out one of our own. If they lay a claim on the Ring, we counterclaim. What we've done to make the outer planets into a viable political force has reaped real benefits, but if we start letting them lead, it could all evaporate."

"We planning to shoot anybody?" Bull asked.

"Hopefully it won't come to that," Fred said.

The gantry's gentle upward slope brought them to a platform arch. In the star-strewn blackness, a great plain of steel and ceramic curved away above them, lit by a thousand lights. Looking out at it was like seeing a landscape—this was too big to be something humans had made. It was like a canyon or a mountain. The meadow-filled caldera of some dead volcano. The scale alone made it impossible to see her as a ship. But she was. The construction mechs crawling along her side were bigger than the house Bull had lived in as a boy, but they looked like football players on a distant field. The long, thin line of the keel elevator stretched along the body of the drum to shuttle personnel from engineering at one end to ops at the other. The secondary car, stored on the exterior, could hold a dozen people. It looked like a grain of salt. The soft curve was studded with turreted rail guns and the rough, angry extrusions of torpedo tubes.

Once, she'd been the *Nauvoo*. A generation ship headed to the stars carrying a load of devout Mormons with only an engineered ecosystem and an unshakable faith in God's grace to see them through. Now she was the *Behemoth*. The biggest, baddest weapons platform in the solar system. Four *Donnager*-class battleships would fit in her belly and not touch the walls. She could accelerate magnetic rounds to a measurable fraction of *c*. She could hold more nuclear torpedoes than the Outer Planets Alliance actually had. Her communications laser was powerful enough to burn through steel if they gave it enough time. Apart from painting teeth on her and welding on an apartment building–sized shark-fin, nothing could have been more clearly or effectively built to intimidate.

Which was good, because she was a retrofitted piece of crap, and if they ever got in a real fight, they were boned. Bull slid a glance at Ashford. The captain's chin was tilted high and his eyes were bright with pride. Bull sucked his teeth.

The last threads of weight let go as the platform and gantry matched to the stillness of the *Behemoth*. One of the distant construction mechs burst into a sun-white flare as the welding started.

"How long before we take her out?" Ashford asked.

"Three days," Fred said.

"Engineering report said the ship'll be ready in about ten," Bull said. "We planning to work on her while we're flying?"

"That was the intention," Fred said.

"Because we could wait another few days here, do the work in dock, and burn a little harder going out, get the same arrival."

The silence was uncomfortable. Bull had known it would be, but it had to be said.

"The crew's comfort and morale need as much support as the ship," Fred said, diplomacy changing the shapes of the words. Bull had known him long enough to hear it. *The Belters don't want a hard burn.* "Besides which, it's easier to get the in-transit work done in lower g. It's all been min-maxed, Bull. You ship out in three."

"Is that a problem?" Ashford said.

Bull pulled the goofy grin he used when he wanted to tell the truth and not get in trouble for it.

"We're heading out to throw gang signs at Earth and Mars while the Ring does a bunch of scary alien mystery stuff. We've got a crew that's never worked together, a ship that's half salvage, and not enough time to shake it all down. Sure it's a problem, but it's not one we can fix, so we'll do it anyway. Worst can happen is we'll all die."

"Cheerful thought," Ashford said. The disapproval dripped off him. Bull's grin widened and he shrugged.

"Going to happen sooner or later."

Bull's quarters on Tycho Station were luxurious. Four rooms, high ceilings, a private head with an actual water supply. Even as a kid back on Earth, he hadn't lived this well. He'd spent his childhood in a housing complex in the New Mexican Shared Interest Zone, living with his parents, grandmother, two uncles, three aunts, and about a thousand cousins, seemed like. When he turned sixteen and declined to go on basic, he'd headed south to Alamogordo and worked his two-year service stripping down ancient solar electricity stations from the bad old days before fusion. He'd shared a dorm with ten other guys. He could still picture them, the way they'd been back then, all skinny and muscled with their shirts off or tied around their heads. He could still feel the New Mexican sun pressing against his chest like a hand as he basked in the radiation and heat of an uncontrolled fusion reaction, protected only by distance and the wide blue sky.

When his two-year stint was up, he tried tech school, but he'd gotten distracted by hormones and alcohol. Once he'd dropped out, his choices were pretty much just the military or basic. He'd chosen the one that felt less like death. In the Marines, he'd never had a bunk larger than the front room of his Tycho Station quarters. He hadn't even had a place that was really his own until he mustered out. Ceres Station hadn't been a good place for him. The hole he'd taken had been up near the center of spin, low g and high Coriolis. It hadn't been much more than a place to go sleep off last night's drunk, but it had been his. The bare, polished-stone walls, the ship surplus bed with restraining straps for low g. Some previous owner had chiseled the words BESSO O NADIE into the wall. It was Belter cant for *better or nothing*. He hadn't known it was a political slogan at the time. The things he'd gotten since coming to Tycho Station—the frame cycling through a dozen good family pictures from Earth, the tin Santos candleholder that his ex-girlfriend hadn't taken when she left, the civilian clothes—would have filled his old place on Ceres and not left room for him to sleep. He had too much stuff. He needed to pare it down.

But not for this assignment. The XO's suite on the *Behemoth* was bigger.

The system chimed, letting him know someone was at the door. From long habit, Bull checked the video feed before he opened the door. Fred was shifting from one foot to the other. He was in civilian clothes. A white button-down and grandpa pants that tried to forgive the sag of his belly. It was a losing fight. Fred wasn't out of shape any more than Bull was. They were just getting old.

"Hey," Bull said. "Grab a chair anywhere. I'm just getting it all together."

"Heading over now?"

"Want to spend some time on the ship before we take her out," Bull said. "Check for stray Mormons."

Fred looked pained.

"I'm pretty sure we got them all out the first time," he said, playing along. "But it's a big place. You can look around if you want."

Bull opened his dresser, his fingers counting through T-shirts. He had ten. There was a sign of decadence. Who needed ten T-shirts? He pulled out five and dropped them on the chair by his footlocker.

"It's going to be all kinds of hell if they get rights to the *Nauvoo* back," he said. "All the changes we're making to her."

"They won't," Fred said. "Commandeering the ship was perfectly legal. It was an emergency. I could list you ten hours of precedent."

"Yeah, but then we salvaged it ourselves and called it ours," Bull said. "That's like saying I've got to borrow your truck, but since I ran it into a ditch and hauled it back out, it's mine now."

"Law is a many-splendored thing, Bull," Fred said. He sounded tired. Something else was bothering him. Bull opened another drawer, threw half his socks into the recycler, and put the others on his T-shirts.

"Just if the judge doesn't see it that way, could be awkward," Bull said.

"The judges on Earth don't have jurisdiction," Fred said. "And the ones in our court system are loyal to the OPA. They know the big picture. They're not going to take our biggest ship off the board and hand it back over. Worst case, they'll order compensation."

"Can we afford that?"

"Not right now, no," Fred said.

Bull snorted out a little laugh. "Ever wonder what we did wrong that got us here? You're driving one of the biggest desks in the OPA, and I'm XO to Ashford. That ain't a sign we've been living our lives right, man."

"About that," Fred said. "We've had a little change of plan."

Bull opened his closet, his lips pressing thin. Fred hadn't just come to chew the fat. There was a problem. Bull took two suits out of the closet, both still wrapped in sticky preservative film. He hadn't worn either one in years. They probably didn't fit.

"Ashford thought it would be better to have Michio Pa as the XO. We talked about it. I'm reassigning you as chief security officer."

"Third-in-command now," Bull said. "What? Ashford think I was going to frag him and take his chair?"

Fred leaned forward, his fingers laced. The gravity of his

expression said he knew it was a crap situation but was making the best of it.

"It's all about how it looks," Fred said. "This is the OPA's navy. The *Behemoth* is the Belt's answer to Mars' and Earth's heaviest hitters. Having an Earther on the bridge doesn't send the right message."

"All right," Bull said.

"I'm in the same position. You know that. Even after all this time, I have to work twice as hard to command loyalty and respect because of where I'm from. Even the ones who like having me around because they think I make Earth look weak don't want to take orders from me. I've had to earn and re-earn every scrap of respect."

"Okay," Bull said. Security officer was going to mean less time in uniform. With a sigh, he put both suits on the chair.

"I'm not saying that you haven't," Fred said. "No one knows better than I do that you're the best of the best. There are just some constraints we have to live with. To get the job done."

Bull leaned against the wall, his arms crossed. Fred looked up at him from under frost-colored brows.

"Sir, I been flying with you for a long time," Bull said. "If you need to ask me something, you can just do it."

"I need you to make this work," Fred said. "What's going on out there is the most important thing in the system, and we don't know what it is. If we embarrass ourselves or give the inner planets some critical advantage, we stand to lose a lot of ground. Ashford and Pa are good people, but they're Belters. They don't have the same experience working with Earth forces that you and I do."

"You think they're going to start something?"

"No. Ashford will try his hardest to do the right thing, but he'll react like a Belter and be surprised when other people don't."

"Ashford has only *ever* done a right thing because he's afraid of being embarrassed. He's a pretty uniform surrounding vacuum. And you can't rely on that."

"I'm not," Fred agreed. "I'm sending you out there because I trust you to make it work."

"But you're not giving me command."

"But I'm not giving you command."

"How about a raise?"

"Not that either," Fred said.

"Well, heck," Bull said. "All the responsibility and none of the power? How can I turn down an offer like that?"

"No joking. We're screwing you over, and the reasons are all optics and political bullshit. But I need you to take it."

"So I'll take it," Bull said.

For a moment, the only sound was the quiet ticking of the air recycler. Bull turned back to the task of putting his life in a footlocker again. Somewhere far above him, hidden by tons of steel and ceramic, raw stone and vacuum, *Behemoth* waited.

Chapter Three: Melba

When she walked into the gambling house, Melba felt eyes on her. The room was lit by the displays on the game decks, pink and blue and gold. Most of them were themed around sex or violence, or both. Press a button, spend your money, and watch the girls put foreign and offensive objects inside themselves while you waited to see whether you'd won. Slot machines, poker, real-time lotteries. The men who played them exuded an atmosphere of stupidity, desperation, and an almost tangible hatred of women.

"Darling," an immensely fat man said from behind the counter. "Don't know where you think you come to, but you come in the wrong place. Maybe best you walk back out."

"I have an appointment," she said. "Travin."

The fat man's eyes widened under their thick lids. Someone in the gloom called out a vulgarity meant to unease her. It did, but she didn't let it show.

"Travin in the back, you want him, darling," the fat man said, nodding. At the far end of the room, through the gauntlet of leers and threat, a red metal door.

All of her instincts came from before, when she was Clarissa, and so they were all wrong now. From the time she'd been old enough to walk, she'd been trained in self-defense, but it had all been anti-kidnapping. How to attract the attention of the authorities, how to deescalate situations with her captors. There had been other work, of course. Physical training had been part of it, but the goal had always been to break away. To run. To find help.

Now that there was no one to help her, nothing quite applied. But it was what she had, so it was what she used. Melba—not Clarissa, *Melba*—nodded to the fat man and walked through the close-packed, dim room. The full gravity of Earth pulled on her like an illness. On one of the gambling decks, a cartoon woman was being sexually assaulted by three small gray aliens while a flying saucer floated above them. Someone had won a minor jackpot. Melba looked away. Behind her, an unseen man laughed, and she felt the skin at the back of her neck tighten.

Of all her siblings, she had most enjoyed the physical training. When it ended, she began studying tai chi with the self-defense instructor. Then, when she was fourteen, her father had made a joke about it at a family gathering. How learning to fight might make sense—he could respect that—but dancing while pretending to fight looked stupid and wasted time. She'd never trained again. That was ten years ago.

She opened the red door and walked through it. The office seemed almost bright. A small desk with a built-in display tuned to a cheap accounting system. White frosted glass that let in the sunlight but hid the streets of Baltimore. A formed plastic couch upholstered with the corporate logo of a cheap brand of beer that even people on basic could afford. Two hulking men sat on the couch. One had implanted sunglasses that made him look like an insect. The other wore a T-shirt that strained at his steroidal shoulders. She'd seen them before.

Travin was at the desk, leaning his thigh against it. His hair was cut close to the scalp, a dusting of white at the temples. His beard was hardly longer. He wore what passed for a good suit in his circles. Father wouldn't have worn it as a costume.

"Ah, look, the inimitable Melba."

"You knew I was here," she said. There were no chairs. No place to sit that wasn't already occupied. She stood.

" 'Course I did," Travin said. "Soon as you came off the street."

"Are we doing business?" she asked. Her voice cut the air. Travin grinned. His teeth were uncorrected and gray at the gums. It was an affectation of wealth, a statement that he was so powerful mere cosmesis was beneath him. She felt a hot rush of scorn. He was like an old cargo cultist; imitating the empty displays of power and no idea what they really meant. She was reduced to dealing with him, but at least she had the grace to be embarrassed by it.

"It's all done, miss," Travin said. "Melba Alzbeta Koh. Born on Luna to Alscie, Becca, and Sergio Koh, all deceased. No siblings. No taxation indenture. Licensed electrochemical technician. Your new self awaits, ah?"

"And the contract?"

"The *Cerisier* ships out, civilian support for the grand mission to the Ring. Our Miss Koh, she's on it. Senior class, even. Little staff to oversee, don't have to get your hands dirty."

Travin pulled a white plastic envelope from his pocket. The shadow of a cheap hand terminal showed through the tissue.

"All here, all ready," he said. "You take it and walk through the door a new woman, ah?"

Melba took her own hand terminal out of her pocket. It was smaller than the one in Travin's hand, and better made. She'd miss it. She thumbed in her code, authorized the transfer, and slid it back in her pocket.

"All right," she said. "The money's yours. I'll take delivery."

"Ah, there is still *one* problem," Travin said.

"We have an agreement," Melba said. "I did my part."

"And it speaks well of you," Travin said. "But doing business with you? I enjoy it, I think. Exciting discoveries to be made. Creating this new you, we have to put the DNA in the tables. We have to scrub out doubled records. I think you haven't been entirely honest with me."

She swallowed, trying to loosen the knot in her throat. The insect-eyed man on the couch shifted, his weight making the couch squeak.

"My money spends," she said.

"As it should, as it should," Travin said. "Clarissa Melpomene Mao, daughter to Jules-Pierre Mao of Mao-Kwikowski Mercantile. Very interesting name."

"Mao-Kwikowski was nationalized when my father went to jail," Melba said. "It doesn't exist anymore."

"Corporate death sentence," Travin said as he put the envelope on the desk display. "Very sad. But not for you, ah? Rich men know money. They find ways to put it where little eyes can't find. Get it to their wives, maybe. Their daughters."

She crossed her arms, scowling. On the couch, the bodybuilder stifled a yawn. It might even have been genuine. She let the silence stretch not because she wanted to pressure Travin to speak next, but because she didn't know what to say. He was right, of course. Daddy had taken care of all of them as best he could. He always had. Even the persecution of the United Nations couldn't reach everything. Clarissa had had enough money to live a quiet, retiring life on Luna or Mars and die of old age before the capital ran out. But she wasn't Clarissa anymore, and Melba's situation was different.

"I can give you another ten thousand," she said. "That's all I've got."

Travin smiled his gray smile.

"All that pretty money flown away, ah? And what takes you out into the darkness, eh? I wondered. So I looked. You are very, very good. Even knowing to squint, I didn't see more than shadows. Didn't hear more than echoes. But—" He put the envelope on the desk before him, keeping one finger on it the way her brother Petyr did when he was almost sure of a chess move but hadn't brought himself to commit. It was a gesture of ownership. "I have something no one else does. I know to look at the Ring."

"Ten thousand is all I have. Honestly. I've spent the rest."

"Would you need more, then?" Travin asked. "Investment capital, call it? Our little Melba can have ten thousand, if you want it. Fifty thousand if you need it. But I will want more back. Much more."

She felt her throat tighten. When she tilted her head, the movement felt too fast, too tight. Birdlike. Scared.

"What are you talking about?" she asked, willing her voice to sound solid. Formless threat hung in the air like bad cologne: masculine and cheap. When he spoke again, false friendliness curved all of his vowels.

"Partners. You are doing something big. Something with the Ring and the flotilla, ah? All these people heading out in the dark to face the monsters. And you are going with them. It seems to me that such a risk means you expect a very great return. The sort one expects from a Mao. You tell me what is your plan, I help you how I can help you, and what comes your way from this, we divide."

"No deal." The words were like a reflex. They came from her spine, the decision too obvious to require her brain.

Travin pulled back the envelope, the plastic hissing against the table. The soft tutting sound of tongue against teeth was as sympathetic as it was false.

"You have moved heaven and earth," he said. "You have bribed. You have bought. You have arranged. And when you say that you have held nothing in reserve, I believe you. So now you come to my table and tell me no deal? No deal is no deal."

"I paid you."

"I don't care. We are partners. *Full* partners. Whatever you are getting from this, I am getting too. Or else there are other people, I think, who would be very interested to hear about what the infamous Mao have been so quietly doing."

The two men on the couch were paying attention to her now. Their gazes were on her. She turned to look over her shoulder. The door to the gamblers' den was metal, and it was locked. The window was wide. The security wire in it was the sort that retracted if you wanted the glass to open and let the filthy breeze of the city in to soil the air. The insect-eyed one stood up.

Her implants were triggered by rubbing her tongue against the roof of her mouth. Two circles, counterclockwise. It was a private movement, invisible. Internal. Oddly sensual. It was almost as easy as just thinking. The suite of manufactured glands tucked in her throat and head and abdomen squeezed their little bladders empty, pouring complex chemistry into her blood. She shuddered. It felt like orgasm without the pleasure. She could feel conscience and inhibition sliding away like bad dreams. She was fully awake and alive.

All the sounds in the room—the roar of street traffic, the muffled cacophony of the gambling decks, Travin's nasty voice—went quieter, as if the cocktail flowing into her had stuffed foam in her ears. Her muscles grew tense and tight. The taste of copper filled her mouth. Time slowed.

What to do? What to do?

The thugs by the couch were the first threat. She moved over to them, gravity's oppressive grip forgotten. She kicked the bodybuilder in the kneecap as he rose, the little beer coaster of bone ripping free of its tendons and sliding up his thigh. His face was a cartoon of surprise and alarm. As he began to crumple, she lifted her other knee, driving it up into his descending larynx. She'd been aiming for his face. *Throat just as good*, she thought as the cartilage collapsed against her knee.

The insect-eyed one lunged for her. He moved quickly, his own body modified somehow. Fused muscular neurons, probably. Something to streamline the long, slow gap when the neurotransmitters floated across the synapses. Something to give him an edge when he was fighting some other thug. His hand fastened on her shoulder, wide, hard fingers grabbing at her. She turned in toward him, dropping to pull him down. Palm strike to the inside of the elbow to break his power, then both her hands around his wrist, bending it. None of her attacks were conscious or intentional. The movements came flowing out of a hindbrain that had been freed of restraint and given the time to plan its mayhem. It was no more a martial art than a crocodile taking down a water buffalo was; just speed, strength, and a couple billion years of survival instinct unleashed. Her tai chi instructor would have looked away in embarrassment.

The bodybuilder sloped down to the floor, blood pouring from his mouth. The insect-eyed man pulled away from her, which was the wrong thing to do. She hugged his locked joints close to her body and swung from her hips. He was bigger than she was, had lived in the gravity well all his life. He buffed up with steroids and his own cheap augmentations. She didn't need to be stronger than him, though. Just stronger than the little bones in his wrist and elbow. He broke, dropping to his knee.

Melba—not Clarissa—swung around him, sliding her right arm around his neck, then locking it with the left, protecting her own head from the thrashing that was about to come. She didn't need to be stronger than him, just stronger than the soft arteries that carried blood to his brain.

Travin's gun fired, gouging a hole in the couch. The little puff of foam was like a sponge exploding. No time. She shrieked, pulling the power of the scream into her arms, her shoulders. She felt the insect-eyed man's neck snap. Travin fired again. If he hit her, she'd die. She felt no fear, though. It had been locked away where she couldn't experience it. That would come soon. Very soon. It had to be done quickly.

He should have tried for a third bullet. It was the smart thing. The wise one. He was neither smart nor wise. He did what his body told him to and tried to get away. He was a monkey, and millions of years of evolution told him to flee from the predator. He didn't have time for another mistake. She felt another scream growing in her throat.

Time skipped. Her fingers were wrapped around Travin's neck. She'd been driving his skull into the corner of his desk. There was blood and scalp adhering to it. She pushed again, but he was heavy. There was no force behind her blow. She dropped him, and he fell to the floor moaning.

Moaning.

Alive, she thought. The fear was back now, and the first presentiment of nausea. He was still alive. He couldn't still be alive when the crash came. He'd had a gun. She had to find what had happened to it. With fingers quickly growing numb, she pulled the little pistol from under him.

"Partners," she said, and fired two rounds into his head. Even over the gambling decks, they had to have heard it. She forced herself to the metal door and checked the lock. It was bolted. Unless someone had a key or cut through it, she was all right. She could rest. They wouldn't call the police. She hoped they wouldn't call the police.

She slid to the floor. Sweat poured down her face and she began shaking. It seemed unfair that she'd lose time during the glorious and redemptive violence and have to fight to stay conscious through the physiological crash that followed, but she couldn't afford to sleep. Not here. She hugged her knees to her chest, sobbing not because she felt sorrow or fear, but because it was what her flesh did when she was coming down. Someone was knocking at the door, but the sound was uncertain. Tentative. Just a few minutes, and she'd be... not all right. Not that. But good enough. Just a few minutes.

This was why glandular modification had never taken root in the military culture. A squad of soldiers without hesitation or doubt, so full of adrenaline they could tear their own muscles and not care, might win battles. But the same fighters curled up and mewling for five minutes afterward would lose them again. It was a failed technology, but not an unavailable one. Enough money, enough favors to call in, and enough men of science who had been cured of conscience. It was easy. The easiest part of her plan, really.

Her sobs intensified, shifted. The vomiting started. She knew from experience that it wouldn't last long. Between retching, she watched the bodybuilder's chest heaving for air through his ruined throat, but he was already gone. The smell of blood and puke thickened the air. Melba caught her breath, wiping the back of her hand against her lips. Her sinuses ached, and she didn't know if it was from the retching or the false glands that lay in that tender flesh. It didn't matter.

The knocking at the door was more desperate now. She could make out the voice of the fat man by the door. No more time. She took the plastic envelope and shoved it in her pocket. Melba Alzbeta Koh crawled out the window and dropped to the street. She stank. There was blood on her hands. She was trembling with every step. The dim sunlight hurt, and she used the shadows of her hands to hide from it. In this part of Baltimore, a thousand people could see her and not have seen anything. The blanket of anonymity that the drug dealers and pimps and slavers arranged and enforced also protected her.

She'd be okay. She'd made it. The last tool was in place, and all she had to do was get to her hotel, drink something to put her electrolytes back in balance, and sleep a little. And then, in a few days, report for duty on the *Cerisier* and begin her long journey out to the edge of the solar system. Holding her spine straight, walking down the street, avoiding people's eyes, the dozen blocks to her room seemed longer. But she would do it. She would do whatever had to be done.

She had been Clarissa Melpomene Mao. Her family had controlled the fates of cities, colonies, and planets. And now Father sat in an anonymous prison, barred from speaking with anyone besides his lawyer, living out his days in disgrace. Her mother lived in a private compound on Luna slowly medicating herself to death. The siblings—the ones that were still alive—had scattered to whatever shelter they could find from the hatred of two worlds. Once, her family's name had been written in starlight and blood, and now they'd been made to seem like villains. They'd been destroyed.

She could make it right, though. It hadn't been easy, and it wouldn't be now. Some nights, the sacrifices felt almost unbearable, but she would do it. She could make them all see the injustice in what James Holden had done to her family. She would expose him. Humiliate him.

And then she would destroy him.

Chapter Four: Anna

Annushka Volovodov, Pastor Anna to her congregation on Europa—or Reverend Doctor Volovodov to people she didn't like—was sitting in the high-backed leather chair in her office when the wife beater arrived.

"Nicholas," she said, trying to put as much warmth into her voice as she could manage. "Thank you for taking the time."

"Nick," he said, then sat on one of the metal chairs in front of her desk. The metal chairs were lower than her own, which gave the room a vaguely courtroom-like setting, with her in the position of judge. It was why she never sat behind the desk when meeting with one of her parishioners. There was a comfortable couch along the back wall that was much better for personal conversations and counseling. But every now and then, the air of authority the big chair and heavy desk gave her was useful.

Like now.

"Nick," she said, then pressed her fingertips together and rested her chin on them. "Sophia came to see me this morning."

Nick shrugged, looking away like a schoolboy caught cheating on an exam. He was a tall man, with the narrow, raw-boned look outer planets types got from hard physical labor. Anna knew he worked in surface construction. Here on Europa, that meant long days in a heavy vacuum suit. The people who did that job were as tough as nails. Nick had the attitude of a man who knew how he looked to others, and used his air of physical competence to intimidate.

Anna smiled at him. *It won't work on me.*

"She wouldn't tell me what happened at first," she said. "It took a while to get her to lift her shirt. I didn't need to see the bruises, I knew they'd be there. But I did need pictures."

When she said *pictures*, he leaned forward, his eyes narrowing and shifting from side to side. He probably thought it made him look tough, threatening. Instead it made him look like a rodent.

"She fell—" he started.

"In the kitchen," Anna finished for him. "I know, she told me. And then she cried for a very long time. And then she told me you'd started hitting her again. Do you remember what I said would happen if you hit her again?"

Nick shifted in his chair, his long legs bouncing in front of him with nervous energy. His large, bony hands squeezing each other until the knuckles turned white. He wouldn't look directly at her. "I didn't mean to," he said. "It just happened. I could try the counseling again, I guess."

Anna cleared her throat, and when he looked at her she stared back until his legs stopped bouncing. "No, too late. We gave you the anger counseling. The church paid for you to go right up until you quit. We did that part. That part is done."

His expression went hard.

"Gonna give me one of those Jesus speeches? I am sick right up to here"—Nick held his hand under his chin—"with that shit. Sophia won't shut up about it. 'Pastor Anna says!' You know what? Fuck what Pastor fucking Anna says."

"No," Anna said. "No Jesus speeches. We're done with that too."

"Then what are we doing here?"

"Do you," she said, drawing the words out, "remember what I said would happen if you hit her again?"

He shrugged again, then pushed up out of the chair and walked away, putting his back to her. While pretending to stare at one of the diplomas hanging on the wall he said, "Why should I give a fuck what you say, *Pastor Anna*?"

Anna breathed a quiet sigh of relief. Preparing for this meeting, she'd been unsure if she'd actually be able to do what was needed. She had a strong, visceral dislike of dishonesty, and she was about to destroy someone by lying. Or if not lying, at least deceit. She justified it to herself by believing that the real purpose was to save someone. But she knew that wouldn't be enough. She'd pay for what she was about to do for a long time in sleepless nights and second-guessing. At least his anger would make it easy in the short term.

Anna offered a quick prayer: *Please help me save Sophia from this man who's going to kill her if I don't stop him.*

"I said," Anna continued at Nick's back, "that I would make sure you went to jail for it."

Nick turned around at that, a rodent's low cunning back on his face. "Oh yeah?"

"Yes."

He moved toward her in the low-gravity version of a saunter. It was intended to look threatening, but to Anna, who'd grown up down the well on Earth, it just looked silly. She suppressed a laugh.

"Sophia won't say shit," Nick said, walking up to her desk to stare down at her. "She knows better. She fell down in the kitchen, and she'll say it to the magistrates."

"That's true," Anna said, then opened the drawer of her desk and took the taser out. She held it in her lap where Nick couldn't see it. "She's terrified of you. But I'm not. I don't care about you at all anymore."

"Is that right?" Nick said, leaning forward, trying to frighten her by pushing into her personal space. Anna leaned toward him.

"But Sophia is a member of this congregation, and she is my friend. Her children play with my daughter. I love them. And if I don't do something, you're going to kill her."

"Like what?"

"I'm going to call the police and tell them you threatened me." She reached for her desk terminal with her left hand. It was a gesture meant to provoke. She might as well have said, *Stop me.*

He gave her a feral grin and grabbed her arm, squeezing the bones in her wrist together hard enough to ache. Hard enough to bruise. She pointed the taser at him with her other hand.

"What's that?"

"Thank you," she said, "for making this easier."

She shot him, and he drifted to the ground spasming. She felt a faint echo of the shock through his hand on her arm. It made her hair stand up. She pulled up her desk terminal and called Sophia.

"Sophia, honey, this is Pastor Anna. Please listen to me. The police are going to be coming to your house soon to ask about Nick. You need to show them the bruises. You need to tell them what happened. Nick will already be in jail. You'll be safe. But Nick confronted me when I asked him about what happened to you, and if you want to keep us both safe, you need to be honest with them."

After a few minutes of coaxing, she finally got Sophia to say she would talk to the police when they came. Nick was starting to move his arms and legs feebly.

"Don't move," Anna said to him. "We're almost done here."

She called the New Dolinsk Police Department. The Earth corporation that had once had the contract was gone, but there still seemed to be police in the tunnels, so someone had picked it up. Maybe a Belter company. Or the OPA itself. It didn't matter.

"Hello, my name is Reverend Doctor Annushka Volovodov. I'm the pastor at St. John's United. I'm calling to report an assault on my person. A man named Nicholas Trubachev tried to attack me when I confronted him about beating his wife. No, he didn't hurt me, just a few bruises on my wrist. I had a taser in my desk and used it before he could do anything worse. Yes, I'd be happy to give a statement when you arrive. Thank you."

"Bitch," Nick spat, trying to get off the floor on shaky limbs.

Anna shot him again.

"Tough day?" Nono asked when Anna finally got home. Nono was dandling their daughter on her lap, and little Nami gave a squeal and reached for Anna as soon as she closed the door behind her.

"How's my girl?" Anna said, and dropped onto the couch next to them with a long sigh. Nono handed the baby to her, and Nami immediately set about undoing Anna's bun and trying to pull her hair. Anna squeezed her daughter and took a long sniff off the top of her head. The subtle and powerful scent Nami had given off when they'd first brought her home had faded, but a faint trace of it was still there. Scientists might claim that humans lacked the ability to interact at the pheromonal level, but Anna knew that was baloney. Whatever chemicals Nami had been pumping out as a newborn were the most powerful drug Anna had ever experienced. It made her want to have another child just to smell it again.

"Namono, no hair pulling," Nono said, trying to untwist Anna's long red hair from the baby's fist. "Don't want to talk about it?" she said to Anna.

Nono's full name was Namono too. But she'd been Nono ever since her older twin had been able to speak. When Anna and Nono named their daughter after her, the name had somehow morphed into Nami. Most people probably had no idea the baby was named after one of her mothers.

"Eventually, yes," Anna said. "But I need baby time first."

She kissed Nami on her pug nose. The same broad flat nose as Nono, just below Anna's own bright green eyes. She had Nono's coffee-colored skin, but Anna's sharp chin. Anna could sit and stare at Nami for hours at a time, drinking in the astonishing melding of herself and the woman she loved. The experience was so powerful it bordered on the sacred. Nami stuck a lock of Anna's hair in her mouth, and Anna gently pulled it back out again, then blew a raspberry at her. "No eating the hair!" she said, and Nami laughed as though this was the funniest thing ever spoken.

Nono took Anna's hand and held it tightly. They didn't move for a long time.

Nono was cooking mushrooms and rice. She'd put some reconstituted onion in with it, and the strong scent filled the kitchen. Anna cut up apples at the table for a salad. The apples were small and not very crisp. Not good for munching, but they'd be fine in a Waldorf with enough other flavors and textures to hide their imperfections. And they were lucky to have them at all. The fruit was part of the first harvest to come off of Ganymede since the troubles there. Anna didn't like to think how hungry everyone would be without that moon's remarkable recovery.

"Nami will be asleep for at least another hour," Nono said. "Are you ready to talk about your day?"

"I hurt someone and I lied to the police today," Anna said. She pushed too hard on the knife and it slipped through the soft apple and scored her thumb. It wasn't deep enough to bleed.

"Well... okay, you'll have to explain that," Nono said, stirring a small bowl of broth into her rice and mushroom mix.

"No, I really can't. Some of what I know was told in confidence."

"This lie you told, it was to help someone?"

"I think so. I hope so," Anna said, putting the last bits of apple in the bowl, then adding nuts and raisins. She stirred in the dressing.

Nono stopped and turned to stare at her. "What will you do if you get caught in the lie?"

"Apologize," Anna said.

Nono nodded, then turned back to the pot of rice. "I turned on your desk terminal today to check my mail. You were still logged in. There was a message from the United Nations about the secretary-general's humanitarian committee project. All those people who they're sending out to the Ring."

Anna felt the sharp twist of guilt. Of having been caught out at something.

"Shit," she said. She didn't like profanity, but some occasions demanded it. "I haven't responded yet." It felt like another lie.

"Were we going to talk about it before you decided?"

"Of course, I—"

"Nami is almost two," Nono said. "We've been here two years. At some point, deciding to stay is deciding who Nami is going to be for the rest of her life. She has family in Russia and Uganda who've never seen her. If she stays here much longer, they never will."

Nami was being fed the same drug cocktail all newborns in the outer planets received. It encouraged bone growth and fought off the worst of the effects low-gravity environments had on childhood development. But Nono was right. If they stayed much longer, Nami would begin to develop the long, thin frame that came with life out there. To life in low gravity. Anna would be sentencing her to a life outside her home world forever.

"Europa was always supposed to be temporary," Anna said. "It was a good posting. I speak Russian, the congregation here is small and fragile..."

Nono turned off the stove and came to sit by her, holding her hand on the table. For the first time, the faux wood tabletop looked cheap to Anna. Tacky. She saw with startling clarity a future in which Nami never lived anywhere with real wood. It felt like a punch to the stomach.

"I'm not mad at you for coming here," Nono said. "This was our dream. Coming to places like this. But when you asked for the transfer out here, you were three months pregnant."

"I was so unlikely to be chosen," Anna said, and she could hear the defensiveness in her own voice.

Nono nodded. "But you *were* chosen. And this thing for the UN. Flying out to the Ring as part of the secretary-general's advisory group. And our baby not even two."

"I think two hundred people signed up for the same slot," Anna said.

"They chose you. They want you to go."

"It was so unlikely—" Anna started.

"They always choose you," Nono interrupted. "Because you are very special. Everyone can see it. I can see it. I saw it the first time I met you, giving your speech at the faith conference in Uganda. So nervous you dropped your notes, but I could've heard a pin drop in that auditorium. You couldn't help but shine."

"I stole you from your country," Anna said. It was what she always said when Nono brought up how they met. "The Ugandan church could have used a young minister like you."

"I stole you," Nono said, like she always said, only this time it had a disconcertingly pro forma feel. As though it were an annoying ritual to be rushed through. "But you always say this. 'There were so many others. I was so unlikely to be picked.' "

"It's true."

"It's the excuse you use. You've always been one to ask for forgiveness rather than permission."

"I won't go," Anna said, pushing her hand against her eyes and the tears that threatened there. Her elbow banged into the salad bowl, nearly knocking it off the table. "I haven't said yes to them. I'll tell them it was a mistake."

"Annushka," Nono said, squeezing her hand. "You *will* go. But I am taking Nami back to Moscow with me. She can meet her grandparents. Grow up in real gravity."

Anna felt a white-hot spike of fear shoot through her stomach. "You're leaving me?"

Nono's smile was a mix of exasperation and love.

"No. *You're* leaving *us*. For a little while. And when you come back, we will be waiting for you in Moscow. Your family. I will find us a nice place to live there, and Nami and I will make it a home. A place where we can be happy. But we will not go with you."

"Why?" was all Anna could think to say.

Nono got up and took two plates out of the cupboard, then dished up dinner and put it on the table. As she spooned Waldorf salad onto her plate she said, "I'm very afraid of that thing. The thing from Venus. I'm afraid of what it will mean for everything we care about. Humanity, God, our place in His universe. I'm afraid of what it will do, of course, but much more afraid of what it *means*."

"I am too," Anna said. It was the truth. In fact, it was part of the reason she'd asked to join the expedition when she heard it was being assembled. That same fear Nono was talking about. Anna wanted to look it in the eye. Give God a chance to help her understand it. Only then could she help anyone else with it.

"So go find the answers," Nono said. "Your family will be waiting for you when you get back."

"Thank you," Anna said, a little awed by what Nono was offering her.

"I think," Nono said around a mouthful of mushrooms and rice, "that maybe they will need people like you out there."

"Like me?"

"People who don't ask permission."

Chapter Five: Bull

"It's not in the budget," Michio Pa, executive officer of the *Behemoth*, said. If she'd been an Earther, she would have been a small woman, but a lifetime in microgravity had changed her the way it did all of them. Her arms, legs, and spine were all slightly elongated—not thin exactly. Just put together differently. Her head was larger than it would have been, and walking in the mild one-third-g thrust gravity, she stood as tall as Bull but still seemed perversely childlike. It made him feel shorter than he was.

"We might need to adjust that," he said. "When they put in the rail gun, they were treating it like we had standard bulkheads and supports. Thing is, the Mormons were really trying to cut back on mass. They used a lot of ceramics and silicates where the metals usually go. Directional stuff. We fire a round right now, we could shear the skin off."

Pa walked down the long, curving corridor. The ceiling arched above her, white and easily twice as high as required, an aesthetic gesture by designers who hadn't known they were building a warship. Her stride a little wider than his, moving a little more comfortably in the low g and making him trot slightly to keep up. It was one of a thousand small ways Belters reminded earthborn men and women that they didn't belong here. The XO shook her head.

"We came out here with an operational plan," she said. "If we start rewriting it every time we find an adjustment we'd like to make, we might as well not have bothered."

Privately, Bull thought the same thing, but with a different inflection. If he'd been XO, the operational plan would have been called a suggested guideline and only opened when he wanted a good laugh. Pa probably knew that. They reached the transit ramp, a softly sloping curve that led from the command and control levels at the head of the *Behemoth* down to the massive drum of her body. From Pa's domain to his.

"Look," Pa said, her mouth twitching into a conciliatory smile, "I'll make note of it for the refit, but I'm not going to start reallocating until I have an idea of the big picture. I mean, if I start pulling resources out of environmental control to cover this, and next week we find something that needs doing there, I'll just be pushing it back, right?"

Bull looked down the ramp. Soft lights recessed in the walls filled the air with a shadowless glow like a cheesy vision of heaven. Pa put her hand on his shoulder. She probably meant it to be sympathetic, but it felt like condescension.

"Yeah, okay," he said.

"It'll be all right, chief," she said, giving his trapezius a little squeeze. He nodded and walked down the ramp to the transfer platform. Her footsteps vanished behind him, submerging in the hum of air recyclers. Bull fought the urge to spit.

The *Behemoth*, back when she'd been the *Nauvoo*, had been built with a different life in mind. Most ships built for travel between the planets were like massive buildings, one floor above another with the thrust of the Epstein drive at the bottom providing the feeling of weight for whole voyages apart from a few hours in the middle when the ship flipped around to change from acceleration to slowing down. But Epstein or not, no ship could afford the power requirements or the heat generated by accelerating forever. Plus, Einstein had a thing or two to say about trying to move mass at relativistic speeds. The *Nauvoo* had been a generation ship, its journey measured in light-years rather than light-minutes. The percentage of its life span it could afford to spend under thrust was tiny by comparison. The command and control at the top of the ship and the main engines and the associated parts of engineering at the bottom could almost have belonged to a standard craft connected by a pair of kilometers-long shafts, one for a keel elevator to move people and another that gave access to the skin of the drum.

Everything else was built to spin.

For the centuries out to Tau Ceti, the body of the *Nauvoo* was meant to turn. Ten levels of environmental engineering, crew quarters, temples, schools, wastewater treatment, machine shops, and forges, and at the center, the vast interior. It would have been a piece of Earth curved back on itself. Soil and farmland and the illusion of open air with a central core of fusion-driven light and heat as gentle and warm as a summer day.

All the rooms and corridors in the body section—the vast majority of the ship—were built with that long, slow, endless season in mind. The brief periods of acceleration and deceleration at the journey's ends hardly mattered. Except that they were all the ship had now. Those places that should have been floors were all walls, and would be forever. The vast reinforced decks meant to carry a tiny world's worth of soil were the sides of a nearly unusable well. Someone slipping from the connection where the command and control levels met the great chamber could fall for nearly two full kilometers. Water systems built to take advantage of spin gravity and Coriolis stood on their sides, useless. The *Nauvoo* had been a marvel of human optimism and engineering, a statement of faith in the twinned powers of God and rigorous engineering. The *Behemoth* was a salvage job with mass accelerators strapped to her side that would do more damage to herself than to an enemy.

And Bull wasn't even allowed to fix the problems he knew about.

He passed through the transfer station and down toward his office. The rooms and corridors here were all built aslant, waiting for the spin gravity that would never come. Stretches of bare metal and exposed ducting spoke of the rush to finish it, and then to salvage and remake it. Just walking past them left Bull depressed.

Samara Rosenberg, longtime repair honcho on Tycho Station and now chief engineer on the *Behemoth*, was waiting in the anteroom, talking with Bull's new deputy. Serge, his name was, and Bull wasn't sure what he thought of the man. Serge had been part of the OPA before that was a safe thing to be. He had the traditional split circle insignia tattooed on his neck and wore it proudly. But like the rest of the security force, he'd been recruited by Michio Pa, and Bull didn't know exactly how things stood. He didn't trust the man yet, and distrust kept him from thinking all that well of him.

Sam, on the other hand, he liked.

"Hey, Bull," she said as he dropped onto the foam-core couch. "Did you get a chance to talk to the XO?"

"We talked," Bull said.

"What's the plan?" Sam said, folding her arms in a way that meant she already knew.

Bull ran a hand through his hair. When he'd been younger, his hair had been soft. Now it was like he could feel each strand individually against his fingertips. He pulled out his hand terminal and scrolled through. There were five reports waiting, three routine security reports and two occasionals—an injury report and a larceny complaint. Nothing that couldn't wait.

"Hey, Serge," Bull said. "You hold the fort here for an hour?"

"Anything you want, chief," Serge said with a grin. It was probably just paranoia that left Bull hearing contempt in the words.

"All right, then. Come on, Sam. I'll buy you a drink."

In a Coalition ship, back when there'd been an Earth-Mars Coalition, there would have been a commissary. In the OPA, there was a bar and a couple mom-and-pop restaurants along with a bare-bones keep-you-alive supply of prepack meals that anyone could get for the asking. The bar was in a wide space that might have been meant for a gymnasium or a ball court, big enough for a hundred people but Bull hadn't seen it with more than a couple dozen. The lighting had been swapped out for blue-and-white LEDs set behind sand-textured plastic. The tables were flat black and magnetized to hold the bulbs of beer and liquor to them. Nothing was served in glasses.

"Che-che!" the bartender called as Bull and Sam stepped through the door. "Moergen! Alles-mesa, you."

"Meh-ya," Sam replied, as comfortable with the mishmash Belter patois as Bull was with Spanish or English. It was her native tongue.

"What're you having?" Bull asked as he slid into one of the booths. He liked the ones where he could see the door. It was an old habit.

"I'm on duty," she said, sitting across from him.

Bull leaned forward, catching the barkeep's eye, and held up two fingers.

"Lemonades," he said.

"Sa sa!" the barkeep replied, lifting a fist in the equivalent of a nod. Bull sat back and looked at Sam. She was a pretty enough woman. Cute, with pixie-cut hair and a quick smile. There had been about a minute when they'd first met that Bull had seriously considered whether he found her attractive. But if he'd seen the same calculus in her, they'd gotten past it.

"Didn't go so good?" Sam asked.

"No."

Sam lifted her eyebrows and leaned her elbows against the tabletop. He sketched out Pa's objections and rationale, and Sam's expression shifted slowly into a fatalistic amusement.

"Waiting for the refit's all well and good," she said when he was done, "but if we try and test-fire that bad boy, it's going to make an awfully big owie."

"You're sure about that?"

"Not a hundred percent," she said. "High eighties, though."

Bull sighed out a tired obscenity as the barkeep brought the bulbs of lemonade. They were about the size of Bull's balled fists, citrus yellow with Плодоовощ малыша потехи printed on the side in bright red script.

"Maybe I should talk to her," Sam said. "If it came straight from me..."

"It came straight from you, probably it would work," he said, "and they get to tell me no on everything from now on. 'Bull asked for it? Well, if it was important, he'd have sent the Belter.' Right?"

"You really think it's about you not getting born up here?"

"Yeah."

"Well...you're probably right," Sam said. "Sorry about that."

"Comes with the territory," Bull said, pretending that it didn't bother him.

Sam plucked her lemonade off the table and took a long, thoughtful drink. The bulb clicked when the magnet readhered to the tabletop. "I've got nothing against inners. Worked with a lot of you guys, and didn't run into a higher percentage of assholes than when I'm dealing with Belters. But I have to get that rail gun's mounts reinforced. If there's a way to do that without undercutting you, I'm all for it."

"But if it's that or mess up the ship," Bull said, nodding. "Gimme a little time. I'll think of something."

"Start when you want to shoot someone and count back eighteen days," Sam said. "That's my deadline. Even if everyone's sober and working balls-out, my crew can't get it done faster than that."

"I'll think of something," Bull said.

The larceny complaint turned out to be from a repair and maintenance crew who couldn't agree how to store their tools. The injury report was a kid who got caught between a stretch of deck plating and someone driving a salvage mech. The cartilage in the kid's knee had gotten ground into about a dozen different bits of custard; the medic said a good clean bone break would have been better. The injured man would be fine, but he was off active duty for at least a month while all his pieces got glued back together.

The security reports were boilerplate, which either meant that things were going well or that the problems were getting glossed over, but probably they were going well. The trip out to the Ring was a shakedown cruise, and that always meant there'd be a little honeymoon period when the crew were all figuratively standing shoulder to shoulder and taking on the work. Everyone expected there'd be problems, so there was a grace period when morale didn't start heading down.

Chief security officer on an OPA ship was a half-assed kind of position, one part cop, one part efficiency expert, and pretty much all den mother to a crew of a thousand people with their own agendas and petty power struggles and opinions on how he should be doing his job better. A good security chief kept bullshit off the captain's plate as a full-time job.

The worst part, though, was that all Bull's formal duties were focused inward, on the ship. Right now, a flotilla of Earth ships was burning out into the deep night. A matching force of Martian war vessels—the remnants of the navy that had survived two let's-not-call-them-wars—was burning out on a converging path. The *Behemoth* was lumbering along too with a head start that came from being farther from the sun and the hobble of low-g acceleration to keep her slow. And all of it was focused on the Ring.

Reports would be filling Captain Ashford's queue, and as his XO, Pa would be reading them too. Bull had whatever scraps they let him have or else the same mix of pabulum and panic that filled the newsfeeds. Ashford and Pa would be in conference for most of their shifts, working over strategies and options and playing through scenarios for how things might go down when they reached the Ring. Bull was going to worry about all the trivial stuff so that they didn't have to.

And somehow, he was going to make the mission work. Because Fred had asked him to.

"Hey, chief," Serge said. Bull looked up from the terminal feed in his desk. Serge stood in the office doorway. "Shift's up, and I'm out."

"All right," Bull said. "I still got some stuff. I can lock up when I'm done."

"Bien alles," Serge said with a nod. His light, shuffling footsteps hissed through the front room. In the corridor, Gutmansdottir stroked his white beard and Casimir said something that made them both chuckle. Corin lifted her chin to Serge as he stepped out. The door closed behind him. When he was sure he was alone, Bull pulled up the operational plan and started hunting. He didn't have authority to change it, but that didn't mean he couldn't change anything.

Two hours later, when he was done, he turned off the screen and stood. The office was dark and colder than he liked it. The hum of the ventilation system comforted him. If it were ever completely silent, that would be the time to worry. He stretched, the vertebrae between his shoulder blades crunching like gravel.

They would still be in the bar, most likely. Serge and Corin and Casimir. Macondo and Garza, so similar they could have been brothers. Jojo. His people, to the degree that they were his. He should go. Be with them. Make friends.

He should go to his bunk.

"Come on, old man," he said. "Time to get some rest."

He had closed and locked the office door before Sam's voice came to him in his memory. *Even if everyone's sober and working balls-out, my crew can't get it done faster than that.* He hesitated, his wide fingers over the keypad. It was late. He needed food and sleep and an hour or so checking in with the family aggregator his cousin had set up three years before to help everyone keep track of who was living where. He had a container of flash-frozen green chile from Hatch, back on Earth, waiting for him. It was all going to be there in the morning, and more besides. He didn't need to make more work for himself. No one was going to thank him for it.

He went back in, turned his desk back on, and reread the injury report.

Sam had a good laugh. One that came from the gut. It filled the machining bay, echoing off ceiling and walls until it sounded like there was a crowd of her. Two of the techs on the far side turned to look toward her, smiling without knowing what they were smiling about.

"Technical support?" she said. "You've got to be kidding."

"Rail gun's a pretty technical piece of equipment," Bull said. "It needs support."

"So you redefined what I do as technical support."

"Yeah."

"That's never going to fly," she said.

"Then get the job done quick," Bull said.

"Ashford will pull you up for disciplinary action," she said, the amusement fading but not quite gone yet.

"He has that right. But there's this other thing I wanted to talk about. You said something yesterday about how long it would take to do the job if everyone on your crew was sober?"

It was like turning off a light. The smile left Sam's face as if it had never been there. She crossed her arms. Tiny half-moon shapes dented in at the corners of her mouth, making her look older than she was. Bull nodded to her like she'd said something.

"You've got techs coming to work high," he said.

"Sometimes," she said. And then, reluctantly, "Some of it's alcohol, but mostly it's pixie dust to make up for lack of sleep."

"I got a report about a kid got his knee blown out. His blood was clean, but it doesn't look like anyone tested the guy who was driving the mech. Driver isn't even named in the report. Weird, eh?"

"If you say so," she said.

Bull looked down at his feet. The gray-and-black service utility boots. The spotless floor.

"I need a name, Sam."

"You know I can't do that," she said. "These assholes are my crew. If I lose their respect, we're done here."

"I won't bust your guys unless they're dealing."

"You can't ask me to pick sides. And sorry for saying this, but you already don't have a lot of friends around here. You should be careful how you alienate people."

Across the bay, the two technicians lifted a broken mech onto a steel repair hoist. The murmur of their conversation was just the sound of words without the words themselves. If he couldn't hear them, Bull figured they couldn't hear him.

"Yeah. So Sam?"

"Bull."

"I'm gonna need you to pick sides."

He watched her vacillate. It only took a few seconds. Then he looked across the bay. The technicians had the mech open, pulling an electric motor out of its spine. It was smaller than a six-pack of beer and built to put out enough torque to rip steel. Not the sort of thing to play with drunk. Sam followed his gaze and his train of thought.

"For a guy who bends so many rules, you can be pretty fucking uncompromising."

"Strong believer in doing what needs to get done."

It took her another minute, but she gave him a name.

Chapter Six: Holden

Uranus is really far away," Naomi said as they walked along the corridor to the docking bay. It was the third objection to the contract that she'd listed so far, and something in her voice told Holden there were a lot more points on her list. Under other circumstances, he would have thought she was just angry that he'd accepted the job. She *was* angry. But not *just*.

"Yes," he said. "It is."

"And Titania is a shitty little moon with one tiny little science base on it," Naomi continued.

"Yes."

"We could *buy* Titania for what it cost these people to hire us to fly out there," Naomi said.

Holden shrugged. This part of Ceres was a maze of cheap warehouse tunnels and even cheaper office space. The walls were the grungy off-white of spray-on insulation foam. Someone with a pocketknife and a few minutes to kill could reach the bedrock of Ceres without much effort. From the ratty look of the corridor, there were a lot of people with knives and idle time.

A small forklift came down the corridor toward them with an electric whine and a constant high-pitched beep. Holden backed up against the wall and pulled Naomi to him to get her out of its way. The driver gave Holden a tiny nod of thanks as she drove by.

"So why are they hiring us?" she asked. Demanded.

"Because we're awesome?"

"Titania has, what, a couple hundred people living at the science base?" Naomi said. "You know how they usually send supplies out there? They load them into a single-use braking rocket, and fling them at Uranus' orbit with a rail gun."

"Usually," Holden agreed.

"And the company? Outer Fringe Exports? If I was making a cheap, disposable shell corporation, you know what I'd call it?"

"Outer Fringe Exports?"

"Outer Fringe Exports," she said.

Naomi stopped at the entry hatch that opened to the rental docking bay and the *Rocinante*. The sign overhead listed the present user: Outer Fringe Exports. Holden started to reach for the controls to cycle the pressure doors open, but Naomi put a hand on his arm.

"These people are hiring a warship to transport something to Titania," she said, lowering her voice as though afraid someone might be listening. "How can they possibly afford to do that? Our cargo hold is the size of a hatbox."

"We gave them a good rate?" Holden said, trying for funny and failing.

"What would someone be sending to Titania that requires a fast, stealthy, and heavily armed ship? Have you asked what's in those crates we signed up to carry?"

"No," Holden said. "No, I haven't. And I normally would, but I'm trying really hard not to find out."

Naomi frowned at him, her face shifting between angry and concerned. "Why?"

Holden pulled out his hand terminal and called up an orbital map of the solar system. "See this, all the way on this edge? This is the Ring." He scrolled the display to the other edge of the solar system. "And this is Uranus. They are literally the two spots furthest from each other in the universe that have humans near them."

"And?" Naomi said.

Holden took a deep breath. He could feel a surge of the anxiety he always tried to deny leaping up in him, and he pushed it back down.

"And I know I don't talk about it much, but something really unpleasant and really big with a really high body count knows my name, and it's connected to the Ring."

"Miller," Naomi said.

"The Ring opened, and he *knew when it happened*. It was the closest thing to making sense he's done since..."

Since he rose from the dead. The words didn't fit in his throat, and Naomi didn't make him say them. Her nod was enough. She understood. In an act of legendary cowardice, he was running away to the other side of the solar system to avoid Miller and the Ring and everything that had to do with them. If they had to transport black market human organs or drugs or sexbots or whatever was in those crates, he'd do it. Because he was scared.

Her eyes were unreadable. After all this time, she could still keep her thoughts out of her expression when she wanted to.

"Okay," Naomi said, and pushed the entry door open for him.

At the outer edge of Ceres where the spin gravity was greatest, Holden almost felt like he could have been on Luna or Mars. Loading gantries fed into the skin of the station like thick veins, waiting for the mechs to load in the cargo. Poorly patched scars marked the walls where accidents had marred them. The air smelled of coolant and the kind of cheap air filters that reminded Holden of urinal cakes. Amos lounged on a small electric power lift, his eyes closed.

"We get the job?"

"We did," Naomi said.

Amos cracked an eye open as they came near. A single frown line drew itself on his broad forehead.

"We happy about that?" he asked.

"We're fine with it," Naomi said. "Let's get the lift warmed up. Cargo's due in ten minutes and we probably want to get it off station as quickly as we can without raising suspicion."

There was a beauty in the efficiency that came from a crew that had flown together as long as they had. A fluidity and intimacy and grace that grew from long experience. Eight minutes after Holden and Naomi had come in, the *Roci* was ready to take on cargo. Ten minutes later, nothing happened. Then twenty. Then an hour. Holden paced the gantry nearest the entry hatch with an uncomfortable tingling crawling up the back of his neck.

"You *sure* we got this job?" Amos asked.

"These guys seemed really sketchy to me," Naomi said over the comm from her station in ops. "I'd think we've been scammed, except we haven't given anyone our account numbers."

"We're on the clock here, boss," Alex said from the cockpit. "These loading docks charge by the minute."

Holden bit back his irritation and said, "I'll call again."

He pulled out his terminal and connected to the export company's office. Their messaging system responded, as it had the last three times he'd requested a connection. He waited for the beep that would let him leave another message. Before he could, his display lit up with an incoming connection request from the same office. He switched to it.

"Holden here."

"This is a courtesy call, Captain Holden," the voice on the other end said. The video feed was the Outer Fringe Exports logo on a gray background. "We're withdrawing the contract, and you might want to consider leaving that dock very, very soon."

"You can't back out now," Holden said, trying to keep his voice calm and professional against the rising panic he felt. "We've signed the deal. We've got your deposit. It's non-refundable."

"Keep it," his caller said. "But we consider your failure to inform us of your current situation as a prior breach."

Situation? Holden thought. They couldn't know about Miller. He didn't think they could. "I don't—"

"The party that's tracking you left our offices about five minutes ago, so you should probably get off Ceres in a hurry. Goodbye, Mr. Holden—"

"Wait!" Holden said. "Who was there? What's going on?"

The call ended.

Amos was rubbing his pale, stubble-covered scalp with both hands. He sighed and said, "We got a problem, right?"

"Yep."

"Be right back," Amos replied, and climbed off the forklift.

"Alex? How long till we can clear this dock?" Holden asked. He loped across the bay to the entry hatch. There didn't seem to be any way to lock it from his side. Why would there be? The bays were temporary rental space for loading and unloading cargo. No need for security.

"She's warmed up," Alex replied, not asking the obvious question. Holden was grateful for that. "Gimme ten to run the decouplin' sequence, that should do it."

"Start now," Holden said, hurrying back toward the airlock. "Leave the 'lock open till the last minute. Amos and I will be out here making sure no one interferes."

"Roger that, Cap," Alex replied, and dropped the connection.

"Interferes?" Naomi said. "What's going on... Okay, why is Amos going out there with a shotgun?"

"Those sketchy, scary gangster types we just signed on with?"

"Yes?"

"They just dropped *us*. And whatever scared them into doing it is coming here right now. I don't think guns are an overreaction."

Amos ran down the ramp, holding his auto-shotgun in his right hand and an assault rifle in his left. He tossed the rifle to Holden, then took up a cover position behind the forklift and aimed at the bay's entry hatch. Like Alex, he didn't ask why.

"Want me to come out?" Naomi asked.

"No, but prepare to defend the ship if they get past me and Amos," Holden replied, then moved over to the forklift's recharging station. It was the only other cover in the otherwise empty bay.

In a conversational tone, Amos said, "Any idea what we're expecting here?"

"Nope," Holden said. He clicked the rifle to autofire and felt a faint nausea rising in his throat.

"All right, then," Amos said cheerfully.

"Eight minutes," Naomi said from his hand terminal. Not a long time, but if they were trying to hold the bay under hostile fire, it would seem like an eternity.

The entry warning light at the cargo bay entrance flashed yellow three times, and the hatch slid open.

"Don't shoot unless I do," Holden said quietly. Amos grunted back at him.

A tall blond woman walked into the bay. She had an Earther's build, a video star's face, and couldn't have been more than twenty. When she saw the two guns pointed at her, she raised her hands and wiggled her fingers. "Not armed," she said. Her cheeks dimpled into a grin. Holden tried to imagine why a supermodel would be looking for him.

"Hi," Amos said. He was grinning back at her.

"Who are you?" Holden said, keeping his gun trained on her.

"My name's Adri. Are you James Holden?"

"I can be," Amos said, "if you want." She smiled. Amos smiled back, but his weapon was still in a carefully neutral position.

"What've we got down there?" Naomi asked, her voice tense in his ear. "Do we have a threat?"

"I don't know yet," Holden said.

"You are, though, right? You're James Holden," Adri said, walking toward him. The assault rifle in his hands didn't seem to bother her at all. Up close, she smelled like strawberries and vanilla. "*Captain* James Holden, of the *Rocinante*?"

"Yes," he said.

She held out a slim, throwaway hand terminal. He took it automatically. The terminal displayed a picture of him, along with his name and his UN citizen and UN naval ID numbers.

"You've been served," she said. "Sorry. It was nice meeting you, though."

She turned back to the door and walked away.

"What the fuck?" Amos said to no one, dropping the muzzle of his gun to the floor and rubbing his scalp again.

"Jim?" Naomi said.

"Give me a minute."

He paged through the summons, jumping past seven pages of legalese to get to the point: The Martians wanted their ship back. Official proceedings had been started against him in both Earth and Martian courts challenging the salvage claim to the *Rocinante*. Only they were calling it the *Tachi*. The ship was under an order of impound pending adjudication, effective immediately.

His short conversation with Outer Fringe Exports suddenly made a lot more sense.

"Cap?" Alex said through the connection. "I'm getting a red light on the docking clamp release. I'm puttin' a query in. Once I get that cleared, we can pop the cork."

"What's going on out there?" Naomi asked. "Are we still leaving?"

Holden took a long, deep breath, sighed, and said something obscene.

The longest layover the *Rocinante* had taken since Holden and the others had gone independent had been five and a half weeks. The twelve days that the *Roci* spent in lockup seemed longer. Naomi and Alex were on the ship most of the time, putting inquiries through to lawyers and legal aid societies around the system. With every letter and conversation, the consensus grew. Mars had been smart to begin legal proceedings in Earth courts as well as their own. Even if Holden and the *Roci* slipped the leash at Ceres, all major ports would be denied them. They'd have to skulk from one gray-market Belter port to the next. Even if there was enough work, they might not be able to find supplies to keep them flying.

If they took the case before a magistrate, they might or might not lose the ship, but it would be expensive to find out. Accounts that Holden had thought of as comfortably full suddenly looked an order of magnitude too small. Staying on Ceres Station made him antsy; being on the *Roci* left him sad.

There had been any number of times in his travels on the *Roci* that he'd imagined—even expected—it all to come to a tragic end. But those scenarios had involved firefights or alien monstrosities or desperate dives into some planetary atmosphere. He'd imagined with a sick thrill of dread what it would be like if Alex died, or Amos. Or Naomi. He'd wondered whether the three of them would go on without him. He hadn't considered that the end might find all of them perfectly fine. That the *Rocinante* might be the one to go.

Hope, when it came, was a documentary streamcast team from UN Public Broadcasting. Monica Stuart, the team lead, was an auburn-haired freckled woman with a professionally sculpted beauty that made her seem vaguely familiar when he saw her on the screen of the pilot's deck. She hadn't come in person.

"How many people are we talking about?" Holden asked.

"Four," she said. "Two camera jockeys, my sound guy, and me."

Holden ran a hand across eight days' worth of patchy beard. The sense of inevitability sat in his gut like a stone.

"To the Ring," he said.

"To the Ring," she agreed. "We need to make it a hard burn to get there before the Martians, the Earth flotilla, and the *Behemoth*. And we'd like some measure of safety once we're out there, which the *Rocinante* would be able to give us."

Naomi cleared her throat, and the documentarian shifted her attention to her.

"You're sure you can get the hold taken off the *Roci*?" Naomi asked.

"I am protected by the Freedom of Journalism Act. I have the right to the reasonable use of hired materials and personnel in the pursuit of a story. Otherwise, anyone could stop any story they didn't like by malicious use of injunctions like the one on the *Roci.* I have a backdated contract that says I hired you a month ago, before I arrived at Ceres. I have a team of lawyers ten benches deep who can drown anyone that objects in enough paperwork to last a lifetime."

"So we've been working for you all along," Holden said.

"Only if you want to get that docking lock rescinded. But it's more than just a ride I'm looking for. That's what makes it reasonable that I can't just hire a different ship."

"I knew there was a but," Holden said.

"I want to interview the crew too. While there are a half dozen ships I could get for the trip out, yours is the one that comes with the survivors of Eros."

Naomi looked across at him. Her eyes were carefully neutral. Was it better to be here, trapped on Ceres while the *Roci* was pulled away from him by centimeters, or flying straight into the abyss with his crew? And the Ring.

"I have to think about it," he said. "I'll be in touch."

"I respect that," Monica said. "But please don't take long. If we're not going with you, we've still got to go with someone."

He dropped the connection. In the silence, the deck seemed larger than it was.

"This isn't coincidence," Holden said. "We just *happen* to get locked down by Mars, and the only thing that can get us out of the docking clamps just *happens* to be heading for the Ring? No way. We're being manipulated. Someone's planning this. It's him."

"Jim—"

"It's him. It's Miller."

"It's not Miller. He can barely string together a coherent sentence," Naomi said. "How is he going to engineer something like this?"

Holden leaned forward and the seat under him shifted. His head felt like it was stuffed with wool.

"If we leave, they can still take her away from us," he said. "Once this story is done, we won't be in any better position than we are right now."

"Except that we wouldn't be locked on Ceres," Naomi said. "And it's a long way out there. A long way back. A lot could change."

"That wasn't as comforting as you meant it to be."

Naomi's smile was thin but not bitter.

"Fair point," she said.

The *Rocinante* hummed around them, the systems running through their automatic maintenance checks, the air cycling gently through the ducts. The ship breathing and dreaming. Their home, at rest. Holden reached out a hand, lacing his fingers with Naomi's.

"We still have some money. We can take out a loan," she said. "We could buy a different ship. Not a good one, but... It wouldn't have to be the end of it all."

"It would be, though."

"Probably."

"No choice, then," Holden said. "Let's go to Nineveh."

Monica and her team arrived in the early hours of the morning, loading a few small crates of equipment that they carried themselves. In person, Monica was thinner than she seemed on screen. Her camera crew were a sturdy Earth woman named Okju and a brown-skinned Martian man who went by Clip. The cameras they carried looked like shoulder-mounted weapons, alloy casings that could telescope out to almost two meters or retract to fit around the tightest corner in the ship.

The soundman was blind. He had a dusting of short white hair and opaque black glasses. His teeth were yellowed like old ivory, and his smile was gentle and humane. According to the paperwork, his name was Elio Casti, but for some reason the documentary team all called him Cohen.

They assembled in the galley, Holden's four people and Monica's. He could see each group quietly considering the other. They'd be living in one another's laps for months. Strangers trapped in a metal-and-ceramic box in the vast ocean of the vacuum. Holden cleared his throat.

"Welcome aboard," he said.

Chapter Seven: Melba

If the Earth-Mars alliance hadn't collapsed, if there hadn't been a war—or two wars depending on how the line between battles was marked—civilian ships like the *Cerisier* would have had no place in the great convoy. The ships lost at Ganymede and in the Belt, the skirmishes to control those asteroids best placed to push down a gravity well. Hundreds of ships had been lost, from massive engines of war like the *Donnager*, the *Agatha King*, and the *Hyperion* to countless small three- and four-person support ships.

Nor, Melba knew, were those the only scars. Phobos with its listening station had become a thin, nearly invisible ring around Mars. Eros was gone. Phoebe had been subjected to a sustained nuclear hell and pushed into Saturn. The farms at Ganymede had collapsed. Venus had been used and abandoned by the alien protomolecule. Protogen and the Mao-Kwikowski empire, once one of the great shipping and transport companies in the system, had been gutted, stolen, and sold.

The *Cerisier* began her life as an exploration vessel. Now she was a flying toolshed. The bays of scientific equipment were machine shops now. What had once been sealed labs were stacked from deck to deck with the mundane necessities of environmental control networks—scrubbers, ducting, sealants, and alarm arrays. She lumbered through the uncaring vacuum on the fusion plume of her Epstein drive. The crew of a hundred and six souls was made of a small elite of ship command—no more than a dozen, all told—and a vast body of technicians, machinists, and industrial chemists.

Once, Melba thought, this ship had been on the bleeding edge of human exploration. Once it had burned through the skies of Jovian moons, seeing things humanity had never seen before. Now it was the handservant of the government, discovering nothing more exotic than what had been flushed into the water reclamation tanks. The degradation gave Melba a sense of kinship with the ship's narrow halls and gray plastic ladders. Once, Clarissa Melpomene Mao had been the light of her school. Popular and beautiful, and suffused with the power and influence of her father's name. Now her father was a numbered prisoner in a nameless prison, allowed only a few minutes of external connection every day, and those to his lawyer, not his wife or children.

And she was Melba Koh, sleeping on a gel couch that smelled of someone else's body in a cabin smaller than a closet. She commanded a team of four electrochemical technicians: Stanni, Ren, Bob, and Soledad. Stanni and Bob were decades older than her. Soledad, three years younger, had been on two sixteen-month tours. Ren, her official second, was a Belter and, like all Belters, passionate about environmental control systems the way normal people were with sex or religion. She didn't ask how he'd ended up on an Earth ship, and he didn't volunteer the information.

She had known the months going out to the Ring would be hard, but she'd misunderstood what the worst parts would be.

"She's a fucking bitch, right?" Stanni said. It was a private channel between him and Ren. If she'd been who she pretended to be, she wouldn't have been able to hear it. "She doesn't know dick."

Ren grunted, neither defending her nor joining the attack.

"If you hadn't caught that brownout buffer wrong way on the *Macedon* last week, it would have been another cascade failure, si no? Would have had to throw off the whole schedule to go back and fix it."

"Might've," Ren said.

She was a level above them. The destroyer *Seung Un* muttered around her. The crew was on a maintenance run. Scheduled, routine, predictable. They'd left the *Cerisier* ten hours earlier in one of the dozen transports that clung to the maintenance ship's skin. They would be here for another fifteen hours, changing out the high-yield scrubbers and checking the air supply continuity. The greatest danger, she'd learned, was condensation degrading the seals.

It was the kind of detail she should have known.

She pulled herself through the access shaft. Her tool kit hung heavy on her front in the full-g thrust gravity. She imagined it was what being pregnant would feel like. Unless something strange had happened, Soledad and Bob were sleeping in the boat. Ren and Stanni were a level down, and going lower with every hour. They were expecting her to make the final inspection of their work. And, it seemed, they were expecting her to do it poorly.

It was true, of course. She didn't know why a real electrochemical technician seeing her inexperience should embarrass her as deeply as it did. She'd read a few manuals, run through a few tutorials. All that mattered was that they think she was an authentic semicompetent overseer. It didn't matter whether they respected her. They weren't her friends.

She should have switched to the private frequencies for Soledad and Bob to be certain neither had woken unexpectedly and might come looking for her. This part of the plan was important. She couldn't let any of them find her. But somehow, she couldn't bring herself to shift away from Ren and Stanni.

"She don't do anything is all. Keeps to her cabin, don't help on the project. She just come out the end, look up, look down, sign off, and go back to her cabin."

"True."

The junction was hard to miss. The bulkhead was reinforced and clearly marked with bright orange safety warnings in five languages. She paused before it, her hands on her hips, and waited to feel some sense of accomplishment. And she did, only it wasn't as pure as she'd hoped. She looked up and down the passageway, though the chances of being interrupted here were minimal.

The explosive was strapped against her belly, the heat of her skin keeping it malleable and bright green. As it cooled to ambient, the putty would harden and fade to gray. It surprised her again with its density. Pressing it along the seams of the junction, she felt like she was forming lead with her bare hands. The effort left her knuckles aching before she was halfway done. She'd budgeted half an hour, but it took her almost twice that. The detonator was a black dot four millimeters across with ten black ceramic contacts that pressed into the already stiffening putty. It looked like a tick.

When she was done, she wiped her hands down with cleaning towelettes twice, making sure none of the explosive was caught under her fingernails or on her clothes. She'd expected to skip her inspection of just the one level, but Ren and Stanni had made good time, and she took the lift down two levels instead. They were still talking, but not about her now. Stanni was considering getting a crush on Soledad. In laconic Belt-inflected half phrases, Ren was advising against it. Smart man, her second.

The lift paused and three soldiers got on it, all men. Melba pressed herself back to make room for them, and the nearest nodded his polite gratitude. His uniform identified him as Marcos. She nodded back, then stared hard at her feet, willing them not to look at her. Her uniform felt like a costume. Even though she knew better, it felt like they would see through her disguise if they looked too close. Like her past was written on her skin.

My name is Melba Koh, she thought. *I've never been anyone else.*

The lift stopped at her level and the three soldiers made way for her. She wondered, when the time came, whether Marcos would die.

She had never been to her father's prison, and even if he'd been allowed visitors, the visit would have been in a prescribed room, monitored, transcribed. Any real human emotion would have been pressed out of it by the weight of official attention. She would never have been permitted to see the hallways he walked down or the cell where he slept, but after his incarceration by the United Nations, she'd researched prison design. Her room was three centimeters narrower, a centimeter and a half longer. The crash couch she slept in was gimbaled to allow for changes in acceleration, while his would be welded to the floor. She could squeeze out whenever she wanted and go to the gang showers or the mess. Her door locked from the inside, and there were no cameras or microphones in her room.

In every way that mattered, she had more freedom than her father. That she likely spent as much time in isolation was a matter of choice for her, and that made all the difference. Tomorrow would be a fresh rotation out. Another ship, another round of maintenance that she could pretend to oversee. Tonight she could lie in her couch dressed in the simple cotton underclothes that she'd bought as the kind of thing Melba would wear. Her hand terminal had fifteen tutorials in local memory and dozens more on the ship's shared storage. They covered everything from microorganic nutrient reclamation to coolant system specifications to management policies. She should have been reading them through. Or if not that, at least she shouldn't have been reviewing her own secret files.

On the screen, Jim Holden looked like a zealot. The composite was built from dozens of hours of broadcast footage of the man taken over the previous years, with weight given to the most recent images and stills. The software she'd used to make a perfect visual simulacrum of the man cost more than her Melba persona had. The fake Holden had to be good enough to fool both people and computers, at least for a little while. On the screen, his brown eyes squinted with an idiot's earnestness. His jaw had the first presentiment of jowls, only half hidden by the microgravity. The smarmy half smile told her everything she needed to know about the man who had destroyed her family.

"This is Captain James Holden," he said. "What you've just seen is a demonstration of the danger you are in. My associates have placed similar devices on every ship presently in proximity to the Ring. You will all stand down as I am assuming sole and absolute control over the Ring in the name of the Outer Planets Alliance. Any ship that approaches the Ring without my *personal* permission will be destroyed without—"

She paused it, freezing her small, artificial Holden in mid-gesture. Her fingertip traced the outline of his shoulder, across his cheek, and then stabbed at his eyes. She wished now that she'd picked a more inflammatory script. On Earth, making her preparations, it had seemed enough to have him take unilateral control of the Ring. Now each time she watched it, it seemed tamer.

Killing Holden would have been easier. Assassinations were cheap by comparison, but she knew enough about image control and social dynamics to see where it would have led. Martyrdom, canonization, love. A host of conspiracy theories that implicated anyone from the OPA to her father. That was precisely not the point. Holden had to be humiliated in a way that passed backward in time. Someone coming to his legacy had to be able to look back at all the things Holden had done, all the pronouncements he'd given, all the high-handed, self-righteous decisions made on behalf of others while never leaving his control and see that of course it had all led to this. His name put in with the great traitors, con men, and self-aggrandizing egomaniacs of history. When she was done, everything Holden had touched would be tainted by association, including the destruction of her family. Her father.

Somewhere deep in the structure of the *Cerisier*, one of the navigators started a minor correction burn and gravity shifted a half a degree. The couch moved under her, and she tried not to notice it. She preferred the times when she could pretend that she was in a gravity well to the little reminders that she was the puppet of acceleration and inertia.

Her hand terminal chimed once, announcing the arrival of a message. To anyone who didn't look carefully, it would seem like just another advertisement. An investment opportunity she would be a fool to ignore with a video presentation attached that would seem like corrupted data to anyone who didn't have the decryption key. She sat up, swinging her legs over the edge of the couch, and leaned close to the hand terminal.

The man who appeared on her screen wore black glasses dark enough to be opaque. His hair was cropped close to his skull, but she could see from the way it moved that he was under heavy burn. The soundman cleared his throat.

"The package is delivered and ready for testing. I'd appreciate the balance transfer as soon as you've confirmed. I've got some bills coming due, and I'm a little under the wire." Something in the background hissed, and a distant voice started laughing. A woman. The file ended.

She replayed it four more times. Her heart was racing and her fingers felt like little electric currents were running through them. She'd need to confirm, of course. But this was the last, most dangerous step. The *Rocinante* had been cutting-edge military hardware when it had fallen into Holden's hands. There could also have been any number of changes made to the security systems in the years since. She set up a simple remote connection looped through a disposable commercial account on Ceres Station. It might take days for the *Rocinante*'s acknowledgment to come back to her saying that the back door was installed and functioning, that the ship was hers. But if it did...

It was the last piece. Everything in place. A sense of almost religious well-being washed over her. The thin room with its scratched walls and too-bright LEDs had never seemed so benign. She levered herself up out of the couch. She wanted to celebrate, though of course there was no one she could tell. Talk to might be enough.

The halls of the *Cerisier* were so narrow that it was impossible to walk abreast or to pass someone coming the opposite way without turning sideways. The mess would fit twenty people sitting with their hips touching. The nearest thing to an open area was the fitness center off the medical bay. The treadmills and exercise machines required enough room that no one would be caught in the joints and belts. Safety regulations made it the widest, freest air in the ship, and so a good place to be around people.

Of her team, only Ren was present. In the usual microgravity, he would probably have been neck deep in a tank of resistance gel. With the full-g burn, he was on a regular treadmill. His pale skin was bright with sweat, his carrot-orange hair pulled back in a frizzed ponytail. It was strange watching him. His large head was made larger by his hair, and the thinness of his body made him seem more like something from a children's program than an actual man.

He nodded to her as she came in.

"Ren," she said, walking to the front of his machine. She felt the gazes of other crewmen on her, but on the *Cerisier* she didn't feel as exposed. Or maybe it was the good news that carried her. "Do you have a minute?"

"Chief," he said instead of yes, but he thumbed down the treadmill to a cool-down walk. "Que sa?"

"I heard some of the things Stanni was saying about me," she said. Ren's expression closed down. "I just wanted…"

She frowned, looked down, and then gave in to the impulse welling up in her.

"He's right," she said. "I'm in over my head with this job. I got it because of some political favors. I'm not qualified to do what I'm doing."

He blinked rapidly. He shot a glance around her, checking to see if anyone had overheard them. She didn't particularly care, but she thought it was sweet that he did.

"Not so bad, you," he said. "I mean, little off here, little off there. But I've been under worse."

"I need help," she said. "To do all the work the way it should be done, I need help. I need someone I can trust. Someone I can count on."

Ren nodded, but his forehead roughened. He blew out his breath and stepped off the treadmill.

"I want to get the work done right," she said. "Not miss anything. And I want the team to respect me."

"Okay, sure."

"I know you should have had this job."

Ren blew out another breath, his cheeks ballooning. It was more expressive than she'd ever seen him before. He leaned against the wall. When he met her gaze, it was like he was seeing her for the first time.

"Appreciate you saying it, chief, but we're both of us outsiders here," he said. "Stick together, bien?"

"Good," she said, leaning against the wall next to him. "So. The brownout buffers? What did I get wrong?"

Ren sighed.

"The buffers are smart, but the design's stupid," he said. "They talk to each other, so they're also a separate network, yah? Thing is, you put one in the wrong way? Works okay. But next time it resets, the signal down the line looks wrong. Triggers a diagnostic run in the next one down, and then the next one down. Whole network starts blinking like Christmas. Too many errors on the network and it fails closed, takes down the whole grid. And then you got us going through checking each one by hand. With flashlights and the supervisor chewing our nuts."

"That's...that can't be right," she said. "Seriously? It could have shut down the *grid*?"

"I know, right?" Ren said, smiling. "And all it would take

is change the design so it don't fit in if you got it wrong. But they never do. A lot of what we do is like that, boss. We try to catch the little ones before they get big. Some things, you get them wrong, it's nothing. Some things, and it's a big mess."

The words felt like a church bell being struck. They resonated. She was that fault, that error. She didn't know what she was doing, not really, and she'd get away with it. She'd pass. Until she didn't, and then everything would fall apart. Her throat felt tighter. She almost wished she hadn't said anything.

She was a brownout buffer pointed the wrong way. A flaw that was easy to overlook, with the potential to wreck everything.

"For the others... don't take them harsh. Blowing off steam, mostly. Not you so much as it's anything. Fear-biting."

"Fear?"

"Sure," he said. "Everyone on this boat's scared dry. Try not to show it, do the work, but we all getting nightmares. Natural, right?"

"What are they afraid of?" she asked.

Behind her the door cycled open and shut. A man said something in a language she didn't know. Ren tilted his head, and she had the sick, sinking feeling that she'd done something wrong. She hadn't acted normal, and she didn't know what her misstep was.

"Ring," he said at last. "It's what killed Eros. Could have killed Mars. All that weird stuff it did on Venus, no one knows what it was. Deaded that slingshot kid who went through. Half everyone thinks we should be pitching nukes at it, other half thinks we'd only piss it off. We're going out as deep as anyone ever has just so we can look in the devil's eye, and Stanni and Solé and Bob? They're all scared as shit of what we see in it. Me too."

"Ah," she said. "All right. I understand that."

Ren tried on a smile.

"You? It don't scare you?"

"It's not something I think about."

Chapter Eight: Anna

Nami and Nono left for Earth a week before Anna's shuttle. Those last days living alone in those rooms, knowing that she would never be back—that they would never be back—was like a gentle presentiment of death: profoundly melancholy and, shamefully, a little exhilarating.

The shuttle from Europa was one of the last to join the flotilla, and it meant eighteen hours of hard burn. By the time she set foot on the deck of the UNN *Thomas Prince*, all she wanted was a bunk and twelve hours' sleep. The young yeoman who'd been sent to greet and escort her had other plans, though, and the effort it would have taken to be rude about it was more than she could muster.

"The *Prince* is a *Xerxes*-class battleship, or what we sometimes refer to as a third-generation dreadnought," he said, gesturing to the white ceramic-over-gel of the hangar's interior walls. The shuttle she'd arrived on nestled in its bay looking small under the cathedral-huge arch. "We call it a third-generation battleship because it is the third redesign since the buildup during the first Earth-Mars conflict."

Not that it had been much of a conflict, Anna thought. The Martians had made noises about independence, the UN had built a lot of ships, Mars had built a few. And then Solomon Epstein had gone from being a Martian yachting hobbyist to the inventor of the first fusion drive that solved the heat buildup and rapid fuel consumption problems of constant thrust. Suddenly Mars had a few ships that went really, really fast. They'd said, *Hey, we're about to go colonize the rest of the solar system. Want to stay mad at us, or want to come with?* The UN had made the sensible choice, and most people would agree: Giving up Mars in exchange for half of the solar system had probably been a pretty good deal.

It didn't mean that both sides hadn't kept on designing new ways to kill each other. Just in case.

"...just over half a kilometer long, and two hundred meters wide at its broadest point," the yeoman was saying.

"Impressive," Anna replied, trying to bring her wandering attention back.

The yeoman pulled her luggage on a small rolling cart to a bank of elevator lifts.

"These elevators run the length of the ship," he said as he punched a button on the control panel. "We call them the keel elevators—"

"Because they run along the belly of the ship?" Anna said.

"Yes! That's what the bottom of seagoing vessels was called, and space-based navies have kept the nomenclature."

Anna nodded. His enthusiasm was exhausting and charming at the same time. He wanted to impress her, so she resolved to be impressed. It was a small enough thing to give someone.

"Of course, the belly of the ship is largely an arbitrary distinction," he continued as the elevator climbed. "Because we use thrust gravity, the deck is always in the direction thrust is coming from, the aft of the ship. Up is always away from the engines. There's not really much to distinguish the other four directions from each other. Some smaller ships can land on planetary surfaces, and in those ships the belly of the ship contains landing gear and thrusters for liftoff."

"I imagine the *Prince* is too large for that," Anna said.

"By quite a lot, actually! But our shuttles and corvettes are capable of surface landings, though it doesn't happen very often."

The elevator doors opened with another ding, and the yeoman pushed her luggage out into the hall. "After we drop off your baggage at your stateroom, we can continue the tour."

"Yeoman?" Anna said. "Is that the right way to address you?"

"Certainly. Or Mister Ichigawa. Or even Jin, since you're a civilian."

"Jin," Anna continued. "Would it be all right if I just stayed in my room for a while? I'm very tired."

He stopped pulling her baggage and blinked twice. "But the captain said all of the VIP guests should get a complete tour. Including the bridge, which is usually off-limits to non-duty personnel."

Anna put a hand on the boy's arm. "I understand that's quite a privilege, but I'd rather see it when I can keep my eyes open. You understand, don't you?" She gave his arm a squeeze and smiled her best smile at him.

"Certainly," he said, smiling back. "Come this way, ma'am."

Looking around her, Anna wasn't sure if she actually wanted to see the rest of the ship. Every corridor looked the same: Slick gray material with something spongy underneath covered most walls. Anna supposed it was some sort of protective surface, to keep sailors from injury if they banged into it during maneuvers. And anything that wasn't gray fabric was gray metal. The things that would be impressive to most people about the ship would be its various mechanisms for killing other ships. Those were the parts of the ship she was least interested in.

"Is that okay?" Ichigawa said after a moment. Anna had no idea what he was talking about. "Calling you ma'am, I mean. Some of the VIPs have titles. Pastor, or Reverend, or Minister. I don't want to offend."

"Well, if I didn't like you I'd ask you to call me Reverend Doctor, but I do like you very much, so please don't," she said.

"Thank you," Jin said, and the back of his neck blushed.

"And if you were a member of my congregation, I'd have you call me Pastor Anna. Buddhist?"

"Only when I'm at my grandmother's house," Jin said with a wink. "The rest of the time I'm a navy man."

"Is that a religion now?" Anna asked with a laugh.

"The navy thinks so."

"Okay." She laughed again. "So why don't you just call me Anna?"

"Yes, ma'am," Jin said. He stopped at a gray door marked OQ 297-11 and handed her a small metal card. "This is your room. Just having the card on you unlocks the door. It will stay locked when you're inside unless you press the yellow button on the wall panel."

"Sounds very safe," Anna said, taking the key from Jin and shaking his hand.

"This is the battleship *Thomas Prince*, ma'am. It's the safest place in the solar system."

Her stateroom was three meters wide by four meters long. Luxurious by navy standards, normal for a poor Europan, coffinlike to an Earther. Anna felt a brief moment of vertigo as the two different Annas she'd been reacted to the space in three different ways. She'd felt the same sense of disconnection when she'd first boarded the *Prince* and felt the full gravity pressing her down. The Earther she'd been most of her life felt euphoric as, for the first time in years, her weight felt *right*. The Europan in her just felt tired, drained by the excessive pull on her bones.

She wondered how long it would take Nono to get her Earth legs back. How long it would take before Nami could walk there. They were both spending the entire trip back pumped full of muscle and bone growth stimulators, but drugs can only take a person so far. There would still be the agonizing weeks or months as their bodies adapted to the new gravity. Anna could almost see little Nami struggling to get up onto her hands and knees like she did on Europa. Could almost hear her cries of frustration while she built up the strength to move on her own again. She was such a determined little thing. It would infuriate her to lose the hard-won physical skills she'd developed over the last two years.

Thinking about it made Anna's chest ache, just behind her breastbone.

She tapped the shiny black surface of the console in her room, and the room's terminal came on. She spent a moment learning the user interface. It was limited to browsing the ship's library and to sending and receiving text or audio/video messages.

She tapped the button to record a message and said, "Hi Nono, hi Nami!" She waved at the camera. "I'm on the ship, and we're on our way. I—" She stopped and looked around the room, at the sterile gray walls and spartan bed. She grabbed a pillow off of it and turned back to the camera. "I miss you both already." She hugged the pillow to her chest, tight. "This is you. This is both of you."

She turned the recording off before she got teary. She was washing her face when the console buzzed a new-message alert. Even though it didn't seem possible Nami could have gotten the message and replied already, her heart gave a little leap. She rushed over and opened the message. It was a simple text message reminding her of the VIP "meet and greet" in the officers' mess at 1900 hours. The clock said it was currently 1300.

Anna tapped the button to RSVP to the event and then climbed under the covers of her bed with her clothes on and cried herself to sleep.

"Reverend Doctor Volovodov," a booming male voice said as soon as she walked into the officers' mess.

The room was laid out for a party, with tables covered in food ringing the room, and a hundred or more people talking in loose clumps in the center. In one corner, an ad hoc bar with four bartenders was doing brisk business. A tall, dark-skinned man with perfectly coiffed white hair and an immaculate gray suit walked out of the crowd like Venus rising from the waves. Anna wondered how he managed the effect. He reached out and took her hand with his. "I'm so happy to have you with us. I've heard so much about the powerful work you're doing on Europa, and I don't see how the Methodist World Council could have chosen anyone else for this important trip."

Anna shook his hand, then carefully extricated herself from his grasp. Doctor Hector Cortez, Father Hank on his live streamcasts that went out to over a hundred million people each week, and close personal friend and spiritual advisor to the secretary-general himself. She couldn't imagine how he knew anything about her. Her tiny congregation of less than a hundred people on Europa wouldn't even be a rounding error to his solar system–wide audience. She found herself caught between feeling flattered, uncomfortable, and vaguely suspicious.

"Doctor Cortez," Anna said. "So nice to meet you. I've seen your show before, of course."

"Of course," he said, smiling vaguely and already looking around the room for someone else to talk to. She had the sense that he'd come to greet her less out of the pleasure of her arrival than as a chance to extricate himself from whatever conversation he'd been having before, and she didn't know whether to be relieved or insulted. She settled on amused.

Like a smaller object dragged into some larger gravity well, an elderly man in formal Roman Catholic garb pulled away from the central crowd and drifted in Doctor Cortez's direction.

She started to introduce herself when Doctor Cortez cut in with that booming voice and said, "Father Michel. Say hello to my friend Reverend Doctor Annushka Volovodov, a worker for God's glory with the Europa congregation of Methodists."

"Reverend Volovodov," the Catholic man said. "I'm Father Michel, with the Archdiocese of Rome."

"Oh, very nice to meet—" Anna started.

"Don't let him fool you with that humble old country priest act," Cortez boomed over the top of her. "He's a bishop on the short list for cardinal."

"Congratulations," Anna said.

"Oh, it's nothing. All exaggeration and smoke." The old man beamed. "Nothing will happen until it fits with God's plan."

"You wouldn't be here if that were true," Cortez said.

The bishop chuckled.

A woman in an expensive blue dress followed one of the uniformed waiters with his tray of champagne. She and Father Michel reached for a glass at the same moment. Anna smiled a no at the offered champagne, and the waiter vanished into the crowd at the center of the room.

"Please," the woman said to Anna. "Don't leave me to drink alone with a Catholic. My liver can't take it."

"Thank you, but—"

"What about you, Hank? I've heard you can put down a few drinks." She punctuated this with a swig from her glass. Cortez's smile could have meant anything.

"I'm Anna," Anna said, reaching out to shake the woman's hand. "I love your dress."

"Thank you. I am Mrs. Robert Fagan," the woman replied with mock formality. "Tilly if you aren't asking for money."

"Nice to meet you, Tilly," Anna said. "I'm sorry, but I don't drink."

"God, save me from temperance," Tilly said. "You haven't seen a party till you get a group of Anglicans and Catholics trying to beat each other to the bottom of a bottle."

"Now, that's not nice, Mrs. Fagan," Father Michel said. "I've never met an Anglican that could keep up with me."

"Hank, why is Esteban letting you out of his sight?" It took Anna a moment to realize that Tilly was talking about the secretary-general of the United Nations.

Cortez shook his head and feigned a wounded look without losing his ever-present toothy grin. "Mrs. Fagan, I'm humbled by the secretary-general's faith and trust in me, as we speed off toward the single most important event in human history since the death of our Lord."

Tilly snorted. "You mean his faith and trust in the hundred million voters you can throw his way in June."

"Ma'am," Cortez said, turning to look at Tilly's face for the first time. His grin never changed, but something chilled the air between them. "Maybe you've had a bit too much champagne."

"Oh, not nearly enough."

Father Michel charged in to the rescue, taking Tilly's hand and saying, "I think our dear secretary-general is probably even more grateful for your husband's many campaign contributions. Though that does make this the most expensive cruise in history, for you."

Tilly snorted and looked away from Cortez. "Robert can fucking afford it."

The obscenity created an awkward silence for a few moments, and Father Michel gave Anna an apologetic smile. She smiled back, so far out of her depth that she'd abandoned trying to keep up.

"What's he getting with them, I wonder?" Tilly said, pointing attention at anyone other than herself. "These artists and writers and actors. How many votes does a performance artist bring to the table? Do they even vote?"

"It's symbolic," Father Michel said, his face taking on a well-practiced expression of thoughtfulness. "We are all of humanity coming together to explore the great question of our time. The secular and the divine come to stand together before that overwhelming mystery: What is the Ring?"

"Nice," Tilly said. "Rehearsal pays off."

"Thank you," the bishop said.

"What is the Ring?" Anna said with a frown. "It's a wormhole gate. There's no question, right? We've been talking about these on a theoretical basis for centuries. They look just like this. Something goes through it and the place on the other side isn't here. We get the transmission signals bleeding back out and attenuating. It's a wormhole."

"That's certainly a possibility," Father Michel said. Tilly smiled at the sourness in his voice. "How do you see our mission here, Anna?"

"It isn't what it *is* that's at issue," she said, glad to be back in a conversation she understood. "It's what it *means*. This changes everything, and even if it's something wonderful, it'll be displacing. People will need to understand how to fit this in with their understanding of the universe. Of what this means about God, what this new thing tells us about Him. By being here, we can offer comfort that we couldn't otherwise."

"I agree," Cortez said. "Our work is to help people come to grips with the great mysteries, and this one's a doozy."

"No," Anna started, "explaining isn't what I—"

"Play your cards right, and it might get Esteban another four years," Tilly said over the top of her. "Then we can call it a miracle."

Cortez grinned a white grin at someone across the room. A man in a small group of men and women in loose orange robes raised his hand, waving at them.

"Can you *believe* those people?" Tilly asked.

"I believe those are delegates from the Church of Humanity Ascendant," Anna said.

Tilly shook her head. "Humanity Ascendant. I mean, really. Let's just make up our own religion and pretend we're the gods."

"Careful," Cortez said. "They're not the only ones."

Seeing Anna's discomfort, Father Michel attempted to rescue her. "Doctor Volovodov, I know the elder of that group. Wonderful woman. I'd love to introduce you. If you all would excuse us."

"Excuse me," Anna started, then stopped when the room suddenly went silent. Father Michel and Cortez were both looking toward something at the center of the gathering near the bar, and Anna moved around Tilly to get a better view. It was hard to see at first, because everyone in the room was moving away toward the walls. But eventually, a young man dressed in a hideous bright red suit was revealed. He'd poured something all over himself; his hair and the shoulders of his jacket were dripping a clear fluid onto the floor. A strong alcohol scent filled the room.

"This is for the people's Ashtun Collective!" the young man yelled out in a voice that trembled with fear and excitement. "Free Etienne Barbara! And free the Afghan people!"

"Oh dear God," Father Michel said. "He's going to—"

Anna never saw what started the fire, but suddenly the young man was engulfed in flames. Tilly screamed. Anna's shocked brain only registered annoyance at the sound. Really, when had someone screaming ever solved a problem? She recognized her fixation on this irritation as her own way of avoiding the horror in front of her, but only in a distant and dreamy sort of way. She was about to tell Tilly to just shut up when the fire-suppression system activated and five streams of foam shot out of hidden turrets in the walls and ceiling. The fiery man was covered in white bubbles and extinguished in seconds. The smell of burnt hair competed with the alcohol stench for dominance.

Before anyone else could react, naval personnel were streaming into the room. Stern-faced young men and women with holstered sidearms calmly told everyone to remain still while emergency crews worked. Medical technicians came in and scraped foam off the would-be suicide. He seemed more surprised than hurt. They handcuffed him and loaded him onto a stretcher. He was out of the room in less than a minute. Once he was gone, the people with guns seemed to relax a little.

"They certainly put him out fast," Anna said to the armed young woman closest to her. "That's good."

The young woman, looking hardly older than a schoolgirl,

laughed. "This is a battleship, ma'am. Our fire-suppression systems are robust."

Cortez had darted across the room and was speaking to the ranking naval officer in a booming voice. He sounded upset. Father Michel seemed to be quietly praying, and Anna felt a strong urge to join him.

"Well," Tilly said, waving at the room with her empty champagne glass. Her face was pale apart from two bright red dots on her cheeks "Maybe this trip won't be boring after all."

Chapter Nine: Bull

It would have gone faster if Bull had asked for more help, but until he knew who was doing what, he didn't want to trust too many people. Or anyone.

A thousand people in the crew more or less made things a little muddier than they would have been in some ways. With a crew that big, the security chief could look for things like crew members from unlikely departments meeting up at odd times. Deviations from the pattern that every ship had. Since this was the shakedown voyage, the *Behemoth* didn't have any patterns yet. It was still in a state of chaos, crew and ship getting to know one another. Making decisions, forming habits and customs and culture. Nothing was normal yet, and so nothing was strange.

On the other hand, it was only a thousand people.

Every ship had a black economy. Someone on the *Behemoth* would be trading sex for favors. Someone would run a card game or set up a pachinko parlor or start a little protection racket. People would be bribed to do things or not do things. It was what happened when you put people together. Bull's job wasn't to stamp it all out. His job was to keep it at a level that kept the ship moving and safe. And to set boundaries.

Alexi Myerson-Freud was a nutritionist. He'd worked mid-level jobs on Tycho, mostly in the yeast vats, tuning the bioengineering to produce the right mix of chemicals, minerals, and salts for keeping humans alive. He'd been married twice, had a kid he hadn't seen in five years, was part of a network war-gaming group that simulated ancient battles, pitting themselves against the great generals of history. He was eight years younger than Bull. He had mouse-ass brown hair, an awkward smile, and a side business selling a combination stimulant and euphoric the Belters called pixie dust. Bull had worked it all until he was certain.

And even once he knew, he'd waited a few days. Not long. Just enough that he could follow Alexi around on the security system. He needed to make sure there wasn't a bigger fish above him, a partner who was keeping a lower profile, or a connection to Bull's own team—or else, God forbid, Ashford's. There wasn't.

Truth was, he didn't want to do it. He knew what had to happen, and it was always easier to put it off for another fifteen minutes, or until after lunch, or until tomorrow. Only every time he did, it meant someone else was going on shift stoned, maybe making a stupid mistake, breaking the ship, getting injured, or getting killed.

The moment came in the middle of second shift. Bull turned down his console, stood up, took a couple of guns from the armory, and made a connection on his hand terminal.

"Serge?"

"Boss."

"I'm gonna need you and one other. We're going to go bust a drug dealer."

The silence on the line sounded like surprise. Bull waited. This would tell him something too.

"You got it," Serge said. "Be right there."

Serge came into the office ten minutes later with another security grunt, a broad-shouldered, grim-faced woman named Corin. She was a good choice. Bull made a mental note in Serge's favor, and handed them both guns. Corin checked the magazine, holstered it, and waited. Serge flipped his from hand to hand, judging the weight and feel, then shrugged.

"What's the plan?" he asked.

"Come with me," Bull said. "Someone tries to keep me from doing my job, warn them once, then shoot them."

"Straightforward," Serge said, and there was a sense of approval in the word.

The food processing complex was deep inside the ship, close to the massive, empty inner surface. In the long voyage to the stars, it would have been next to the farmlands of the small internal world of the *Nauvoo*. In the *Behemoth*, it wasn't anywhere in particular. What had been logical became dumb, and all it took was changing the context. Bull drove them, the little electric cart's foam wheels buzzing against the ramps. In the halls and corridors, people stopped, watched. Some stared. It said something that three armed security agents traveling together stood out. Bull wasn't sure it was something good.

Near the vats, the air smelled different. There were more volatiles and unfiltered particulates. The processing complex itself was a network of tubs and vats and distilling columns. Half of the place was shut down, the extra capacity mothballed and waiting for a larger population to feed. Or else waiting to be torn out.

They found Alexi knee deep in one of the water treatment baths, orange rubber waders clinging to his legs and his hands full of thick green kelp. Bull pointed to him, and then to the catwalk on which he, Serge, and Corin stood. There might have been a flicker of unease in Alexi's expression. It was hard to say.

"I can't get out right now," the dealer said, holding up a broad wet leaf. "I'm in the middle of something."

Bull nodded and turned to Serge.

"You two stay here. Don't let him go anywhere. I'll be right back."

"Sa sa, boss," Serge said.

The locker room was down a ladder and through a hall. The bank of pea-green private storage bins had been pulled out of the wall, turned ninety degrees, and put back in to match the direction of thrust. Blobs and filaments of caulk still showed at the edges where it failed to sit quite flush. Two other water processing techs were sitting on the bench in different levels of undress, talking and flirting. They went silent when Bull walked in. He smiled at them, nodded, and walked past to a locker on the far end. When he reached it, he turned back.

"This belong to anyone?" he asked.

The two techs looked at each other.

"No, sir," the woman said, pulling her jumpsuit a little more closed. "Most of these are just empty."

"Okay, then," Bull said. He thumbed in his override code and pulled the door open. The duffel bag inside was green and gray, the kind of thing he'd have put his clothes in when he went to work out. He ran a finger along the seal. About a hundred vials of yellow-white powder, a little more grainy than powdered milk. He closed the bag, put it on his shoulder.

"Is there a problem?" the male tech asked. His voice was tentative, but not scared. Curious, more. Excited. Well, God loved rubberneckers, and so did Bull.

"Myerson-Freud just stopped selling pixie dust on the side," Bull said. "Should go tell all your friends, eh?"

The techs looked at each other, eyebrows raised, as Bull headed out. Back at the kelp tank, he dropped the bag, then pointed to Alexi and to the catwalk beside him, the same motions he'd used before. This time Alexi's face went grim. Bull waited while the tech slogged through the deep water and pulled himself up.

"What's the problem?" Alexi said. "What's in the bag?"

Bull shook his head slowly, and only once. The chagrin on Alexi's face was like a confession. Not that Bull had needed one.

"Hey, ese," Bull said. "Just want you to know, I'm sorry about this."

He punched Alexi in the nose. Cartilage and bone gave way under his knuckle and a bright red fountain of blood spilled slowly past the tech's startled mouth.

"Put him on the back of the cart," Bull said. "Where folks can see him."

Serge and Corin exchanged a look that was a lot like the pair in the locker room.

"We heading to the brig, boss?" Serge asked, and his tone of voice meant he already knew the answer.

"We have a brig?" Bull asked as he scooped up the duffel bag.

"Pretty don't."

"Then we're not going there."

Bull had planned the route to pass through all the most populated public areas between the innermost areas of the ship and its skin. Word was already going around, and there were spectators all along the way. Alexi was making a high keening sound when he wasn't shouting or begging or demanding to see the captain. Bull had the sudden, visceral memory of seeing a pig carried to the slaughter when he'd been younger. He didn't know when it had happened; the memory was just there, floating unconnected from the rest of his life.

It took almost half an hour to reach the airlock. A crowd had gathered, a small sea of faces, most of them on wide heads and thin bodies. The Belters watching the Earther kill one of their own. Bull ignored them. He keyed in his passcode, opened the inner door of the lock, walked back to the cart, and hefted Alexi with one arm. In the low gravity it should have been easy, but Bull felt himself getting winded before he got back to the lock. It didn't help that Alexi was thrashing. Bull pushed him in, closed the inner door, put in the override code, and opened the exterior door without evacuating the air first. The pop rang through the metal deck like a distant bell. The monitor showed that the lock was empty. Bull closed the exterior door. While the lock refilled, he walked back to the cart. He stood on the back of the cart where Alexi had been, the duffel bag over his head in both hands. Blood stained his sleeve and his left knee.

"This is pixie dust, right?" he said to the crowd. He didn't use his terminal to amplify his voice. He didn't need to. "I'm gonna leave this in the airlock for sixteen hours, then I'm spacing it. Any other dust comes in to join it before then, well, it just happened. No big deal. Any of this goes away, and that's a problem. So everybody go tell everybody. And the next pendejo signs on shift high comes and talks to me."

He walked back to the airlock slowly, letting everyone see him. He opened the inner door, slung the bag through, and turned away, leaving the door open behind him. Climbing back behind the wheel of the cart, he could feel the tension in the crowd, and it didn't bother him at all. Other things did. What he'd just done was the easy part. What came next was harder, because he had less control over it.

"You want to set a guard on that, boss?" Serge asked.

"Think we need to?" Bull asked. He didn't expect an answer, and he didn't get one. The cart lurched forward, the spectators parting before it like a herd of antelope before a lion. Bull aimed them back toward the ramps that would take him to the security offices.

"Hardcore," Corin said. She made it sound like a good thing.

Religious art decorated the captain's office. Angels in blue and gold held the parabolas of the archways that rose overhead to meet at the image of a calm and bearded God. A beneficent Christ looked down from the wall behind Ashford's desk, Caucasian features calm and serene. He didn't look anything like the bloody, bent, crucified man Bull was familiar with. Arrayed at the Savior's side were images of plenty: wheat, corn, goats, cows, and stars. Captain Ashford paced back and forth by Jesus' knees, his face dark with blood and fury. Michio Pa was seated in the other guest chair, carefully not looking at Ashford or at Bull. Whatever the situation was with the Martian science ships and their military escort, with the massive Earth flotilla, it was forgotten for the moment.

Bull didn't let the anxiety show in his face.

"This is unacceptable, Mister Baca."

"Why do you think that, sir?"

Ashford stopped, put his wide hands on the desk, and leaned forward. Bull looked into his bloodshot eyes and wondered whether the captain was getting enough sleep.

"You killed a member of my crew," Ashford said. "You did it with clear premeditation. You did it in front of a hundred witnesses."

"Shit, you want witnesses, there's surveillance footage," Bull said. It wasn't the right thing to do.

"You are relieved of duty, Mister Baca. And confined to quarters until we return to Tycho Station, where you will stand trial for murder."

"He was selling drugs to the crew."

"Then he should have been *arrested*!"

Bull took a deep breath, exhaling slowly through his nose.

"You think we're more running a warship or a space station, sir?" he asked. Ashford's brow furrowed, and he shook his head. To Bull's right, Pa shifted in her seat. When neither of them spoke, Bull went on. "Reason I ask is if I'm a cop, then yeah, I should have taken him to the brig, if we had a brig. He should have gotten a lawyer. We could have done that whole thing. Me? I don't think this is a station. I think it's a battleship. I'm here to maintain military discipline in a potential combat zone. Not Earth navy discipline. Not Martian navy discipline. OPA discipline. The Belter way."

Ashford stood up.

"We aren't anarchists," he said, his voice dripping with scorn.

"OPA tradition, maybe I'm wrong, is that someone does something that intentionally endangers the ship, they get to hitchhike back to wherever there's air," Bull said.

"You hauled him out of a water vat. How was he endangering the ship? Was he going to throw kelp at it?" Pa said, her voice brittle.

"People been coming on shift high," Bull said, lacing his fingers together on one knee. "Don't trust me. Ask around. And, c'mon. Of course they are, right? We've got three times as much work needs to get done as we can do. Pixie dust, and they don't feel tired. Don't take breaks. Don't slow down. Get more done. Thing about bad judgment? You got to have good judgment to notice you've got it. We already got people hurt. Matter of time before someone died. Or worse."

"You're saying this man was responsible for all those other people performing badly at their work, so you killed him?" Ashford said, but the wind was out of his sails. He was going to fold like wet cardboard. Bull recognized that Ashford's weakness was going to work to his advantage this time, but he still hated it.

"I'm saying he was putting the ship at risk for his own financial gain, just like he was stealing air filters. And sure he did. There was a demand, he filled it. If I lock him up, that makes it so that the risk is higher. Prices are higher. Get caught, you maybe go to jail when we get back to Tycho."

"And you made it so that the risk is death."

"No," Bull said. "I mean, yeah, but I don't shoot him. I do what you do to people who risk the ship. Belters know what getting spaced means, right? It frames the issue."

"This was a mistake."

"I've got a list of fifty people he sold to," Bull said. "Some of them are skilled technicians. A couple are mid-level overseers. We could lock 'em all up, but then we've got less people to do the work. And anyway, they won't be doing it anymore. Supply's gone. But if you want I could talk to them. Let 'em know I'm keeping an eye open."

Pa's chuckle was mirthless.

"That would be difficult if you're in the brig on charges," she said.

"We don't have a brig," Bull said. "Plan was the church elders were just gonna talk everything out." He kept his tone carefully free of sarcasm.

Ashford waffled. It was like watching a cat trying to decide whether to jump from one tree limb to another. His expression was calculating, internal, uncertain. Bull waited.

"This never happens again," Ashford said. "You decide someone needs to go out the airlock, you come to me. I'll be the one that pushes the button."

"All right."

"All right, what?" Ashford bit the words. Bull lowered his head, looking at the deck. He'd gotten what he came for. He could let Ashford feel like he'd gotten a little win too.

"I mean, yes, sir, Captain. Solid copy. I understand and will comply."

"You're damn right you will," Ashford said. "Now get the hell back to work."

"Yes, sir."

When the door closed behind him, Bull leaned against the wall and took a few deep breaths. He was intensely aware of the sound of the ship—low hum of the air recyclers, the distant murmur of voices, the chimes and beeps of a thousand different system alerts. The air smelled of plastic and ozone. He'd taken his calculated risk, and he'd pulled it off.

Walking back down, level by level, he felt the attention on him. In the lift, a man tried not to stare at him. In the hall outside the security office, a woman smiled at him and nodded, nervous as a mouse that smells cat. Bull smiled back.

In the security office, Serge and another man from the team—a Europan named Casimir—lifted their fists, greeting him in the physical idiom of the Belt. Bull returned the gesture and ambled over.

"What we got?" Bull asked.

"A couple dozen people came to pay respects," Serge said. "I figure about half a kilo more dust just appeared out of nowhere."

"Okay, then."

"I've got a file of everyone who went in. You want me to flag them in the system?"

"Nope," Bull said. "I told them it was no big deal. It's no big deal. You can kill the file."

"You got it, boss."

"I'll be in my office," Bull said. "Let me know if something comes up. And somebody start a pot of coffee."

He sat down on the desk, his feet resting on the seat of his chair, and leaned forward. He was suddenly exhausted. It had been a long, bad day, and losing the dread he'd been carrying for the weeks leading up to it was like being released from prison. It took a minute or two to notice he had a message waiting from Michio Pa. The XO hadn't requested a connection. She didn't want to talk to him, then. She just wanted to say something.

In the recording, her face was lit from below with the backsplash of her hand terminal screen. Her smile was thin and tight and sort of faded away somewhere around her cheekbones.

"I saw what you did there. That was very nice. Very clever. Wrapping yourself in the OPA flag, making the old man wonder if the crew wouldn't take your side. More-Belter-than-thou. It was *graceful*."

Bull scratched his chin. The stubble that had grown in since morning made his fingernails sound like a rasp. It was probably too much to ask that he not make any enemies with this, but he was sorry it was Pa.

"You can't sugarcoat it with me. We both know that killing someone doesn't make you admirable. I'm not about to forget this. I just hope you have enough soul left that what you've done still bothers you."

The recording ended, and Bull smiled at the blank screen wearily.

"Every time," he told the hand terminal. "And next time too."

Chapter Ten: Holden

The *Rocinante* was not a small ship. Her normal crew complement was over a dozen navy personnel and officers, and on many missions she'd also carry six marines. Running the *Roci* with four people meant each of them did several jobs, and that didn't leave a lot of downtime. It also meant that it was pretty easy at first to avoid the four strangers living on the ship. With the documentary crew restricted from entering ops, the airlock deck, the machine shop, or engineering, they were stuck on the two crew decks with access only to their quarters, the head, the galley, and sick bay.

Monica was a lovely person. Calm, friendly, charismatic. If even a part of her charm translated to the other side of the camera, it was easy to see how she'd succeeded. The others—Okju, Clip, Cohen—made clear overtures of friendship, cracking jokes with the *Rocinante*'s crew, making dinners. Reaching out, but it wasn't clear to Holden whether it was the usual honeymoon period that came when any crew first came together for a long voyage or something more calculated. Maybe a little of both.

What he did see was his own crew drawing back. After two days of the documentary team being on board, Naomi simply retreated to the ops deck where she couldn't be found. Amos had made a halfhearted pass at Monica, and a slightly more serious attempt with Okju. When both failed, he began spending most of his time in the machine shop. Of them all, only Alex took time to socialize with their passengers, and him not all that often. He'd taken to sometimes sleeping in the pilot's couch.

They'd agreed to being interviewed, and Holden knew they couldn't avoid it forever. They hadn't been out for a full week yet, and even on a fairly high burn it would be months to their destination. Besides, it was in their contract. The discomfort of it was almost enough to distract him from the fact that every day brought them closer to the Ring and whatever it was that Miller wanted him out there for. Almost.

"It's Saturday," Naomi said. She was lounging in a crash couch near the comm station. She hadn't cut her hair for a while, and it was getting long enough to become an annoyance to her. For the last ten minutes, she'd been trying to braid it. The thick black curls resisted her efforts, seeming to move with a will of their own. Based on past experience, Holden knew this was the precursor to cutting half of it off in exasperation. Naomi liked the idea of growing her hair very long, but not the reality. Holden sat at the combat ops panel watching her struggle with it and letting his mind drift.

"Did you hear me?" she said.

"It's Saturday."

"Are we inviting our guests to dinner?"

It had become custom on the ship that no matter what else was going on, the crew tried to have dinner as a group once a week. By unspoken agreement it was usually Saturday. Which day of the week it happened to be didn't really matter much on a ship, but by holding their dinner on Saturday, Holden thought they were doing some small bit to celebrate the passing of a week, the beginning of another. A gentle reminder that there was still a solar system outside of the four of them.

But he hadn't considered inviting the documentary crew to join them. It felt like an invasion. The Saturday dinner was for *crew.*

"We can't keep them out of it." He sighed. "Can we?"

"Not unless we want to eat up here. You did give them the run of the galley."

"Dammit," he said. "Should have confined them to quarters."

"For four months?"

"We could have shoved ration bars and catheter bags under the door to them."

She smiled and said, "It's Amos' turn to cook."

"Right, I'll call and let him know it's dinner for eight."

Amos made pasta and mushrooms, heavy on the garlic, heavy on the Parmesan. It was his favorite, and he always splurged to buy real cloves of garlic and actual Parmesan cheese to grate. Another small luxury they wouldn't be able to afford if they wound up in a courtroom battle with Mars.

While Amos finished sautéing the mushrooms and garlic, Alex set the table and took drink orders. Holden sat next to Naomi on one side of the table, while the documentary crew sat together on the other. The banter was polite and friendly, and if there was an uncomfortable undercurrent to it all, he still wasn't quite sure why.

Holden had asked them not to bring cameras or recording equipment to the dinner table, and Monica had agreed. Clip, the Martian, was talking about sports history with Alex. Okju and Cohen, sitting across from Naomi, were telling stories about the last assignment they'd been on, covering a new scientific station that was in stationary orbit around Mercury. It should have been almost pleasant, and it just wasn't.

Holden said, "We don't usually eat this well while flying, but we try to do something nice for our weekly dinner together."

Okju smiled and said, "Smells lovely." She was wearing half a dozen rings, a blouse with buttons on it, a silver pendant, and an ivory-colored comb holding back her frizzy brown hair. The soundman gazed serenely at nothing, his black glasses hiding the top of his face, his expression calm and open. Monica watched him look over her crew, saying nothing, a faint smile on her lips.

"Chow," Amos said, then began putting bowls of food on the table. While the meal was handed around in a slow circuit, Okju bowed her head and mumbled something. It took Holden a moment to realize she was praying. He hadn't seen anyone do it for years, not since he'd left home. One of his fathers, Caesar, had sometimes prayed before meals. Holden waited for her to finish before he started eating.

"This is very nice," Monica said. "Thank you."

"You're welcome," said Holden.

"We're a week out of Ceres," she said, "and I think we're all settled in. Was wondering if we could start scheduling some preliminary interviews? It's mostly so we can test out the equipment."

"You can interview me," Amos said, not quite hiding his leer.

Monica smiled at him and speared a mushroom with her fork, then stared at him while she popped it into her mouth and chewed slowly.

"Okay," she said. "We can start with background work. Baltimore?"

The silence was suddenly brittle. Amos started to stand, but a gentle hand on his arm from Naomi stopped him. He opened his mouth, closed it, then looked down at his plate while the pale skin on his scalp and neck turned bright red. Monica looked down at her plate, her expression at the friction point between embarrassed and annoyed.

"That's not a good idea," Holden said.

"Captain, I'm sensitive to privacy issues for you and your crew, but we have an agreement. And with all respect, you've been treating me and mine like we're unwelcome."

Around the table, the food was starting to cool off. It had hardly been touched. "I get it. You held up your end of the deal," Holden said. "You got me out of Ceres, and you put money in our pockets. We haven't been holding up our end. I get it. I'll set aside an hour tomorrow for starters, does that work?"

"Sure," she said. "Let's eat."

"Baltimore, huh?" Clip said to Amos. "Football fan?"

Amos said nothing, and Clip didn't press it.

After the uncomfortable dinner, Holden wanted nothing more than to climb into bed. But while he was in the head brushing his teeth, Alex pretended to casually wander in and said, "Come on up to ops, Cap. Got something to talk about."

When Holden followed him up, he found Amos and Naomi already waiting. Naomi was leaning back with her hands behind her head, but Amos sat on the edge of a crash couch, both feet on the floor and his hands clenched into a doubled fist in front of him. His expression was still dark with anger.

"So, Jim," Alex said, walking over to another crash couch and dropping into it, "this ain't a good start."

"She's looking stuff up about us," Amos said to no one in particular, his gaze still on the floor. "Stuff she shouldn't know."

Holden knew what Amos meant. Monica's reference to Baltimore was an allusion to Amos' childhood as the product of a particularly nasty brand of unlicensed prostitution. But Holden couldn't admit he knew it. He himself only knew because of an overheard conversation. He had no interest in humiliating Amos further.

"She's a journalist, they do background research," he said.

"She's more than that," Naomi said. "She's a nice person. She's charming and she's friendly, and every one of us on this ship wants to like her."

"That's a problem?" Holden said.

"That's a big fucking problem," Amos said.

"I was on the *Canterbury* for a reason, Jim," Alex said. His Mariner Valley drawl had stopped sounding silly, and just seemed sad instead. "I don't need someone diggin' up my skeletons to air them out."

The *Canterbury*, the ice hauler they'd all worked on together before the Eros incident, was a bottom-of-the-barrel job for those who flew for a living. It attracted people who'd failed down to the level of their incompetence, or those who couldn't pass the background checks a better job might require. Or, in his own case, those who had a dishonorable military discharge staining their record. After having served with his small crew for years, Holden knew it wasn't incompetence that had put any of them on that ship.

"I know," he started.

"Same here, Cap'n," Amos said. "I got a lot of past in my past."

"So do I," Naomi said.

Holden started to reply, then stopped when the import of her words hit him. Naomi was hiding something that had driven her to take a glorified mechanic's job on the *Canterbury*. Well, of course she was. Holden hadn't wanted to think about it, but it was obvious. She was about the most talented engineer he'd ever met. He knew she had degrees from two universities, and had completed her three-year flight officer training in two. She'd started her career on an obvious command track. Something had happened, but she'd never talked about what it had been. He frowned a question at her, but she stopped him with a tiny shake of her head.

The fragility of their little family struck him full force. The paths that had pulled them all together had been so diverse, as improbable and unlikely as those kinds of things ever were. And the universe could just as easily take them apart. It left him feeling small and vulnerable and a little defensive.

"Everyone remembers why we did this, right?" Holden asked. "The lockdown? Mars coming after the *Rocinante*?"

"We didn't have a choice," Naomi replied. "We know. We all agreed to take this job."

Amos nodded in agreement. Alex said, "No one's sayin' we shouldn't have taken the job. What we're sayin' is that you're the frontman for this band."

"Yes," Naomi said. "You need to be so interesting that this documentary crew forgets all about the rest of us. That's your job for the rest of this flight. That's the only way this works."

"No," Amos said, still not looking up. "There *is* another way, but I've never tossed a blind man out an airlock. Don't know how I'd feel about that. Might not be fun."

"Okay," Holden said, patting the air with his hands in a calming motion. "I get it. I'll keep the cameras out of your faces as much as I can, but this is a long trip. Be patient. When we get to the Ring, maybe they'll be tired of us and we can pawn them off on some other ship."

They were silent for a moment, then Alex shook his head.

"Well," he said, "I think we just found the only thing that'll make me look forward to getting *there*."

Holden woke with a start, rubbing furiously at an itch on his nose. He had a half-remembered feeling of something trying to climb inside it. No bugs on the ship, so it had to have been a dream. The itch was real, though.

As he scratched, he said, "Sorry, bad dream or something," and patted the bed next to him. It was empty. Naomi must have gone to the bathroom. He inhaled and exhaled loudly through his nose several times, trying to get rid of the itchy sensation inside. On the third exhale, a blue firefly popped out and flew away. Holden became aware of a faint scent of acetate in the air.

"We need to talk," said a familiar voice in the darkness.

Holden's throat went tight. His heart began to pound. He pulled a pillow over his face and suppressed an urge to scream as much from frustration and rage as the old familiar fear that tightened his chest.

"So. There was this rookie," Miller started. "Good kid, you'd have hated him."

"I can't take this shit," Holden said, yanking the pillow away from his face and throwing it in the direction of Miller's voice. He slapped the panel by the bed and the room's lights came on. Miller was standing by the door, the pillow behind him, wearing the same rumpled gray suit and porkpie hat, fidgeting like he had a rash.

"He never really learned to clear a room, you know?" Miller continued. His lips were black. "Corners and doorways. I tried to tell him. It's always corners and doorways."

Holden reached for the comm panel to call Naomi, then stopped. He wanted her to be there, to make the ghost vanish the way it always had before. And he was also afraid that this time, it wouldn't.

"Listen, you've gotta clear the room," Miller said, his face twisted with confusion and intensity, like a drugged man trying to remember something important. "If you don't clear the room, the room *eats* you."

"What do you want from me?" Holden said. "Why are you making me go out there?"

A thick exasperation twisted Miller's expression.

"What the hell are you hearing me *say*? You see a room full of bones, only thing you know is something got *killed.* You're the predator right up until you're prey." He stopped, staring at Holden. Waiting for an answer. When Holden didn't respond, Miller moved a step closer to the bed. Something on his face made Holden think of the times he'd watched the cop shoot people. He opened a cabinet by the bed and took out his sidearm.

"Don't get any closer," Holden said, not pointing the gun at Miller yet. "But be honest, if I shot you, would you even die?"

Miller laughed. His expression became almost human. "Depends."

The door opened and Miller blinked out. Naomi came in wearing a robe and carrying a bulb of water.

"You awake?"

Holden nodded, then opened the cabinet and put the gun away. His expression must have told Naomi everything.

"Are you all right?"

"Yeah. He vanished when you opened the door."

"You look terrified," Naomi said, putting her water down and sliding under the covers next to him.

"He's scarier now. Before, I thought...I don't know what I thought. But ever since he knew about the gate, I keep trying to figure out what he really means. It was easier when I could think it was some kind of static. That it didn't...that it didn't mean anything."

Naomi curled up against his side, putting her arms around him. He felt his muscles relaxing.

"We can't let Monica and her crew ever know about this," he said. Naomi's smile was half sorrow. "What?"

"James Holden not telling everyone everything," she said.

"This is different."

"I know."

"What did he say?" Naomi asked. "Did it make sense?"

"No. But it was all about death. Everything he says is about death."

Over the course of the following weeks, the ship fell into a routine that, while not comfortable, was at least collegial. Holden spent time with the documentary crew, being filmed, showing them the ship, answering questions. What was his childhood like? Loving and complex and bittersweet. Had he really saved Earth by talking the half-aware girl who'd been the protomolecule's seed crystal into rerouting to Venus? No, mostly that had just worked out well. Did he have any regrets?

He smiled and took it and pretended he wasn't holding anything back. That the only thing leading him out to the Ring was his contract with them. That he hadn't been chosen by the protomolecule for something else that he hadn't yet begun to understand.

Sometimes, Monica turned to the others, but Alex and Naomi kept their answers friendly, polite, and shallow. Amos laced his responses with cheerful and explicit profanity until it was almost impossible to edit into something for a civilized audience.

Cohen turned out to be more than a sound engineer. The dark glasses he wore were a sonar feedback system that allowed him to create a three-dimensional model of any space he occupied. When Amos asked why he didn't have prosthetics instead, Cohen had told them that the accident that claimed his eyes also burned the optic nerves away. The attempted nerve regrowth therapy had failed and almost killed him with an out-of-control brain tumor. But the interface that allowed his brain to translate sonar data into a working 3D landscape also made him an extraordinary visual effects modeler. While Monica spun a narrative of Holden's life following the destruction of his ship the *Canterbury*, Cohen created beautiful visual renderings of the scenes. At one point, he showed the crew a short clip of Holden speaking, describing the escape from Eros after the initial protomolecule infection, all while he appeared to be moving down perfectly rendered Erosian corridors filled with bodies.

Part of Holden had almost come to enjoy the interviews, but he could only watch the Eros graphics for a few seconds before he asked Cohen to turn it off. He'd been sure that seeing it would somehow invoke Miller, but it hadn't. Holden didn't like the memories that came with their story. The documentary crew made accommodations, not forcing him further than he was willing to go. Their being nice about it somehow only made him feel worse.

A week out from the Ring, they caught up to the *Behemoth*. Monica was sitting on the ops deck with the crew when the massive OPA ship finally got close enough for the *Roci*'s telescopes to get a good view of her. Holden had allowed the restrictions on where the documentary crew were permitted to just sort of fade away.

They were doing a slow pan of the *Behemoth*'s hull when Alex whistled and pointed at a protrusion on the side. "Damn, boss, the Mormons are better armed than I remember. That's a rail gun turret right there. And I'd bet a week's desserts those things are torpedo tubes."

"I liked her better when she was a generation ship," Holden replied. He called up combat ops and told the *Rocinante* to classify the new hull as the *Behemoth*-class dreadnought and add all the hardpoints and weapons to her threat profile.

"That's the kind of stealing only governments can get away with," Amos said. "I guess the OPA is a real thing now."

"Yeah," Alex replied with a laugh.

"Mars is making a similar claim against us," Holden said.

"And if *we'd* been the ones to blow up their battleship before we flew off in this boat, they'd have an argument to make," Amos said. "Last I checked, that was the bad guys, though."

Naomi didn't chime in. She was working at something on the comm panel. Holden could tell it was a complex problem because she was quietly humming to herself.

"You've been on the *Nauvoo* before, right?" Monica asked.

"No," Holden said. The *Rocinante* began rapidly throwing data onto his screen. The ship's calculations of the *Behemoth*'s actual combat strength. "They were still working on it the first time I was on Tycho Station. By the time I started working for Fred Johnson, they'd already shot the *Nauvoo* at Eros, and she was on her way out of the solar system. I did get to walk through the ship they sent to catch her, once."

The *Rocinante* was displaying puzzling projections at him. The ship seemed to think that the *Behemoth* didn't have the structural strength to support the number and size of weapon hardpoints she currently sported. In fact, she seemed to think that if the OPA battleship ever actually fired two of its six capital-ship-class rail guns at the same time, there was a 34 percent chance the hull would rip apart. Just to have something to do, Holden told the *Roci* to create a tactical package for fighting the *Behemoth* and send it to Alex and Naomi. Probably, they'd never need it.

"You didn't like working for the OPA?" Monica asked. She had the little smile she got when she asked a question she already knew the answer to. Holden suspected the documentarian was also a terrible poker player, but so far he hadn't been able to get her into a game.

"It was a mixed bag," he said, forcing himself to smile. To be the James Holden that Monica wanted and expected. To sacrifice himself to her attention so she'd leave the others be.

"Jim?" Naomi said, finally looking up from her panel. "You know that memory leak in comms that I've been hunting for a month? It's getting worse. It's driving me nuts."

"How bad?" Alex asked.

"Fluctuating between .0021 and .033 percent," she said. "I'm having to flush and reboot every couple of days now."

Amos laughed. "Do we care about that? Because I'll raise you a power leak in the head that's almost a whole percent."

Naomi turned to look at him with a frown. "You didn't tell me?"

"I'll bet you a month's pay it's a worn lead to the lights. I'll yank the fucker out when I get a chance."

"Do those things happen a lot?" Monica asked.

"Hell no," Alex replied before Holden could. "The *Roci* is solid."

"Yeah," Amos chimed in. "She's so well put together, we gotta obsess over bullshit like crusty memory bubbles and shitty light bulbs just to have something to do." The smile he aimed at Monica was indistinguishable from the real thing.

"So you didn't really answer my question about the OPA," Monica said, swiveling her chair to face Holden. She pointed at the threat map the *Roci* had created of the *Behemoth*, the weapon hardpoints like angry red blisters dotting her skin. "Everything okay between you?"

"Yeah, everyone's still friends," Holden said. "Nothing to worry about."

A proximity light flashed as the *Behemoth* bounced a ranging laser off the *Roci*'s hull. She returned the favor. Not targeting lasers. Just two ships making sure they weren't in any danger of getting too close.

Nothing to worry about.

Yeah, right.

Chapter Eleven: Melba

Stanni stood just behind Melba's left shoulder, looking at the display. His palm rubbed against the slick fabric of his work trousers like he was trying to sooth a cramped quadriceps. Melba had learned to read it as a sign the man was nervous. The narrow architecture of the *Cerisier* put him so close to her, she could feel the subtle warmth of his body against the back of her neck. In any other context, being this close to a man would have meant they were sharing an intimate moment. Here, it meant nothing. She didn't even find it annoying.

"Mira," Stanni said, flapping his hand. "La. Right there."

The monitor was old, a constant green pixel burning in the lower left corner where some steady glitch had been irreparable and not worth replacing. The definition was still better than a hand terminal. To the untrained eye, the power demand profile for the UNN *Thomas Prince* could have been the readout of an

EEG or a seismological reading or the visual representation of a bhangra recording. But over the course of weeks—months now—Melba's eye wasn't untrained.

"I see it," she said, putting her finger on the spike. "And we can't tell where it came from?"

"Fucks me," Stanni said, rubbing his thigh. "I'm seeing it, but I don't know what I'm looking at."

Melba ran her tongue against the back of her teeth, concentrating, trying to remember what the tutorials had shown about tracking power spikes. In an odd way, her inexperience had shifted into an asset for the team. Stanni and Ren, Bob and Soledad all had more hands-on experience than she did, but she'd only just learned the basics. Sometimes she would know some simple thing that all of them had known once, and only she hadn't forgotten. Her analysis was slower, but it didn't skip steps, because she didn't know which steps could be skipped.

"Did it start at the deceleration flip?" she asked.

Stanni grunted like a man struck by a sudden pain.

"They hit null g and one of the regulators reset," he said. "Least it's nothing serious. Embarrassing to blow up all they preachers y sa. We'll need to get back over there and check them, though."

Melba nodded and made a mental note to read through what that process required. All she'd known was the truism repeated in three of her tutorials that when a ship cut thrust halfway through a journey, flipped, and began accelerating in the opposite direction it was a time for especial care.

"I'll put it on the rotation," she said, and pulled up her team's schedule. There was a slot in ten days when there would be enough time to revisit the big ship. She blocked out the time, marked it, and posted it to the full group. All of it felt easy and natural, like the sort of thing she had been doing her whole life. Which in a sense, she had.

The flotilla was coming to the last leg of its journey. They had passed the orbit of Uranus weeks ago, and the sun was a bright star in an overwhelming abyss of night sky. All the plumes of fire were pointed toward the Ring now, bleeding off their velocity with every passing minute. Even though it was the standard pattern for Epstein drive ships, Melba couldn't quite shake the feeling that they were all trying to flee from their destination and being pulled in against their will.

Unless they were discussing work, the only conversation—in the mess hall, on the exercise machines, on the shuttles to and from the ships they maintained—was about the Ring. The Martian science ships and their escort were already there, peering through the void. There had been no official reports given, so instead rumors sprang up like weeds. Every beam of light that passed through the Ring and hit something bounced back, just like in normal space. But a few troubling constants varied as you got close to it. The microwave background from inside the Ring was older than the big bang. People said if you listened carefully to the static from the other side of the Ring, you could hear the voices of the dead of Eros, or of the damned. Melba heard the dread in other people's voices, saw Soledad crossing herself when she thought no one was looking, felt the oppressive weight of the object. She understood their growing fear not because she felt it herself but because her own private crisis point was coming.

The OPA's monstrous battleship was on course to arrive soon, almost at the same time as the Earth flotilla. It wasn't a matter of days yet, but it would be soon. The *Rocinante* had already passed the slower *Behemoth*. She and Holden were rising up out of the sun's domain, and soon their paths would converge. Then there would be the attack, and the public humiliation of James Holden, and with it, his death. And after that…

It was strange to think of an afterward. The more she imagined it, the more she could see herself relaxing back into Melba's life. There was no reason not to. Clarissa Mao had nothing, commanded nothing, was nothing. Melba Koh had work, at least. A history. It was a pretty thought, made prettier by being impossible.

She would go home, become Clarissa again, and do whatever else she could to restore her family's name. Honor required it. If she'd stayed, it would have meant being like Julie.

Growing up, Clarissa had admired and resented her older sister. Julie the pretty one. The smart one. The champion yacht racer. Julie who could make Father laugh. Julie who could do no wrong. Petyr was younger than Clarissa and so would always be less. The twins Michael and Anthea had always been a world unto themselves, sharing jokes and comments that only they understood, and so seemed at times more like long-term guests of the family than part of it. Julie was the oldest, the one Clarissa longed to be. The one to beat. Clarissa hadn't been the only one to see Julie that way. Their mother felt it too. It was the thing that made Clarissa and her mother most alike.

And then something happened. Julie had walked away from them all, cut her hair, dropped out of school, and disappeared up into the darkness. She remembered her father hearing the news over dinner. They'd been having kaju murgh kari in the informal dining room that overlooked the park. She'd just come back from her riding lesson and still smelled a little of horse. Petyr had been talking about mathematics again, boring everyone, when her mother looked up from her plate with a smile and announced that Julie had written a letter to say she'd quit the family. Clarissa's mouth had dropped open. It was like saying that the sun had decided to become a politician or that four had decided to be eight. It wasn't quite incomprehensible, but it lived on the edge.

Her father had laughed. He'd said it was a phase. Julie'd gone to live like the common people and sow a few wild oats, and once she'd had her fill, she'd come home. But she'd seen in his eyes that he didn't believe it. His perfect girl was gone. She'd rejected not only him, but the family. Their name. Forever after, cashews and curry had tasted like victory.

And so Melba would have to be folded up when she was done here. Put back in a box and buried or burned. Clarissa could go live with one of her siblings. Petyr had his own ship now. She could work on it as an electrochemical engineer, she thought with a smile. Or, in the worst case, stay with Mother. If she told them what she'd done, how she'd saved the family name, then Clarissa could start to rebuild the company. Remake their empire in her own name. Possibly even free her father from imprisonment and exile.

The thought left her feeling both hopeful and tired.

A loud clang and the distant sound of laughter brought her back to herself. She reviewed the maintenance schedule for the next ten-day cycle—maintenance on the electrical systems of three of the minor warships and a physical inventory of the electrical cards—marked the ship's time, and shut down her terminal. The mess hall was half full when she got there, members of half a dozen other teams eating together and talking and watching the newsfeeds about the Ring, about themselves going to meet it. Soledad was sitting by herself, gaze fixed on her hand terminal while she ate a green-brown paste that looked like feces but smelled like the finest-cooked beef in the world. Melba told herself to think of it as pâté, and then it wasn't so bad.

Melba got herself a plate and a bulb of lemon water and slid in across from Soledad. The other woman's eyes flicked up with a small but genuine smile.

"Hoy, boss," she said. "How's it go?"

"Everything's copacetic." Melba smiled. She smiled more than Clarissa did. That was an interesting thought. "What did I miss?"

"Report from Mars. Data, this time. The ship that went through? Not on the drift."

"Really?" Melba said. After they'd picked up the faint transmission from the little cobbled-together ship that had started all this, the assumption had been that it had been crippled by something that lived on the other side of the Ring. That it was floating free. "It's under power?"

"Maybe," Soledad said. "Data shows it's moving, and a lot slower than it went in. And the probes they sent in? One of *them* got grabbed too. Normal burn, and then boom, stopped.

The signal's all fucked up, but it looks like the same course that the ship's on. Like they're being...taken to the same place. Or something."

"Weird," Melba said. "But I guess weird is kind of what we expect. After Eros."

"My dad was on Eros," Soledad said, and Melba felt a strange tightening in her throat. "He worked one of the casinos. Security to make sure no one hacked the games, right? Been there fifteen years. Said he was going to retire there, get a little hole up where he didn't weigh so much and just live off his retirement."

"I'm sorry."

Soledad shrugged.

"Everyone dies," she said gruffly, then wiped the back of her hand against her eyes and turned back to the screen.

"My sister was there," Melba said. It was truth, and more than truth. "My sister was one of the first ones it took."

"Shit," Soledad said, looking up at her now, terminal forgotten.

"Yeah."

The two were quiet for a long moment. At another table, a Belter man no more than twenty barked his knees against the edge of the table and started cursing squat little Earth designers, to the amusement of his friends.

"You think they're still there?" Soledad said softly, nodding at her terminal. "There were those voices. The transmissions that came off Eros. You know. After. It was people, right?"

"They're dead," Melba said. "Everyone on Eros died."

"Changed, anyway," Soledad said. "Some guy said it took the patterns off them, right? Their bodies. Their brains. I think about maybe they never really died. Just got *remade*, you know? What if their brains never stopped working and just got..."

She shrugged, looking for a word, but Melba knew what she meant. Change, even profound change, wasn't the same as death. She was proof enough of that.

"Does it matter?"

"What if their souls never got loose?" Soledad said, with real pain in her voice. "What if it caught them all, right? Your sister. My dad. What if they aren't dead, and Ring's got all their souls still?"

There are no souls, Melba thought with a touch of pity. *We are bags of meat with a little electricity running through them. No ghosts, no spirits, no souls. The only thing that survives is the story people tell about you. The only thing that matters is your name.* It was the kind of thing Clarissa would think. The kind of thing her father would have said. She didn't say it aloud.

"Maybe that's why Earth's bringing all those priests," Soledad said and took a scoop of her food. "To put them all to rest."

"Someone should," Melba agreed, and then she turned to her meal.

Her hand terminal chimed: Ren requesting a private conversation. Melba frowned and accepted the connection.

"What's up?" she said.

His voice, when it came, was strained.

"I got something I was wondering if you could look at. An anomaly."

"On my way," Melba said. She dropped the connection and downed her remaining meat paste in two huge swallows, then dropped the plate into the recycler on her way out. Ren was at a workstation in one of the storage bays. It was one of the new spaces he could work in that had a ceiling high enough that he wouldn't have to hunch. Around him, blue plastic crates stood fixed to the floor or one another with powerful electromagnets. Her footsteps were the only sound.

"What've you got?" she asked.

He stood back and nodded at the monitor.

"Air filter data from the *Seung Un*," he said.

Her blood went cold.

"Why?" she said too sharply, too quickly.

"It's catching a lot of outliers. Raised a flag. I'm looking at the profile, and it's all high-energy ganga. Nitroethenes y sa."

She hadn't thought of this. She'd known that the ships did passive gas monitoring, but it had never occurred to her that stray molecules of her explosive would get caught in the filters, or that anyone would check. Ren took her silence as confusion.

"Built a profile," he said. "Ninety percent fit with a moldable explosive."

"So they've got explosives on board," Melba said. "It's a warship. Explosives is what they do, right?" Despair and embarrassment warred in her chest. She'd screwed up. She just wanted Ren to be quiet, to not say the things he was saying. That he was *going* to say.

"This is more like what they'd use for mining and excavation," he said. "You inspected that deck. You remember seeing anything funny? Might have been hard to see. This stuff's putty until it hits air."

"You think it's a bomb?" she said.

Ren shrugged.

"Inners hauling full load of gekke. A guy tried to light himself on fire. Hunger strike lady. The one coyo did that thing with the camera."

"That wasn't political," she said. "He's a performance artist."

"All I mean, we put together a lot of different kinds of people think a lot of different kinds of things. Doesn't bring out the best in people. I was a kid, I watched me eltern end a marriage over whether the madhi was going to be a Belter. And everybody know everybody back down the well's watching. That kind of attention changes people, and it don't make them better. Maybe someone's planning to make a statement, si no?"

"Did you alert their security?" she asked.

"Check with you first. But something like this, shikata ga nai. We got to."

I have to kill him, she thought like someone whispering in her ear. She saw how to do it. Get him to look at his screen, hunch over it just a little. Enough to bare the back of his neck. Then she would press her tongue against the roof of her mouth, the rough of the tastebuds tickling her palate a little, and the strength would come. She'd break him here and then...take him back to her quarters. She could clear out her locker, fit him in. And there was packing sealant that would keep the smell of the body from getting out. She'd file a report, say he was missing. She could act as confused as anyone. By the time she gave up the room and they found him, Melba would already be gone. Even if they worked out that she'd also planted the bomb, they'd just assume she was one of Holden's agents.

Ren was looking at her, his brown eyes mild, his carrot-orange hair back in a wiry ponytail that left the skin of his neck exposed. She thought of him explaining about the brownout buffers. The gentleness in his expression. The kindness.

I'm sorry, she thought. *This isn't my fault. I have to.*

"Let's check the data again," she said, angling her body toward the monitor. "Show me where the anomalies are."

He nodded, turning with her. Like everything on the *Cerisier*, the controls were built for someone a little shorter than Ren. He had to bend a little to reach them. A thickness rose up at the back of her neck, filled her throat. Dread felt like drowning. Ren's ponytail shifted, pulled to the side. There was a mole, brown and ovoid, just where his spine met his skull, like a target.

"So I'm looking on this report here," he said, tapping the screen.

Melba pressed her tongue against the roof of her mouth. What about Soledad? She'd been there when Ren called her. She knew Melba had gone to see him. She might have to kill her too. Where would she put that body? There would have to be an accident. Something plausible. She couldn't let them stop her. She was so close.

"It's not going up, though," he said. "Steady levels."

She circled her tongue counterclockwise once, then paused. She felt light-headed. Short of breath. One of the artificial glands leaking out, maybe, in preparation for the flood. Ren was speaking, but she couldn't hear him. The sounds of her own breath and the blood in her ears was too loud.

I have to kill him. Her fingers were jittering. Her heart raced.

He turned to her, blew a breath out his nostrils. He wasn't a person. He was just a sack of meat with a little electricity. She could do this. For her father. For her family. It needed to be done.

When Ren spoke, his voice seemed to come from a distance.

"Was denkt tu? You want to make the call, you want me to?"

Her mind moved too quickly and too slowly. He was asking if they should alert the *Seung Un* about the bomb. That was what he meant.

"Ren?" she said. Her voice sounded small, querulous. It was the voice of someone much younger than she was. Someone who was very frightened, or very sad. Concern bloomed in his expression, drew his brows together.

"Hey? You all right, boss?"

She touched the screen with the tip of her finger.

"Look again," she said softly. "Look close."

He turned, bending toward the data as if there were something there to discover. She looked at his bent neck like she might have looked at a statue in a museum: an object. Nothing more. She circled her tongue against the roof of her mouth twice, and calm descended on her.

His neck popped when it broke, the cartilaginous disks ripping free, the bundle of nerves and connective tissue that his life had run through coming apart. She kept striking the base of his skull until she felt the bone give way beneath her palm, and then it was time to move the body. Quickly. Before anyone walked in on them. Before the crash came.

Fortunately, there was only a little blood.

Chapter Twelve: Anna

Two hours into an interfaith prayer meeting, and for the very first time in her life, Anna was tired of prayer. She'd always found a deep comfort in praying. A profound sense of connection to something infinitely larger than herself. Her atheist friends called it awe in the face of an infinite cosmos. She called it God. That they might be talking about the same thing didn't bother her at all. It was possible she was hurling her prayers at a cold and unfeeling universe that didn't hear them, but that wasn't how it felt. Science had given mankind many gifts, and she valued it. But the one important thing it had taken away was the value of subjective, personal experience. That had been replaced with the idea that only measurable and testable concepts had value. But humans didn't work that way, and Anna suspected the universe didn't either. *In God's image*, after all, being a tenet of her faith.

At first, the meeting had been pleasant. Father Michel had a lovely deep voice that had mellowed with age like fine wine. His lengthy and heartfelt prayer for God's guidance to be upon those who would study the Ring had sent shivers down her spine. He was followed by an elder of the Church of Humanity Ascendent who led the group through several meditations and breathing exercises that left Anna feeling energized and refreshed. She made a note in her hand terminal to download a copy of their book on meditation and give it a read. Not all of the faiths and traditions represented on board took a turn, of course. The imam would not pray in front of non-Muslims, though he did give a short speech in Arabic that someone translated for her through her earbud. When he ended with *Allah hu akbar*, several people in the audience repeated it back. Anna was one of them. Why not? It seemed polite, and it was a sentiment she agreed with.

But after two hours, even the most heartfelt and poetic of the prayers had begun to wear on her. She began counting the little plastic domes that hid fire-suppression turrets. She'd gotten good at spotting them since the attempted suicide at the first party. She found her mind wandering off to think about the message she'd send to Nono later. The chair she sat in had a very faint vibration that she could almost hear if she remained very still. It must have been the ship's massive drive, and as Anna listened for it, it began to develop a rhythmic pulse. The pulse turned into music, and she began humming under her breath. She stopped when an Episcopalian in the seat next to her pointedly cleared his throat.

Hank Cortez was, of course, scheduled to go last. In the weeks and months Anna had been on the *Prince*, it had become apparent that while no one was officially in charge of the interfaith portion of the Ring expedition, Doctor Hank was treated as a sort of "first among equals." Anna suspected this was because of his close ties to the secretary-general, who'd made the whole mission possible. He also seemed to be on a first-name basis with many of the important artists, politicians, and economic consultants in the civilian contingent of the group.

It didn't really bother her. No matter how egalitarian a group might start out, someone always wound up taking a leadership role. Better Doctor Hank than herself.

When the Neo-Wiccan priestess currently at the podium finally finished her rites, Doctor Hank was nowhere to be seen. Anna felt a little surge of hope that the prayer service would end early.

But no. Doctor Hank made his entrance into the auditorium trailed by a camera crew and bulled his way up to the podium like an actor taking the stage. He flashed his gleaming smile across the audience, making sure to end with the section the camera people had set up in.

"Brothers and sisters," he said, "let us bow our heads and offer thanks to the Almighty and seek His counsel and guidance as we draw ever closer to the end of this historic journey."

He managed to rattle on that way for another twenty minutes.

Anna started humming again.

After, Anna met Tilly for lunch at the officers' mess that had been set aside for civilian use. Anna wasn't exactly sure how she'd wound up being Tilly's best and only friend on the trip, but the woman had latched on to her after their first meeting and burrowed in like a tick. No, that wasn't really fair. Even though the only thing she and Tilly had in common was their carbon base, it wasn't like Anna had a lot of friends on the ship either. And while Tilly could appear flighty and exasperating, Anna had gradually seen through the mask to the deeply lonely woman underneath. Her husband's obscene contributions to the secretary-general's reelection campaign had bought her way onto the flight as a civilian consultant. She had no purpose on the mission other than to be seen, an extended reminder of her husband's enormous wealth and power. That she had nothing else to offer the group only made the real point clearer. She knew it, and everyone else knew it too. Most of the other civilians on the flight treated her with barely concealed contempt.

While they waited for their food to arrive, Tilly popped a

lozenge in her mouth and chewed it. The faint smell of nicotine and mint filled the air. No smoking on military ships, of course.

"How'd your thing go?" Tilly asked, playing with her silver-inlaid lozenge box and looking around the room. She was wearing a pants and blouse combination that probably cost more than Anna's house on Europa had. It was the kind of thing she wore when she wanted to appear casual.

"The prayer meeting?" Anna said. "Good. And then not as good. Long. Very, very long."

Tilly looked at her, the honesty getting her attention. "God, don't I know it. No one can blather on like a holy man with a trapped audience. Well, maybe a politician."

Their food arrived, a navy boy acting as waiter for the VIP civilians. Anna wondered what he thought of that. The UN military was all volunteer. He'd probably had a vision of what his military life would be like, and she doubted this was it. He carefully placed their food in front of them with the ease of long practice, gave them both a smile, and vanished back into the kitchen.

Galley. They called it a galley on ships.

Tilly picked halfheartedly at a farm-grown tomato and real mozzarella salad that Anna could have afforded on Europa by selling a kidney, and said, "Have you heard from Namono?"

Anna nodded while she finished chewing a piece of fried tofu. "I got another video last night. Nami gets bigger in every one. She's getting used to the gravity, but the drugs make her cranky. We're thinking about taking her off of them early, even if it means more physical therapy."

"Awww," Tilly said. It had a pro forma feel to it. Anna waited for her to change the subject.

"Robert hasn't checked in for a week now," Tilly said. She seemed resigned rather than sad.

"You don't think he—"

"Cheating?" Tilly said with a laugh. "I wish. That would at least be interesting. When he locks himself away in his office at 2 a.m., you know what I catch him looking at? Business reports, stock values, spreadsheets. Robert is the least sexual creature I've ever met. At least until they invent a way to fuck money."

Tilly's casual obscenity had very quickly stopped bothering Anna. There was no anger in it. Like most of the things Tilly did, it struck her as another way to be noticed. To get people to pay attention to her. "How's the campaign coming?" Anna said.

"Esteban? Who knows? Robert's job is to be rich and have rich friends. I'm sure that part is coming along just fine."

They ate in silence for a while, then without planning to, Anna said, "I don't think I should have come."

Tilly nodded gravely, as though Anna had just quoted gospel at her. "None of us should have."

"We pray, and we get photographed, and we have meetings about interfaith cooperation," Anna continued. "You know what we never talk about?"

"The Ring?"

"No. I mean yes. I mean we talk about the Ring all the time. What is it, what's it for, why did the protomolecule make it."

Tilly pushed her salad away and chewed another lozenge. "Then what?"

"What I thought we came here to do. To talk about what it *means.* Nearly a hundred spiritual leaders and theologians on this ship. And none of us is talking about what the Ring means."

"For God?"

"Well, at least *about* God. Theological anthropology is a lot simpler when humans are the only ones with souls."

Tilly waved at the waiter and ordered a cocktail Anna had never heard of. The waiter seemed to know, though, and darted off to get it. "This seems like the kind of thing I'll need a drink for," she said. "Go on."

"But how does the protomolecule fit into that? Is it alive? It murders us, but it also builds amazing structures that are astonishingly advanced. Is it a tool used by someone more like us, only smarter? And if so, are they creatures with a sense of the divine? Do they have faith? What does that look like?"

"If they're even from the same God," Tilly said, using a short straw to mix her drink, then taking a sip.

"Well, for some of us there's only one," Anna replied, then asked the waiter for tea. When he'd left again, she said, "It calls into question the entire concept of Grace. Well, not entirely, but it complicates it at the very least. The things that made the protomolecule are intelligent. Does that mean they have souls? They invade our solar system, kill us indiscriminately, steal our resources. All things we would consider sins if we were doing them. Does that mean they're fallen? Did Christ die for them too? Or are they intelligent but soulless, and everything the protomolecule's done is just like a virus doing what it's programmed for?"

A group of workers in civilian jumpsuits came into the dining area and sat down. They ordered food from the waiter and talked noisily among themselves. Anna let them distract her while her mind chewed over the worries she hadn't let herself articulate before today.

"And, really, it's all pretty theoretical, even to me," she continued. "Maybe none of that should matter to *our* faith at all, except that I have this feeling it will. That to most people, it will matter."

Tilly was sipping her drink, which Anna knew from experience meant she was taking the conversation seriously. "Have you mentioned this to anyone?" Tilly said, prompting her to continue.

"Cortez acts like he's in charge," Anna replied. Her tea arrived and she blew on it for a while to cool it. "I guess I should talk to him."

"Cortez is a politician," Tilly said with a condescending smirk. "Don't let his folksy Father Hank bullshit snow you. He's here because as long as Esteban is in office, Cortez is a powerful man. This dog and pony show? This is all about votes."

"I hate that," Anna said. "I believe you. You understand this all better than I do. But I hate that you're right. What a waste."

"What would you ask Cortez for?"

"I'd like to organize some groups. Have the conversation."

"Do you need his permission?" Tilly asked.

Anna thought of her last conversation with Nono and laughed. When she spoke, her voice sounded thoughtful even to her.

"No," she said. "I guess I don't."

That night Anna was awakened from a dream about taking Nami to Earth and watching her bones break as the gravity crushed her, to a blaring alarm. It lasted only a few seconds, then stopped. A voice from her comm panel said, "All hands to action stations."

Anna assumed this didn't mean her, as she had no idea what an action station was. There were no more alarms, and the voice from the comm panel didn't return with more dire pronouncements, but being startled out of her nightmare left her feeling wide awake and jumpy. She climbed out of her bunk, sent a short video message to Nono and Nami, and then put on some clothes.

There was very little traffic in the corridor and lifts. The military people she did see looked tense, though to her relief, not particularly frightened. Just aware. Vigilant.

Having nowhere else to go, she wandered into the officers' mess and ordered a glass of milk. When it arrived, she was stunned to discover it was actual milk that had at some point come out of a cow. How much was the UN spending on this civilian "dog and pony show"?

The only other people in the mess hall were a few military people with officers' uniforms, and a small knot of the civilian contractors drinking coffee and slumping in their seats like workers in the middle of an all-nighter. A dozen metal tables were bolted to the floor with magnetic chairs at their sides. Wall displays scrolled information for the ship's officers, all of it gibberish to her. A row of cutouts opened into the galley, letting through plates of food and the sounds of industrial dishwashers and the smell of floor cleaner. It was like sitting too near the kitchen in a very, very clean restaurant.

Anna drank her milk slowly, savoring the rich texture and ridiculous luxury of it. A bell chimed on someone's hand terminal, and two of the civilian workers got up and left. One stayed, a beautiful but sad-faced woman who looked down at a terminal on the table with a vacant, thousand-yard stare.

"Excuse me, ma'am," said a voice behind her, almost making Anna jump out of her chair. A young man in a naval officer's uniform moved into her field of view and gestured awkwardly at the chair next to her. "Mind if I sit?"

Anna recovered enough to smile at him, and he took it as assent, stiffly folding himself into the seat. He was very tall for an Earther, with short blond hair and the thick shoulders and narrow waist all of the young officers seemed to have regardless of gender.

Anna reached across the table to shake his hand and said, "Anna Volovodov."

"Chris Williams," the young officer replied, giving her hand a short but firm shake. "And yes, ma'am, I know who you are."

"You do?"

"Yes, ma'am. My people in Minnesota are Methodists, going back as far as we can trace them. When I saw you listed on the civilian roster, I made sure to remember the name."

Anna nodded and sipped her milk. If the boy had singled her out because she was a minister of his faith, then he wanted to talk to her as a member of the congregation. She mentally shifted gears to become Pastor Anna and said, "What can I do for you, Chris?"

"Love your accent, ma'am," Chris replied. He needed time to build up to whatever it was that he'd approached her about, so Anna gave it to him.

"I grew up in Moscow," she replied. "Though after two years on Europa I can almost do Belter now, sa sa?"

Chris laughed, some of the tension draining out of his face. "That's not bad, ma'am. But you get those guys going at full speed, I can't understand a word the skinnies say."

Anna chose to ignore the slur. "Please, no more 'ma'am.' Makes me feel a hundred years old. Anna, please, or Pastor Anna if you have to."

"All right," Chris said. "Pastor Anna."

They sat together in companionable silence for a few moments while Anna watched Chris work up to whatever he needed to say.

"You heard the alarm, right?" he finally said. "Bet it woke you up."

"It's why I'm here," Anna replied.

"Yeah. Action stations. It's because of the dusters— I mean, Martians, you know."

"Martians?" Anna found herself wanting another glass of the delicious milk, but thought it might distract Chris, so she didn't wave at the waiter.

"We're in weapons range of their fleet now," he said. "So we go on alert. We can't share sky with the dusters anymore without going on alert. Not since, you know, Ganymede."

Anna nodded and waited for him to continue.

"And that Ring, you know, it's already killed somebody. I mean, just a dumb as sand skinny slingshotter, but still. Somebody."

Anna took his hand. He flinched a bit, but relaxed when she smiled at him. "That scares you?"

"Sure. Of course. But that ain't it."

Anna waited, keeping her face carefully neutral. The pretty civilian girl across the room got up suddenly, as though leaving. Her lips moved, talking to herself, then she sat back down, put her arms on the table, and leaned her head on them. Someone else scared, waiting out the long watches of the night, all alone in a room full of people.

"I mean," Chris said, breaking into her reverie, "that ain't all of it anyway."

"What else?" Anna said.

"The Ring didn't put us on alert," he said. "It's the Martians. Even with that thing out there, we're still thinking about shooting each other. That's pretty fucked up. Sorry. Messed up."

"It seems like we should be able to see past our human differences when we're confronted with something like this, doesn't it?"

Chris nodded and squeezed her hand tighter, but said nothing.

"Chris, would you like to pray with me?"

He nodded and lowered his head, closing his eyes. When she'd finished, he said, "I know I'm not the only Methodist on the ship. Do you, you know, hold services?"

I do now.

"Sunday, at 10 a.m., in conference room 41," she said, making a mental note to ask someone if she could use conference room 41 on Sunday mornings.

"I'll see if I can get the time off," Chris said with a smile. "Thank you, ma'am. Pastor Anna."

"It was nice talking to you, Chris." *You just gave me a reason to be here.*

When Chris left, Anna found herself very tired, ready to return to her bed, but the pretty girl across the room hadn't moved. Her head was still buried in her arms. Anna walked over to her and gently touched her on the shoulder. The girl's head jerked up, her eyes wild, almost panicked.

"Hi," Anna said. "I'm Anna. What's your name?"

The girl stared up, as if the question were a difficult one. Anna sat down across from her.

"I saw you sitting here," Anna said. "It looked like you could use some company. It's okay to be afraid. I understand."

The girl jerked to her feet like a malfunctioning machine. Her eyes were flat, and her head tilted a degree. Anna felt suddenly afraid. It was like she'd gone to pet a dog and found herself with her hand on a lion. Something in the back of her head told her, *This is a bad one. This one will hurt you.*

"I'm sorry," Anna said, standing up with her hands half raised. "I didn't mean to disturb you."

"You don't know me," the girl replied. "You don't know anything." Her hands were clenched into fists at her sides, the tendons in her neck quivering like plucked guitar strings.

"You're right," Anna said, still backing up and patting the air with her hands. "I apologize."

Other people in the room were staring at them now, and Anna felt a surge of relief that she wasn't alone with the girl. The girl stared at her, trembling, for a few more seconds, then darted out of the room.

"What the fuck was that all about?" someone behind Anna said in a quiet voice.

Maybe the girl had woken up from a nightmare too, Anna thought. Or maybe she hadn't.

Chapter Thirteen: Bull

Arriving at the Ring was a political fiction, but that didn't keep it from being real. There was no physical boundary to say that this was within the realm of the object. There was no port to dock at. The *Behemoth*'s sensory arrays had been sucking in data from the Ring since before they'd left Tycho. The Martian science ships and Earth military forces that had been there before the doomed Belter kid had become its first casualty were still there, where they had been, but resupplied now. The new Martian ships had joined them, matched orbit, and were hanging quietly in the sky. The Earth flotilla, like the *Behemoth*, was in the last part of the burn, pulling up to whatever range they'd chosen to stop at. To say, *We have come across the vast abyss to float at this distance and now we are here. We've arrived.*

As far as anyone could tell, the Ring didn't give a damn.

The structure itself was eerie. The surface was a series of twisting ridges that spiraled around its body. At first they appeared uneven, almost messy. The mathematicians, architects, and physicists assured them all that there was a deep regularity there: the height of the ridges in a complex harmony with the width and the spacing between the peaks and valleys. The reports were breathless, finding one layer of complexity after another, the intimations of intention and design all laid bare without any hint of what it all might mean.

"The official Martian reports have been very conservative," the science officer said. His name was Chan Bao-Zhi, and on Earth, he'd have been Chinese. Here, he was a Belter from Pallas Station. "They've given a lot of summary and maybe a tenth of the data they've collected. Fortunately, we've been able to observe most of their experiments and make our own analysis."

"Which Earth will have been doing too," Ashford said.

"Without doubt, sir," Chan said.

Like any ritual, the staff meeting carried more significance than information. The heads of all the major branches of the *Behemoth*'s structural tree were present: Sam for engineering, Bull for security, Chan for the research teams, Bennie Cortland-Mapu for health services, Anamarie Ruiz for infrastructure, and so on, filling the two dozen seats around the great conference table. Ashford sat in the place of honor, another beneficent Christ painted on the wall behind him. Pa sat at his right hand, and Bull—by tradition—at his left.

"What have we got?" Ashford said. "Short form."

"It's fucking weird, sir," Chan said, and everyone chuckled. "Our best analysis is that the Ring is an artificially sustained Einstein-Rosen bridge. You go through the Ring, you don't come out the other side here."

"So it's a gate," Ashford said.

"Yes, sir. It appears that the protomolecule or Phoebe bug or whatever you want to call it was launched at the solar system several billion years ago, aiming for Earth with the intention of hijacking primitive life to build a gateway. We're positing that whoever created the protomolecule did it as a first step toward making travel to the solar system more convenient and practical later."

Bull took a deep breath and let it out slowly. It was what everyone had been thinking, but hearing it spoken in this official setting made it seem more real. The Ring was a way for something to get here. Not just a gateway. A beachhead.

"When the *Y Que* went through it, the mass and velocity of the ship triggered some mechanism in the Ring," Chan said. "The Martians have a good dataset from the moment it happened, and there was a massive outpouring of energy within the Ring structure and a whole cascade of microlevel conformation changes. The entire object went up to about five thousand degrees Kelvin, and it has been cooling regularly ever since. So it took a lot of effort to get that thing running, but it looks like not much to maintain."

"What do we know about what's on the other side?" Pa asked. Her expression was neutral, her voice pleasant and unemotional. She could have been asking him to justify a line item in his budget.

"It's hard to know much," Chan said. "We're peeking through a keyhole, and the Ring itself seems to be generating interference and radiation that makes getting consistent readings difficult. We know the *Y Que* wasn't destroyed. We're still getting the video feed that the kid was spewing when he went through, it's just not showing us much."

"Stars?" Ashford said. "Something we can start to navigate from?"

"No, sir," Chan said. "The far side of the Ring doesn't have any stars, and the background microwave radiation is significantly different from what we'd expect."

"Meaning what?" Ashford said.

"Meaning, 'Huh, that's weird,' " Chan said. "Sir."

Ashford's smile was cool as he motioned the science officer to continue. Chan coughed before he went on.

"We have a couple of other anomalies that we aren't quite sure what to make of. It looks like there's a maximum speed on the other side."

"Can you unpack that, please?" Pa said.

"The *Y Que* went through the Ring going very fast," Chan said. "About seven-tenths of a second after it reached the other side, it started a massive deceleration. Bled off almost all its speed in about five seconds. It looks like the nearly instant deceleration was what killed the pilot. Since then, it seems as if the ship is being moved out away from the Ring and deeper into whatever's on the other side."

"We know that when the protomolecule's active, it's been able to...alter what we'd expect from inertia," Sam said. "Is that how it stopped the ship?"

"That's entirely possible," Chan said. "Mars has been pitching probes through the Ring, and it looks like we start seeing the effect right around six hundred meters per second. Under that, mass behaves just the way we expect it to. Over that, it stops dead and then moves off in approximately the same direction that the *Y Que* is going."

Sam whistled under her breath.

"That's *really* slow," she said. "The main drives would be almost useless."

"It's slower than a rifle shot," Chan said. "The good news is it only affects mass above the quantum level. The electromagnetic spectrum seems to behave normally, including visible light."

"Thank God for small favors," Sam said.

"What else are the probes telling us?"

"There's something out there," Chan said, and for the first time a sense of dread leaked into his voice. "The probes are seeing objects. Large ones. But there's not much light except what we're shining through the Ring or mounting on the probes. And, as I said, the Ring has always given inconsistent returns. If whatever's in there is made of the same stuff, who knows?"

"Ships?" Ashford said.

"Maybe."

"How many?"

"Over a hundred, under a hundred thousand. Probably."

Bull leaned forward, his elbows on the table. Ashford and Pa were looking around the table at the graying faces. They'd known before, because they weren't going to wait for a staff meeting to get their information. Now they were judging the reactions. So he'd give them a reaction. Control the fall.

"Be weirder if there wasn't anything there. If it was an attack fleet, they'd have attacked by now."

"Yeah," Ruiz said, latching on to the words.

Ashford opened the floor for questions. How many probes had Mars fired through? How long would it take something going at six hundred meters per second to reach one of the structures? Had they tried sending small probes in? Had there been any contact from the protomolecule itself, the stolen voices of humans, the way there had been with Eros? Chan did his best to be reassuring without actually having anything more that he could say. Bull assumed there was a deeper report that Ashford and Pa were getting, and he wondered what was in it. Being kept out chafed.

"All right. This is all interesting, but it's not our focus," Ashford said, bringing the Q-and-A session to a halt. "We're not here to send probes through the Ring. We're not here to start a fight. We're just making sure that whatever the inner planets do, we're at the table. If something comes out of the Ring, we'll worry about it then."

"Yes, sir," Bull said, throwing his own weight behind Ashford's. It wasn't like there was another strategy. Better that the crew see them all unified. People were watching how this all came down, and not just the crew.

"Mister Pa?" Ashford said. The XO nodded and glanced at Bull. Instinct dropped a weight in his gut.

"There have been some irregularities in the ship's accounting structure," Pa said. "Chief Engineer Rosenberg?"

Sam nodded, surprise on her face. "XO?" she said.

"I'm afraid I'm going to have to restrict you to quarters and revoke your access privileges until this is all clarified. Chief Watanabe will relieve you. Mister Baca, you'll see to it."

The room was just as silent, but the meaning behind it was different now. Sam's eyes were wide with disbelief and rising fury.

"Excuse me?" she said. Pa met her gaze coolly, and Bull understood all of it in an instant.

"Records show you've been drawing resources from work and materials budgets that weren't appropriate," Pa said, "and until the matter is resolved—"

"If this is about the tech support thing, that's on me," Bull said. "I authorized that. It's got nothing to do with Sam."

"I'm conducting a full audit, Mister Baca. If I find you've been drawing resources inappropriately, I'll take the actions I deem appropriate. As your executive officer, I am informing you that Samara Rosenberg is to be confined to quarters and her access to ship's systems blocked. Do you have any questions about that?"

She'd waited until they'd made the trip, until they'd gotten where they were going, and now it was time to establish that she was in control. To get back at him for the drug dealer he'd spaced and punish Sam for being his ally. Would have been stupid to do until their shakedown run was over. But now it was.

Bull laced his fingers together. The refusal was on the back of his tongue, waiting. It would have been insubordination, and it would have been easy as breathing out. There were years—decades even—when he'd have done it, and taken the consequences as a badge of honor. It had been his call, and standing by while Sam was punished for it was more than dishonorable, it was disloyal. Pa knew that. Anyone who'd read his service records would know it. If it had just been his mission, his career on the line, he'd have done it, but Fred Johnson had asked him to make this work. So there was only one play to make.

"No questions," he said, rising from his chair. "Sam. You should come with me now."

The others were silent as he led her out of the conference room. They all looked stunned and confused, except Ashford and Pa. Pa wore a poker face, and Ashford had a little shadow of smugness in the corners of his mouth. Sam's breath shook. Outrage and adrenaline left her skin pale. He helped her into the side seat of his security cart, then got behind the controls. They lurched into motion, four small engines whirring and whining. They were almost at the elevators when Sam laughed. A short, mirthless sound as much like a cry of pain as anything.

"Holy shit," Sam said.

Bull couldn't think of anything to say that would pull the punch, so he only nodded and took the cart into the wide elevator car. Sam wept, but there was nothing that looked like sorrow in her expression. He guessed that she'd never suffered that kind of disciplinary humiliation before. Or if she had, it hadn't been often enough to build up a callus. The dishonor of letting her take the hit was like he'd swallowed something before he'd chewed it enough, and now it wouldn't go down.

Back at the security office, Serge was at the main desk. The man's eyebrows rose as Bull came in the room.

"Hoy, bossman," the duty officer said. A hardcore OPA bruiser named Jojo. "Que pasa?"

"Nothing good. What did I miss?"

"Complaint from a carnicería down by engineering about a missing goat. Got a note from one of the Earth ships lost one of their crew, wondering if we'd come up with an extra. A couple coyos got shit-faced and we locked 'em in quarters, told 'em we'd sic the Bull on 'em."

"How'd they take that?"

"We had them mop up after."

Bull chuckled before he sighed.

"So. I've got Samara Rosenberg in the cart outside," he said. "XO wants her confined to quarters for unauthorized use of resources."

"I want a pony in a wetsuit." Jojo grinned.

"XO gave an order," Bull said. "I want you to take her to her quarters. I'll get her access pulled. We'll need to set a guard while we're at it. She's pissed."

Jojo scratched at his neck. "We're doing it?"

"Yeah."

Jojo's face closed. Bull nodded toward the door. Jojo left, and Bull took his place at the desk, identifying himself to the system and starting the process of locking Sam out of her own ship. While the security system ran its check against each of the *Behemoth*'s subsystems, he leaned on his elbows and watched.

The first time Fred Johnson saved Bull's life, he'd done it with a rifle and a mobile medical unit. The second time, he'd done it with a credit chip. Bull had mustered out at thirty and took his pension to Ceres. For three years, he'd just lived. Ate cheap, drank too much, slept in his own bed not knowing if he was sick from the alcohol or the spin. Not caring much. He got into a few fights, had a few disagreements with the local law. He didn't see that he had a problem until it was unmistakable, and by then it was a hell of a problem.

Depression ran in his family. Self-medicating did too. His grandfather had died of the pair. His mother had been in therapy a couple times. His brother had graduated to heroin and lived five years in a treatment center in Roswell. None of it had seemed to have anything to do with Bull. He was a marine. He'd turned away from a life on basic to live in the stars, or if not the stars, at least the rocks that floated free in the night sky. He'd killed men. Bottle couldn't beat him. But it almost had.

The day Fred Johnson had appeared at his door, it had been stranger than a dream. His former commanding officer looked different. Older, stronger. Truth was, their birthdays weren't all that far apart, but Johnson had always been the Old Man. Bull had followed the news about the fallout from Anderson Station, and Fred's changing sides. Some of the other marines he knew on Ceres had been angry about it. He'd just figured the Old Man knew what he was doing. He wouldn't have done it without a reason.

Bull, Fred had said. Just that, at first. He could still remember Fred's dark eyes meeting his. The shame had made Bull try to stand straighter, to suck in his gut a little. In that moment, he saw how far he'd fallen. Two seconds of seeing himself through Fred Johnson's eyes was all it took for that.

Sir, Bull had replied, then stood back and let Johnson into the hole. The place stank of yeast and old tofu. And flop sweat. Fred ignored it all. *I need you back on duty, soldier.*

Okay, Bull had said. And the secret he carried with him, the one he'd take to his grave, was this: He hadn't meant it. In that moment, all he'd wanted was for Fred Johnson to go away and let Bull forget him again. Lying to his old commanding officer, to the man who'd kept him from bleeding out under fire, came as naturally as breathing. It didn't have anything to do with Earth or the Belt or Anderson Station. It wasn't some greater loyalty. He just wasn't done destroying himself. And even now, sitting alone at the security desk betraying Sam, he thought that Fred had known. Or guessed.

Fred had pressed a credit chip into his palm. It was one of the cheap, vaguely opalescent ones that the OPA had used to keep its funds untraceable, back in the bad old days. *Get yourself a new uniform.* Bull had saluted, already thinking about the booze he could buy.

The chit carried six months' wages at his old pay grade. If it had been less, Bull wouldn't have gone. Instead, he shaved for the first time in days, got a new suit, packed a valise, and threw out anything that didn't fit in it. He hadn't had a drink since, even on the nights he'd wanted one more than oxygen.

The security system chimed that the lockout was finished. Bull noted it and leaned back in the chair, reading the be-on-alert notice from the *Cerisier* and letting his mind wander. When Gathoni arrived to take the next shift, he walked two corridors down to a little mom-and-pop bodega, bought a blister-pack with four bulbs of beer, and headed over to Sam's quarters. The guard on duty nodded to him. Legally, Bull didn't have to knock. As head of security, he could have walked into Sam's rooms at any time, with or without being welcome. He knocked.

Sam was wearing a simple sweater and black workpants with magnetic strips down the sides. Bull held up the beer. For a long moment, Sam glared at him. She stepped back and to the side. He followed her in.

Her rooms were clean, neat, and cluttered. The air smelled like industrial lubricant and old laundry. She leaned against the arm of a foam couch.

"Peace offering?" she said bitterly.

"Pretty much," Bull said. "Pa's pissed off at me, and she's taking it out on you. She figured either I do it and I lose my best ally or I don't and I'm the one confined to quarters, right? No way to lose for her."

"This is bullshit."

"It is," Bull said. "And I'm sorry as hell about the whole damn thing."

Sam's breath rattled with anger. Bull accepted it. He had it coming. She walked across to him, grabbing the four-pack out of his hand, twisting it to shatter the plastic, and plucking one of the bulbs free.

"You want one?" she asked.

"Just water for me," he said.

"What chafes me," Sam said, "is the way Ashford just sits there like he's so happy about the whole thing. He knows the score. He's as much a part of it as Pa. Or you. Don't think you can buy me off with a few cheap brews. You're just as much at fault as they are."

"I am."

"I got into engineering because I didn't want all the petty social birdshit. And now look at me."

"Yeah," Bull said.

Sam dropped to the couch with a sigh and said something obscene and colorful. Bull sat down across from her.

"Okay, stop that," she said.

"What?"

"That looking repentant thing. I feel like I'm supposed to genuflect or something. It's creepy." She took a long pull at the bulb, the soft plastic collapsing under the suction, then expanding out a little as the beer outgassed. "Look, you and Pa are both doing what you think you ought to, and I'm getting screwed. I get it. Doesn't mean I have to be happy about it. Thing is, you're right. She wants you to lose allies. So no matter how much I want to tell you to go put your dick in a vise? I'm not going to, just because it would mean Pa won."

"Thank you for that, Sam."

"Go put your dick in a vise, Bull."

Bull's hand terminal chimed.

"Mister Baca?" Gathoni's voice said. "You should come back to the office, maybe."

Sam's expression sobered and she put down the bulb. Bull's belly tightened.

"What's going on?" he asked. When Gathoni answered, her voice was controlled and calm as a medic calling for more pressure.

"Earth destroyer *Seung-Un*? It just blew up."

Chapter Fourteen: Melba

When she'd thought about it, planning the final, closing stages of her vengeance, she'd pictured herself as the conductor of a private symphony, moving her baton to the orchestrated chaos. It didn't happen that way at all. The morning she went to the *Thomas Prince*, she didn't know that the day had finally come.

"Active hands to stations," a man's voice announced over the general channel.

"Wish to fuck they'd stop doing that," Melba said. "Always makes me feel like I should be doing something."

"Savvy, boss. When they start paying me navy wages, I'll start jumping for their drills," Soledad said, her voice pressed thin by the hand terminal's speaker. "I've got nothing on this couple. Unless Stanni's got it, we got to move down a level, try again."

"Copy that," Melba said. "Stanni, what are you seeing?"

The channel went silent. Melba looked around the service

corridor at a half kilometer of nothing: conduit and pipes and the access grating that could shift to accommodate any direction of thrust. The only sounds were the creaking, hissing, and muttering of the *Thomas Prince*. The seconds stretched.

"*Stanni?*" Soledad said, dread in her voice, and the channel crackled.

"Perdón," Stanni said. "Looking at some weird wiring, but it's not the goose we're hunting. Lost in my head, me. I'm fine. I'm here."

Soledad said something obscene under her breath.

"Sorry," Stanni said again.

"It's okay," Melba said. "Did you check the brownout buffers?"

"Did."

"Then let's just keep moving. Next level."

The thing that surprised her, the one she hadn't seen coming, was how everyone on the *Cerisier* was ready to put Ren's disappearance at the foot of the Ring. It was rare for people to go missing on a ship. The *Cerisier*, like any other long-haul vessel, was a closed system. There was nowhere to go. She'd assumed there would be the usual, human suspicions. Ren had crossed someone, stolen something, slept with the wrong person, and he'd been disposed of. Thrown out an airlock, maybe. Fed into the recycling and reduced to his basic nutrients, then passed into the water or food supply. It wasn't that there were no ways to hide or dispose of a body, it was that there were so few ways for it to go unnoticed. Traveling between the planets had never eliminated murder. So many highly evolved primates in the same box for months on end, a certain death rate had to be expected.

This time, though, it was different. It made sense to people that someone would go missing, vanish, as they approached the Ring. It felt right. The voyage itself was ill-omened, and strange things were supposed to happen when people drew too near the uncanny, the dangerous, the haunted. The others were all on edge, and that gave her cover too. If she started weeping, they'd think they understood why. They'd think it was fear.

Melba packed her diagnostic array back in its sleeve, stood, and headed down to the lift. The internal service lifts were tiny, with hardly enough room for one person and the gear. Traveling between decks here was like stepping into a coffin. As she shifted down to the next level, she imagined the power failing. Being trapped there. Her mind flickered, and for a moment, she saw her own storage locker. The one in her quarters. The one filled with sealant foam and Ren. She shuddered and forced her mind elsewhere.

The *Thomas Prince* was one of the larger ships in the Earth flotilla, the home of the civilian horde that the UN had put together. Artists, poets, philosophers, priests. Even without changing the physical structures of the ship, it gave her the feeling of being less a military vessel and more a poorly appointed, uncomfortable cruise liner. Clarissa had been on yachts and luxury ships most of the times she'd traveled outside Earth's gravity well, and she could imagine the thousand complaints the ship's captain would suffer about the halls not being wide enough and the screens on the walls too low a quality. It was the sort of thing she would have been concerned with, in her previous life. Now it was less than nothing.

It shouldn't have bothered her. One more death, more or less. It shouldn't have mattered. But it was Ren.

"In position," Stanni said.

"Give me a second," Melba said, stepping out of the lift. The new corridor was nearly identical to the one above it. These decks were all quarters and storage, with very little of the variation that she'd see when they reached the lowest levels—engineering, machine shops, hangar bays. Tracking down the electrical anomaly, they'd started here because it was easy. The longer it took, the harder it would get. Like everything.

She found the junction, took the diagnostic array out of its sleeve, and plugged it in.

"Solé?"

"In place," Soledad said.

"Okay," Melba said. "Start the trace."

When it had happened, she'd gotten Ren to her quarters and laid him out on the floor. She'd already felt the crash coming on, so she'd lain down on her bunk and let it come. It might only have been her imagination that made that one seem worse than the ones before. For a long horrified moment at the end, she thought that she'd voided herself, but her uniform was clean. She'd gone then, Ren still on her floor, gotten a bulb of coffee, put Ren's hand terminal in a stall of the group head, and found the security officer. He was a thin Martian named Andre Commenhi, and he'd listened to her informal report with half an ear. Ren had called her and asked her to consult with him. When she'd gone to see him at his usual workstation, he wasn't there. She'd been through the ship, but she hadn't found him, and he wasn't answering connection requests. She was starting to get concerned.

While they'd done a sweep of the ship, she'd gotten the tubes of sealant foam, gone back to her quarters, and entombed him. His hair had seemed brighter, the orange like something from a coral reef. His skin was pale as sunlight where the blood had drained away from it. Purple as a bruise where it had pooled. Rigor hadn't set in, so she was able to fold him together, curled like a fetus, and fill the spaces around him with foam. It had taken minutes to harden. The foam was engineered to be airtight and pressure-resistant. If she'd done it right, the corpse smell would never leak out.

"Nadie," Soledad said, sounding resigned. "You guys got anything?"

"Hey!" Stanni said. "Think I do. I've got a ten percent fluctuation on this box."

"Okay," Melba said. "Let's reset it and see if that clears the issue."

"On it," Stanni said. "Grab some lunch while it run?"

"I'll meet you in the galley," Melba said. Her voice seemed almost normal. She sounded like someone else.

The galley was nearly empty. By the ship's clock, it was the middle of the night, and only a few officers lurked at their tables watching the civilians as they passed. The terms of the service contract meant they got to use the officers' mess. She'd heard there was a certain level of distrust among the navy crews for civilians like her and her team. She would have resented it more if she hadn't been the living example of why their suspicions were justified. Soledad and Stanni were already at a table, drinking coffee from bulbs and sharing a plate of sweet rolls.

"I'm gonna miss these when we cut thrust," Stanni said, holding one of the rolls up. "Best cook flying can't bake right without thrust. How long you think we're going to be on the float?"

"As long as it takes," Melba said. "They're planning for two months."

"Two months at null g," Soledad said, but her voice and the grayness of her face were clear. Two months at the Ring.

"Yeah," Stanni said. "Any word on Bob?"

The fifth of the team—fourth now—was still back on the *Cerisier.* It turned out he and Ren had both been having a relationship with a man on the medical team, and security were rounding up the usual suspects. Most times someone went missing, it was domestic. Melba felt her throat going thick again.

"Nothing yet," she said. "They'll clear him. He wouldn't have done anything."

"Yeah," Soledad said. "Bob wouldn't hurt anyone. He's a good man. Everyone knew about everything, and he loved Ren."

"Could stop the passato," Stanni said. "We don't know he's dead."

"With esse coisa out there, dead's the best thing he could be," Soledad said. "I've been having bad dreams since we flipped. I don't think we're making it back from this run. Not any of us."

"Talking like that won't help," Stanni said.

A woman walked into the galley. Middle-aged, thick red hair pulled into a severe-looking bun that competed with her smile. Melba looked at her to try not to be at the table, then looked away.

"Whatever happened to Ren," she said, "we've got our job to do. And we'll do it."

"Damn right," Stanni said, and then again with a catch in his voice. "Damn right."

They sat together quietly for a moment while the older man wept. Solé put a hand on his arm, and Stanni's shuddering breath slowed. He nodded, swallowed. He looked like an icon of grief and courage. He looked noble. It struck Melba for the first time that Stanni was probably her father's age, and she had never seen her father weep for anyone.

"I'm sorry," she said. She hadn't planned to speak the words, but there they were, coughed up on the table. They seemed obscene.

"It's okay," Stanni said. "I'm all right. Here, boss, have a roll."

Melba reached out, fighting herself not to weep again. Not to speak. She didn't know what she'd say, and she was afraid of herself. The alert chimed on her hand terminal. The diagnostic was finished. It only took a second to see that the spike was still there. Stanni said something profane, then shrugged.

"No rest for the wicked, no peace for the good," he said, standing.

"Go ahead," Melba said. "I'll catch up."

"Pas problema," Soledad said. "You hardly got to drink your coffee, sa sa?"

She watched them go, relieved that they wouldn't be there and wanting to call them back, both at the same time. The thickness in her throat had traveled to her chest. The sweet rolls looked delicious and nauseating. She forced herself to take a few deep breaths.

It was almost over. The fleets were there. The *Rocinante* was there. Everything was going according to her plan, or if not quite that, at least near enough to it. Ren shouldn't have mattered. She'd killed men before him. It was almost inevitable that people would die when the bomb went off. Vengeance called forth blood, because it always did. That was its nature, and she had made herself its instrument.

Ren wasn't her fault, he was Holden's. Holden had killed him by making her presence necessary. If he had respected the honor of her family, none of this would have happened. She stood up, squared herself, prepared to get back to the job of fixing the *Thomas Prince*, just the way the real Melba would have.

"I'm sorry, Ren," she said, thinking it would be the last time, and the sorrow that shook her made her sit back down.

Something was wrong. This wasn't how it was supposed to be. Her control was slipping. She wondered if after all she'd done, she simply wasn't strong enough. Or if there was something else. Maybe the artificial glands had begun to leak their toxins into her bloodstream without being summoned. She was getting more emotionally labile. It could be a symptom. She rested her head on her arms and tried to catch her breath.

He'd been kind to her. He'd been nothing but kind. He'd helped her, and she'd killed him for it. She could still feel his skull giving way under her hand; crisp and soft, like standing at the bank of a river and feeling the ground fall away. Her fingers smelled like sealant foam.

Ren touched her shoulder, and her head snapped up.

"Hi," someone said. "I'm Anna. What's your name?"

It was the redhead who'd been talking to the naval officer a moment ago.

"I saw you sitting here," she said, sitting down. "It looked like you could use some company. It's okay to be afraid. I understand."

She knows.

The thought ran through Melba's body like a sheet of lightning. Even without her tongue touching her palate, she felt the glands and bladders hidden in her flesh engorging. Her face and hands felt cold. Before the woman's eyes could widen, Melba's sorrow and guilt turned to a cold rage. She knew, and she would expose everything, and then all of it would have been wasted.

She didn't remember rising to her feet, but she was there now. The woman stood and took a step back.

I have to kill her.

"I'm sorry. I didn't mean to disturb you."

The woman's hands were half raised, as if that were enough to ward off a blow. It would be simple. She didn't look strong. She didn't know how to fight. Kick her in the gut until she bled out. Nothing simpler.

A small voice in the back of Melba's mind said, *She's one of those idiot priests looking for someone to save. She doesn't know anything. You're in public. If you attack her, they'll catch you.*

"You don't know me," Melba said, struggling to keep her voice calm. "You don't know anything."

At one of the tables nearest the door, a young officer stood up and took two steps toward them, ready to interfere. If this woman got her thrown in the brig, they'd look into Melba's identity. They'd find Ren's body. They'd find out who she was. She had to keep it together.

"You're right. I apologize," the woman said.

Hatred surged up in Melba's mind, pure and black where it wasn't red. A swamp of obscenities rose in her throat, ready to pour out on the idiot priest who was putting everything—everything—in jeopardy. Melba swallowed it all and walked quickly away.

The corridors of the *Thomas Prince* were a vague presence in the unquiet of her mind. She'd let the thing with Ren throw her. It stole her focus and led her into risks she didn't need to take. She hadn't been thinking straight, but now she was. She got into the elevator and selected the level where Stanni and Soledad were checking the electrical system, chasing down the failing component. Then she deselected it and picked the hangar.

"Stanni? Solé?" she said into her hand terminal. "Hold it together for me here. I've got a thing I need to do."

She waited for the inevitable questioning, the prying and suspicion.

"Okay," Soledad said. And that was all.

At the hangar, Melba authorized the flight of her shuttle, waited ten minutes for clearance, and launched out the side of the *Thomas Prince* and into the black. The shuttle monitors were cheap and small, the vastness of space compressed into fifty centimeters by fifty centimeters. She had the computer figure the fastest burn for the *Cerisier*. It was less than an hour. She leaned into the thrust like she was riding a roller coaster and let the torch engines burn. The *Cerisier* appeared in the dusting of stars as a small gray dot that hurtled toward her. The ship, like all the others in the flotilla, was in the last of the deceleration burn to put them at the Ring. Somewhere out past all the glowing drive plumes, it waited. Melba pushed the thought from her mind. It made her think of Stanni and Soledad and their quiet fears. She couldn't think of them now.

Impatience to arrive made it hard to start the flip and the deceleration burn. She wanted to get there, to be there already. She wanted to speed into the *Cerisier* like a witch on a broom, screaming in at speeds that wouldn't have been possible in atmosphere. She waited too long, and did the last half of the jump at almost two g. When she docked, she had a headache and her jaw felt like someone had punched her.

No one asked why she was back early and alone. She listed personal reasons in the log. Walking through the cramped corridors, squeezing past the other crewmen, felt oppressive, familiar, and comforting. It took coming back to recognize how much the wider spaces of the *Thomas Prince* had bothered her. It felt too much like freedom, and she was all about necessity.

Her cell was a mess. All of her things—clothes, terminal jack, tampons, communications deck, toothbrush—were scattered on the floor. She'd have to find a way to secure them all before the burn stopped, or they'd be floating out into the corridor. People would wonder why they weren't packed away. She let herself glance at the metal door under her crash couch. A tiny golden curl of sealant foam stuck out from one corner. She'd get some kind of mesh bag and some magnets. That would do. It didn't matter. That was later. Nothing later mattered.

She picked up the comm deck, turned it on. Ping times to the *Rocinante* were under thirty seconds. Melba loaded the sequence she'd been waiting to load for months. Years. It was a short script. It didn't take a second to prompt her to confirm.

The fear was gone. The hatred was too. For a moment, the tiny room was filled with a sense of having just woken from a dream, and her body felt relaxed. Almost light. She'd come so far and worked so hard, and despite all of the mistakes and screwups and last-minute improvisations, she'd done it. Everything in her life had been aiming toward this moment, and now that she was here, it was almost hard to let it all go. She felt like she was graduating from university or getting married. This moment, this action that fulfilled all the things she'd fought for, and then her world would never be the same.

Carefully, savoring each keystroke, she put in the confirmation code—JULES-PIERRE MAO—and thumbed the send button. The comm deck LED glowed amber. At the speed of light, a tiny packet of information was pulsing out, hardly more than a bit of background static. But the software on the *Rocinante* would recognize it. The communications array on Holden's ship would be slaved to the virtual machine already installed and impossible to stop without scraping the whole system clean. The *Rocinante* would send a clearly recognizable trigger code to the *Seung Un*, wait fifty-three seconds, and announce Holden's responsibility and his demands. And then the virtual machine would power up the weapons and targeting systems. And nothing, no power in the universe, could stop it from happening.

The comm deck got the confirmation response, and the amber LED shifted to red.

Chapter Fifteen: Bull

Bull's hand terminal sat on the cart's thin plastic dashboard, jiggling with every bump in the corridor floor. The siren blatted its standard two-tone, scattering people from his path and calling them out behind him. If they didn't know yet, they all would in minutes. The death of the *Seung Un* wasn't the sort of thing you could overlook.

On the small, jittering screen, the destroyer exploded again. At first it was only a flicker of orange light amidships, something that could have been electrical discharge or a gauss gun finishing its maintenance regimen. Half a second later, sparkles of yellow radiated out from the site. Two seconds after, the major detonation. Between one frame and the next, the destroyer's side bloomed open. Then nothing for ten full seconds before the fusion reactor core emerged slowly from the back, brighter than the sun. Bull watched the intense white gases begin to diffuse out and fade into a massive golden aurora, a drop of gold losing cohesion in the oceanic black.

He looked up to make the turn onto the ramp that would take him back to the office. A young man ambled slowly out of his path, and Bull leaned on the cart's horn.

"There's a siren," Bull yelled as he passed the young man, and got an insolent nod in reply.

"Okay," Serge said from the terminal. "We're getting the first security analysis. Best guess, something blew out in one of the power conduits, fused the safety systems so they couldn't shut it down. Would have taken about that long to turn the whole starboard main circuit to molten slag."

"What blew?" Bull demanded.

"Probably a maneuvering thruster. About the right place for one. Get it hot enough, water skips steam and just goes straight to plasma. Cuts right through the bulkheads around it."

Bull turned the cart around a tight corner and slowed to let a half dozen pedestrians get out of his way.

"Why'd they dump core?"

"Don't know, but probably they thought they'd lose containment. They got six ships diverting now to keep from plowing into that mierda."

"If they'd lost containment it'd be worse. They'd be diverting to avoid bodies and shrapnel. Are there survivors?"

"Yeah. They're putting out the distress request. Medical and evacuation. Sounds pretty fucked up, que no?"

"What about trace data. Can we tell who shot 'em?"

"No one shot 'em. Either it was a straight accident, or..."

"Or?"

"Or it wasn't."

Bull bit his lip. An accident would be bad enough. People on all sides of the system's power structure were on edge, and a reminder that Earth's fleet was aging and poorly maintained wouldn't make anything easier. Sabotage would be worse. The closest thing to good news was that everyone had seen it and there wouldn't be any accusations of enemy action. If there'd been a gauss round or a lucky missile that had slipped through the *Seung Un*'s defenses undetected, the scientific mission could turn into a shooting war faster than Bull wanted to think about.

"Are we offering assistance?" Bull asked.

"Give us a breath, boss," Serge said. "Ashford ain't hearing any of this faster than us."

Bull leaned forward, his hands wrapping the steering controls until his knuckles went white. Serge was right. What happened outside the ship was Ashford's problem. And Pa's. He was security chief, and he needed to think about what needed doing inside the *Behemoth*. People would be scared, and it was his job to make sure that fear didn't turn into hysteria. Watching a ship blow out—even an enemy ship—reminded everyone how tenuous life was with only a thin skin of steel and ceramic to keep the vacuum at bay. It reminded him. The cart hit a larger bump than usual, and his hand terminal slipped onto its side.

"Okay," Bull said. "Look, we're going to need to get relief supplies ready in case the captain decides to offer assistance. How many survivors can we take on?"

Serge's laughter rasped.

"All of them. We're the pinche *Behemoth*. We got enough room for a city, us."

"Okay," Bull said, smiling a little despite himself. "It was a stupid question."

"The only thing we got to worry about is—"

The line went dead.

"Serge? Not funny," Bull said. And then, "Talk to me, mister."

"We got something. Broadcast coming from a private corvette called the *Rocinante*."

"Why do I know that name?" Bull asked.

"Yeah," Serge said. "I'm putting it to you."

The handset screen blacked out, jumped, and then a familiar face appeared. Bull let the cart slow as James Holden, the man whose announcement about the death of the ice hauler *Canterbury* started the first war between Earth and Mars, once again made things worse.

"...ship that approaches the Ring without my *personal* permission will be destroyed without warning. Do not test my resolve."

"Oh no," Bull said. "Oh shit no."

"It has always been a personal mission of mine to assure that information and resources remain free to all people. The efforts of individuals and corporate entities may have helped us to colonize the planets of our solar system and make life possible where it was inconceivable before, but the danger of someone unscrupulous taking control of the Ring is too great. I have proven myself worthy of the trust of the people of the Belt. It is a moral imperative that this shining artifact be protected, and I will spill as much blood as I have to in order to do so."

Bull scooped up the hand terminal and tried to connect to Ashford. The red trefoil of command block blinked on the screen and shunted him to a menu that let him record a message for later. He tried Pa and got the same thing. Holden's message was looping now, the replayed words just as idiotic and toxic the second time through. Bull said something obscene through clenched teeth. He pulled on the cart, turning the wheels as far as they would go, and stamped on the accelerator. The central lifts were only a minute or two away. He could get there. Just please God let Ashford not do anything stupid before he got to the bridge.

"That true, boss?" Serge said. "Did Holden just claim us all the Ring?"

"I want everyone on security mobilized right now," Bull said. "Enemy action protocols. Corridors clear and bulkheads closed. Anyone on a weapons or damage control team, wake 'em up and get 'em dressed. You're in charge of that."

"You got it, boss," Serge said. "Someone asks, where are you?"

"Trying to keep from needing them."

"Bien."

The familiar corridors seemed longer than usual, the awkwardness of floors built to be walls and walls intended as ceilings more surreal. If he'd been on a real battleship, there would have been a simple, direct path. If the Behemoth's great belly had been spinning, it would have been better than this. He willed the cart faster, pushing the engine past what it could do. The alert Klaxon sounded: Serge calling everyone to brace for battle.

A crowd had formed at the lift: men and women trying to get back to their stations. Bull pushed through them, the shortest person there. An Earther, like Holden. At the lift, he activated the security override, called the first car, and stepped in. A tall, dark-skinned man tried to follow him. Bull put a hand on the man's chest, stopping him.

"Take the next one," Bull said. "I'm not going where you want to be."

As the lift rose toward the bridge like it was ascending to heaven, Bull used his hand terminal to grasp for any information. He didn't have access to the secure channels—only the captain and the XO had those—but there was more than enough public chatter. He ran through the open feeds, grasping for a sense of the situation, watching for a few seconds here, a few seconds there.

The Martian science team and their escort were raging at Holden on every feed, calling him a terrorist and a criminal. The Earth flotilla's reaction was quieter. Most of the public conversation was coordinating the rescue efforts on the *Seung Un*. The high-energy gas from the core dump was confusing some of the relief crew's comms, and someone fairly smart had started using the public feeds to coordinate them. It had the grim efficiency of a military operation, and it gave Bull hope for the Earth navy crew still alive on the *Seung Un* as much as it scared him about what was going to come after.

Holden's message was repeating, spilling out over the public feeds. At first it just came from the *Rocinante*, but soon it was being relayed on other feeds along with commentary. Once the signal got back to the Belt and the inner planets, it was going to be the only thing anyone talked about. Bull could already imagine the negotiations between Earth and Mars, could practically hear them reaching the conclusion that the OPA had gotten too confident and needed to be taken down a notch.

Someone on the *Behemoth* put out a copy of Holden's message with the split circle emblem over it and a commentary track saying that it was about time that the Belt take its place and demand the respect it deserved. Bull told Serge to find the feed and shut it down.

After what felt like hours and probably wasn't more than four minutes, the lift reached the bridge, the doors opening silently before him, and let Bull out.

The bridge wasn't designed for battle. Instead of a real war machine's system of multiple stations and controlled lines of command, the *Behemoth*'s bridge was built like the largest tugboat ever made, only with angels blowing golden trumpets adorning the walls. The stations—single stations with a rotating backup scheme—were manned by Belters looking at each other and chatting. The security station was through a separate door and stood unmanned. The bridge crew were acting like children or civilians, their expressions were bright and excited. People who didn't recognize danger when they saw it and assumed that whatever the crisis was, it would all work out in the end.

Ashford and Pa were at the command station. Ashford was speaking into a camera, talking with someone on one of the other ships. Pa, scowling, strode toward Bull. Her eyes were narrow and her lips bloodless.

"What the hell are you doing here, Mister Baca?"

"I've got to talk to the captain," Bull said.

"Captain Ashford's busy right now," Pa said. "You might have noticed we have a situation on our hands. I would have expected you to be at your duty station."

"Yes, XO, but—"

"Your station isn't on the bridge. You should leave now."

Bull clenched his jaw. He wanted to shout at her, but this wasn't the time for it. He was here to make it work, and that wasn't going to help.

"We've got to shoot him, ma'am," Bull said. "We've got to fire on the *Rocinante*, and we've got to do it now."

All heads had turned toward them. Ashford ended his transmission and stepped toward them. Uncertainty made him look haughty. The captain's eyes flickered toward the crew members at their stations and back again. Bull could see how aware Ashford was that he was being watched. It deformed all his decisions, but there wasn't time for privacy.

"I have this under control, Mister Baca," Ashford said.

"All respect, Captain," Bull said, "but we've got to shoot down Holden, and we have to do it before anyone else does."

"We're not going to do a damn thing until we know what's going on, mister," Ashford said, his voice taking a dangerous buzz. "I've sent back a request for clarification to Ceres to see whether the higher-ups authorized Holden's action, and I am monitoring the activity of the Earther fleet."

The slip was telling. Not UN. Earther. Bull felt the blood in his neck. Ashford's casual racism and incompetence was about to get them all killed. He gritted his teeth, lowered his head, and raised his voice.

"Sir, there's a calculation happening right now with Earth and Mars both—"

"This is a potentially volatile situation, Mister Baca—"

"—where they have to decide whether to take direct response or let Holden win—"

"—and I am not going to be the one to throw gas on the fire. Escalating to violence at this point—"

"—and once they start shooting at *him*, they're going to start shooting at *us*."

Pa's voice cut through the air like a single flute in a bass symphony.

"He's right, sir."

Bull and Ashford turned toward her. Ashford's surprise was a mirror of his own. The man at the sensor station muttered something to the woman next to him, the hiss of his voice carrying in the sudden silence.

"Mister Baca's right," Pa said. "Holden's identified himself as a representative of the OPA. He's taken violent action against the Earth forces. The opposing commanders will have to look on us as his backup."

"Holden isn't a representative of the OPA," Ashford said. The bluster made him sound unsure.

"You called Ceres," Bull said. "If you're not sure, they're not either."

Ashford's face flushed red.

"Holden hasn't had any official status with the OPA since Fred Johnson fired him over his handling of Ganymede. If there's a question, I can clarify with the other commanders that Holden doesn't speak for us, but no one's taking any action. The best thing is to wait and let things cool down."

Pa looked down, then up again. It didn't matter that she'd humiliated Bull and Sam in front of the command staff. All that counted was doing this next part right. Bull wanted to reach out, touch her arm, lend her the courage to stand up to Ashford.

It turned out she didn't need it.

"Sir, if we don't take the initiative, someone else will, and then it's going to be too late for clarifications. Denials are fine if they're believed, but Holden and his crew were known to be working with us previously and they're claiming to represent us now. We're four hours' lag to Ceres. We can't wait for answers. We have to make the division between us and Holden unequivocal. Mister Baca's right. We need to engage the *Rocinante*."

Ashford's face was gray.

"I'm not going to start a shooting war," he said.

"You listening to the same feeds as me, Captain?" Bull asked. "Everyone already thinks we did."

"The *Rocinante*'s one ship. We can take her out," Pa said. "If we fight Earth or Mars, we'll lose."

The truth lay on the floor between them. Ashford put a hand to his chin. His eyes were flickering back and forth like he was reading something that wasn't there. Every second he didn't respond, his cowardice showed through, and Bull could see that the man knew it. Resented it. Ashford was responsible, and didn't want the responsibility. He was more afraid of looking bad than of losing.

"Mister Chen," Ashford said. "Get a tightbeam to the *Rocinante*. Tell Captain Holden that it's an urgent matter."

"Yes, sir," the communications officer said, and then a moment later, "The *Rocinante* isn't accepting the connection, sir."

"Captain?" the man at the sensor array said. "The *Rocinante*'s changing course."

"Where's she going?" Ashford demanded, his gaze still locked on Bull.

"Um. Toward us? Sir?"

Ashford closed his eyes.

"Mister Corley," he growled. "Power up the port missile array. Mister Chen, I want tightbeam connections to the Earth and Mars command ships, and I want them now."

Bull let himself sag back. The sense of urgency giving way to relief and a kind of melancholy. *One more time, Colonel Johnson. We dodged the bullet one more time.*

"Weapons board is green, sir," the weapons officer said, her voice crisp and excited as a kid at an arcade.

"Lock target," Ashford said. "Do I have those tightbeams yet?"

"We're acknowledged and pending, sir," Chen said. "They know we want to talk."

"That'll do," Ashford said, and began pacing the bridge like an old-time captain on a wooden quarterdeck. His hands were clasped behind his back.

"We have lock," the weapons officer said. Then, "The *Rocinante*'s weapons systems are powering up."

Ashford sank into his couch. His expression was sour. He'd been hoping, Bull realized, that it might be true. That the OPA might be making a play to control the Ring.

The man was an idiot.

"Should we fire, sir?" the weapons officer asked, the strain in her voice like a dog on a leash. She wanted to. Badly. Bull didn't think better of her for it. He glanced at Pa, but she was making a point of not looking at him.

"Yes," Ashford said. "Go ahead. Fire."

"One away, sir," the weapons officer said.

"I'm getting an error code," the operations officer said. "We're getting feedback from the launcher."

Bull's mouth tasted like a penny. If Holden had put a bomb on the *Behemoth* too, their problems might only be starting.

"Is the missile out?" Pa snapped. "Tell me we don't have an armed torpedo stuck in the tube."

"Yes, sir," the weapons officer said. "The missile is away. We have confirmation."

"The *Rocinante* is taking evasive maneuvers."

"Is she returning fire?" Ashford said.

"No, sir. Not yet, sir."

"I'm getting errors in the electrical grid, sir. I think something's shorted out. We might—"

The bridge went dark.

"—lose power. Sir."

The monitors were black. The lights were off. The only sound was the hum of the air recyclers, running, Bull imagined, off the battery backups. Ashford's voice came out of the darkness.

"Mister Pa, did we ever test-fire the missile systems?"

"I believe it's on the schedule for next week, sir," the XO said. Bull tuned his hand terminal screen to its brightest, lifting it like a torch. He glanced up at the emergency lighting set into the walls all around the room, sitting there as dark as everything else. Another system that hadn't been tested yet.

A few seconds later, half of the bridge crew pulled flashlights out of recessed emergency lockers. The light level came up as beams played across the room. No one spoke. No one needed to. If the *Rocinante* fired back, they were a dead target, but the chances were that they wouldn't lose the whole ship. If they'd waited until they were in pitched battle against Earth or Mars or both, the *Behemoth* would have died. Instead, they'd just shown the whole system how unprepared they were. It was the first time Bull was really glad to be just the security officer.

"XO?" Bull said.

"Yes."

"Permission to release the chief engineer from house arrest?"

Pa's face was monochrome gray in the dim light, and solemn as the grave. Still, he thought he saw a glint of bleak amusement in her eyes.

"Permission granted," she said.

Chapter Sixteen: Holden

"Well," Amos said. "That's just fucking peculiar."

The message began to repeat.

"This is Captain James Holden. What you've just seen is a demonstration of the danger you are in..."

The ops deck was in a stunned silence, then Naomi began working the ship ops panel with a quiet fury. In Holden's peripheral vision, Monica motioned to her crew and Okju lifted a camera. The tacit decision to let the "no civilians on the ops deck" rule slide suddenly seemed like it might have been a mistake.

"It's a fake," Holden said. "I never recorded that. That's not me."

"Sort of sounds like you, though," Amos said.

"Jim," Naomi said, panic beginning to distort her voice. "That broadcast is coming from us. It's coming from the *Roci* right now."

Holden shook his head, denying the assertion outright. The

only thing more ridiculous than the message itself was the idea that it was coming from *his* ship.

"That broadcast is coming from us," Naomi said, slamming her hand against her screen. "And I can't stop it!"

Everything seemed to recede from Holden, the noises in the room coming from far away. He recognized it as a panic reaction, but he gave in to it, accepted the short moment of peace it brought. Monica was shouting questions at him he could barely hear. Naomi was furiously pounding on her workstation, flipping through menu screens faster than he could follow. Over the ship's comm, Alex was shouting demands for orders. From across the room, Amos was staring at him with a look of almost comical puzzlement. The two camera operators, equipment still clutched in one hand, were trying to belt themselves into crash couches with the other. Cohen floated in the middle of the room, lips pursed in a faint frown.

"This was the setup," Holden said. "This is what it was for."

Everything: the Martian lawsuit, the loss of his Titania job, the camera crew going to the Ring, all leading to this. The only thing he couldn't imagine was why.

"What do you mean?" Monica asked, pushing close to get into the shot with him. "What setup?"

Amos put a hand on her shoulder and shook his head once.

"Naomi," Holden said, "is the only system you've lost control of comms?"

"I don't know. I think so."

"Then kill it. If you can't, help Amos isolate the entire comm system from the power grid. Cut it out of the damn ship if you have to."

She nodded again and then turned to Amos.

"Alex," Holden said. Monica started to say something to him, but he held up one finger to silence her, and she closed her mouth with a snap. "Get us burning toward the *Behemoth*. We're not really claiming the Ring for the OPA, but as long as everyone thinks we are, they're the team least likely to shoot us."

"What can you tell me about what's going on?" Monica said. "Are we in danger here? Is this dangerous?" Her usual smirk was gone. Open fear had replaced it.

"Strap in," Holden said. "All of you. Do it now."

Okju and Clip were already belted into crash couches, and Monica and Cohen quickly followed suit. The entire documentary crew had the good sense to stay quiet.

"Cap," Alex said. His voice had taken on the almost sleepy tone he got when in a high-stress situation. "The *Behemoth* just lit us up with their targeting laser."

Holden belted himself into the combat ops station and warmed it up. The *Roci* began counting ships within their threat radius. It turned out to be all of them. The ship asked him if any should be marked as hostiles.

"Your guess is as good as mine, honey."

"Huh?" Naomi asked.

"Um," Alex said. "Are you guys warming up the weapons?"

"No," Holden said.

"Oh, I'm really sorry to hear that," Alex said. "Weapons systems are coming online."

"Are we shooting at anyone?"

"Not yet?"

Holden told the *Roci* to mark anything that hit them with a targeting system as hostile and was relieved when the system actually responded. The *Behemoth* shifted to red on the display. Then, after a moment's thought, he told the ship to lump all the Martians and Earth ships into two groups. If they wound up fighting with one ship in a group, they'd be fighting them all.

There were too many. The *Roci* was caught between Fred Johnson's two-kilometer-long OPA overcompensation and most of the remaining Martian navy. And beyond the Martians, the Ring.

"Okay," he said, desperately trying to think of what to do now. They were as far from a hiding spot as it was possible to be in the solar system. It was a two-month trip just to the nearest rock bigger than their ship. He doubted he could outrun three fleets and all their torpedoes for two months. Or two minutes, really, if it came to that. "How's that radio coming?"

"Down," Amos said. "Easy enough to just pull the plug."

"Do we have any way to tell everyone that the broadcast wasn't us? I will happily signal full and complete surrender at this point," Holden said.

"Not without turning it back on," Amos replied.

"Everyone out there is probably trying to contact us," Holden said. "The longer we don't answer, the worse this will look. What about the weapons?"

"Warmed up, not shooting," Amos said. "And not responding to us."

"Can we pull power on those too?"

"We can," Amos said, looking pained. "But damn, I sure don't want to."

"Fast mover!" Naomi yelled.

"Holy shit," Alex said. "The OPA just fired a torpedo at us."

On Holden's panel, a yellow dot separated from the *Behemoth* and shifted to orange as it took off at high g.

"Go evasive!" Holden said. "Naomi, can you blind it?"

"No. No laser," she replied, her voice surprisingly calm now. "And no radio. Countermeasures aren't responding."

"Fuck me," Amos said. "Why did someone drag us all the way out here just to kill us? Coulda done that at Ceres, saved us the trip."

"Alex, here's your course." Holden sent the pilot a vector that would take them right through the heart of the Martian fleet. As far as he knew, the Martians only wanted to arrest him. That sounded okay. "Has the *Behemoth* fired again?"

"No," Naomi replied. "They've gone dark. No active sensors, no drives."

"Kinda big and kinda close to be trying for sneaky," Alex said without any real humor. "Here comes the juice."

While the couches pumped them full of drugs to keep the high g from killing them, apropos of nothing Cohen said, "Fucking *bitch*."

Before Holden could ask what he meant, Alex opened up the *Roci*'s throttle and the ship took off like a racehorse feeling the spurs. The sudden acceleration slammed Holden into his couch hard enough to daze him for a second. The ship buzzed him back to his senses when a missile proximity alarm warned him the *Behemoth*'s torpedo was getting closer. Helpless to do anything about it, Holden watched the orange dot that meant all their deaths creeping ever closer to the fleeing *Rocinante*. He looked up at Naomi, and she was looking back, as helpless as he was, all her best tricks taken away when the comm array was powered down.

The gravity dropped suddenly. "Got an idea," Alex said over the comm, then the ship jerked through several sharp maneuvers, and the gravity went away again. The *Rocinante* had added a new alarm to her song. A collision warning was sounding. Holden realized he'd never actually heard a collision alarm outside of drills. When do spaceships run *into* each other?

He turned on the exterior cameras to a field of uniform black. For a second, he thought they were broken, but then Alex took control of them, panning out along the vast expanse of a Martian cruiser's skin. The target lock buzzer cut out, the missile losing them.

"Put this Martian heavy between us and the missile," Alex said, almost whispering it, as though the missile might hear if he spoke too loud.

"How close are we to them?" Holden asked, his voice matching Alex's.

" 'Bout ten meters," Alex said, pride in his voice. "More or less."

"This is really going to piss them off if the missile keeps coming," Amos said. Then, almost meditatively, "I don't even know what a point defense cannon does at a range like this."

As if in answer, the cruiser hit them with a targeting laser. Then all of the other Martian ships did as well, adding a few dozen more alarms to the cacophony.

"Shit," Alex said, and the gravity came back like a boulder rolled onto Holden's chest. None of the Martian ships fired, but the original missile shot back into view on the scope. The Martians were guiding it in, now that the *Behemoth* seemed to be out of action. Holden marveled that he'd lived *just* long enough to finally see real Martian-OPA cooperation. It wasn't as gratifying as he'd hoped.

Martian ships whipped past on both sides as the *Rocinante* accelerated through the main cluster of their fleet. Holden could imagine the targeting arrays and point defense cannons swiveling to track them as they went by. Once past them, there was nothing but the Ring and infinite star-speckled black all around it.

The plan came to mind with the sick, sinking feeling of something horrible he'd always known and tried to forget. The missile was coming, and even if they avoided it, there would be others. He couldn't dodge forever. He couldn't surrender. For all he knew, his weapons might start firing at any second. For a moment, the ops deck seemed to go still, time slowing the way it did when something catastrophic was happening. He was intensely aware of Naomi, pressed back in her couch. Monica and Okju, their eyes wide with fear and thrust. Clip, his hand pressed awkwardly into the gel by his side. Cohen's slack jaw and pale face.

"Huh," Holden gurgled to himself, the g forces crushing his throat when he vocalized. He signaled Alex to cut thrust, and the gravity dropped away again.

"The Ring," Holden said. "Aim for the Ring. Go."

The gravity came back with a slap, and Holden rotated his chair to his workstation and brought up the navigational console. Watching the rapidly approaching orange dot out of the corner of his eye, he built a navigational package for Alex that would take them at high speed to the Ring, then spin them for a massive and almost suicidally dangerous deceleration burn just before they went in. He could slide them in under the velocity cap that had stopped the *Y Que* and all the fast-moving probes since. With any luck, the missile would be caught by whatever was on the other side, and the *Roci*, going slower, wouldn't. The ship warned him that such high-g forces had a 3 percent chance to kill one of the crew members even during a short burn.

The missile would kill them all.

Holden sent the nav package to Alex, half expecting him to refuse. Hoping. Instead, the *Roci* accelerated for an endless twenty-seven minutes, followed by a nauseating zero-g spin that lasted less than four seconds, and a deceleration burn that lasted four and a half minutes and knocked every single person on the ship unconscious.

"Wake up," Miller said in the darkness.

The ship was in free fall. Holden began coughing furiously as his lungs attempted to find their normal shape again after the punishing deceleration burn. Miller floated beside him. No one else seemed to be awake yet. Naomi wasn't moving at all. Holden watched her until he could see the gentle rise and fall of her rib cage. She was alive.

"Doors and corners," Miller said. His voice was soft and rough. "I tell you check your doors and corners, and you blow into the middle of the room with your dick hanging out. Lucky sonofabitch. Give you this, though, you're consistent."

Something about the way he spoke seemed saner than usual. More controlled. As if guessing his thoughts, the detective turned to look at him. Smiled.

"Are you here?" Holden asked. His mind was still fuzzy, his brain abused by thrust and oxygen loss. "Are you real?"

"You're not thinking straight. Take your time. Catch up. There's no hurry."

Holden pulled up the exterior cameras and blew out one long exhale that almost ended in a sob. The OPA missile was floating outside the ship, just over a hundred meters from the nose of the *Roci*. The torpedo's drive was still firing, its tail a furious white torch stretching nearly a kilometer behind it. But the missile hung in space, motionless.

Holden didn't know if the missile had been that close when they went through. He suspected not. More likely, they'd just wound up that close once they'd both stopped moving. Even so, the sight of the massive weapon, engine burning as it still fought to reach him, made a shiver go down his spine and his balls creep up into his belly. Ten meters closer and they'd have been in proximity. It would have detonated.

As he watched, the missile was slowly pulled away, dragged off to who knew where by whatever power set the speed limit on this side of the Ring.

"We made it," he said. "We're through."

"Yeah," Miller said.

"This is what you wanted, isn't it? This is why you did it."

"You're giving me too much credit."

Amos and Naomi both groaned as they started to wake. The documentary crew was motionless. They might even be dead. Holden couldn't tell without unstrapping, and his body wouldn't allow that yet. Miller leaned close to the screen, squinting at it like he was searching for something. Holden pulled up the sensor data. A host of information flooded in. Numerous objects, clustered within a million kilometers, close as seeds in a pod. And past them, nothing. Not even starlight.

"What are they?" Holden asked. "What's out there?"

Miller glanced down at the display. His face was expressionless.

"*Nothing*," the dead man said. And then, "It scares the shit out of me."

Chapter Seventeen: Bull

The hell are we?" Serge said, floating gently by the security desk. "Security or fucking babysitters?"

"We're whatever gets the job done," Bull said, but he couldn't put much force behind the words.

It was thirty hours since the *Behemoth* had gone dark, and he had slept for six of them. Serge, Casimir, Jojo, and Corin had been trading off duty at the desk, coordinating the recovery. The rest of the security staff had been in ad hoc teams, putting down two little panic riots, coordinating the physical resources to free a dozen people trapped in storage bays where the air recycler hadn't booted back up, arresting a couple of mech jockeys who'd taken the chaos as opportunity to settle a personal score.

The lights were on all across the ship now. The damage control systems, woken from their coma, were working double time to catch up. The crews were exhausted and frightened and on edge, and James fucking Holden had escaped through the Ring into whatever was on the other side. The security office smelled like old sweat and the bean curd masala that Casimir had brought in yesterday. For the first day, there had been an unconscious effort to keep a consistent physical orientation—feet toward the floor, head toward the ceiling. Now they all floated in whatever direction they happened to fall into. It seemed almost natural to the Belters. Bull still suffered the occasional bout of vertigo.

"Amen alles amen," Serge said with a laugh. "Lube for the machine, us."

"Least fun I've ever had with lube," Corin said. Bull noted that when Corin got tired, she got raunchy. In his experience, everyone dealt with pushing too hard differently. Some got angry and irritable, some got sad. At a guess, it was all loss of inhibition. Wear down the façade with too much work or fear or both, and whoever was waiting underneath came out.

"All right," Bull said. "You two go take a rest. I'll watch the shop until the others get back. You two have done more than—"

The security desk chimed. The connection request was from Sam. Bull lifted a finger to Serge and Corin, and pulled himself over to the desk.

"Sam?" he said.

"Bull," she replied, and the single syllable, short and sharp, carried a weight of annoyance and anger that verged on rage. "I need you to come down here."

"You can call whoever you want," a man's voice said in the background. "I don't care, you hear? I don't care anymore. You do whatever you want."

Bull checked the connection location. She was down near the machine shops. It wasn't too far.

"I need to bring a sidearm?" Bull asked.

"I won't stop you, sweetie," Sam said.

"On my way," he said, and dropped the connection.

"Gehst du," Corin said to Serge. "You've been up longer. I'll keep the place from burning."

"You going to be all right?" Serge asked, and it took Bull a second to realize the man was talking to him.

"Unstoppable," Bull said, trying to mean it.

Being exhausted in zero gravity wasn't the same as it was under thrust or down a gravity well. Growing up, Bull had been dead tired pretty often, and the sense of weight, of his muscles falling off the bone like overcooked chicken, was what desperate fatigue meant. He'd been off of Earth for more years now than he'd been on it, and it still confused him on an almost cellular level to be worn to the point of collapse and not feel it in his joints. Intellectually, he knew it left him feeling that he could do more than he actually could. There were other signs: the grit against his eyes, the headache that bloomed slowly out from the center of his skull, the mild nausea. None of them had the same power, and none of them convinced.

The corridors weren't empty, but they weren't crowded. Even at full alert, with every team working double shifts and busting ass, the *Behemoth* was mostly empty. He moved through the ship, launching himself handhold to handhold, sailing down each long straightaway like he was in a dream. He was tempted to speed up, slapping at the handholds and ladders as they passed and adding just a touch of kinetic energy to his float the way he and his men had back in his days as a marine. More than one concussion had come out of the game, and he didn't have time for it now. He wasn't young anymore either.

He found Sam and her crew in a massive service bay. Four men in welding rigs floated near the wall, fixing lengths of conduit to the bulkhead with showers of sparks and lights brighter than staring at the sun. Sam floated nearby, her body at a forty-five-degree angle from the work. A young Belter floated near her, his body at an angle that pointed his feet toward her. Bull understood it was an insult.

"Bull," Sam said. The young man's face was a pale mask of rage. "This is Gareth. He's decided laying conduit's icky."

"I'm an *engineer*," Gareth said, spitting out the word so violently it gave him a degree of spin. "Did eight years on Tycho Station! I'm not going to get used like a fucking *technician.*"

The other welders didn't turn from their work, but Bull could see them all listening. He looked at Sam, and her face was closed. Bull couldn't tell if calling him in for help had been hard for her or if it was part of how she expected him to make things right to her after the thing with Pa. That it had been the shortest detention on record didn't pull the sting of being caught up in his political struggles. Either way, she'd escalated the problem to him, and so it was his now.

Bull took a deep breath.

"So what are we working on here?" he asked, less because he cared than that it would give him a few extra seconds to think and his brain wasn't at its best.

"I've got a major line faulting out," Sam said. "I can take three days and diagnose the whole thing or I can take twenty hours and put up a workaround."

"And the conduit's for the workaround?"

"Is."

Bull lifted his fist in the Belter's equivalent of a nod and then turned his attention to the boy. Gareth was young and he was tired and he was an OPA Belter, which meant he'd never been through any kind of real military indoctrination. Bull had to figure Sam had yelled at him enough before she'd called for backup.

"All right, then," Bull said.

"Está-hey bullshit is," the man said, his educated grammar fracturing.

"I understand," Bull said. "You can go. Just help me get your rig on first."

Gareth blinked. Bull thought he saw the ghost of a smile in the corners of Sam's bloodshot eyes, but that could have meant anything. Pleasure at the weariness in Bull's voice or at Gareth's confusion, or maybe she'd understood what Bull was doing and she thought he was really clever.

"I talk to the guys on the other ships some," Bull said. "Earth or Mars. Someone'll be sending a ship back. I'll see if I can't get you a ride as far as Ceres anyway."

Gareth's mouth opened and closed like a goldfish. Sam pushed off, hooking the welder's rig with one hand, pulling it close to speed up the turn and then extending her arm to slow it. Bull took it from her and started pulling on the straps.

"You know how to do this?" Sam asked.

"Good enough to hang conduit," Bull said.

"Security can lose you?"

"Shift's done," Bull said. "I was just heading for my bunk, but this needs doing, I can do it."

"All right, then," Sam said. "Take the length at the end, and I'll have someone join it up with Marca's. I'll come check your work in a minute."

"Sounds good," Bull said. He was spinning just a few degrees each second and he let the momentum carry him around to face the boy. The rage was still there, but it was sinking under a layer of embarrassment. All his arguments and bluster about not doing something because it was beneath him, and now the head of security was using his off-shift to do the same work. Bull could feel the attention of the other welders on them. Bull lit his torch, just testing it out, and the air between them went white for a second. "Okay, then. I got this. You can go if you want."

The boy shifted, getting ready to launch himself back across the bay and out into the ship. Bull tried to remember the last time he'd actually welded something with no gravity. He was pretty sure he could do it, but he'd have to start slow. Then Gareth's shoulders cupped forward, and he knew he wouldn't have to. Bull started taking off the straps, and Gareth moved forward to help him.

"You're tired," Bull said, his voice low enough not to carry to the others. "You been working too hard, and it got to you a little. Happens to everyone."

"Bien."

He put the torch in the boy's hand and squeezed it there.

"This is a privilege," Bull said. "Being out here, doing this bullshit, working our asses off for no one to give a shit? It's a privilege. Next time you undermine Chief Engineer Rosenberg's authority, I will ship your ass home with a note that says you couldn't handle it."

The boy muttered something Bull couldn't make out. The flare from the other torches made the boy's face dance white and brown and white again. Bull put a hand on his arm.

"Yes, sir," Gareth said. Bull let go, and the boy pushed off to the wall, situating himself over the length of pipe that was waiting there for him. Sam appeared at Bull's elbow, sliding down from the blind spot above and behind him.

"That worked," she said.

"Yeah."

"Didn't hurt that you're an Earther."

"Didn't. How's it all coming?"

"Apart," Sam said. "But we'll stick it back together with bubblegum if we have to."

"Least no one was shooting at us."

Sam's laugh had some warmth in it.

"They wouldn't have had to do it twice."

The alert tone came from all their hand terminals at once, simultaneous with the ship address system. Bull felt his lips press thin.

"Well, that timing's a little ominous," Sam said before Captain Ashford's voice rang out through the ship. The openness of the spaces and the different speakers made the words echo like the voice of God.

"This is your captain speaking. I have just received confirmation from the OPA central authority that the actions undertaken by the criminal James Holden were unauthorized by any part of the Outer Planets Alliance. His actions put not only this ship but the reputation and good standing of the alliance in threat. I have informed the central authority that we took swift and decisive action against Holden, and that he escaped from us only by retreating through the Ring."

"Thanks for that, by the way," Sam said.

"De nada."

"I have requested and received," Ashford continued, "the authority to continue action to address this insult as I deem fit. The evidence of our own sensors and of the Martian and Earth feeds to which we have access all show that the *Rocinante* has passed through the Ring in good condition and appears to have sustained no damage despite the physical anomalies on the other side.

"In light of that, I have made the decision to follow Holden through the Ring and take him and his crew into custody. I will be sending out specific instructions to all department heads outlining what preparations we will need to complete before we begin our burn, but I expect to be in pursuit within the next six hours. It is imperative for the pride, dignity, and honor of the OPA that this insult not go unanswered and that the hands that bring Holden to justice be ours.

"I want you all to know that I am honored to serve with such a valiant crew, and that together we will make history. Take these next hours, all of you, to rest and prepare. God bless each and every one of you, and the Outer Planets Alliance."

With a resounding click from a hundred speakers, Ashford dropped the connection. The flashing white light of the welding torches was gone, and the bay was darker. Laughter warred against despair in Bull's gut.

"Is he drunk, do you think?" Sam said.

"Worse. Embarrassed. He's trying to save face," Bull said.

"The *Behemoth* filled its diddies in front of God and everyone, so now we're going to be the biggest badass in the system to make up for it?"

"Pretty much."

"Gonna talk him out of it?"

"Gonna try."

Sam scratched her cheek.

"Could be hard to back down after that little once-more-into-the-breach thing."

"He won't," Bull said. "But I've got to try."

The inner planets came out to the black with an understanding that they were soldiers sent to a foreign land. Bull remembered the feeling from when he'd first shipped out: the sense that his home was behind him. For the inners, the expansion out into the solar system had always had the military at its core.

The Belters didn't have that. They were the natives here. The forces that had brought their ancestors out to the Belt had roots in trade, commerce, and the overwhelming promise of freedom. The OPA had begun its life more like a labor union than a nation. The difference was subtle but powerful, and it showed in strange ways.

If they had been in any of the Earth or Mars ships that floated now in the darkness near the Ring, Bull would have come from his thorough and profound dressing down by the captain to seek out XO Pa in a galley or mess hall. But this was the *Behemoth*, so he found her in a bar.

It was a small place with bulbs of alcohol, chocolate, coffee, and tea all set with temperature controls in the nipple, so the uniformly tepid drinks could come out anywhere from almost boiling to just this side of ice. The décor was cheap nightclub, with colored lights and cheap graphic films to hide the walls. Half a dozen people floated on handholds or tethers, and Pa was one of them.

His first thought as he pulled himself toward her was that she needed a haircut. With the false gravity of acceleration gone, her hair floated around her, too short to tie back but still long enough to interfere with her vision and creep into her mouth. His second thought was that she looked as tired as he was.

"Mister Baca," Pa said.

"XO. You mind if I join you?"

"I was expecting you. You've been to see the captain?"

Bull wished he could sit down, not for any actual reason so much as the small physical punctuation it would have given their conversation.

"I have. He wasn't happy to see me. Showed me the proposal you'd built up on how to remove me from my position."

"It was a contingency plan," she said.

"Yeah. So this idea where we take the *Behemoth* through the Ring? We can't do that. We start any kind of serious burn, we're going to have two navies on our butts. And we don't know what's on the other side except that it's way more powerful than we are."

"Do you want an alien civilization taking its ideas of humanity from Jim Holden?"

Ashford had said the same thing, word for word. It had been his most cogent argument, and now Bull knew where he'd borrowed it from. He'd had the long trip down in the lift to let his sleep-deprived brain come up with its counterargument.

"That's not even going to come into play if they shoot our nuts off before we get there," he said. "You really think Earth and Mars are going to go for the whole 'we're just playing sheriff' line? There's going to be a bunch of them who still think whatever Holden was up to, we were in on it. But even if they don't, the part where they stand to the side and let us take the lead isn't going to happen. You can bet your ass the head of the Mars force is asking his XO if they want an alien civilization taking its ideas of humanity from Ashford."

"That was nice," Pa said. "The reversal thing? That was good."

"The inner planets may not be making threats yet," Bull said, "but—"

"They are. Mars has threatened to open fire on us if we get within a hundred thousand kilometers of the Ring."

Bull put his hand to his mouth. He could feel his mind struggling to make sense of the words. The Martian navy had already laid down an ultimatum. Ashford hadn't even mentioned it.

"So what the hell are we doing?"

"We're preparing for burn in four and three-quarter hours, Mister Baca," Pa said. "Because that's what we've been ordered to do."

The bitterness wasn't only in her voice. It was in her eyes and the angle of her mouth. Sympathy and outrage battled in Bull's mind, and underneath them a rising panic. He was too tired to be having this conversation. Too tired to be doing what had to get done. It had stripped away all the protections that would have made him hesitate to speak. If he could have gotten just one good cycle's rest, maybe he could have found another way, but this was the hand he'd been dealt, so it was the hand he'd play.

"You don't agree with him," Bull said. "If it was your call, you wouldn't do it."

Pa took a long pull at her bulb, the flexible foil buckling under the suction. Bull was pretty sure she wasn't drinking for the taste, and the urge to get some whiskey for himself came on him like an unexpected blow.

"It doesn't matter what I would or wouldn't do," Pa said. "It's not my command, so it's not my decision."

"Unless something happens to the captain," Bull said. "Then it would be."

Pa went still. The sound of the music, the shifting patterns of lights, all of it seemed to recede. They were in their own small universe together. Pa thumbed on the bulb's magnet and stuck it to the wall beside her.

"There are still hours before the burn starts. And then travel time. The situation may change, but I won't take part in mutiny," she said.

"Maybe you wouldn't have to. Doesn't have to have anything to do with you. But unless you're going to specifically order me not to—"

"I am specifically ordering you, Mister Baca. I am ordering you not to take any action against the captain. I am ordering you to respect the chain of command. And if that means I have to commit to following through on Ashford's orders, then I'll make that commitment. Do you understand me?"

"Yeah," Bull said slowly. "Either we're all going to die, or we're going through the Ring."

Chapter Eighteen: Anna

Eleven people showed up for Anna's first worship service. The contrast with her congregation on Europa was unsettling at first. On Europa, she'd have had twenty or so families straggling in over the half hour before the service began, and a few drifting in late. They'd have been all ages, from grandparents rolling in on personal mobility devices to screaming children and infants. Some would come in their Sunday best formal wear, others in ratty casual clothes. The buzz of conversation prior to the service would be in mixed Russian, English, and outer planets polyglot. By the end of the worship meeting, a few might be snoring in their pews.

Her UNN congregation showed up in a single group at exactly 9:55 a.m. Instead of walking in and taking seats, they floated in as a loose clump and then just hovered in a disconcerting cloud in front of her podium. They wore spotless dress uniforms so crisply pressed they looked sharp enough to cut skin. They didn't speak, they just stared at her expectantly. And they were all so young. The oldest couldn't have been more than twenty-five.

The unusual circumstances rendered her standard worship service inappropriate—no need for a children's message or church announcements—so Anna launched directly into a prayer, followed by a scripture reading and a short sermon. She'd considered doing a sermon on duty and sacrifice; it seemed appropriate in the martial setting. But she had instead decided to speak mostly on God's love. Given the fear Chris had expressed a few days prior, it felt like the better choice.

When she'd finished, she closed with another prayer, then served communion. The gentle ritual seemed to ease the tension she felt in the room. Each of her eleven young soldiers came up to her makeshift table, took a bulb of grape juice and a wafer, and returned to their prior position floating nearby. She read the familiar words in Matthew and Luke, then spoke the blessing. They ate the bread and drank from the bulb. And, as had always happened since the very first church service she could remember, Anna felt something vast and quiet settle on her. She also felt the shiver that tried to crawl up her spine competing with a threatening belly laugh. She had a sudden vision of Jesus, who'd asked His disciples to keep doing this in remembrance of Him, watching her little congregation as they floated in microgravity and drank reconstituted grape beverage out of suction bulbs. It seemed to stretch the boundaries of what He'd meant by *this*.

A final prayer and the service was over. Not one of her congregation pushed toward the door to leave. Eleven young faces stared at her, waiting. The oppressive aura of fear she'd managed to push away during the communion crept back into the room.

Anna pulled herself around the podium and joined their loose cloud. "Should I expect anyone next week? You guys are making me nervous."

Chris spoke first. "No, it was real nice." He seemed to want to say more, but stopped and looked down at his hands instead.

"Back on Europa, people would have brought snacks and coffee for after the service," Anna said. "We could do that next time, if you want."

A few halfhearted nods. A muscular young woman in a marine uniform pulled her hand terminal halfway out of her pocket to check the time. Anna felt herself losing them. They needed something else from her, but they weren't going to ask for it. And it definitely wasn't coffee and snacks.

"I had a whole sermon on David," she said, keeping her tone casual. Conversational. "On the burden we place on our soldiers. The sacrifices we ask you to make for the rest of us."

Chris looked up from his hands. The young marine put her hand terminal away. With her podium behind her, the meeting room was just a featureless gray box. The little knot of soldiers floated in front of her, and suddenly the perspective shifted and she was above them, falling toward them. She blinked rapidly to break up the scene and swallowed to get the lemony taste of nausea out of her throat.

"David?" a young man with brown hair and dark skin said. He had an accent that she thought might be Australian.

"King of Israel," another young man said.

"That's just the nice version," the marine countered. "He's the guy who killed one of his own men so he could sleep with his wife."

"He fought for his country and his faith," Anna cut in, using the teacher's voice she used in Bible classes for teenagers. The one that made sure everyone knew she was the voice of authority. "That's the part I care about right now. Before he was a king, he was a soldier. Often unappreciated by those he served. He put his body over and over again between danger and those he'd sworn to protect, even when his leaders were unworthy of him."

A few more nods. No one looking at hand terminals. She felt herself getting them all back.

"And we've been asking that of our soldiers since the beginning of time," she continued. "Everyone here gave up something to be here. Often we're unworthy of you and you do it anyway."

"So why didn't you?" Chris asked. "You know, do the David sermon?"

"Because I'm scared," Anna said, taking Chris' hand with her left, and the hand of the Australian boy with her right. Without anyone saying anything, the loose cloud became a circle of held hands. "I'm so afraid. And I don't want to talk about soldiers and sacrifice. I want to talk about God watching me. Caring about what happens to me. And I thought maybe other people would too."

More nods. Chris said, "When the skinnies blew that ship, I thought we were all dead."

"No shit," the marine said. She gave Anna an embarrassed look. "Sorry, ma'am."

"It's okay."

"They say they didn't," another woman said. "They shot at Holden."

"Yeah, and then their whole ship mysteriously turned off. If the dusters hadn't pinged Holden, he'd have flown off scot free."

"They're gonna follow him," the young marine said.

"Dusters say they'll smoke them if they go in."

"Fuck the dusters," the Australian said. "We'll grease every one of them if they start anything."

"Okay," Anna cut in, keeping her voice gentle. "Dusters are Martians. They prefer Martians. And calling people from the outer planets skinnies is also rude. Epithets like that are an attempt to dehumanize a group so that you won't feel as bad about killing them."

The marine snorted and looked away.

"And," Anna continued, "fighting out here is the last thing we should be doing. Am I right?"

"Yeah," Chris said. "If we fight out here, we'll all die. No support, no reinforcements, nothing to hide behind. Three armed fleets and nothing bigger than a stray hydrogen atom for cover. This is what we call the kill box."

The silence stretched for a moment, then the Australian sighed and said, "Yeah."

"And something may come out of the Ring."

Saying the thing out loud and then acknowledging it drained the tension out of the air. With everyone floating in microgravity, no one could slump. But shoulders and foreheads relaxed. There were a few sad smiles. Even her angry young marine ran a hand through her blond crew cut and nodded without looking at anyone.

"Let's do this again next week," Anna said while she still had them. "We can celebrate communion, then maybe just chat for a while. And in the meantime, my door is always open. Please call me if you need to talk."

The group began to break up, heading for the door. Anna kept hold of Chris' hand. "Could you wait a moment? I need to ask you about something."

"Chris," the marine said with a mocking singsong voice. "Gonna get a little preacher action."

"That's not funny," Anna said, using the full weight of her teacher voice. The marine had the grace to blush.

"Sorry, ma'am."

"You may leave," Anna said, and her marine did. "Chris, do you remember the young woman who was in the officers' mess that first time we met?"

He shrugged. "There were lots of people coming and going."

"This one had long dark hair. She looked very sad. She was wearing civilian clothes."

"Oh," Chris said with a grin. "The cute one. Yeah, I remember her."

"Do you know her?"

"No. Just a civvy contractor fixing the plumbing, I'd guess. We have a couple ships full of them in the fleet. Why?"

That was a good question. She honestly wasn't sure why the angry young woman weighed on her mind so much over the last few days. But something about her stuck in Anna's memory like a burr in her clothing. She'd feel irritated and antsy and suddenly the girl's face would pop into her mind. The anger, the sense of threat she'd radiated. The proximity of that encounter to the sudden hostilities and damaged ships and people shooting at each other. There was nothing that tied them all together, but Anna couldn't shake the feeling that they were connected.

"I'm worried about her?" Anna finally said. At least it wasn't a lie.

Chris was tinkering with his hand terminal. After a few seconds, he said, "Melba Koh. Electrochemical engineer. She'll probably be on and off the ship here and all the way home. Maybe you'll run into her."

"Great," Anna said, wondering if she actually wanted that to happen.

"You know what sucks?" Tilly asked. Before Anna could say anything, Tilly said, "*This* sucks."

She didn't have to elaborate. They were floating together near a table in the civilian commissary. A small plastic box was attached to the table with magnetic feet. Inside it was a variety of tubes filled with protein and carbohydrate pastes in an array of colors and flavors. Next to the box sat two bulbs. Anna's held tea. Tilly's coffee. The officers' mess, with its polite waiters, custom-cooked meals, and open bar, was a distant memory. Tilly hadn't had an alcoholic drink in several days. Neither of them had eaten anything that required chewing in as long.

"The oat and raisin isn't bad. I think it might actually have real honey in it," Anna said, holding up one of the white plastic squeeze packs. Tilly was no stranger to space travel. Her husband owned estates on every major rock in the solar system. But Anna suspected she'd never eaten food out of a plastic tube in her entire life before this. Any pilot who had the poor planning to put Tilly's ship at null g during one of her meals was probably fired at the next port.

Tilly picked up a packet of the oat mush, wrinkled her lip at it, and flicked it away with her fingers. It sat spinning next to her head like a miniature helicopter.

"Annie," Tilly said. "If I wanted to suck vile fluids out of a flaccid and indifferent tube, I'd have stayed on Earth with my husband."

At some point Anna had become Annie to Tilly, and her objection to this nickname hadn't fazed Tilly at all. "You have to eat, eventually. Who knows how long we'll be out here."

"Not much longer, if I have anything to say about it," said a booming voice from behind Anna.

If she'd been touching the floor, she would have jumped. But floating in the air, all she managed was an undignified jerk and squeak.

"Sorry to startle you," Cortez continued, sliding into her field of view. "But I had hoped we might speak."

He was scuffing across the floor wearing the magnetic booties the navy had handed out. Anna had tried them, but drifting free while your feet remained pinned to the floor had given her an uncomfortable underwater sensation that made her even sicker than just floating around did. She never used them.

Cortez nodded to Tilly, his too-white smile beaming at her in his nut-brown face. Without asking if he could join them, he used the menu screen on the table to order himself a soda water. Tilly smiled back. It was the fake *I don't really see you* smile she used on people who carried her luggage or waited on her table. Their mutual contempt established, Tilly sipped her coffee and ignored his presence. Cortez placed one large hand on Anna's shoulder and said, "Doctor Volovodov, I am putting together a coalition of the important civilian counselors on this ship to make a request of the captain, and I'd like your support."

Anna admired the absolute sincerity Cortez managed to pack into a sentence that was almost entirely composed of flattery. Cortez was here because he was the spiritual advisor to the UN secretary-general. Anna was here because the United Methodist

Council could spare her, and her home happened to be on the way. If she was on any list of important counselors, then the bar was set pretty low.

"I'm happy to talk about it, Doctor Cortez," Anna said, then reached for her tea bulb. It gave her an excuse to extricate her arm from his grip. "How can I help?"

"First, I have to commend you on your initiative in arranging worship services for the women and men on the ship. I'm ashamed I didn't think of it first, but I'm happy to follow your lead. We're already arranging for similar meetings with leaders of the various faiths on board."

Anna felt a blush come up, even though she suspected that everything Cortez said was manipulative. He was so good, he could get the response he wanted even when you knew exactly what he was up to. Anna couldn't help but admire it a little.

"I'm sure the sailors appreciate it."

"But there is other work we can be doing," Cortez said. "Greater work. And that's what I came to ask you about."

Tilly turned back to the table and gave Cortez a sharp look. "What are you up to, Hank?"

Cortez ignored her. "Anna, may I call you Anna?"

"Here it comes, Annie," Tilly said.

"Annie?"

"No," Anna cut in. "Anna is fine. Please call me Anna."

Cortez nodded his big white-and-brown head at her, blinding her with his smile. "Thank you, Anna. What I want to ask you to do is sign a petition I'm circulating, and add your voice to ours."

"Ours?"

"You know that the *Behemoth* has begun to burn toward the Ring?"

"I'd heard."

"We're asking the captain to accompany it."

Anna blinked twice, then opened her mouth to speak and found nothing to say. She closed it with a snap when she realized both Cortez and Tilly were staring at her. Go *into* the Ring? Holden had made it inside, and it looked like he was still alive. But actually entering the Ring had never been part of the mission plan, at least not for the civilian contingent.

No one had any idea what the structures were that waited beyond the Ring, or what changes passing through the wormhole might make on humans. Or even if the Ring would stay open. It might have a preset mass limit, or a limited power supply, or anything. It might just slam shut after enough ships had gone through. It might slam shut with half a ship going through. Anna pictured the *Prince* cut in half, the two pieces drifting in space a billion light-years apart, humans spilling into vacuum from both sides.

"We're also asking the Martians to come with us," Cortez continued. "Now hear me out. If we join together in this—"

"Yes," Anna said before she knew she was going to say it. She didn't know why Cortez was pushing for it, and she didn't care. Maybe it was to get votes in the Earth elections. Maybe it was a way for Cortez to exert control over the military commanders. Maybe he felt it was his calling. They hadn't come here as explorers, not really. They'd come here to be seen by the people back at home who were watching. It was why they'd had so many protests and dramas on the way out. Once, this had been about the spectacle, but now things had changed, and this was the answer to the fear she'd seen at church.

The immediate danger wasn't the Ring. At least not right now. It was humans taking their anxiety out on the nearest enemy they could actually see: each other. If the OPA went ahead with its plan to follow Holden into the Ring, and the UN and Martian forces joined together to follow, no one would have any reason to shoot anyone else. They'd be what they'd started out as again. They'd be a joint task force exploring the most important discovery in human history. If they stayed, they were three angry fleets trying to keep one another from getting an advantage. The whole thing spilled into Anna's mind feeling very much like relief.

"Yes," she said again. "I'll sign it. The things we need to know, the things we need to learn and take back with us to all those frightened people back home. That's where we'll learn them. Not here. On the other side. Thank you for asking me, Doctor Cortez."

"Hank, Anna. Please call me Hank."

"Oh," Tilly said, her coffee bulb floating forgotten in the air in front of her. "We are *so* fucked."

"Hi Nono," Anna said to the video camera in her room's communication panel. "Hi Nami! Mom loves you. She loves you so much." She hugged her pillow to her chest, squeezing it tight. "This is you. This is both of you."

She put the pillow down, taking a moment to compose herself.

"Nono, I'm calling to apologize again."

Chapter Nineteen: Melba

The injustice of it shrieked in the back of her skull; it wouldn't let her sleep. It had come so close to working. So much of it *had* worked. But then Holden dove into the Ring, and something had saved him, and Melba felt a huge invisible fist drive itself into her gut. And it was still there.

She'd watched the whole thing unfold in her quarters, sitting cross-legged on her crash couch, her hand terminal seeking information from any feed. The network had been so swamped with other people doing the same thing, her own signal wouldn't stand out. No one would wonder why she was watching when everyone else was doing the same. When the OPA had opened fire, she'd heard the Earth forces bracing for a wave of sabotage explosions that never came. The anger at Holden, the condemnations and recriminations had been like pouring cool water on a burn. Her team had been called up on an emergency run to the *Seung Un*, repairing the damage she'd done, but she'd checked in whenever there was a free moment. When Mars had turned its targeting lasers on the *Rocinante*, guiding the missile to him, she'd laughed out loud. Holden had stopped her outgoing message, but at the expense of killing his whole communications array. There was no way he could send out a retraction in time.

When he'd passed through the Ring, she'd been in three conversations simultaneously and watching an electrical meter for dangerous fluctuations. She didn't find out until they were being rotated back to the *Cerisier* that Holden hadn't died. That he wasn't going to. The missile had been stopped and the enemy had been spared.

Back on her ship, she'd gone straight to her bunk, curled up on the crash couch, and tried not to panic. Her brain felt like it had come untied; her thoughts ran in random directions. If the Martians had just launched a few missiles of their own instead of waiting for the OPA's to do the job, Holden would be dead. If the *Rocinante* had been a few thousand kilometers closer to the *Behemoth* when it fired, Holden would be dead. The gimbaling under her couch hushed back and forth in the last of the deceleration burn, and she realized she was shaking her body, banging her back against the gel. If the thing that made the protomolecule—the nameless, evil thing that was hunched in the abyssal black on the other side of the Ring—hadn't changed the laws of physics, Holden would be dead.

Holden was alive.

She'd always known that the destruction of James Holden was a fragile thing. Discrepancies would be there if anyone looked closely. She couldn't match her announcement to the exact burn that the *Rocinante* would be on when she sprang her trap. There would be artifacts in the video that a sufficiently close analysis would detect. By the time that happened, though, it would have been too late. The story of James Holden would have been set. New evidence could be dismissed as crackpots and conspiracy theorists. But it required that Holden and his crew be *dead*. It was something she'd always heard her father say. If the other man's dead, the judge only has one story to follow. When he put his communication array back together, the investigation would begin. She'd be caught. They'd find out it was her.

And—the thought had the copper taste of fear—they'd find Ren. They'd know she killed him. Her father would know. Word would reach him in his cell that she had beaten Ren to death, and that would be worse than anything. Not that she'd done it, Melba thought. That she'd been caught doing it.

The sound came from her door, three hard thumps, and she screamed despite herself. Her heart was racing, the blood tapping at the inside of her throat, banging at her ribs.

"Miss Koh?" Soledad's voice came. "You in there? Can I... I need to talk if you've..."

Hearing fear in someone else's voice felt like vertigo. Melba got to her feet. Either the pilot was repositioning the ship or she was just unsteady. She couldn't tell which. She looked in her mirror, and the woman looking out could almost have been a normal person woken from a deep sleep.

"Just a minute," she said, running her fingers through her hair, pressing the dark locks against her scalp. Her face felt clammy. Nothing to be done. She opened the door.

Soledad stood in the thin, cramped corridor. The muscles in her jaw worked like she was chewing something. Her wide eyes skittered over Melba, away and back, away and back.

"I'm sorry, Miss Koh, but I can't... I can't do it. I can't go there. They can fire me, but I can't go." Melba reached out and put her hand on the woman's arm. The touch seemed to startle them both.

"All right," she said. "It'll be all right. Where can't you go?"

The ship shifted. That one wasn't her imagination, because Solé moved too.

"The *Prince*," she said. "I don't want... I don't want to volunteer."

"Volunteer for what?" Melba asked. She felt like she was coaxing the girl back from some sort of mental break. There was enough self-awareness left in her to appreciate the irony.

"Didn't you get the message? It's from the contracts supervisor."

Melba looked back over her shoulder. Her hand terminal was on the crash couch, a green-and-red band on the screen showing that there was a priority message waiting. She raised a finger, keeping Soledad out of the room and away from the locker, and grabbed the terminal. The message had come through ten hours before, marked URGENT AND MUST REPLY. Melba wondered how long she'd been lying in her couch, lost in her panic fugue. She thumbed the message accept. A stream of tight legal script poured onto the screen, brash as a shout.

Danis General Contracting, owners and operators of half the civilian support craft in the fleet, including the *Cerisier*, was invoking the exceptional actions clause of the standard contract. Each functional team would choose a designated volunteer for temporary duty on the UNN *Thomas Prince*. The remuneration would remain at the standard level until completion of the contract, when any hazard bonuses or exemptions would be assessed.

Melba had to read the words three times to understand them.

"I can't go in there," Soledad was saying, somewhere away to her left. The voice had taken on an irritating whine. "My father. I told you about him. You understand. Your sister was there too. You have to tell Bob or Stanni to do it. I can't."

They were going after Holden. They were going through the Ring after Holden. Her panic didn't fall away so much as click into focus.

"None of you are going," Melba said. "This one's mine."

The official transfer was the easiest thing she'd done since she came aboard. She sent a message to the contracts officer with her ID number and a short message saying that she'd accept transfer to the *Prince*. Two minutes later, she had her orders. Three hours to finish her affairs on the *Cerisier*, then into the transport and gone. It was intended, she knew, as a time to meet with her team, make the transition easy. She had other fish to fry.

Filling a locker with industrial sealant was one thing. The foam was made to apply quickly and remain malleable for a few seconds before the yellow mush dimmed to gold and set. The excess could be cut away with a sharp knife for the next hour. After that, nothing would move it except the right kind of solvent, and even that was an ugly, arduous process.

But leaving the body where it could be found wasn't an option. Someone would be assigned to her bunk, and they'd want to use the locker. Besides which, leaving Ren behind seemed somehow wrong. And so with two and a half hours before she left the ship, Melba took a pair of shoulder-length latex gloves, three cans of solvent, a roll of absorbent towels, and a vacuum-rated large personal tool case into her room and locked the door behind her.

The locker door didn't want to open at first, fixed in place by a drop of sealant she hadn't noticed, but a few sprays of solvent degraded it until she could pull it open with her fingers. The sealant was a single rough-textured face of gold, like a cliff made small. She opened the tool case, took a deep breath, and faced the grave.

"I'm sorry about this," she said. "I'm really, really sorry."

At first the solvent spray didn't seem to do anything beyond a sharp smell, but then the sealant began ticking, like a thousand insects walking over stone. Gouges and crevasses formed in the sealant wall, then a small runnel of slime. She rolled up a few of the towels, setting them on the floor to catch the flow.

Ren's knee was the first part to appear, the round cap of the bone and death-blackened skin emerging from the melting foam like a fossil. The fabric of his uniform was soaked with fluid rot. The smell hit her, but it wasn't as bad as she'd expected. She'd imagined herself retching and weeping, but it was gentler than that. When she took his legs to draw him out, they fell away from his pelvis, so she cut the trousers, wrapped the legs in towels, and put them in the toolbox. Her mind was quiet and still, like an archaeologist pulling the dead of centuries before out into the light. Here was his spine. This was the vile slush where the hydrochloric acid in his gut, no longer held in check by the mechanisms of life, had digested his stomach, his liver, his intestines. She drew out his head last, the bright red hair darkened and flecked with matter like an overused kitchen mop.

She lifted the bones into the toolbox, packed them with the gore- and corruption-soaked towels, then closed his new coffin, triggered the seal, and set the lock combination. She had forty minutes left.

She spent another ten minutes cleaning out the locker where Ren had spent his death, then stripped off the gloves and threw them in the recycler. She bathed, trying to scrub off the stink, and noticed distantly that she was sobbing. She ignored the fact, and by the time she'd changed into her new uniform, the crying seemed to have stopped. She picked up the last of her things, threw them in a pack, put her still-wet hair in a ponytail, and hauled Ren to the loading bay where the other supplies would be taken across to the *Prince*. It didn't allow her time to say her goodbyes to Soledad or Stanni or Bob. She was sorry for that, but it was a burden she could bear.

There were about thirty of them, all told. Men and women she'd seen around the ship, heard their names once or twice, nodded to in the galley or on the exercise machines. Once they reached the *Prince*, they were all brought into a small white conference room with benches that bolted to the floor like pews. They were already under thrust, already moving for the Ring and whatever was on the other side. While the overly enthusiastic yeoman prattled on about the *Thomas Prince*, she glanced at the faces around her. An old man with a scruffy white beard and ice-blue eyes. A stocky blond woman who was probably younger than she was with poorly applied eyeliner and a grim look about the jowls. They'd all come here of their own free will. Or free will as bounded by the terms of their work contracts. They were all going through the Ring, into the mouth of whatever was on the other side. She wondered what would motivate them to do it, what kinds of secrets they'd hidden in *their* tool chests.

"You will need to keep your identification cards with you at all times," the yeoman was saying, holding up a white plastic card on a lanyard. "Not only are these the keys to get into your quarters, they'll also get you food in the civilian commissary. And they'll let you know if you're where you're supposed to be."

The blond woman turned toward Melba and glared. Melba looked away, blushing. She hadn't intended to stare. Never be rude unintentionally, her father had always said.

The yeoman's white card turned a deep, bloody red.

"If you see this," he said, "it means you're in a restricted area and need to leave immediately. Don't worry too much. She's a big ship, and we all get a little turned around sometimes. I got buzzed four times the first week I was here. No one's going to get bent out of shape over an honest mistake, but security will be following up on them, so be prepared."

Melba looked at her own white card. It had her name, a picture of her unsmiling face. The yeoman was talking about how much they were appreciated, and how their service was an honor to the ship and to themselves. All in this together, one big team. The first stirring of hatred for the man shifted in her gut, and she tried to distract herself.

She didn't know what she'd do once they were all on the other side, but she had to find Holden. She had to destroy him. The soundman too. Anything that led back to her had to be destroyed or discredited. She wondered if there was a way to get a fake card, or one that belonged to someone with a lot more clearance than Melba Koh would have. Maybe one that could check out a shuttle. She'd need to look into it. She was improvising now, and getting the best tools she could manage would be critical.

Around her, people began standing up. From the bored looks and the quiet, she figured they were beginning the walking tour. She'd been through the *Thomas Prince* before. She was already familiar with the high ceilings and wide corridors where three people could walk abreast. She might not know where everything was, but she could fake it. She fell in line with the others.

"In case of emergency, all you'll have to do is get back to your quarters and strap in," the yeoman said, walking backward so that he could keep lecturing them while they all moved, bumping against each other like cattle. Someone behind her made a soft mooing sound, and someone else chuckled. The joke had gone out to the darkness of space even where cows hadn't.

"Now, through here is the civilian commissary," the yeoman said as they passed through a pair of sliding steel doors. "Those of you who were working here before might be used to getting your food and coffee from the officers' mess, but now that we're on a military operation, this is going to be the place to go."

The civilian commissary was a low gray box of a room with tables and chairs bolted to the floor, and a dozen people of all ages and dress sat scattered around. A thin man with improbably pale hair leaned against a crash-padded wall, drinking something from a bulb. Two older men in black robes and clerical collars sat huddled together like the unpopular kids at a cafeteria. Melba was already beginning to turn inward again, ignoring them all, when something caught her. A familiar voice.

Twenty feet away, Tilly Fagan leaned in toward an older man who looked like he was struggling between annoyance and flirtation. Her hair was up and her laughter caustic in a way that recalled long, uncomfortable dinner parties with both of their families. Melba felt a sudden atavistic shame at being so underdressed. For a sickening moment, her false self slipped away and she was Clarissa again.

Forcing herself to move slowly, calmly, she drifted to the back of the crowd, making herself as small and difficult to notice as she could. Tilly glanced over at the nattering yeoman and his herd of technicians with undisguised annoyance, but didn't notice Melba. Not this time. The yeoman led them all back out of the commissary, down the long hallway to their new quarters. Melba took her ponytail down and brushed her hair in close around her face. She'd known, of course, that the *Prince* had the delegation from Earth, but she'd discounted them. Now she wondered how many other people here knew Clarissa Mao. She had the horrible image of turning a corner and seeing Micha Krauss or Steven Comer. She could see their eyes going wide with surprise, and she wondered whether she could bring herself to kill them too. If she couldn't, the brig and the newsfeeds and a prison cell like her father's would follow.

The yeoman was talking about their quarters, assigning them out one by one to all the volunteer technicians. They were tiny, but the need for each person to have a crash couch in case of emergency meant they wouldn't be hot-bunking. She could stay in there, bribe one of the others to bring her food. Except, holed up like a rat, tracking and killing Holden became exponentially more difficult. There had to be a way...

The yeoman called her name, and she realized it wasn't the first time.

"Here," she said. "Sorry."

She scuttled into her room, the door recognizing her white card and unlocking for her, then closing once she was inside. She stood for a long moment, scratching her arm. The room was bright and clean and as unlike the *Cerisier* as Nepal was from Colombia.

"You came to improvise," she said, and her voice sounded like it came from someone else. "Well, here you are. Start improvising."

Chapter Twenty: Holden

Instead of putting him at ease, the weeks and months of interviews had given Holden a new persona. A version of himself that stood in front of a camera and answered questions. That explained things and told stories in ways entertaining enough to keep the focus on himself. It wasn't the sort of thing that he'd have expected to have any practical application.

One more surprise among many.

"This," Holden said, gesturing to the large video monitor behind him on the operations deck, "is what we are calling the slow zone."

"That's a terrible name," Naomi said. She was at the ship operations panel, just out of view of the documentary crew's cameras. "Slow zone? Really?"

"You have a better name?" Monica asked. She whispered something to Clip and he shifted a few degrees to his left, camera moving with him in a slow pan. The burst blood vessel in his eye was starting to fade. The high-g burn through the Ring had been hard on all of them.

"I still like Alex's name," Naomi replied.

"Dandelion sky?" Monica said with a snort. "First of all, only people from Earth and Mars have even the slightest idea what a dandelion is. And second of all, no, it sounds stupid."

Holden knew he was still on camera, so he just smiled and let the two of them hash it out. The truth was, he'd been partial to Alex's name. Where they sat, looking out, it did sort of look like being at the center of a dandelion, the sky filled with fragile-looking structures in an enormous sphere around them.

"Can we finish this?" Monica asked, shooting the comment at Naomi without looking at her.

"Sorry I interrupted," Naomi replied, not looking sorry at all. She winked at Holden and he grinned back.

"And, three...two..." Monica pointed at him.

"The slow zone, based on the sensor data we're able to get, is approximately one million kilometers across." Holden pointed at the 3D representation on the screen behind him. "There are no visible stars, so the location of the zone is impossible to determine. The boundary is made up of one thousand three hundred and seventy-three individual rings evenly spaced into a sphere. So far, the only one we've been able to find that's 'open' is the one we came through. The fleets we traveled out with are still visible on the other side, though the Ring seems to distort visual and sensor data, making readings through it unreliable."

Holden tapped on the monitor, and the center of the image enlarged rapidly.

"We're calling this Ring Station, for lack of a better term. It appears to be a solid sphere of a metallic substance, measuring about five kilometers in diameter. Around it is a slow-moving ring of other objects, including all of the probes we've fired into the slow zone, and the Belter ship *Y Que*. The torpedo that chased us through the Ring is headed toward the station in a trajectory that seems to indicate it will become part of the garbage ring too."

Another tap and the central sphere took up the entire screen. "We're calling it a station pretty much only because it sits at the center of the slow zone, and we're making the entirely unfounded assumption that some sort of control station for the gates would be located there. The station has no visible breaks in its surface. Nothing that looks like an airlock, or an antenna, or a sensor array, or anything. Just that big silvery blue glowing ball."

Holden turned off the monitor and both of the camera operators swiveled to put him at the center of their shots.

"But the most intriguing factor of the slow zone, and the one that gives it its name, is the absolute speed limit of six hundred meters per second. Any object above the quantum level traveling faster than that is locked down by what seems to be an inertial dampening field, and then dragged off to join the garbage circling the central station. At a guess, this is some sort of defensive system that protects the Ring Station and the gates themselves. Light and radar still work normally, but radiation made up of larger particles like alpha and beta radiation does not exist inside the slow zone. At least outside the ship, that is. Whatever controls the speeds here only seems concerned by the exterior of the objects, not the interior. We've done radiation and object speed tests inside the ship, and so far everything works as normal. But the last probe we fired was immediately grabbed by the field and is now making its way down to the garbage ring. The lack of alpha and beta radiation leads me to believe that there's a thin cloud of loose electrons and helium nuclei orbiting that station as part of the garbage ring."

"Can you tell us what your plan is now?" Monica said from off camera. Cohen pointed his mic at her, then back at Holden.

"Our plan now is to remain motionless, avoid attracting the Ring Station's attention, and keep studying the slow zone using what instruments we have. We can't leave until we repair the comm array and let everyone outside know that we aren't psychotic murderers bent on claiming the Ring for ourselves."

"Great!" Monica said, giving him the thumbs-up. Clip and

Okju moved around the room getting shots to cut in later. They shot the instrument panels, the monitor behind Holden, even Naomi lounging in her ops station crash couch. She smiled sweetly and flipped them off.

"How's everyone doing after the burn?" Holden asked, Clip's blood-pinked eye still drawing his attention.

Cohen touched his side and grimaced. "Got a rib that I think just slid back into place this morning. I've never been on a ship doing maneuvers that violent before. It gave me a little more respect for the navy."

Holden pushed off the bulkhead and drifted over to Naomi. In a low voice he said, "Speaking of the navy, how's that comm array coming along? I'd really love to start protesting my innocence before someone figures out a way to lob a slow-moving torpedo in here after us."

She blew out an exasperated breath at him and started tugging on her hair like she did when she was lost in a complex problem. "That little Trojan horse that keeps grabbing control? Every time I wipe and reboot, it finds its way back in. I've got comms totally isolated from the other systems, and it's still getting in."

"And the weapons?"

"They keep on powering up, but they never fire."

"So there has to be some connection."

"Yes," Naomi said, and waited. Holden felt a self-conscious discomfort.

"That doesn't tell you anything you didn't know."

"No."

Holden pulled himself down into the crash couch next to hers and buckled in. He was trying to play it cool, but the truth was the longer they went without presenting a defense or at least a denial to the fleets outside, the more risk there was that someone would find a way to destroy the *Roci*, slow zone or not. The fact that Naomi couldn't figure it out only added to the worry. If whoever was doing this was clever enough to outsmart Naomi with an engineering problem, they were in a lot of trouble.

"What's the next plan?" he asked, trying to keep the impatience out of his voice. Naomi heard it anyway.

"We're taking a break from it," she said. "I've got Alex doing ladar sweeps of all the other rings that make up the boundary of the slow zone. Just to see if one is different in some way. And I've got Amos fixing that light bulb in the head. There's nothing else to do, and I wanted him out of my hair while I come up with another way to attack this comm problem."

"What can I do to help?" Holden asked. He'd already gone through every other system on the ship three times looking for malicious and hidden programs. He hadn't found any, and he couldn't think of anything else that might be useful.

"You're doing it," Naomi said, subtly moving her head toward Monica without actually looking at her.

"I feel like I've got the shit job here."

"Oh, please," Naomi said with a grin. "You love the attention."

The deck hatch slid open with a bang, and Amos came up the crew ladder. "Mother*fucker*!" he yelled as the hatch closed behind him.

"What?" Holden started, but Amos kept yelling.

"When I peeled that twitchy power circuit open in the head, I found this little bastard hiding in the LED housing, sucking off our juice."

Amos threw something, and Holden barely managed to catch it before it hit him in the face. It looked like a small transmitter with power leads coming off one end. He held it up to Naomi, and her face darkened.

"That's it," she said, reaching out to take it from Holden.

"You're fucking right that's it," Amos bellowed. "Someone hid that in the head, and it's been loading the software hijacker onto our system every time we boot up."

"Someone with access to the ship's head," Naomi said, looking at Holden, but he'd already gone past that and was unbuckling his restraints.

"Are you armed?" Holden asked Amos. The big mechanic

pulled a large-caliber pistol out of his pocket and held it against his thigh. In the microgravity it would shove Amos around if he fired it, but surrounded by bulkheads that wouldn't be too much of a problem.

"Hey," Monica said, her face shifting from confusion to fear.

"One of you hijacked my comm array," Holden said. "One of you is working for whoever is doing this to us. Whoever it is should really just tell me now."

"You forgot to threaten us," Cohen said. He sounded almost ill.

"No. I didn't."

Naomi had unbuckled her harness as well, and was floating next to him now. She tapped a wall panel and said, "Alex, get down here."

"Look," Monica said, patting the air with her hands. "You're making a mistake blaming us for this." Clip and Okju moved behind her, pulling Cohen to them. The documentary crew formed a small circle facing outward, unconsciously creating a defensive perimeter. More Pleistocene-age behavior that humans still carried with them. Alex drifted down from the cockpit; his usually jolly face had a hard expression on it. He was carrying a heavy wrench.

"Tell me who did it," Holden repeated. "I swear by everything holy that I will space the whole damn lot of you to protect this ship if I have to."

"It wasn't *us*," Monica said, the fear on her face draining the bland video star prettiness away, making her look older, gaunt.

"Fuck this," Amos said, pointing the gun at them. "Let me drag one of 'em down to the airlock and space them right now. Even if only one of them did it, I got me a twenty-five percent chance to get the right one. Got a thirty-three percent chance with the second one I toss. Fifty-fifty by the third, and those are odds I'll take any day."

Holden didn't acknowledge the threat, but he didn't argue with it either. Let them sweat.

"Shit," Cohen said. "I don't suppose it will matter that I got set up just as bad as you guys, will it?"

Monica's eyes went wide. Okju and Clip turned to stare at the blind man.

"You?" Holden said. It didn't make any sense not to, not really, but he honestly hadn't suspected the blind guy. It made him feel betrayed and guilty of his prejudices at the same time.

"I got paid to stick that rig on the ship," Cohen said, moving out of the defensive circle and floating a half meter closer to Holden. Pulling himself out of the group, so that if anything happened, they wouldn't get hurt. Holden respected him for that. "I had no idea what it would do. I figured someone was spying on your comms, is all. When that broadcast went out and the missiles started flying, I was just as surprised as you guys. And my ass was just as much on the line."

"Motherfucker," Amos said again, this time without the heat. Holden knew him well enough to know that angry Amos was not nearly as dangerous as cold Amos. "I was thinking I'd have a tough time spacing a blind guy, but turns out I'm gonna be just fine with it."

"Not yet," Holden said, waving Amos off. "Who paid you to do this. Lie to me and I let Amos have his way."

Cohen held up both hands in surrender. "Hey, you got me, boss. I know my ass is hanging by a thread right now. I got no reason not to come clean."

"Then do."

"I only met her once," Cohen continued. "Young woman. Nice voice. Had lots of money. Asked me to plant this thing. I said, 'Sure, get me on that ship and I plant whatever you want.' Next thing I know Monica's got a gig doing this doc about you and the Ring. Damned if I know how she swung that."

"Son of a bitch," Monica said, clearly as surprised by this revelation as anyone else. That actually made Holden feel a little better.

"Who was this young woman with all the money?" Holden asked. Amos hadn't moved, but he wasn't pointing the gun at anyone anymore. Cohen's tone didn't have a hint of deception in it. He sounded like a man who knew that his life hung on every word.

"Never got a name, but I can sculpt her pretty easy."

"Do that," Holden said, then watched as Cohen plugged his modeling software into the big monitor. Over the next several minutes, the image of a woman slowly formed. It was all one color, of course, and the hair was a sculpted lump, not individual strands. But when Cohen had finished, Holden had no doubt about who it was. She was changed, but not so much that he couldn't recognize the dead girl.

Julie Mao.

The ship was quiet. Monica and her two camera operators had been confined to the crew decks again, and last time Holden had checked they were together in the galley, not talking. Cohen's betrayal had taken them by surprise as well, and they were still working through it. Cohen himself was in the airlock. It was the closest thing they had to a brig. Holden had to assume the man was quietly panicking.

Alex was back in the cockpit. After Amos had thrown Cohen into the airlock he'd disappeared back down to his machine shop to brood. Holden had let him go. Of them all, Amos took betrayal the hardest. Holden knew that Cohen's life was hanging on whether Amos could get past it or not. If he decided to take action, Holden wouldn't be able to stop him, and didn't even know if he'd want to try.

So he and Naomi sat alone together on the ops deck as she made the last few adjustments to get the comm array back up and running. With Cohen's device disabled, they'd been able to reboot it without being hijacked.

Naomi was waiting for him to speak. He could feel the tension in her shoulders from across the room. But he had no idea what to say. For a year, Miller had been a confused phantasm that appeared randomly and spouted nonsense. Now everything

Miller had said over the last year took on the weight of dark portents. Prophetic riddles whose meaning must be teased out or risk catastrophe. And Miller wasn't the only ghost haunting Holden.

Julie Mao had joined the game.

Somehow, while Miller had followed Holden around the solar system, the protomolecule had been using Julie, working on its own secret plans. Julie had arranged for the Martian lawsuit that stripped him of safe ports and employment. She'd arranged to have a documentary crew placed on his ship to send him to the Ring. And now it appeared she'd engineered an elaborate betrayal that forced him to actually go through the Ring to stay alive. The ghost Julie didn't resemble his Miller at all. It was working with very specific purpose. It had access to money and powerful connections. The only thing it had in common with Miller was that it seemed to be focused on him. And if this was all true, then everything it had done had been with a single purpose in mind.

To bring him here. To *force* him to go through the Ring.

A shiver crawled its way up his spine, sending all the hairs on his arms and neck standing straight up. He turned on the closest workstation and brought up the external telescopes. Nothing at all in this starless void except a lot of inactive rings and the massive blue ball at its center. As he watched, the missile that had chased them through the gate drifted into view and joined the slowly circling ring of flotsam that orbited the station.

Everything comes to me, eventually, the station seemed to be saying.

"I have to go there," he said out loud even as the thought popped into his head.

"Where?" Naomi asked, turning away from her work on the comm. The relief he could see on her face now that he'd finally said something wouldn't last long. He felt a pang of guilt for that.

"The station. Or whatever it is. I have to go there."

"No you don't," she said.

"Everything that's happened over the last year has been to bring me here, now." Holden rubbed his face with both hands, itching his eyes and hiding from Naomi's scrutiny at the same time. "And that thing is the only place in here. There's nothing else. No other open gates, no planets, no other ships. Nothing."

"Jim," Naomi said, a warning in her voice. "This thing where you always have to be the guy who goes..."

"I'll never know why the protomolecule is talking to me until I get there, face-to-face."

"Eros, Ganymede, the *Agatha King*," Naomi continued. "You always think you have to go."

Holden stopped rubbing his face and looked at her. She stared back, beautiful and angry and sad. He felt his throat threaten to close up, so he said, "Am I wrong? Tell me I'm wrong and we'll think of something else. Tell me how all of what's happened means something else and I'm just not seeing it."

"No," she said again, meaning something else this time.

"Okay." He sighed. "Okay then."

"It's getting old being the one who stays behind."

"You're not staying behind," Holden said. "You're keeping the crew alive while I do something really stupid. It's why we're an awesome team. You're the captain now."

"That's a shit job and you know it."

Chapter Twenty-One: Bull

In the last hours before they shot the Ring, a kind of calm descended on the *Behemoth*. In the halls and galleries, people talked, but their voices were controlled, quiet, brittle. The independent feeds, always a problem, were pretty subdued. The complaints coming to the security desk fell to nothing. Bull kept an eye on the places people could get liquored up and stupid, but there were no flare-ups. The traffic going through the comm laser back toward Tycho Station and all points sunward spiked to six times its usual bandwidth. A lot of people on the ship wanted to say something to someone—a kid, a sister, a dad, a lover—before they passed through the signal-warping circumference and into whatever was on the other side.

Bull had thought about doing it too. He'd logged into the family group feed for the first time in months, and let the minutiae of the extended Baca family wash over him. One cousin was engaged, another one was divorcing, and they were trading notes and worldviews. His aunt on Earth was having trouble with her hip, but since she was on basic, she was on a waiting list to get a doctor to look at it. His brother had dropped a note to say that he'd gotten a job on Luna, but he didn't say what it was or anything about it. Bull listened to the voices of the family he never saw except on a screen, the lives that didn't intersect his own. The love he felt for them surprised him, and kept him from putting his own report in among them. It would only scare them, and they wouldn't understand it. He could already hear his cousins telling him to jump ship, get on something that wasn't going through. By the time the message got there, he'd already have gone anyway.

Instead, he recorded a private video for Fred Johnson, and all he said in it was, "After this, you owe *me* one."

With an hour to go before they passed through, Bull put the whole ship on battle-ready status. Everyone in their couches, one per. No sharing. All tools and personal items secured, all carts in their stations and locked down, the bulkheads closed between major sections so that if something happened, they'd only lose air one deck at a time. He got a few complaints, but they were mostly just grousing.

They made the transit slowly, the thrust gravity hardly more than a tendency for things to drift toward the floor. Bull couldn't say whether that was a technical decision on Sam's part meant to keep them from moving too quickly in the uncanny reduced speed beyond the ring, or Ashford giving the Earth and Mars ships the time to catch up so that they'd all be passing through at more or less the same time. Only if it was that, it wouldn't have been Ashford. That kind of diplomatic thinking was Pa.

Probably it was just that the main drive couldn't go slow enough, and this was as fast as the maneuvering thrusters could move them.

Bull wasn't that worried about the Earth forces. They'd been the ones to broker the deal, and they had civilians on board. Mars, on the other hand, might call itself a science mission, but its escort was explicitly military, and until Earth stepped in they'd been willing to poke holes in the *Behemoth* until the air ran out.

Too many people with too many agendas, and everyone was worried that the other guy would shoot them in the back. Of all the ways to go and meet the God-like alien whatever-they-were that built the protomolecule, this was the stupidest, the most dangerous, and—for Bull's money—the most human.

The transit actually took a measurable amount of time, the great bulk of the *Behemoth* sulking through the Ring in a few seconds. An eerie fluting groan passed through the ship, and Bull, in his crash couch at the security office waiting for the next disaster, felt the gooseflesh on his arms and neck. He flipped through the security monitors like a dad walking through the house to see if the windows were all locked, all the kids safely in their beds. Memories of the Eros feed tugged at the back of his mind: black whorls of filament covering the corridors; the bodies of the innocent and the guilty alike warping, falling apart, and becoming something else without actually dying in between; the blue firefly glow that no one had yet explained. With every new monitor, he expected to see the *Behemoth* in that same light, and every time he didn't, his dread moved on to the one still to come.

He moved to the external sensor feed. The luminous blue object in the center of a sphere of anomalies that the computers interpreted as being approximately the same size as the Ring. Gates to God knew where.

"I don't know what the hell we're doing here," he said under his breath.

"A-chatté-men, brother," Serge said, pale-faced, from his desk.

A connect request popped on Bull's hand terminal, the alert-red of senior staff. With dread growing at the back of his throat, Bull accepted it. Sam appeared on the screen.

"Hey," she said. "This whole act-like-we're-in-a-battle thing where we aren't supposed to get out of our crash couches? I'd really appreciate it if you could ease up enough to let us make sure the ship isn't falling apart."

"You getting alerts?"

"No," Sam admitted. "But we just sailed the *Behemoth* into a region of space with different, y'know, laws of *physics* and stuff? Makes me want to take a peek."

"We got eight ships coming in right behind us," Bull said. "Hold tight until we see how that shakes down."

Sam smiled in a way that expressed her annoyance with him perfectly.

"You can get the teensiest bit paternalistic sometimes, Bull. You know that?"

A new alert popped up by Sam's face. A high-priority message was coming into the comm array. From the *Rocinante*.

"Sam, I got something here. I'll get back to you."

"I'll be sitting here in my couch doing nothing," she said.

He flipped over to the incoming message. It was a broadcast. A Belter woman, with black hair pulled back from her face in a style that gave Bull the impression she'd been welding something before she'd begun the broadcast and would be again as soon as she was finished, looked into the camera.

"...Nagata, executive officer of the *Rocinante*. I want to make it very clear that the previous broadcast claiming our ownership of the Ring was a fake. Our communications array was hijacked, and we were locked out of it. The saboteur on board has confessed, and I am including a datafile at the end of this transmission with all the evidence we have about the real perpetrator of these crimes. I am also including a short documentary presentation on what we've discovered in the time we've been here that Monica Stuart and her team produced. I want to reiterate here, Captain Holden had no mandate from anyone to claim the Ring, he had no intention of doing so, and none of us had any participation in or knowledge of the bomb on the *Seung Un* or on any other ship. We were here solely as transport and support for a documentary team, and pose no intentional threat whatsoever to any other vessel."

Serge grunted, unconvinced. "You think they fragged him?"

"Keep Jim Holden from grabbing the camera? Fragged him or

tied him up," Bull said. It was a joke, but there was something in it. Why *wasn't* the *Rocinante*'s captain the one making the announcement?

"We will not surrender our ship," the Belter said, "but we will invite inspectors aboard to verify what we've reported, with the following conditions. First, the inspectors will have to comply with basic safety—"

Five more communication alerts popped up, all from different ships. All broadcast. If they were flying into the teeth of a vast and malefic alien intelligence, by God, they we're going to go down squabbling.

"—unacceptable. We demand the immediate surrender of the *Tachi* and all accompanying—"

"—what confirmation you can provide that—"

"—James Holden at once for interrogation. If your claims are verified, we will—"

"—Message repeats. Please confirm and clarify EVA activity, *Rocinante.* Who've you got out there, and where are they going?"

Bull pulled up the sensor array and began a careful sweep of the area around Holden's ship. It took him half a minute to find it. A single EVA suit, burning away from the ship and heading for the blue-glowing structure in the center of the sphere. He said something obscene. Five minutes later, the XO of the *Rocinante* spoke again to confirm Bull's worst suspicions.

"This is Naomi Nagata," she said, "executive officer and acting captain of the *Rocinante.* Captain Holden is not presently available to take questions, meet with any representatives, or surrender himself into anybody's custody. He is..." She looked down. Bull couldn't tell if it was fear or embarrassment or a little of both. The Belter took a deep breath and continued, "He is conducting an EVA approach of the base at the middle of the slow zone. We have reason to believe he was...called there."

Bull's laughter pulled Serge's attention. Serge lifted his hand, the physical Belter idiom for asking a question. Bull shook his head.

"Just trying to think of a way we could be doing this worse," he said.

Ashford insisted that they meet in person, so even though Bull had ordered that all crew members not performing essential functions remain in their couches, he himself floated to the lift and headed to the bridge.

The crew was a muted cacophony. Every station was juggling telemetry and signal switching and sensor data, even though basically nothing was going on. It was just that the excitement demanded that everything be busy and serious and fraught. The excitement or else the fear. The monitors were set to a tactical display, Earth in blue, Mars in red, the *Behemoth* in orange, and the artifact at the center of the sphere in a deep forest green. The debris ring was marked in white. And two dots of gold: one for the *Rocinante*, well ahead of the other ships, and another for her captain. The scale was so small, Bull could see the shapes of the larger ships, boxy and awkward in the way that structures built for vacuum could be. The universe, shrunk down to a knot smaller than the sun and still unthinkably vast.

And in that bubble of darkness, mystery, and dread, two matched dots—one blue, the other red—moving steadily toward the little gold Holden. Marine skiffs, hardly more than a wide couch strapped on the end of a fusion drive. Bull had ridden on boats like them so long ago it seemed like a different lifetime, but if he closed his eyes, he could still feel the rattle of the thrusters transferred through the shell of his armor. Some things he would never forget.

"How long," Ashford said, "until you can put together a matching force?"

Bull rubbed his palm against his chin, shrugged.

"How long'd it take to get back to Tycho?"

Ashford's face went red.

"I'm not interested in your sense of humor, Mister Baca. Earth and Mars have both launched interception teams against the outlaw

James Holden. If we don't have a force of our own out there, we look weak. We're here to make sure the OPA remains the equal of the inner planets, and we're going to do that, whatever it takes. Am I clear?"

"You're clear, sir."

"So how long would it take?"

Bull looked at Pa. Her face was carefully blank. She knew the answer as well as he did, but she wasn't going to say it. Leaving the shit job for the Earther. Well, all right.

"It can't be done," Bull said. "Each one of those skiffs is carrying half a dozen marines in full battle dress. Powered armor. Maybe Goliath class for the Martians, Reaver class for the Earthers. Either way, I don't have anything in that league. And the soldiers inside those suits have trained for exactly this kind of combat every day for years. I've got a bunch of plumbers with rifles I could put on a shuttle."

The bridge went quiet. Ashford crossed his arms.

"Plumbers. With rifles. Is that how you see us, Mister Baca?"

"I don't question the bravery or commitment of anyone on this crew," Bull said. "I believe that any team we sent over there would be willing to lay down their lives for the cause. Of course, that would only take about fifteen seconds, and I won't send our people into that."

The implication floated in the air as gently as they did. *You're the captain. You can make the order, but you'll own the consequences. And they'll know the Earther told you what would happen.* Pa's eyes were narrow and looked away.

"Thank you, Mister Baca," Ashford said. "You're dismissed."

Bull saluted, turned, and launched himself for the lift. Behind him, the bridge crew started talking again, but not as loud. Probably they'd all get reamed once Bull was gone just because they'd been in the room when Ashford got embarrassed. The chances were slim that they'd be sending anyone to the thing. Nucleus, base, whatever it was. Bull couldn't think of a way to do any better than that, so that would count for a win.

On the way back to his station, he looked over the datafile the *Rocinante* had sent out. The saboteur seemed legitimate enough. Bull had seen enough faked confessions to recognize the signs, and this didn't have them. After that, though, the whole damn thing turned into a fairy tale. A mysterious woman who manipulated governments and civilians, who was willing to kill dozens of people and risk thousands in order to...do what? Put James Holden through the Ring, where he was going now?

The image the prisoner had built looked like it had been carved from ice. No one had added color. Bull put on an even olive flesh tone and brown hair, and the face didn't look familiar. Juliette Mao, they said. She hadn't been the first person infected with the protomolecule, but everyone before her had gotten thrown in an autoclave one way or the other. She'd been the seed crystal that Eros had used to make itself, to make the Ring. So who was to say she couldn't be wandering around hiring traitors and placing bombs?

The problem with living with miracles was that they made everything seem plausible. An alien weapon had been lurking in orbit around Saturn for billions of years. It had eaten thousands of people, hijacking the mechanisms of their bodies for its own ends. It had built a wormhole gate into a kind of haunted sphere. So why not the rest? If all that was possible, everything was.

Bull didn't buy it.

Back at the security desk, he checked the status. The skiff of Earth marines had gone too fast, trying to race ahead of the Martian force. The slow zone had caught them, and the skiff was drifting off toward the ring of debris. Chances were that all the men in it were dead. The Martian skiff was still on track, but Holden would reach the structure before they got to him. It was too bad, in a way. The Martians had been the trigger-happy ones all along. Chances of someone getting to question Holden were looking pretty long.

Bull sucked his teeth, half-formed ideas shifting in the back of his mind. Holden wasn't getting interrogated, but that didn't mean no one would. He checked his security codes. Ashford hadn't blocked him from using the comm laser. Protocol would have been to discuss this with Ashford or at least Pa, but they had their hands full right now anyway. And if it worked, it would be hard for them to object. They'd have a bargaining chip.

The *Rocinante*'s XO appeared on the screen.

"What can I do for you, *Behemoth*?"

"Carlos Baca here. I'm security chief. Wanted to talk about maybe taking a problem off your hands."

She hoisted her eyebrows, her head shaking like she was trying to stay awake. She had a smart face.

"I've got a lot of problems right now," she said. "Which one were you thinking about?"

"You got a bunch of civvies on your ship. One of 'em under arrest. Mars is still saying you're flying their ship. Earth is wondering whether you blew the shit out of one of theirs. I can take custody of your prisoner and give the rest of them a safer place than you can."

"Last I checked, the OPA was the only one that's actually shot at us so far," she said. She had a good smile. Too young for him, but ten years ago he'd have been asking her if he could make her dinner around now. "Doesn't put you at the top of my list."

"That was me," Bull said. "I won't do it this time." It got him a chuckle, but it was the bleak kind. The one that came from someone wading through hell. "Look, you got a lot going on, and you've got a bunch of people on there who aren't your crew. You got to keep them safe, and it's a distraction. You send 'em over here, and everyone'll see you aren't trying to control access to them. Makes this whole thing about how it wasn't you that blew the shit out of the *Seung Un* that much easier for people to believe."

"I think we're past goodwill gestures," she said.

"I think goodwill gestures are the only chance you have to avoid a field promotion," Bull said. "They're sending killers after your captain. Good ones. No one's thinking straight here. You and me, we can start cooling things down. Acting like grown-ups. And if we do, maybe they do too. No one else needs to get killed."

"Thin hope," she said.

"It's all the hope I got. You got nothing to hide, then show them that. Show everyone."

It took her twenty seconds.

"All right," she said. "You can have them."

Chapter Twenty-Two: Holden

"Wow," Holden said to himself, "I really don't want to do this."

The sound echoed in his helmet, competing only with the faint hiss of his radio.

"I tried to talk you out of it," Naomi replied, her voice somehow managing to be intimate even flattened and distorted by his suit's small speakers.

"Sorry, I didn't think you were listening."

"Ah," she said. "Irony."

Holden tore his eyes way from the slowly growing sphere that was his destination and spun around to look for the *Rocinante* behind him. She wasn't visible until Alex fired a maneuvering thruster and a gossamer cone of steam reflected some of the sphere's blue glow. His suit told him that the *Roci* was over thirty thousand kilometers away—more than twice as far as any two people on Earth could ever be from each other—and receding.

And here he was, in a suit of vacuum armor, wearing a disposable EVA pack that had about five minutes of thrust in it. He'd burned one minute accelerating toward the sphere. He'd burn another slowing down when he got there. That left enough to fly back to the *Roci* when he was done.

Optimism expressed as conservation of delta V.

Ships from the three fleets had begun coming through the gate even before he'd started his trip. The *Roci* was now protected from them only by the absolute speed limit of the slow zone. She was drifting off at just under that limit to put as much space between her and the fleets as possible. They had a sphere a million kilometers in diameter to play with, even without going beyond the area marked by the gates. The gates had close to fifty thousand kilometers of empty space between them, but the idea of flying out of the slow zone and into that starless void beyond made Holden's skin crawl. He and Naomi had agreed it would be a maneuver of last resort.

As long as no one could fire a ballistic weapon, the *Roci* should be plenty safe with five hundred quadrillion square kilometers to move around in.

Holden spun back around, using two quarter-second blasts from his EVA pack, and took a range reading to the sphere. He was still hours away. The minute-long burst he'd fired from the pack to start his journey had accelerated him to a slow crawl, astronomically speaking, and the *Roci* had come to a relative stop before releasing him. He'd never have had enough juice in the EVA pack to stop himself if the ship had flung him out at the slow zone's maximum speed.

Ahead in the middle of all that starless black, the blue sphere waited.

It had waited for two billion years for someone to come through his particular gate, if the researchers were right about how long ago Phoebe had been captured by Saturn. But lately the strangeness surrounding the protomolecule and the Ring left Holden with the disquieting feeling that maybe all of the assumptions they'd made about its origins and purpose were wrong.

Protogen had named the protomolecule and decided it was a tool that could redefine what it meant to be human. Jules-Pierre Mao had treated it like a weapon. It killed humans, therefore it was a weapon. But radiation killed humans, and a medical X-ray machine wasn't intended as a weapon. Holden was starting to feel like they were all monkeys playing with a microwave. Push a button, a light comes on inside, so it's a light. Push a different button and stick your hand inside, it burns you, so it's a weapon. Learn to open and close the door, it's a place to hide things. Never grasping what it actually did, and maybe not even having the framework necessary to figure it out. No monkey ever reheated a frozen burrito.

So here the monkeys were, poking the shiny box and making guesses about what it did. Holden could tell himself that in his case the box was asking to be poked, but even that was making a lot of assumptions. Miller looked human, had *been* human once, so it was easy to think of him as having human motivations. Miller wanted to communicate. He wanted Holden to know or do something. But it was just as likely—more likely, maybe—that Holden was anthropomorphizing something far stranger.

He imagined himself landing on the station, and Miller saying, *James Holden, you and only you in the universe have the correct chemical composition to make a perfect wormhole fuel!* then stuffing him into a machine to be processed.

"Everything okay?" Naomi asked in response to his chuckle.

"Still just thinking about how incredibly stupid this is. Why didn't I let you talk me out of it?"

"It looks like you did, but it took a couple of hours for it to process. Want us to come get you?"

"No. If I bail out now, I'll never have the balls to try it again," Holden said. "How's it look out there?"

"The fleets came through with about two dozen ships, mostly heavies. Alex has figured out the math on doing short torpedo burns to get one up to the speed limit but not over. Which means everyone on those other ships are doing the same thing. So far no one has fired at us."

"Maybe your protestations of my innocence worked?"

"Maybe," she said. "There were a couple of small ships detaching from the fleet on an intercept course with you. The *Roci* is calling them landing skiffs."

"Shit, they're sending the Marines after me?"

"They've burned up to the speed limit, but the *Roci* says you make stationfall before they catch you. But *just* before."

"Damn," Holden said. "I really hope there's a door."

"They lost the UN ship. The other is Martian. So maybe they brought Bobbie. She can make sure the others are nice to you."

"No," Holden said with a sigh. "No, these will be the ones that are still mad at me."

Knowing the marines were following made the back of his neck itch. Being in a space suit just added that to his already lengthy list of insoluble problems.

"On the good news level, Monica's team is getting evacuated to the *Behemoth*."

"You never did like her."

"Not much, no."

"Why not?"

"Her job is digging up old things," Naomi said, the lightness of her tone almost covering her anxieties. "And digging up old things leads to messes like this one."

When Holden was nine, Rufus the family Labrador died. He'd already been an adult dog when Holden was born, so Holden had only ever known Rufus as a big black slobbering bundle of love. He'd taken some of his first steps clutching the dog's fur in one stubby fist. He'd run around their Montana farm not much bigger than a toddler with Rufus as his only babysitter. Holden had loved the dog with the simple intensity only children and dogs share.

But when he was nine, Rufus was fifteen, and old for such a big dog. He slowed down. He stopped running with Holden, barely managing a trot to catch up, then gradually only a slow walk. He stopped eating. And one night he flopped onto his side next to a heater vent and started panting. Mother Elise had told him that Rufus probably wouldn't last the night, and even if he did they'd have to call the vet in the morning. Holden had tearfully sworn to stay by the dog's side. For the first couple of hours, he held Rufus' head on his lap and cried, as Rufus struggled to breathe and occasionally gave one halfhearted thump of his tail.

By the third, against his will and every good thought he'd had about himself, Holden was bored.

It was a lesson he'd never forgotten. That humans only have so much emotional energy. No matter how intense the situation, or how powerful the feelings, it was impossible to maintain a heightened emotional state forever. Eventually you'd just get tired and want it to end.

For the first hours drifting toward the glowing blue station, Holden had felt awe at the immensity of empty starless space around him. He'd felt fear of what the protomolecule might want from him, fear of the marines following him, fear that he'd made the wrong choice and that he'd arrive at the station to find nothing at all. Most of all fear that he'd never see Naomi or his crew again.

But after four hours of being alone in his space suit, even the fear burned out. He just wanted it all to be over with.

With the infinite and unbroken black all around him, and the only visible spot of light coming from the blue sphere directly ahead, it was easy to feel like he was in some vast tunnel, slowly moving toward the exit. The human mind didn't do well with infinite spaces. It wanted walls, horizons, limits. It would create them if it had to.

His suit beeped at him to let him know it was time to replenish his O2 supply. He pulled a spare bottle out of the webbing clipped to his EVA pack and attached it to the suit's nipple. The gauge on his HUD climbed back up to four hours and stopped. The next time he had to refill, he'd be on the station or in Marine custody.

One way or the other, he wouldn't be alone anymore, and that was a relief. He wondered what his mothers would have thought about all this, whether they would have approved of the choices he'd made, how he could arrange to have a dog for their children since Naomi wouldn't be able to live at the bottom of the gravity well. His attention wandered, and then his mind.

He awoke to a harsh buzzing sound, and for a few seconds slapped his hand at empty space trying to turn his alarm off. When he finally opened sleep-gummed eyes, he saw his HUD flashing a proximity warning. He'd somehow managed to fall asleep until the station was only a few kilometers away.

At that distance, it loomed like a gently curving wall of metallic blue, glowing with its own inner light. No radiation alarms were flashing, so whatever made it glow wasn't anything his suit thought was dangerous to him. The flight program Alex had written for him was spooling out on the HUD, counting down to the moment when he'd need to do his minute-long deceleration burn. Waving his hand around when he first woke up had put him into a gentle rotation, and the flight program was prompting him to allow it to make course corrections. Since he trusted Alex completely on matters of navigation, Holden authorized the suit to handle the descent automatically.

A few quick bursts of compressed gas later, he was facing out into the black, the sphere at his back. Then came a minute-long burn from the pack to slow him to a gentle half meter per second for landing. He kicked on his boot magnets, not knowing if they'd actually help or not—the sphere looked like metal, but that didn't mean much—and turned around.

The wall of glowing blue was less than five meters away. Holden bent his knees, bracing for the impact of hitting the surface, and hoping to absorb enough energy that he didn't just bounce off. The half meters ticked away, each second taking too long and passing too quickly. With only a meter before impact, he realized he'd been holding his breath and let out a long exhale.

"Here we go," he said to no one.

"Hey, boss?" Alex said in a burst of radio static.

Before Holden could reply, the surface of the sphere irised open and swallowed him up.

After Holden passed through the portal into the interior of the sphere he landed on the gently curving floor of a room shaped like an inverted dome. The walls were the metallic blue of the sphere's exterior. The surfaces were textured almost like moss, and tiny lights seemed to flicker in and out of existence like fireflies. His suit reported a thin atmosphere made mostly of benzene compounds and neon. The ceiling irised closed again, its flat unbroken surface showing no sign that there had ever been an opening.

Miller stood a few meters from where Holden landed, his rumpled gray suit and porkpie hat made both mundane and exotic by the alien setting. The lack of breathable air didn't seem to bother him at all.

Holden straightened his knees, and was surprised to feel something like gravity's resistance. He'd felt the weight of spin and of thrust, and the natural deep pull of a gravity well. The EVA pack was heavy on his back, but the quality of it was different. He almost felt like something was pushing down on him from above instead of the ground coming up to meet him.

"Hey, boss?" Alex repeated, a note of worry in his voice. Miller held up a hand in a don't-mind-me gesture. Wordless permission for Holden to answer.

"Receiving, Alex. Go ahead."

"The sphere just swallowed you," Alex said. "You okay in there?"

"Yep, five by five. But you called before I went in. What's up?"

"Just wanted to warn you that company's comin' pretty close on. You can expect them in about five minutes at best guess."

"Thanks for the report. I'm hoping Miller won't let them in."

"Miller?" Alex and Naomi said at the same time. She must have been monitoring the exchange.

"I'll call when I know more," Holden said with a grunt as he finished getting the EVA pack off. It fell to the floor with a thud.

That was odd.

Holden turned on the suit's external speakers and said, "Miller?" He heard the sound of his own voice echoing off of the walls and around the room. The atmosphere shouldn't have been thick enough for that.

"Hey," Miller replied, his voice unmuffled by the space suit, as if they were standing together on the deck of the *Roci*. He nodded slowly, his sad basset hound face twisting into something resembling a smile. "There are others coming. They yours?"

"Not mine, no," Holden replied. "That would be the skiff full of Martian recon marines that are coming to arrest me. Or maybe just shoot me. It's complicated."

"You've been making friends without me," Miller said, his tone sardonic and amused.

"How are you doing?" Holden asked. "You seem more coherent than usual."

Miller gave a short Belter shrug. "How do you mean?"

"Usually when we talk, it's like only half the signal's getting through."

The old detective's eyebrows rose in surprise.

"You've seen me before?"

"On and off for the last year or so."

"Well, that's pretty disturbing," Miller said. "If they're planning to shoot you, we'd better get going."

Miller seemed to flicker out of existence, reappearing at the edge of the mosslike walls. Holden followed, his body fighting with the nauseating sense of being weightless and heavy at the same time. When he drew close, he could see the spirals within the moss on the walls. He'd seen something like this before where the protomolecule had been, but this was lush by comparison. Complex and rich and deep. A vast ripple seemed to pass over the wall like a stone thrown in a pond, and despite having his own isolated air supply, Holden smelled something like orange peels and rain.

"Hey," Miller said.

"Sorry," Holden said. "What?"

"We better get going?" the dead man said. He gestured toward what looked like a fold of the strange moss, but when Holden came close, he saw a fissure behind it. The hole looked soft as flesh at the edges, and it glistened with something. It wept.

"Where are we going?"

"Deeper," Miller said. "Since we're here, there's something we should probably do. I have to tell you, though, you got a lot of balls."

"For what?" Holden said, and his hand slid against the wall. A layer of slime stuck to the fingers of his suit.

"Coming here."

"You told me to," Holden said. "You brought me. Julie brought me."

"I don't want to talk about what happened to Julie," the dead man said.

Holden followed him into the narrow tunnel. Its walls were slick and organic. It was like crawling through a deep cave or down the throat of a vast animal.

"You're definitely making more sense than usual."

"There are tools here," Miller said. "They're not...they're not right, but they're here at least."

"Does this mean you might still say something enigmatic and vanish in a puff of blue fireflies?"

"Probably."

Miller didn't expand on this, so Holden followed him for several dozen meters through the tunnel until it turned again and Miller led him into a much larger room.

"Uh, wow," he managed to say.

Because the floor of the first room and the tunnel that led out of it had both had a consistent "down," Holden had thought he was moving laterally just under the skin of the station. That couldn't have been right, because the room the tunnel opened into had a much higher ceiling than was possible if that were true. The space stretched out from the tunnel into a cathedral-vast opening, hundreds of meters across. The walls slanted inward into a domed ceiling that was twenty meters off the floor in the center. Scattered across the room in seemingly random places were two-meter-thick columns of something that looked like blue glass with black, branching veins shooting through it. The columns pulsed with light, and each pulse was accompanied by a subsonic throb that Holden could feel in his bones and teeth. It felt like enormous power, carefully restrained. A giant, whispering.

"Holy shit," he finally said when his breath came back. "We're in a lot of trouble, aren't we?"

"Yeah," Miller said. "You should not have come."

Miller walked off across the room, and Holden hurried to catch up. "Wait, what?" he said. "I thought you wanted me here!"

Miller walked around something that from a distance had looked like a blue statue of an insect, but up close was a massive confusion of metallic limbs and protrusions, like a construction mech folded up on itself. Holden tried to guess at its purpose and failed.

"Why would you think that?" Miller said as he walked. "You don't know what's *in* here. Doors and corners. Never walk into a crime scene until you know there's not someone there waiting to put you down. You've got to clear the room first. But maybe we got lucky. For now. Wouldn't recommend doing it again, though."

"I don't understand."

They came to a place in the floor that was covered in what looked like cilia or plant stalks, gently rippling in a nonexistent wind. Miller walked around it. Holden was careful to do the same. As they passed, a swarm of blue fireflies burst out of the ground cover and flew up to a vent in the ceiling where they vanished.

"So there was this unlicensed brothel down in sector 18. We went thinking we'd be hauling fifteen, twenty people in. More, maybe. Got there, and the place was stripped to the stone," Miller said. "It wasn't that they'd gotten wind of us, though. The Loca Greiga had heard about the place, sent their guys to clean it up.

Took about a week to find the bodies. According to forensics, they'd all been shot twice in the head pretty much while we were getting one last cup of coffee. If we'd been a little bit faster, we'd have walked in on it. Nothing says fucked like opening the door on a bunch of kids who thought they'd make a quick buck off the sex trade and having an organized kill squad there for the meet and greet instead."

"What has that got to do with anything?"

"This place is the same," Miller said. "There was supposed to be something. A lot of something. There was supposed to be... shit, I don't have the right words. An empire. A civilization. A home. More than a home, a *master*. Instead, there's a bunch of locked doors and the lights on a timer. I don't want you charging into the middle of that. You'll get your ass killed."

"What the hell do you mean?" Holden said. "You, or the protomolecule, or Julie Mao, or whatever, *you* set this whole thing up. The job, the attack, all of it."

That stopped Miller. He turned around with a frown on his face. "Julie's dead, kid. *Miller's* dead. I'm just the machine for finding lost things."

"I don't understand," Holden said. "If you didn't do this, then who did?"

"See now, *that's* a good question, on several levels. Depending on what you mean by 'this.' " Miller's head lifted like a dog catching an unfamiliar scent on the wind. "Your friends are here. We should go." He moved off at a faster walk toward the far wall of the room.

"The marines," Holden said. "Could you stop them?"

"No," Miller said. "I don't protect anything. I can tell the station they're a threat. There'd be consequences, though."

Holden felt a punch of dread in his gut.

"That sounds bad."

"It wouldn't be good. Come on. If we're going to do this, we need to stay ahead of them."

The halls and passages widened and narrowed, meeting and

falling away from each other like blood vessels of some massive organism. Holden's suit lights seemed almost lost in the vast darkness, and the blue firefly flickers came in waves and vanished again. Along the way they passed more of the metallic blue insect-like constructs.

"What are these?" Holden asked, pointing to an especially large and dangerous-looking model as they passed it.

"Whatever they need to be," Miller replied without turning around.

"Oh, great, so we're back to inscrutable, are we?"

Miller spun around, a worried look on his face, and blinked out of existence. Holden turned.

Far across the huge room, a form was coming out of the tunnel. Holden had seen similar armor before. A Martian marine's powered armor was made of equal parts efficiency and threat.

There was no escaping it. Anyone in those suits could run him down without trying. Holden switched his suit to an open frequency.

"Hey! I'm right here. Let's talk about this," he said, then started to walk toward the group. As one, all eight marines raised their right arms and opened fire. Holden braced himself for death even while part of his mind knew that he shouldn't have time to brace for death. At the distance they were, the rounds from their high-velocity guns would be hitting in a fraction of a second. He'd be dead long before the sound of the shots reached him.

He heard the rapid and deafening buzzsaw sound of the guns firing, but nothing hit him.

A diffuse cloud of gray formed in front of the marines. When the firing finally stopped, the cloud drifted away toward the walls of the room. Bullets. They'd stopped centimeters from the gun barrels, and were now being drawn away just like the objects outside the station.

The marines broke into a fast run across the room, and Holden tried to scramble away. They were beautiful in their way, the lethal power of the suits harnessed by years of training to make their movements seem like a dance. Even without their weapons, they could tear him limb from limb. One punch from that armor would break all the bones he had and change his viscera to a thin slurry. His only chance was to outrun them, and he couldn't outrun them.

He almost didn't see the movement when it came. His focus was locked on the Martians, on the danger he knew. He didn't consciously notice that one of the insectlike things had started moving until the marines turned to it.

The alien thing's movements were fast and jagged, like a clockwork mechanism that only had full speed and full stop. It clicked toward the marines, jerking with each step, and it loomed larger than the tallest of them by almost half a meter.

They panicked in the way that people trained to expect violence panic. Two started firing, with the same results as before. Another marine's suit shifted something in its arm, and a larger barrel appeared. Holden scooted away from the confrontation. He was sure there was shouting going on in those armored suits, but it wasn't a frequency he had access to. The large barrel went white with muzzle flash, and a slow-arcing slug of metal the size of Holden's fist took to the strange air.

A grenade.

The ticking monster ignored it, stepping closer to the marines, and the grenade detonated at its insectile feet where it landed. The alien thing jerked back, its appendages flailing and dust falling from its severed limbs like a smoke of fungal spores. The complex carpet of moss glowed with orange embers where the blast had burned it.

And all around the marines, a dozen other alien statues came to life. They moved faster this time. Before the marines could begin to react, the one who'd launched the grenade was lifted gently up and ripped apart. Blood sprayed up into the air, hanging, Holden thought numbly, too long before it drifted back to the ground. The surviving marines began to fall back, their guns pointing to the alien creatures that were swarming the dead man. While

Holden watched, the marines retreated into the far tunnel, falling back. Regrouping.

The alien things fell on their own injured fellow, ripping and clawing, slaughtering it as if it were the enemy as much as the marines had been. And then, when it was gone, five of the monsters gathered together in the burned spot where the explosion had been. They shuddered, went still, shuddered again, and then from all five of them, a thin stream of opaque yellow goo spattered out onto the scar. Holden felt fascination and revulsion as the moss grabbed on to the stuff, regrowing like it had never been damaged. Like the attack hadn't even existed.

"Consequences," Miller said at his side. He sounded tired.

"Did they...did they just turn that poor bastard into spackle?"

"They did," Miller said. "He had it coming, though. That guy got happy with his grenade launcher? Just killed a lot of people."

"What? How?"

"He taught the station that something moving as fast as a good baseball pitch might still be a threat."

"Is it going to take revenge?"

"No," Miller said. "It's just going to protect itself. Reevaluate what counts as dangerous. Take control of all the ships that might be a problem."

"What does that even mean?"

"Means a really bad day for a whole lot of people. When it slows you down, it ain't gentle."

Holden felt a cold hand close on his heart.

"The *Roci*..."

A look of sorrow, even sympathy, passed over the detective's face.

"Maybe. I don't know," Miller said with a rueful shrug. "One way or the other, a whole lot of people just died."

Chapter Twenty-Three: Melba

Julie saved her. There was no other way to look at it.

True to style, Holden's proxy had given everything away. Cohen, discovered, told everything he knew, and put the image he'd stolen along with it. Melba had it on her hand terminal: a portrait of the young woman as ice sculpture. She hadn't known the soundman had taken the data when she'd met with him, but she should have guessed he would. The mistake was obvious in retrospect.

It ought to have ended the chase. The people in power should have seen it, shrugged, and thrown her out an airlock. Except that it came with its own misinterpretation. *Here*, Holden said, *is Julie Mao*, and that's what everyone saw. The differences that were obvious to her became invisible to others. They expected to see the protomolecule infiltrating and threatening and raising the dead, and so they saw it.

She did what she could to keep anyone from noticing the similarities. She'd met Cohen on Earth with a full g pulling down. With the *Thomas Prince* already close to the Ring's velocity limit, there was no acceleration thrust. Her cheeks looked fuller, her face round. She'd had her hair down then, so now she pulled it back in a braid. The image had no color, so she wore a little makeup to alter the shape of her eyes and lips. Doing something radical would only call attention, so she went small. She might not even have needed to do that.

Her schedule in the *Thomas Prince* was full. They were going to work her—work all of them—like dogs. She didn't care. The service gantries and accessways would be safe. No one who knew Clarissa Mao would be there. She would stay away from the public parts of the ship as much as she could, and more often than not she could get one of the other techs to grab a tube of something from the commissary and bring it to her.

In the off-shifts, she would build her arsenal.

Holden was beyond her reach for the time being. It was almost funny. She'd gone to so much effort to make him seem like an unrepentant megalomaniac, and then left to his own devices, he named himself de facto ambassador of the whole human race. Julie had fooled him too. With any luck at all, he'd die in a firefight or get killed by the protomolecule. Her work had narrowed to destroying the evidence of Holden's innocence. It wouldn't be hard.

The *Rocinante* had begun its life as an escort corvette on the battleship *Donnager*. It was well designed and well constructed, but also now years past its last upgrade. The weaknesses in its defense were simple: The cargo doors nearest the reactor had been damaged and repaired, and would almost certainly be weaker than the original. The forward airlock had been built with a software glitch vulnerable to hacking; real Martian naval ships would have been updated as a matter of course, but Holden might have been sloppy.

Her first hope was the airlock. A short-range access transmitter built for troubleshooting malfunctioning airlocks had found its way in among her things. If that failed, getting through the cargo door was harder. She hoped for something explosive, but the *Thomas Prince* took its munitions very seriously. The equipment manifests did include a half-suit exoskeleton mech. It would fit over her chest and arms—it wasn't designed for legs—and with a cutting torch to make the initial breach, it could probably bend the plating enough to let her through. It was also small and lightweight enough to carry, and her access card was a high enough grade for the system to let her take one away.

Once she was on, it would be simple. Kill everyone, overload the reactor, and blow the ship to atoms. With any luck at all, it would reignite suspicions about the bomb on the *Seung Un*. If she got out, fine. If she didn't, she didn't.

The only tricks now were getting there, and waiting like everyone else to hear what happened on the station.

She was dreaming when catastrophe came.

In it, she was walking through a field outside a schoolhouse. She knew that it was on fire, that she had to find a way in. She heard fire engine sirens, but their dark shapes never appeared in the sky. There were people trapped inside and she was supposed to get to them. To free them or to keep them from escaping or both.

She was on the roof, going down through a hole. Smoke billowed out around her, but she could still breathe because she'd been immunized against flames. She stretched down, fingertips brushing against low-g handholds. She realized someone was holding her wrist, supporting her as she strained in toward the darkness and fire. Ren. She couldn't look at him. Sorrow and guilt welled up in her like a flood and she collapsed into a blue-lit bar with crash couches where all the tables should have been. Couples ate dinner and talked and screwed in the dim around her. The man across from her was both Holden and her father. She tried to speak, to say that she didn't want to do this. The man took her by the shoulders, pressing her into the soft gel. She was afraid for a moment that he'd crawl on top of her, but he brought his fists down on her chest with a killing impact and she woke up to the sound of Klaxons and droplets of blood floating in the air.

The pain in her body was so profound and inexplicable that it didn't feel like pain; it was only the sense that something was wrong. She coughed, launching a spray of blood across the room. She thought that somehow she'd triggered her false glands in her sleep, that what was wrong was only her, but the ship alarms argued that it was something worse. She reached for her hand terminal, but it wasn't in its holder. She found it floating half a meter from the door, rotating in the air. A star-shaped fracture in the resin case showed where it had hit something hard enough to break. The network access displayed a bright red bar. No status. System down.

Melba pulled herself to the door and cycled it open.

The dead woman floating in the corridor had her arms out before her, her hair splayed around her like someone drowned. The left side of her face was oddly shaped, softer and rounder and bluer than it should have been. Her eyes were half open, the whites the bright red of burst vessels. Melba pushed past the corpse. Farther down the corridor, a sphere of blood the size of a soccer ball floated slowly toward the air intake with no sign where it had come from.

In the wider corridors toward the middle of the ship, things were worse. Bodies floated at every door, in every passageway. Everything not bolted down floated now by the walls, thrown toward the bow. The soft gray walls were covered with dents where hand terminals and tools and heads had struck them. The air smelled like blood and something else, deeper and more intimate.

Outside the commissary, three soldiers were using sealant foam to stick the dead to the walls, keeping them out of the way. In gravity, they would have been stacking bodies like cordwood.

"You all right?" one of them said. It took Melba a second to realize that the woman was speaking to her.

"I'm okay," Melba said. "What happened?"

"Who the fuck knows? You're one of the maintenance techs, yes?" the woman said sharply.

"I am," Melba said. "Melba Koh. Electrochemical."

"Well, you can get your ass to environmental, Koh," the woman said. "I'm guessing they need you there."

Melba nodded, the motion sending her spinning a little until the woman put out a hand to steady her.

She'd never been in a battle or at the scene of a natural disaster. The nearest had been a hurricane that hit São Paulo when she was eight, and her father had hidden the family in the corporate shelters until the flooding was gone. She'd seen more of that damage on the newsfeeds than in person. The *Thomas Prince* was a scene from hell. She passed knots of people working frantically, but the dead and dying were everywhere. Droplets of blood and chips of shattered plastic formed clouds where the eddies of the recyclers pushed them together. In zero g, blood pooled in the wounds and wouldn't clear. Inflammation was worse. Lungs filled with fluid more easily. However many had died already, more would. Soon. If she hadn't been in her crash couch, she'd have been thrown into a wall at six hundred meters per second, just like all the others. No, that couldn't be right. No one would have survived that.

She hadn't spent much of her time on environmental decks. Most of her work before with Stanni and Soledad had been with power routing. The air and water systems had technicians of their own, specialists at a higher pay grade than hers. The architecture of the rooms kept everything close without being as cramped as the *Cerisier.* She floated in with a sense of relief, as if reaching her goal accomplished something in itself. As if it gave her some measure of control.

The air smelled of ozone and burned hair. A young man, face covered with blue-black bruises, was stuck to the bulkhead with a rope and two electromagnets. He waved something similar to a broom with a massive mesh of fabric on the end like a gigantic fly swatter. Clearing blood from the air. His damaged face was impassive, shocked. A thickening layer of tears encased his eyes, blinding him.

"You! Who the hell are you?"

Melba turned. The new man wore a navy uniform. His right leg was in an inflatable pressure cast. The foot sticking out the end was a bluish purple, and his breath was labored in a way that made her think of pneumonia, of internal bleeding.

"Melba Koh. Civilian electrochemical tech off the *Cerisier.*"

"Who do you answer to?"

"Mikelson's my group supervisor," she said, struggling to remember the man's name. She had only met him once, and he hadn't left much of an impression on her.

"My name's Nikos," the broken-legged man said. "You work for me now. Come on."

He pushed off more gracefully than should have been possible. She followed him a little too fast and had to grab a handhold to keep from running into his back. He led her through a long passageway into engineering. A huge array of thin metal and ceramic sheets stood at one wall, warnings in eight languages printed along its side. Scorch marks drew circles on the outermost plate, and the air stank of burnt plastic and something else. A hole two feet across had been punched through the center. A human body was still in it, held in place by shards of metal.

"You know what that is, Koh?"

"Air processing," she said.

"That's the primary atmosphere processing unit," he said as if she hadn't spoken. "And it's a big damn problem. Secondary processor's still on fire just at the moment, and the tertiary backups will get us through for about seven hours. Everyone on my team is busted or dead, so you're about to rebuild this one. Understand?"

I can't do that, she thought. *I'm not really an electrochemical technician. I don't know how to do this.*

"I'll... get my tools."

"Don't let me stop you," he said. "If I find someone can help out, I'll send 'em your way."

"That would be good," she said. "What about you? Are you all right? Can you help?"

"At a guess? Crushed pelvis, maybe something worse going on in my gut. Keep passing out a little," he said with a grin. "But I'm high as a kite on the emergency speed, and there's work. So hop to."

She pushed off. Her throat was tight, and she could feel her mind starting to shut down. Overstimulation. Shock. She made her way through the carnage and wreckage to the storage bay where the toolboxes from the *Cerisier* were. Her card unlocked them. One had shattered, the remains of a testing deck floating in the air, green ceramic shards and bits of gold wire. Ren was there, his coffin toolbox shifted in place despite the electromagnetic clamps. For a moment, the dream of the fire washed over her. She wondered if she might still be sleeping, the wave of death just part of the same blackness in her own brain. She put her hand on Ren's box, half expecting to feel him knocking back. A sudden vertigo washed through her, and the sense that she and the ship were falling, that it would land on her. Crush her. All the blood and all the terror, every dead person held in place to keep the corpses from floating, they all began here. Every sin she'd committed, backward and forward in time, had its center in the bones beneath her hand.

"Stop," she said. "Just stop."

She took her tool chest, the real one, and sped back to engineering and the shattered air processing controller. Nikos had found two other people, a man in civilian dress and an older woman in naval uniform.

"You're Koh?" the woman said. "Good, grab his legs."

Melba set her toolbox against the deck and activated the magnets, then pushed over to the hole in the atmosphere processor. The machine had been loosened from its housing, giving the body a little more room to move. Melba put her hands on the dead man's thighs, wadding the cloth of his trousers in her fists. She braced herself against the metal siding of the unit.

"Ready?" the man asked.

"Ready."

The woman counted down from three, and Melba pulled. For a long moment, she thought the corpse wouldn't come out, but then something tore, the vibrations of it transferring through to her hands. The body slid free.

"Score one for the good guys," Nikos said from across the bay. His face was developing an ashy gray tone. Like he was dying. She wished he would go to the medical bays, but they were probably swamped. He could die here doing his work, or there waiting for an open bay. "Clear him away. Got him out, we don't need him drifting back."

Melba nodded, took a firm grip, and pushed off on a trajectory that would land them on the far bulkhead. The back of the corpse's head had been crushed almost flat, but death had come so swiftly, there was very little blood. At the wall, she secured him with a spray of foam and held him for a moment while it set. The dead man's face was close to hers. She could see the whiskers he'd missed when he'd shaved. The brown of his empty eyes. She felt a sudden urge to kiss him and then pushed the impulse away, disgusted.

From his uniform, he'd been an officer. Lieutenant, maybe. The white identity card on the lanyard around his neck had a picture of him looking solemn. She took it in her fingers. Not lieutenant. Lieutenant commander. Lieutenant Commander Stepan Arsenau, who would never have come through the Ring if it weren't for her. Who wouldn't have died here. She tried to feel guilt, but there wasn't room for him inside of her. She had too much blood already.

She was reaching out to tuck his card back in place when the small voice in the back of her mind said, *I bet he could get an EVA pack with this.* Melba blinked. Her mind seemed to click back into focus, and she looked around her, the last wisps of dream or delirium leaving her mind. She had access to the equipment she needed. The ship was in chaos. This was it. This was the opportunity she'd been waiting for. She plucked the card off its lanyard and slipped it in her pocket, then looked around nervously.

No one had noticed.

She licked her lips.

"I'm going to need something to crack this," the young man was saying. "The bolt head's sheared round. I can't get it out."

The older woman swore and turned to her.

"Got anything that'll do the trick?"

"Not here," Melba said. "I have an idea where I could get something to drill it out, though."

"Move fast. We don't want this place gettin' stuffy."

"Okay. You guys do what you can. I'll be right back," Melba lied.

Chapter Twenty-Four: Anna

Eschatology had always been Anna's least favorite study of theology. When asked about Armageddon, she'd tell her parishioners that God Himself had been pretty circumspect on the topic, so it didn't do much good to worry about it. Have faith that God will do what's best, and avoiding His vengeance against the wicked should be the least compelling reason for worship.

But the truth was that she'd always had a deeply held disagreement with most futurist and millennialist interpretations. Not the theology itself, necessarily, since their guess at what the end times prophecies really meant was as good as anyone else's. Her disagreement was primarily with the level of glee over the destruction of the wicked that sometimes crept into the teachings. This was especially true in some millennialist sects that filled their literature with paintings of Armageddon. Pictures of terrified people running away from some formless fiery doom that burned their world down behind them, while smug worshipers—of the correct religion, of course—watched from safety as God got with the smiting. Anna couldn't understand how anyone could see such a depiction as anything but tragic.

She wished she could show them the *Thomas Prince*.

She'd been reading when it happened. Her hand terminal had been propped on her chest with a pillow behind it, her hands behind her head. A three-tone alarm had sounded a high-g alert, but it was late to the party. She was already being mashed into her crash couch so hard that she could feel the plastic of the base right through twenty centimeters of impact gel. It seemed to last forever, but it was probably just a few seconds. Her hand terminal had skidded down her chest, suddenly heavier than Nami the last time she'd picked her daughter up. It left a black-and-blue trail of bruises up her breastbone and slammed into her chin hard enough to split the skin. The pillow mashed into her abdomen like a ten-kilo sandbag, filling her mouth with the taste of stomach acid.

But worst of all was the pain in her shoulders. Both arms had snapped back flat against the bed, temporarily dislocating them. When the endless seconds of deceleration were over, both joints popped back into place with a pain even worse than when they'd come out. The gel of the couch, stressed beyond its design specifications, hadn't gripped her the way it was meant to. Instead, it rebounded back into its prior shape and launched her in slow motion toward the ceiling of her cabin. Trying to put her hands in front of her sent bolts of agony through her shoulders, so she drifted up and hit the ceiling with her face. Her chin left a smear of blood on the fabric-covered foam.

Anna was a gentle person. She'd never in her life been in a fight. She'd never been in a major accident. The worst pain she'd ever felt before was childbirth, and the endorphins that had followed had mostly erased it from her memory. To suddenly be so hurt in so many different places at once left her dazed and with a sort of directionless anger. It wasn't fair that a person could be hurt so much. She wanted to yell at the crash couch that had betrayed her by letting this happen, and she wanted to punch the ceiling for hitting her in the face, even though she'd never thrown a punch in her life and could barely move her arms.

When she could finally move without feeling light-headed she went looking for help and found that the corridor outside her room was worse.

Just a few meters from her door, a young man had been crushed. He looked as though a malevolent giant had stomped on him and then ground him under its heel. The boy was not only smashed, but torn and twisted in ways that barely left him recognizable as a human. His blood splashed the floor and walls and drifted around his corpse in red balls like grisly Christmas ornaments.

Anna yelled for help. Someone yelled back in a voice filled with liquid and pain. Someone from farther down the corridor. Anna carefully pushed off the doorjamb of her room and drifted toward the voice. Two rooms down, another man was half in and half out of his crash couch. He must have been in the process of getting out of bed when the deceleration happened, and everything from his pelvis down was twisted and broken. His upper torso still lay on the bed, arms waving feebly at her, his face a mask of pain.

"Help me," he said, and then coughed up a glob of blood and mucus that drifted away in a red-and-green ball.

Anna drifted up high enough to push the comm panel on the wall without using her shoulder. It was dead. All the lights were the ones she'd been told came on in emergency power failures. Nothing else seemed to be working.

"Help me," the man said again. His voice was weaker and filled with even more of a liquid rasp. Anna recognized him as Alonzo Guzman, a famous poet from the UN's South American region. A favorite of the secretary-general, someone had told her.

"I will," Anna said, not even trying to stop the tears that suddenly blinded her. She wiped her eyes on her shoulder and said, "Let me find someone. I've hurt my arms, but I'll find someone."

The man began weeping softly. Anna pushed back into the corridor with her toes, drifting past the carnage to find someone who wasn't hurt.

This was the part the millennialists never put in their paintings. They loved scenes of righteous Godly vengeance on sinful mankind. They loved to show God's chosen people safe from harm, watching with happy faces as they were proved right to the world. But they never showed the aftermath. They never showed weeping humans, crushed and dying in pools of their own fluids. Young men smashed into piles of red flesh. A young woman cut in half because she was passing through a hatchway when catastrophe hit.

This was Armageddon. This is what it looked like. Blood and torn flesh and cries for help.

Anna reached an intersection of corridors and ran out of strength. Her body hurt too badly to continue. And in all four directions, the corridor floors and walls were covered with the aftermath of violent death. It was too much. Anna drifted in the empty space for a few minutes, and then she gently floated to the wall and stuck to it. Movement. The ship was moving now. Very slow, but enough to push her to the wall. She pushed away from it and floated again. Not still accelerating, then.

She recognized that her interest in the relative movements of the ship was just her mind trying to find a distraction from the scene around her, and started crying again. The idea that she might never come home from this trip crashed in on her. For the first time since coming to the Ring, she saw a future in which she never held Nami again. Never smelled her hair. Never kissed Nono, or climbed into a warm bed beside her and held her close. The pain of those things being ripped away from her was worse than anything physical she'd suffered. She didn't wipe away the tears that came, and they blinded her. That was fine. There was nothing here she wanted to see.

When something grabbed her from behind and spun her around, she tensed, waiting for some new horror to reveal itself.

It was Tilly.

"Oh, thank God," the woman said, hugging Anna tight enough to send new waves of pain through her shoulders. "I went to your room and there was blood on the walls and you weren't there and someone was dead right outside your door..."

Unable to hug back, Anna just put her cheek against Tilly's for a moment. Tilly pushed her out to arm's length, but didn't let go. "Are you okay?" She was looking at the gash on Anna's chin.

"My face is fine. Just a little cut. But my arms are hurt. I can barely move them. We need to get help. Alonzo Guzman's in his room, and he's hurt. Really hurt. Do you know what happened?"

"I haven't met anyone yet who knows," Tilly said, rotating Anna first one way, then the other, looking her over critically. "Move your hands. Okay. Bend your elbows." She felt Anna's shoulders. "They're not dislocated."

"I think they were for a second," Anna said after the gasp of pain Tilly's touch brought. "And everything else hurts. But we have to hurry."

Tilly nodded and pulled a red-and-white backpack off one shoulder. When she opened it, it was filled with dozens of plastic packages with tiny black text on them. Tilly pulled a few out, read them, put them back. After several tries, she stripped the packaging off of three small injection ampules.

"What is that?" Anna said, but Tilly just jabbed her with all three in answer.

Anna felt a rush of euphoria wash over her. Her shoulders stopped hurting. *Everything* stopped hurting. Even her fear about never seeing her family again seemed a distant and minor problem.

"I was sleeping when it happened," Tilly said, tossing the empty ampules into the first aid pack. "But I woke up feeling like a forklift had run over me. I think my ribs were popped out of place. I could barely breathe. So I dug up this pack from the emergency closet in my room."

"I didn't think to look there," Anna said, surprised she hadn't. She had a vague memory of being disoriented by pain, but now she felt *great*. Better than ever before. And sharp. Hyper-aware. Stupid not to think of the emergency supplies. This being, after all, an emergency. She wanted to slap herself on the forehead for being so stupid. Tilly was holding her arms again. Why was she doing that? They had work to do. They had to find the medics and send them after the poet.

"Hey, kiddo," Tilly said, "takes a second for that first rush to ease down a bit. I spent a full minute trying to resuscitate a pile of red paste before I realized how wired I was."

"What is this?" Anna asked, moving her head from side to side, which made the edges of Tilly's face blurry.

Tilly shrugged. "Military-grade amphetamines and painkillers, I'm guessing. I gave you an anti-inflammatory too. Because what the hell."

"Are you a doctor?" Anna asked, marveling at how *smart* Tilly was.

"No, but I can read the directions on the package."

"Okay." Anna nodded, her face serious. "Okay."

"Let's go find someone who knows what's going on," Tilly said, pulling Anna down the corridor with her.

"And after, I need to find my people," Anna said, letting herself be pulled.

"I may have given you too much. Nono and Nami are at home, in Moscow."

"No, my *people*. My congregation. Chris and that other guy and the marine. She's angry, but I think I can talk to her. I need to find them."

"Yeah," Tilly said. "May have overdosed you a bit. But we'll find them. Let's find help first."

Anna thought of the poet and felt her tears threatening to return. If she was sad, maybe the initial rush of the drugs was wearing off a little. She found herself regretting that for a moment.

Tilly stopped at a printed deck map on the wall. It was right next to a black and unresponsive network panel. Of course military ships would have both, Anna thought. They were built with the expectation that things would stop working when the ship got shot. That thought made Anna sad too. Some distant part of her consciousness recognized the drug-fueled emotional roller coaster she was on, but was powerless to do anything about. She started weeping again.

"Security station." Tilly tapped on a spot on the map, then yanked Anna down the corridor after her. They made two turns and wound up at a small room filled with people, guns, and computers that seemed to still be working. A middle-aged man with salt-and-pepper hair and a grim expression on his face pointedly ignored them. The other four people in the room were younger, but equally uninterested in their arrival.

"Get 35C open first," the older man said to the two young men floating to his left. He pointed at something on a map. "There were a dozen civvies in there."

"EMT?" one of the young men asked.

"Don't have them to spare, and that galley doesn't have crash couches. Everyone in there is pasta sauce, but the El Tee says look anyway."

"Roger that," the young man replied, and he and his partner pushed out of the room past Anna and Tilly, barely glancing at them as they went.

"You two do a corridor sweep," the older man said to the other two young sailors in the room. "Tags if you can find them, pictures and swabs if you can't. Everything sent to OPCOM on red two one, got me?"

"Aye-aye," one of them said, and they floated out of the room.

"The man in 295 needs help," Anna said to the security officer. "He's hurt badly. He's a poet."

He tapped something onto his desk terminal and said, "Okay, he's in the queue. EMTs will get there as soon as they can. We're setting up a temporary emergency area in the officers' mess. I suggest you two ladies get there double time."

"What happened?" Tilly asked, and gripped a handhold on the wall like she meant to stay a while. Anna grabbed on to the nearest thing she could find, which turned out to be a rack of weapons.

The security officer looked Tilly up and down once, and seemed to come to the conclusion that giving her what she wanted was the easiest solution. "Hell if I know. We decelerated to a dead stop in just a shade under five seconds. The damage and injuries are all high-g trauma. Whatever grabbed us only grabbed the skin of the ship and didn't give a shit about the stuff inside."

"So the slow zone changed?" Tilly was asking. Anna looked over the guns in the rack, her emotions more under control, but her mind was still racing. The rack was full of pistols of various kinds. Big blocky ones with large barrels and fat magazines. Smaller ones that looked like the kind you saw on cop shows. And in a special rack all their own, tasers like the one she'd had on Europa. Well, not really like it. These were military models. Gray and sleek and efficient-looking, with a much bigger power pack than hers. In spite of their non-lethal purpose, they managed to appear dangerous. Her old taser at home had looked like a small hair dryer.

"Don't touch those," the security officer said. Anna hadn't even realized she was reaching for one until he said it.

"That could mean a damn lot of casualties," Tilly said. Anna had the feeling she was reentering the conversation after having missed a lot of it.

"Hundreds on the *Prince*," the security officer said. "And we weren't going anywhere near the old speed limit. Some of the ships were. We get no broadcasts from those now."

Anna looked at the various terminals working in the office around her. Damage reports and security feeds and orders. Anna couldn't understand much of them. They used a lot of acronyms and numbers for things. Military jargon. One small monitor was displaying pictures of people. Anna recognized James Holden in one, then another version of him with a patchy beard. Wanted posters? But she didn't recognize any of the other people until the sculpture of the girl that Naomi, Holden's second-in-command, had blamed for the attack.

"Maybe it was the space girl," Anna said before she'd realized she was going to. She still felt stoned, and suppressed an urge to giggle.

The security officer and Tilly were both staring at her.

Anna pointed at the screen. "Julie Mao, the girl from Eros. The one the *Rocinante* blamed. Maybe she did this."

Both the security officer and Tilly turned to look at the screen. A few seconds later the image of Julie the space girl disappeared and was replaced by someone Anna didn't recognize.

"Someone's going to get James Holden in an interrogation room for a few hours, and then we'll have a much better idea of where to put the blame."

Tilly just laughed.

"Is that who they blamed?" she said when she'd finished. "That isn't Julie Mao. And there's no way Claire's out here."

"Claire?" Anna and the officer said at the same time.

"That's Claire. Clarissa Mao. Julie's little sister. She's living on Luna with her mother, last I heard. But that's definitely not Julie."

"Are you sure?" Anna said. "Because the executive officer from the *Rocinante* said—"

"I dandled both those girls on my knee back in the day. The Maos used to be regular guests at our house in Baja. Brought the kids out during the summers to swim and eat fish tacos. And that one is Claire, not Julie."

"Oh," said Anna as her drug-enhanced mind ran out the entire plot. The angry girl she'd seen in the galley, the explosion of the UN ship, the ridiculous message from Holden's ship, followed by the protestations of innocence. "It was her. She blew up the ship."

"Which ship?" the officer asked.

"The UN ship that blew up. The one that made the Belter ship shoot at Holden. And then we all went through the Ring and she's *here*! She's on this ship right now! I saw her in the galley and I *knew* there was something wrong with her. She scared me but I should have said something but I didn't because why would I?"

Tilly and the security man were both staring at her. She could feel her mind running away with her, and her mouth seemed to be working all on its own. They were looking at her like she'd gone insane.

"She's here," Anna said, clamping her mouth shut with an effort.

"Claire?" Tilly asked with a frown.

"I saw her in the galley. She threatened me. She was on this ship."

The security man scowled and tapped something on his terminal, swore, then tapped something else. "I'll be a sonofabitch. Shipwide face recognition says we've got a match in hangar B right now."

"You have to go arrest her," Anna shouted.

"Hangar B is a designated emergency area," the officer said. "She's probably there with the other survivors and broken in five different places. If it's even her. Shitty reproduction like that makes for a lot of false positives."

"You have software that could have found her at any time?" Tilly asked in disbelief. "You didn't *check*?"

"Ma'am, we don't ask 'how high' when James fucking Holden says jump," the officer growled back.

"There's an airlock in there," Anna said, stabbing her hand at the display. "She could leave. She could go anywhere."

"Like *where*?" the officer replied.

As if on cue, a green airlock cycling alarm appeared on the display.

"We have to go get her," Anna said, pulling on Tilly's arm.

"You have to go to the officers' mess," the security man said. "I'll send people to pick her up for questioning as soon as we stop bleeding. Don't worry about it. We've got plenty enough to sort out now. That one'll wait."

"But—"

A young man floated into the room. The left half of his face was covered in blood.

"Need the EMTs to six-alpha, sir. We've got ten civvies."

"I'll see who I can pry free," the officer said. "Do we know anything about the condition of the injured?"

"Bones sticking out, but they're not dead."

Anna pulled Tilly into the corridor.

"We can't wait. She's dangerous. She's already killed people when she blew up the other ship."

"You're stoned," Tilly said, pulling her arm free and drifting across the corridor to bump into the wall. "You're not acting rationally. What are you going to do even if Claire Mao *is* on this ship and has become some sort of terrorist? She blew up a ship. Gonna hit her with your Bible?"

Anna pulled the taser halfway out of her pocket. Tilly sucked in a whistling breath through her teeth. "You *stole* that? Are you insane?" she asked in a loud whisper.

"I'm going to go find her," Anna replied, the drugs singing in her blood having focused down to a fine point. She felt like if she could stop this Claire person, she could save herself from losing her family forever. She recognized this idea as utterly irrational, and gave in to its power anyway. "I have to talk to her."

"You're going to get killed," Tilly said. She looked like she might start crying. "You told security. You did your part. Let it go. You're a minister, not a cop."

"I'll need an EVA pack. Do you know where they keep those? Are they near the airlocks?"

"You're insane," Tilly said. "I can't be part of this."

"It's okay," Anna said. "I'll be back."

Chapter Twenty-Five: Holden

Naomi," Holden said again. "Come in. Please. Please respond."

The silent radio felt like a threat. Miller had paused, his face bleak and apologetic. Holden wondered how many other people had looked at that exact expression on Miller's face. It seemed designed to go with words like *There's been an accident* and *The DNA matches your son's.* Holden could feel his hands trembling. It didn't matter.

"*Rocinante.* Naomi, come *in.*"

"Doesn't mean anything," Miller said. "She could be just fine, but the comm array went down. Or maybe she's busy fixing something."

"Or maybe she's dying by centimeters," Holden said. "I've got to go. I have to get back to her."

Miller shook his head.

"It's a longer trip back out than it was getting here. You can't go as fast anymore. By the time you get back, she'll have figured out whatever needed figuring."

Or she'll be dead, Miller didn't say. Holden wondered what it meant that the protomolecule could put Miller on its hand like a puppet and the detective could still be thoughtful enough to leave out the possibility that everyone on the *Roci* was gone.

"I have to try."

Miller sighed. For a moment, his pupils flickered blue, like there were tiny bathypelagic fish swimming in the deep trenches of his eyeballs.

"You want to help her? You want to help all of them? Come with me. Now. You run back home, we won't get to find out what happened. And you may not get the chance to come back here. Plus, you can bet your friends are regrouping back there, and they can still gently rip your arms off if they catch you."

Holden felt like there were two versions of himself pulling at his mind. Naomi might be hurt. Might be dead. Alex and Amos too. He had to be there for them. But there was also a small, quiet part of himself that knew Miller was right. It was too late.

"You can tell the station that there are people on those ships," he said. "You can ask it to help them."

"I can tell a rock that it ought to be secretary-general. Doesn't mean it's gonna listen. All this?" Miller waved his hands at the dark walls. "It's dumb. Utilitarian. No creativity or complex analysis."

"Really?" Holden said, his curiosity peeking through the panic and anger and fear. "Why not?"

"Some things, it's better if they're predictable. No one wants the station coming up with its own bad ideas. We should hurry."

"Where are we going?" Holden said, pausing for a few deep breaths. He'd been at low g for too long without taking the time for exercise. His cardio had suffered. The dangers of growing rich and lazy.

"I'm going to need you to do something for me," Miller replied. "I need access to the...shit, I don't know. Call 'em records."

Holden finished his panting, then straightened and nodded for Miller to resume their walk. As they moved down the gently sloping corridor he said, "Aren't you already plugged in?"

"I'm aware. The station is in lockdown, and they didn't exactly give me the root password. I need you to open it up for me."

"Not sure what I can do that you can't," Holden said. "Other than be a charming dinner guest."

Miller stopped at another seeming dead end, touched the wall, and a portal irised open. He gestured Holden through, then followed and closed the door behind them. They were in another large chamber, vaguely octagonal and easily fifty meters long on each face. More of the insectile mechs littered the space, but the glass pillars were not in evidence. Instead, at the center of the chamber stood a massive construct of glowing blue metal. It was octagonal, a smaller version of the dimensions of the room, but only a few meters wide on each face. It didn't glow any brighter than the rest of the room, but Holden could feel something coming off of it, an almost physical pressure that made walking toward it difficult. His suit said that the atmosphere had changed, that it was rich with complex organic chemicals and nitrogen.

"Sometimes, having a body at all means you've got a certain level of status. If you aren't pretty damn trusted, you don't get to walk around in the fallen world."

"The fallen world?"

Miller shuddered and leaned his hand out against the wall. It was a profoundly human gesture of distress. The glowing moss of the wall didn't respond at all. Miller's lips were beginning to turn black.

"Fallen world. The substrate. *Matter.*"

"Are you all right?" Holden asked.

Miller nodded, but he looked like he was about to vomit. "There's time's I start knowing things that are too big for my head. It's better in here, but there're going to be some questions that don't fit in me. Just thinking with all this crap connected to the back of my head is a full contact sport, and if I get too much,

I'm pretty sure they'll...ah...call it reboot me. I mean, sure, consciousness is an illusion and blah blah blah, but I'd rather not go there if we can help it. I don't know how much the next one would remember."

Holden stopped walking, then turned and gave Miller a hard shove. Both of them staggered backward. "You seem pretty real to me."

Miller held up his finger. "Seem. Good verb. You ever wondered why I leave as soon as anyone else shows up?"

"I'm special?"

"Yeah, I wouldn't go that far."

"Fine," Holden said. "I'll bite. Why doesn't anyone else see you?"

"I'm not sure we've got time for this, but..." Miller took off his hat and scratched his head. "So your brain has a hundred billion brain cells and about five hundred trillion synapses."

"Will this be on the test?"

"Don't be an asshole," Miller said conversationally, and put his hat back on. "And that shit is custom grown. No two brains are exactly alike. Guess how much processing power it takes to really model even one human brain? More than every human computer ever built put together, and that's before we even start getting to the crap that goes on inside the cells."

"Okay."

"Now picture those synapses as buttons on a keyboard. Five hundred trillion buttons. And say that a brain looking at something and thinking, 'That's a flower' punches a couple billion of those keys in just the right pattern. Except it ain't near that easy. It isn't just a flower, it's a pile of associations. Smells, the way a stem feels in your fingers, the flower you gave your mom once, the flower you gave your girl. A flower you stepped on by accident and it made you sad. And being sad brings on a whole pile of other associations."

"I get it," Holden said, holding up his hands in surrender. "It's complicated."

"Now picture you need to push exactly the right buttons to make someone think of a person, hear them speaking, remember the clothes they wore and the way they smelled and how they would sometimes take off their hat to scratch their head."

"Wait," Holden said. "Are there bits of protomolecule in my brain?"

"Not exactly. You may have noticed I'm non-local."

"What the hell does that even mean?"

"Well," Miller said. "Now you're asking me to explain microwaves to a monkey."

"That's a metaphor I've never actually spoken aloud. If you're aiming for not creeping me the hell out, you need more practice."

"So, yeah. The most complex simulation in the history of your solar system is running right now so that we can pretend I'm here in the same room with you. The correct response is being flattered. Also, doing what the fuck I need you to do."

"That would be?"

"Touching that big thing in the middle of the room."

Holden looked at the construct again, felt the almost subliminal pressure coming off of it. "Why?"

"Because," said Miller, lecturing to a stupid child. "The place is in lockdown. It's not accepting remote connections without a level of authorization I don't have."

"And I do?"

"You're not making a remote connection. You're actually here. In the substrate. In some quarters, that's kind of a big deal."

"But I just walked in here."

"You had some help. I calmed some of the security down to get you this far."

"So you let the marines in too?"

"Unlocked is unlocked. C'mon."

The closer Holden got to the octagon, the harder it was to approach. It wasn't just fear, though the dread swam at the back of his throat and all down his spine. It was physically difficult, like pushing against a magnetic field.

The shape was chipped at the edges, marked with hair-thin lines in patterns that might have been ideograms or patterns of fungal growth or both. He reached out his hand, and his teeth itched.

"What will happen?" he asked.

"How much do you know about quantum mechanics?"

"How much do you?" Holden replied.

"A lot, turns out," Miller said with a lopsided grin. "Do now, anyway."

"I'm not going to burst into flames or something, right?"

Miller gave a small Belter shrug with his hands. "Don't think so. I'm not up on all the defense systems. But I don't *think* so."

"So," Holden said. "*Maybe?*"

"Yeah."

"Okay." Holden sighed and started to reach for the surface. He paused. "You didn't really answer the question, you know."

"You're stalling," Miller said. And then, "Which question was that?"

"I get why no one else sees you. But the real question is 'why me' at all? I mean, okay, you're screwing with my brain and that's hard work, and if there's other people for me to interact with it's too hard and all like that. But why *me*? Why not Naomi or the UN secretary-general or something?"

Miller nodded, understanding the question. He frowned, sighed.

"Miller kind of liked you. Thought you were a decent guy."

"That's it?"

"You need more?"

Holden placed his palm flat against the closest surface. He didn't burst into flames. Through the gloves of his EVA suit, he felt a short electric tingle and then nothing, because he was floating in space. He tried to scream and failed.

Sorry, a voice said in his head. It sounded like Miller. *Didn't mean to drag you in here. Just try and relax, all right?*

Holden tried to nod, but failed at that too. He didn't have a head.

His sense of his own body had changed, shifted, expanded past anything he'd imagined before. The simple extent of it was numbing. He felt the stars within him, the vast expanses of space contained by him. With a thought, he could pull his attention to a sun surrounded by unfamiliar planets like he was attending to his finger or the back of his neck. The lights all tasted different, smelled different. He wanted to close his eyes against the flood of sensation, but he couldn't. He didn't have anything so simple as eyes. He had become immeasurably large, and rich, and strange. Thousands of voices, millions, billions, lifted in chorus and he was their song. And at his center, a place where all the threads of his being came together. He recognized the station not by how it looked, but by the deep throb of its heartbeat. The power of a million suns contained, channeled. Here was the nexus that sat between the worlds, the miracle of knowledge and power that gave him heaven. His Babel.

And a star went out.

It wasn't especially unique. It wasn't beautiful. A few voices out of quadrillions went silent, and if the great chorus of his being was lessened by them, it wasn't perceptible. Still, a ripple passed through him. The colors of his consciousness swirled and darkened. Concern, curiosity, alarm. Even delight. Something new had happened for the first time in millennia.

Another star flickered and failed. Another few voices went silent. Now, slowly and instantly both, everything changed. He felt the great debate raging in him as a fever, an illness. He had been beyond anything like a threat for so long that all the reflexes of survival had weakened, atrophied. Holden felt a fear that he knew belonged to him—the man trapped within the machine—because his larger self couldn't remember to feel it. The vast parliament swirled, thoughts and opinions, analysis and poetry blending together and breaking apart. It was beautiful as sunlight on oil, and terrifying.

Three suns failed, and now Holden felt himself growing smaller. It was still very little, almost nothing. A white spot on the back of his hand, a sore that wouldn't heal. The plague was still only a symptom, but it was one his vast self couldn't ignore.

From the station at his core, he reached out into the places he had been, the darkened systems that were lost to him, and he reached out through the gates with fire. The fallen stars, mere matter now, empty and dead, bloated. Filled their systems in a rage of radiation and heat, sheared the electrons from every atom, and detonated. Their final deaths echoed, and Holden felt a sense of mourning and of peace. The cancer had struck, and been burned away. The loss of the minds that had been would never be redeemed. Mortality had returned from exile, but it had been cleansed with fire.

A hundred stars failed.

What had been a song became a shriek. Holden felt his body shifting against itself, furious as a swarm of bees trapped and dying. In despair, the hundred suns were burned away, the station hurling destruction through the gates as fast as the darkness appeared, but the growing shadow could not be stopped. All through his flesh, stars were going out, voices were falling into silence. Death rode the vacuum, faster than light and implacable.

He felt the decision like a seed crystal giving form to the chaos around it, solid, hard, resolute. Desperation, mourning, and a million farewells, one to the other. The word *quarantine* came to him, and with the logic of dreams, it carried an unsupportable weight of horror. But within it, like the last voice in Pandora's box, the promise of reunion. One day, when the solution was found, everything that had been lost would be regained. The gates reopened. The vast mind restored.

The moment of dissolution came, sudden and expected, and Holden blew apart.

He was in darkness. Empty and tiny and lost, waiting for the promise to be fulfilled, waiting for the silent chorus to whisper again that Armageddon had been stopped, that all was not lost. And the silence reigned.

Huh, Miller thought at him. *That was weird.*

Like being pulled backward through an infinitely long tunnel of light, Holden was returned to his body. For one vertiginous moment he felt too small, like the tiny wrapping of skin and meat would explode trying to contain him.

Then he just felt tired, and sat down on the floor with a thump.

"Okay," Miller said, rubbing his cheek with an open palm. "I guess that's a start. Sort of explains everything, sort of nothing. Pain in the ass."

Holden flopped onto his back. He felt like someone had run him through a shredder and then badly welded him back together. Trying to remember what it felt like to be the size of a galaxy gave him a splitting headache, so he stopped.

"Tell me everything it explains," he said when he could remember how to speak. Being forced to move moist flaps of meat in order to form the words felt sensual and obscene.

"They quarantined the systems. Shut down the network to stop whatever was capping the locals."

"So, behind each of those gates is a solar system full of whatever made the protomolecule?"

Miller laughed. Something in the sound of it sent a shiver down Holden's spine. "That seems pretty fucking unlikely."

"Why?"

"This station has been waiting for the all-clear signal to open the network back up for about two billion years. If they'd found a solve, they wouldn't still be waiting. Whatever it was, I think it got them all."

"All of them but you," Holden said.

"Nah, kid. I'm one of them like the *Rocinante* is one of you. The *Roci*'s smart for a machine. It knows a lot about you. It could probably gin up a rough simulation of you if someone told it to. Those things? The ones you felt like? Compared to them, I'm a fancy kind of hand terminal."

"And the nothing it explains," Holden said. "You mean what killed them."

"Well, if we're gonna be fair, it's not really nothing," Miller said, crossing his arms. "We know it ate a galaxy spanning hive consciousness like it was popcorn, so that's something. And we know it survived a sterilization that was a couple hundred solar systems wide."

Holden had a powerfully vivid memory of watching the station hurl fire through the ring gates, of the stars on the other side blowing up like balloons, of the gates themselves abandoned to the fire and disappearing. Even just the echo of it nearly blinded him with remembered pain. "Seriously, did they blow up those *stars* to stop it?"

Holden's image of Miller patted the column at the center of the room, though he knew now that Miller wasn't really touching it. Something was pressing the right buttons on his synaptic keyboard to make him think Miller was.

"Yup. Autoclaved the whole joint. Fed a bunch of extra energy in and popped 'em like balloons."

"They can't still do that, though, right? I mean, if the things that ran this are all gone, no one to pull that trigger. It won't do that to us."

Miller's grim smile chilled Holden's blood. "I keep telling you. This station is in war mode, kid. It's playing for keeps."

"Is there a way we can make it feel better about things?"

"Sure. Now I'm in here, I can take off the lockdown," Miller said, "but you're going to have to—"

Miller vanished.

"To what?" Holden shouted. "I'm going to have to *what*?"

From behind came an electronically amplified voice. "James Holden, by authority of the Martian Congressional Republic, you are placed under arrest. Get down on your knees and place your hands on your head. Any attempt to resist will be met with lethal response."

Holden did as he was told, but turned his head to look behind. Seven marines in recon armor had come into the room. They weren't bothering to point their guns at him, but Holden knew they could catch him and tear him to pieces just using the strength of their suits.

"Guys, seriously, you couldn't have given me five more minutes?"

Chapter Twenty-Six: Bull

Voices. Light. A sense of wrongness deep in places he couldn't identify. Bull tried to grit his teeth and found his jaw already clenched hard enough to ache. Someone cried out, but he didn't know where from.

The light caught his attention. Simple white LED with a sanded backsplash to diffuse it. An emergency light. The kind that came on when power was down. It hurt to look at, but he did, using it to focus. If he could make that make sense, everything else would come. A chiming alarm kept tugging at his attention, coming from outside. In the corridor. Bull's mind tried to slide that way, going into the corridor, out into the wide, formless chaos, and he pulled it back to the light. It was like trying to wake up except he was already awake.

Slowly, he recognized the alarm as something he'd hear in the medical bay. He was in the medical bay, strapped onto a bed. The tugging sensation at his arm was a forced IV. With a moment of nauseating vertigo, his perception of the world shifted—he wasn't standing, he was lying down. Meaningless distinctions without gravity, but human brains couldn't seem to help trying to assert direction on the directionless. His neck ached. His head ached. Something else felt wrong.

There were other people in the bay. Men and women on every bed, most with their eyes closed. A new alarm sounded, the woman in the bay across from him losing blood pressure. Crashing. Dying. He shouted, and a man in a nurse's uniform came floating past. He adjusted something on her bed's control board, then pushed off and away. Bull tried to grab him as he went by, but he couldn't.

He'd been in his office. Serge had already gone for the night. A few minor incidents were piled up from the day, the constant friction of a large, poorly disciplined crew. Like everyone else, he'd been waiting to see whether Holden and the Martians came back out of the station. Or if something else would. The fear had made sleep unlikely. He started watching the presentation that the *Rocinante* had sent, James Holden looking surprisingly young and charming saying, *This is what we're calling the slow zone.* He remembered noticing that everyone had accepted Holden's name for the place, and wondered whether it was just that the man had gotten there first or if there was something about charisma that translated across the void.

And then he'd been here. Someone had attacked, then. A torpedo had gotten past their defenses or else sabotage. Maybe the whole damn ship was just coming apart.

There was a comm interface on the bed. He pulled it over, logged in, and used his security override to open its range to the full ship and not just the nurses' station. He requested a connection to Sam, and a few heartbeats later she appeared on the screen. Her hair was floating around her head. Null g always made him think of drowned people. The sclera of her left eye was the bright red of fresh blood.

"Bull," she said with a grin that looked like relief. "Jesus Christ with a side of chips, but I never thought I'd be glad to hear from you."

"Need a status report."

"Yeah," she said. "I better come by for this one. You in your office?"

"Medical bay," Bull said.

"Be there in a jiff," she said.

"Sam. What happened?"

"You remember that asshole who shot the Ring and got turned into a thin paste when his ship hit the slow zone? Same thing."

"We went too fast?" Bull said.

"We didn't. Something changed the rules on us. I've got a couple techs doing some quick-and-dirty tests to figure out what the new top speed is, but we're captured and floating into that big ring of ships. Along with *everybody* else."

"The whole flotilla?"

"Everybody and their sisters," Sam said. A sense of grim despair undercut the lightness of her words. "No one's under their own power now except the shuttles that were inside the bays when it happened, and no one's willing to send them going too fast either. The *Behemoth* was probably going the slowest when it happened. Other ships, it's worse."

How bad floated in his mind, but something about the words refused to be asked. His mind skated over them, flickering. The deep sense of wrongness welled up in him.

"First convenience," he said.

"On my way," Sam said, and the connection dropped. He wanted to sag back into a pillow, wanted to feel the comforting hand of gravity pressing him down. He wanted the New Mexican sun streaming in through a glass window and the open air and blue sky. None of it was there. None of it ever would be.

Rest when you're dead, he thought, and thumbed the comm terminal on again. Ashford and Pa weren't accepting connections, but they both took messages. He was in the process of connecting to the security office when a doctor came by and started talking with him. Mihn Sterling, her name was. Bennie Cortland-Mapu's second. He listened to her with half his attention. A third of the crew had been in their rest cycle, safely in their crash couches. The other two-thirds—him included—had slammed into walls or decks, the hand terminals they'd been looking at accelerating into projectiles. Something about network regrowth and zero gravity and spinal fluid. Bull wondered where Pa was. If she was dead and Ashford alive, it would be a problem.

Disaster recovery could only go two ways. Either everyone pulled together and people lived, or they kept on with their tribal differences and fear, and more people died.

He had to find a way to coordinate with Earth and Mars. Everyone was going to be stressed for medical supplies. If he was going to make this work, he had to bring people together. He needed to see if Monica Stuart and her team—or anyway the part of her team that wasn't going to be charged with sabotage and executed—were still alive. If he could start putting out his own broadcasts, something along the lines of what she'd done with Holden...

The doctor was getting agitated about something. He didn't notice when Sam came into the room; she was just floating there. Her left leg was in an improvised splint of nylon tape and packing foam. Bull put his palm out to the doctor, motioning for silence, and turned his attention to Sam.

"You've got the report?" he asked.

"I do," Sam said. "And you can have it as soon as you start listening to what she's saying."

"What?"

Sam pointed to Doctor Sterling.

"You have to listen to her, Bull. You have to hear what she's saying. It's important."

"I don't have time or patience—"

"Bull!" Sam snapped. "Can you feel anything—I mean *anything*—lower than your tits?"

The sense of wrongness flooded over him, and with it a visceral, profound fear. Vertigo passed through him again, and he closed his eyes. All the words the doctor had been saying—*crushed spinal cord*, *diffuse blood pooling*, *paraplegic*—finally reached his brain. To his shame, tears welled up in his eyes, blurring the women's faces.

"If the fibers grow back wrong," the doctor said, "the damage will be permanent. Our bodies weren't designed to heal in zero g. We're built to let things drain. You have a bolus of blood and spinal fluid putting pressure on the wound. We have to drain that, and we have to get the bone shards out of the way. We could start the regrowth now, but there are about a dozen people who need the nootropics just to stay alive."

"I understand," Bull said around the lump in his throat, hoping she'd stop talking, but her inertia kept her going on.

"If we can stabilize the damage and get the pressure off and get you under at least one-third g, we have a good chance of getting you back to some level of function."

"All right," Bull said. The background of medical alerts and voices and the hum of the emergency air recyclers stood in for real silence. "What's your recommendation?"

"Medical coma," the doctor said without hesitating. "We can slow down your system. Stabilize you until we can evacuate."

Bull closed his eyes, squeezing the tears between the lids. All he had to say was yes, and it was all someone else's problem. It would all go away, and he'd wake up somewhere under thrust with his body coming back together. Or he wouldn't wake up at all. The moment lasted. He remembered walking among the defunct solar collectors. Climbing them. Bracing a ceramic beam with his knees while one of the other men on his team cut it. Running. He remembered a woman he'd been seeing on Tycho Station, and the way his body had felt against her. He could get it back. Or some part of it. It wasn't gone.

"Thank you for your recommendation," he said. "Sam, I'll have that damage report now."

"Bull, no," Sam said. "You know what happens when one of my networks grows back wrong? I burn it out and start over. This is biology. We can't just yank out your wiring and reboot you. And you can't macho your way through it."

"Is that what I'm doing?" Bull said, and he almost sounded like himself.

"I'm serious," Sam said. "I don't care what you promised Fred Johnson or how tough you think you are. You're going to be a big boy and take your nasty medicine and get *better.* You got it?"

She was on the edge of crying now. Blood was darkening her face. Some of her team were surely dead. People she'd known for years. Maybe her whole life. People she'd worked with every day. With a clarity that felt almost spiritual, he saw the depth of her grief and felt it resonate within him. Everyone was going to be there now. Everyone who'd lived on every ship would have seen people they cared about broken or dead. And when people were grieving, they did things they wouldn't do sober.

"Look where we are, Sam," Bull said gently. "Look what we're doing here. Some things don't go back to normal." Sam wiped her eyes with a sleeve cuff, and Bull turned to the doctor. "I understand and respect your medical advice, but I can't take it right now. Once the ship and crew are out of danger, we'll revisit this, but until then staying on duty is more important. Can you keep me cognitively functioning?"

"For a while, I can," the doctor said. "But you'll pay for it later."

"Thank you," Bull said, his voice soft and warm as flannel. "Now, Chief Engineer Rosenberg, give me the damage report."

It wasn't good.

The best thing Bull could say after reading Sam's report and consulting with the doctors and his own remaining security forces was that the *Behemoth* had weathered the storm better than some of the other ships. Being designed and constructed as a generation ship meant that the joints and environmental systems had been built with an eye for long-term wear. She'd been cruising at under 10 percent the slow zone's previous maximum speed when the change came.

The massive deceleration had happened to all the ships at the same time, slowing them from their previous velocity to the barely perceptible drifting toward the station's captive ring in just under five seconds. If it had been instantaneous, no one would have lived through it. Even with the braking spread out, it had approached the edge of the survivable for many of them. People asleep or at workstations with crash couches had stood a chance. Anyone in an open corridor or getting up for a bulb of coffee at the wrong moment was simply dead. The count stood at two hundred dead and twice that many wounded. Three of the Martian ships that had been significantly faster than the *Behemoth* weren't responding, and the rest reported heavy casualties. The big Earth ships were marginally better.

To make matters worse, the radio and laser signals going back out of the Ring to what was left of the flotilla were bent enough that communication was just about impossible. Not that it would have mattered. The slow zone—shit, now he was thinking of it that way too—was doing everything it could to remind them how vast the distances were within it. At the velocities they had available to them now, getting to the Ring would take as long as it had to reach it from the Belt. Months at least, and that in shuttles. All the ships were captured.

However many of them were left, they were on their own.

The station's grip was pulling them into rough orbit around the glowing blue structure, and no amount of burn was able to affect their paths one way or the other. They couldn't speed up and they couldn't stop. No one was under thrust, and it was making the medical crisis worse as zero g complicated the injuries. The *Behemoth*'s power grid, already weakened and patched after the torpedo launch debacle, had suffered a cascading shipwide failure. Sam's team was trekking through the ship, resetting the tripped safeties, adding new patches to the mess. One of the Earth ships had come close to losing core containment and gone through an automatic shutdown that left it running off batteries, another was battling an environmental systems breakdown with the air recyclers. The Martian navy ships might be fine or they might be in ruins, but the Martian commander wasn't sharing.

If it had been a battle, it would have been a humbling defeat. It hadn't even been an attack.

"Then what would you call it?" Pa asked from the screen of his hand terminal. She and Ashford had both survived. Ashford was riding roughshod over the recovery efforts, trying—Bull thought—to micromanage the crisis out of existence. That left Pa at the helm to coordinate with all the other ships. She was better suited for it anyway. There was a chance, at least, that she would listen.

"If I were doing it, I'd call it progressive restraint," Bull said. "That asshole who shot the Ring came through doing something fierce and he got locked down. There's rules about how fast you can go. Then Holden and those marines go to the station, something happens. Whatever's running the station gets its jock in a twist, and things lock down harder. I don't know the mechanism of how they do it, but the logic's basic training stuff. It's allowing us as much freedom as it can, but the more we screw it up, the tighter the choke."

"Okay," Pa said, running a hand through her hair. She looked tired. "I can see that. So as long as it doesn't feel threatened, maybe things don't get worse."

"But if someone gets pissed," Bull said. "I don't know. Some Martian pendejo just lost all his friends or something? He decides to arm a nuke, walk it to the station, and set it off, maybe things get a lot worse."

"All right."

"We've got to get everyone acting together," Bull said. "Earth, Mars, us. Everyone. Because if this was me, I'd escalate from a restraint, to a coercive restraint, to shooting someone. We don't want to get this thing to follow the same—"

"I said *all right*, Mister Baca!" Pa shouted. "That means I understood your point. You can stop making it. Because the one thing I *don't* need right now is another self-righteous male telling me how high the stakes are and that I'd better not fuck things up. I *got* it. *Thank* you."

Bull blinked, opened his mouth, and closed it again. On his screen, Pa pinched the bridge of her nose. He heard echoes of Ashford in her frustration.

"Sorry, XO," he said. "You're right. I was out of line."

"Don't worry about it, Mister Baca," she said, each syllable pulling a weight behind it. "If you have any concrete, specific recommendations, my door is always open."

"I appreciate that," Bull said. "So the captain...?"

"Captain Ashford's doing his best to keep the ship in condition and responsive. He feels that letting the crew see him will improve morale."

And how's that going, Bull didn't ask. Didn't have to. Pa could see him restraining himself.

"Believe it or not, we are all on the same team," she said.

"I'll keep it in mind."

Her expression clouded and she leaned in toward her screen, a gesture of intimacy totally artificial in the floating world of zero g and video connections and still impossible to entirely escape.

"I heard about your condition. I'm sorry."

"It's all right," he said.

"If I ordered you to accept the medical coma?"

He laughed. Even that felt wrong. Truncated.

"I'll go when I'm ready," he said, only realizing after the fact that the phrase could mean two different things. "We get out of the woods, the docs can take over."

"All right, then," she said and her terminal chimed. She cursed quietly. "I have to go. I'll touch base with you later."

"You got it," Bull said and let the connection drop.

The wise thing would have been to sleep. He'd been awake for fourteen hours, checking in with the security staff who were still alive, remaking a duty roster, doing all the things he could do from the medical bay that would make the ship work. Fourteen hours wasn't all that long a shift in the middle of a crisis, except that he'd been crippled.

Crippled.

With a sick feeling, he walked his fingertips down his throat, to his chest, and to the invisible line where the skin stopped feeling like his own and turned into something else. Meat. His mind skittered off the thought. He'd been hurt before and gotten back from it. He'd damn near died four or five different times. Something always happened that got him back on his feet. He always got lucky. This time would be the same. Somehow, somehow he'd get back. Have another story to tell and no one to tell it to.

He knew he was lying to himself, but what else could he do? Apart from stand aside. And maybe he should. Let Pa take care of it. Give Ashford his shot. No one would give him any shit if he took the medical coma. Not even Fred. Hell, Fred would probably have told him to do it. Ordered him.

Bull closed his eyes. He'd sleep or he wouldn't. Or he'd drift into some half-lucid place that wasn't either. One of the doctors was weeping in the corridor, a slow, autonomic sound, more like being sick than expressing sorrow. Someone coughed wetly. Pneumonia was the worst danger now. Null g messed with the sensors that triggered the kinds of coughing that actually cleared lungs until it was too late. After that, strokes and embolisms as the blood that gravity should have helped to drain pooled and clotted instead. On all the other ships, it was the same. Survivable injuries made deadly just by floating. If they could just get under thrust. Get some gravity…

We're all on the same team, Pa said in his half drowse, and Bull was suddenly completely awake. He scooped up his hand terminal, but Ashford and Pa were both refusing connections. It was the middle of their night. He considered putting through an emergency override, but didn't. Not yet. First, he tried Sam.

"Bull?" she said. Her skin looked grayish, and there were lines at the corners of her mouth that hadn't been there before. Her one blood-red eye seemed like an omen.

"Hey, Sam. Look, we need to get all the other crews from all the other ships onto the *Behemoth*. Bring everyone together so no one does anything stupid."

"You want a pony too?"

"Sure," Bull said. "Thing is, we got to give them a reason to come here. Something they need and they can't get anyplace else."

"Sounds great," Sam said, shaking her head. "Maybe I'm not at my cognitive best here, sweetie, but are you asking me for something?"

"They've all got casualties. They all need gravity. I'm asking you how long it would take you to spin up the drum."

Chapter Twenty-Seven: Melba

The darkness was beautiful and surreal. The ships of the flotilla, drawn together by the uncanny power of the station, hugged closer to each other than they ever would have under human control. The only lights came from the occasional exterior maintenance array and the eerie glow of the station. It was like walking through a graveyard in the moonlight. The ring of ships and debris glittered in a rising arc before her and behind, as if any direction she chose would lead up from where she was now.

The EVA suit had limited propellant, and she wanted to conserve it for her retreat. She scuttled through the vacuum, magnetic boots clicking against the hull of the *Prince* until she reached its edge and launched herself into the gap between vessels, aiming toward a Martian supply ship. The half mech and emergency airlock folded on her back massed almost fifty kilos, but with their courses matched, they were as weightless as she was. It was an illusion, she knew, but in the timeless reach between the *Thomas Prince* and hated *Rocinante*, all her burdens seemed light.

The EVA suit had a simple heads-up display that outlined the *Rocinante* with a thin green line. It wasn't the nearest ship. The trip out to it would take hours, but she didn't mind. It was as trapped as all the others. It couldn't go anyplace.

She hummed to herself as she imagined her arrival. Rehearsed it. She let herself daydream that he would be there: Jim Holden returned from the station. She imagined him raging at her as she destroyed his ship. She imagined him weeping and begging her forgiveness, and seeing the despair in his eyes when she refused. They were beautiful dreams, and folded safely inside them, she could forget the blood and horror behind her. Not just the catastrophe on the *Prince*, but all of it—Ren, her father, Julie, everything. The dim blue light of the not-moon felt like home, and the impending violence like a promise about to be kept.

If there was another part of her, a sliver of Clarissa that hadn't quite been crushed yet that felt differently, it was small enough to ignore.

Of course it was just as likely they'd all be dead when she got there. The catastrophe would have hit them as hard as the *Thomas Prince* or any of the other ships. Holden's crew might be nothing but cooling meat already, only waiting for her to come and light their funeral pyre. There was, she thought, a beauty in that too. She ran across the skins of the ships, leaped from one to the next like a nerve impulse crossing a synapse. Like a bad idea being thought by a massive, moonlit brain.

The air in the suit smelled like old plastic and her own sweat. The impact of the magnetic boots pulling her to the ships and then releasing her again translated up her leg, tug and release, tug and release. And before her, as slowly as the hour hand of an analog clock, the ghost-green *Rocinante* grew larger and nearer.

She knew the ship's specs by heart. She'd studied them for weeks. Martian corvette, originally assigned to the doomed *Donnager*. The entry points were the crew airlock just aft of the ops deck, the aft cargo bay doors, and a maintenance port that ran along beneath the reactor. If the reactor was live, the maintenance access wouldn't work. The fore airlock had almost certainly had its security profile changed once the ship fell into Holden's control. Only a stupid man wouldn't change it, and Melba refused to believe a stupid man could bring down her father. The service records she'd gleaned suggested that the cargo bay had been breached once already. Repairs were always weaker than the original structure. The choice was easy.

The attitude of the ship put the cargo bay on the far side of the ship, the body of the *Rocinante* hiding its flaw from the light. Melba stepped into shadow, shivering as if it could actually be colder in the darkness. She fastened the mech to the ship's skin and assembled it for use under the glare of the EVA suit's work lamps. The mech was the yellow of fresh lemons and police tape. The cautions printed in three alphabets were like little Rosetta stones. She felt an inexplicable fondness for the machine as she strapped it across her back, fitting her hands into the waldoes. The mech hadn't been designed for violence, but it was suited for it. That made her and it the same.

She lit the cutting torch and the EVA suit's mask went dark. Melba clung to the ship and began her slow invasion. Sparks and tiny asteroids of melted steel flew off into the darkness around her. The repair work where the bay doors had been bent out and refitted was almost invisible. If she hadn't known to look, she wouldn't have seen the weaknesses. She wondered if they knew she was coming. She imagined them hunched over their security displays, eyes wide with fear at what was digging its way under the *Rocinante*'s skin. She found herself singing softly, snatches of popular songs and old holiday tunes, whatever came to mind. Bits of lyrics and melody matched to the hum of the torch's vibration.

She breached the *Rocinante*, a patch of glowing steel no wider than her finger popping out. No air vented through the gap into the vacuum. They didn't keep the cargo bay pressurized. That meant the atmosphere wasn't dropping inside, and the ship alarms weren't blaring. One problem solved even without her help. It felt like fate. She killed the torch and unfolded the emergency airlock, sealing it against the hatch. She unzipped the outer layer, closed it, unzipped the inner one, and stepped into the small additional room she'd created. She didn't know how much damage she'd have to do to get into the inner areas of the ship. She didn't want an accidental loss of atmosphere to rob her of her vengeance. Holden needed to know who'd done this to him, not gasp out his last breaths thinking his ship had merely broken.

Gently, she slipped the mech's hand into the hole, braced, and peeled back the cargo door, long strips of steel blooming like an iris blossom. When it was wide enough, she took the sides of the hole in her mechanical hands and pulled herself into the cargo bay. Supply crates lined the walls and floors, held in place by electromagnets. One had shattered, a victim of the catastrophe. A cloud of textured protein packets floated in the air. The LED on the panel beside the interior airlock door was green; the bay hadn't been locked down. Why would it? She punched the button to enter the airlock and begin the cycle. Once the green pressure light came on, she slipped her hands out of the mech and lifted off the helmet. No Klaxons were ringing. No voices shouted or threatened. She'd made it on without alarming anyone. Her grin ached.

Back in the mech, she opened the airlock into the interior of the ship and paused. Still no alarms. Melba pulled herself gently, silently into enemy territory.

The *Rocinante* was built floor by floor from the reactor up to the engineering deck, to the machine shop, then the galley and crew cabins and medical bays, storage deck containing the crew airlock, then on up to the command deck and pilot's station farthest forward. Under thrust, it would be like a narrow building. Without thrust, the ship was directionless.

She had choices to make now. The cargo bay was close enough to give her access to engineering and the reactor. She could sneak in there and start the reactor on its overload. Or she could go up, try taking the crew by surprise, and set the ship to self-destruct from the command deck.

She took a deep breath. The *Rocinante* had four regular crew including Holden, and she didn't know whether the documentary crew were still on board. At least two of the regular crew had military training and experience. She might be able to take them in a fight if she got the drop on them or came across them one at a time.

The risk was too high. The reactor was nearest, it was easiest, and she could get out through the cargo bay. She pulled herself along the corridors she knew only from simulations, toward the reactor and the death of the ship.

When she opened the hatch to engineering, a woman floated above an opened control panel, a soldering iron in one hand and a spool of wire in the other. She had the elongated frame and slightly oversized head of someone who'd grown up under low g. Brown skin and dark hair pulled back in a utilitarian knot. Naomi Nagata. Holden's lover.

Melba felt a sudden urge to tear off the mech suit, swirl her tongue across the roof of her mouth, feel the chemical rush. To grab the narrow Belter's neck in her bare hands and feel the bones snap. It would be a yearlong dream of revenge made tactile and perfect. But two other crew members were on the ship, and she didn't know where they were. The terror she'd felt in that sleazy Baltimore casino came rushing back. Crawling helplessly on the floor in the post-drug collapse while people banged at the door to get in. She couldn't risk a crash until she knew where everyone was.

Naomi looked up at the sound of the door, pleasure in the woman's dark eyes as if the interruption were a happy surprise, and then shock, and then a cold fury.

For a moment, neither one moved.

With a yell, the woman launched herself at Melba, spinning the spool of wire in front of her. Melba tried to dodge, but the bulk of the mech and its slow response made it impossible. The wire hit her left cheek with a sound like a brick falling to earth, and for a moment her head rang. She brought up the mech's arm in a rough block, taking the Belter solidly in the ribs and sending them both spinning. Melba grabbed at a handhold, missed it, and then tried for another. The mech's hand latched on, crushing the metal flat and almost pulling it from the wall, but the Belter was ahead of her, skimming through the air at Melba, teeth bared like a shark. Melba tried to get the mech's free arm up to bat her away, but the Belter was already too close. She grabbed the front of Melba's jumpsuit, balling it in a fist, and used the leverage to swing a hard knee into her ribs, punctuating each blow with a word.

"You. Don't. Get. To hurt. My. *Ship.*"

Melba felt a rib give way. She reached her tongue for the roof of her mouth, but again she didn't make the small private circles that would flush her blood with fire. She had to be awake and functional when the fight was over. She gritted her teeth and curled the mech's free arm in, bending it against itself, and then snapped her hand closed. The Belter screamed. The mech's claw had her by the shoulder. Melba squeezed again and heard the muffled, wet sound of bone breaking.

She threw the Belter across the room as hard as the motors let her. Where the woman bounced off the far wall, a smear of blood marked it. Melba waited, watching the Belter rotate in the air, directionless and loose as a rag doll sinking to the bottom of a swimming pool. A growing sphere of blood adhered to the woman's shoulder and neck.

"I do what I want," Melba said, and the voice sounded like someone else's.

Carefully, she pulled herself to the control panel. The panel was off, fixed to the deck with a length of adhesive tape. The guts within were a mess of wires and plates. The *Rocinante* had taken some damage in the catastrophe, but not so much that Melba couldn't do what was needed. She shrugged out of the mech, cracked her knuckles, traced the major control nodes, and plugged them back into the panel. The local memory check took only a few seconds, and she overrode the full system check. It was nothing she could have done before she left Earth, but Melba Koh had spent months learning about the guts of military ships. This was just the sort of thing Soledad, Stanni, and Bob would have checked on if they'd been working maintenance. It was something Ren would have taught her.

Her fingers curled, stumbling over the keyboard for a moment, but she got it back.

The control specs of the reactor came up. Releasing the magnetic bottle that kept the core from melting through the ship was deliberately designed to be difficult. Changing the limits on the reaction itself until it would eventually outstrip the bottle's ability to contain it was also hard, but less so. And it would give her a little time to tell Holden what she'd done, then get out of the ship and back toward the *Thomas Prince*. In the chaos of the day, no one might even know that someone had survived the death of the *Rocinante*.

A flicker in her peripheral vision was the only warning she had, but it was enough. Melba twisted out of the way, the Belter's massive wrench hissing through the air where her temple had been. Melba pushed back with her legs, struggling frantically to worm back into the mech. She tensed against the coming attack, but no blows came. She shrugged into the metal and jammed her hands into the waldoes, grabbing the wall and spinning back to the fight just as the Belter looked up from the control panel. Blood was crawling up the woman's neck, held to her by surface tension, and her smile was triumphant. The control panel flashed red and a screen of code crawled over it too fast to read. The lights in the room went off, and the emergency LEDs flickered on. Melba felt her throat go tight.

The Belter had dumped core. The reaction Melba had come to overload was dissipating in a cloud of gas behind the ship. The Belter's smile was feral and triumphant.

"Doesn't change anything," Melba said. It hurt to talk. "You have torpedoes. I'll overload one of those."

"Not in my lifetime," the Belter said, and attacked again.

Her swing was lopsided, though. Clumsy. The wrench clanged against the mech's joint, but it didn't do any damage. The Belter launched herself out of reach just as Melba swung an arm at her. The Belter wasn't using her injured arm at all, and she left spinning droplets of blood whenever she changed direction.

Melba wondered why the woman didn't call for help. On little ships like this, opening a communications channel was often as simple as saying it out loud. Either the computer was down, the rest of the crew dead or incapacitated, or it simply hadn't occurred to her. It didn't matter. It didn't change what Melba had to do. She shifted to her right, sliding through the air, moving handhold to handhold, never giving the other woman the chance to catch her unmoored and spin her into the open air at the center of the room. The Belter perched on the wall, her dark eyes darting one way, then other, searching for advantage. There was no fear in them, no sentimentality. Melba had no doubt that if the opportunity came, Naomi would kill her.

She reached the hatch, setting the mech's claw to grip a handhold, and then slipping one arm free to reach for the door's controls. It was a provocation, and it worked. The Belter jumped, not straight at Melba, but to the deck above her, then turned, kicked, off, and drove down, her heels aiming for Melba's head.

Melba drove her arm back into the mech and snapped the free arm up, catching the Belter in mid-flight. Her handhold broke free of the wall, and the pair of them floated together into the open air of the room. The Belter's injured arm was caught in the mech's clamp, and she kicked savagely with her heels. One blow connected, and Melba's vision narrowed for a moment. She pulled the Belter through the air, worrying at her like a terrier with a rat, and then managed to swing the free arm up and catch the woman by the neck.

The Belter's hand flew up to the clamp, panic in her expression. Her eyes went wide and bright. It would take a twitch of

Melba's fingers to crush the woman's throat, and they both knew it. A sense of triumph and overwhelming joy washed through her. Holden might not be here, but she had his lover. She would take someone he loved from him just the way he'd taken her own father from her. This wasn't even fighting anymore. This was justice.

The Belter's face was flushing red, her breath constricted and rough. Melba grinned, enjoying the moment.

"This is his fault," she said. "All of this is what he had coming."

The Belter scratched at the mech's claw. The blood that came away might have been from the old wound, or the mech's grip might already have broken the skin. Melba closed her fingers a fraction, the pressure feather light. The mech's servos buzzed as it closed a millimeter more. The Belter tried to say something, pushing the word out past her failing windpipe, and Melba knew she couldn't let her speak. She couldn't let her beg or weep and cry mercy. If she did, Melba suddenly wasn't sure she could go through with it, and it had to be done. *Sympathy is for the weak*, her father's voice whispered in her ear.

"You're Naomi Nagata," Melba said. "My name is Clarissa Melpomene Mao. You and your people attacked my family. Everything that's happened here? Everything that's going to happen. It's *your fault.*"

The light was fading from the Belter's eyes. Her breath came in ragged gasps. All it would take was a squeeze. All she had to do was make a fist and snap the woman's neck.

With the last of her strength, the Belter woman lifted her free hand in a gesture of obscenity and defiance.

Melba's body buzzed like she'd stepped into the blast from a firehose. Her head bent back, her spine arching against itself. Her hands flexed open, her toes curled back until it seemed like they had to break. She heard herself scream. The mech spread its arms to the side and froze, leaving her crucified in the metal form. The buzzing stopped, but she couldn't move. No matter how much she willed it, her muscles would not respond.

Naomi came to rest against the opposite wall, a knot of panting and blood.

"Who are you?" the Belter croaked.

I am vengeance, Melba thought. *I am your death made flesh.* But the voice that answered came from behind her.

"Anna. My name's Anna. Are you all right?"

Chapter Twenty-Eight: Anna

The woman—Naomi Nagata—replied by coughing up a red glob of blood.

"I'm an idiot, of course you're not all right," Anna said, then floated over to her, pausing to push the still-twitching Melba to the other side of the compartment. Girl and mech drifted across the room, bounced off a bulkhead, and came to a stop several meters away.

"Emergency locker," Naomi croaked, and pointed at a red panel on one wall. Anna opened it to find flashlights, tools, and a red-and-white bag not too different from the one Tilly had been carrying on the *Prince*. She grabbed it. While Anna extracted a package of gauze and a can of coagulant spray for the nasty wound on Naomi's shoulder, the Belter pulled out several hypo ampules and began injecting herself with them one at a time, her movements efficient and businesslike. Anna felt like something was tearing in her shoulders every time she wrapped the gauze around Naomi's upper torso, and she almost asked for another shot for herself.

Years before, Anna had taken a seminar on ministering to people with drug addictions. The instructor, a mental health nurse named Andrew Smoot, had made the point over and over that the drugs didn't only give pleasure and pain. They changed cognition, stripped away the inhibitions, and more often than not, someone's worst habits or tendencies—what he called their "pathological move"—got exaggerated. An introvert would often withdraw, an aggressive person would grow violent. Someone impulsive would become even more so.

Anna had understood the idea intellectually. Almost three hours into her spacewalk, the amphetamines Tilly had given her began to fade and a clarity she hadn't known she lacked began to return to her. She felt she had a deeper, more personal insight into what her own pathological move might be.

Anna had spent only a few years living among Belters and outer planets inhabitants. But that was long enough to know that their philosophy boiled down to "what you don't know kills you." No one growing up on Earth ever really understood that, no matter how much time they later spent in space. No Belter would have thrown on a space suit and EVA pack and rushed out the airlock without first knowing exactly what the environment on the other side was like. It wouldn't even occur to them to do so.

Worse, she'd run out that airlock without stopping to send a message to Nono. *You don't ask for permission, you ask for forgiveness* echoed in her head. If she died doing this, Nono would have it carved as her epitaph. She'd never get that last chance to say she was sorry.

The brightly colored display, which always seemed to float at the edge of her vision no matter which way her face was pointed, had said that she had 83 percent of her air supply remaining. Not knowing how long a full tank would last robbed that information of some much-needed context.

As she'd tried to slow her breathing back down and keep from panicking, the gauge ticked to 82 percent. How long had it been at 83 percent before it did? She couldn't remember. A vague feeling of nausea made her think about how bad throwing up in her space suit would be, which only made the feeling worse.

The girl, Melba, or Claire now, was far ahead and gaining, moving with the easy grace of long practice. Someone for whom walking in a space suit with magnetic boots was normal. Anna tried to hurry and only managed to kick her boot with her other foot and turn the magnet up high enough to lock it to the hull of the ship. The momentum of her step tugged against the powerful magnetic clamp. After several lost seconds figuring out how to fix that problem, she'd found the controls and slid the grip back down to a normal human range. After that, she gave up on haste and aimed for a safe, consistent pace. Slow and steady, but she wasn't winning the race. She lost sight of the girl, but she'd told herself it didn't matter. She guessed well enough where Clarissa Mao was going. Or Melba Koh. Whoever this woman was.

She had seen images of the *Rocinante* on newsfeeds before. It was probably as famous as a ship could be. James Holden's central role in the Eros and Ganymede incidents along with a peppering of dogfights and antipiracy actions had kept his little corvette mentioned in the media on and off for years. As long as there weren't two Martian corvettes parked next to each other, Anna felt confident she'd be able to spot it.

Fifteen long minutes later, she did.

The *Rocinante* was shaped like a stubby black wedge of metal; a fat chisel laid on its side. The flat surface of the hull was occasionally broken up by a domed projection. Anna didn't know enough about ships to know what they were. It was a warship, so sensors or guns, maybe, but definitely not doors. The tail of the ship had been facing her, and the only obvious opening in it was at the center of the massive drive cone. She walked to the edge of the ship she was on and then from side to side trying to get a better look at the rest of the *Rocinante* before jumping over to it. The irony of looking before she leapt at this late stage of the game made her laugh, and she felt some of the tension and nausea fading.

Just to the right of the drive cone was a bubble of plastic attached to the ship, pale as a blister. A moment later she was through the wound in the ship's cargo doors and inside. It had occurred to her, as she looked at the maze of crates locked against the hull with magnets much like the ones on her own feet, that she hadn't thought her plan through past this. Did this room connect to the rest of the ship? The doors behind her didn't have an airlock, which probably meant that this space was usually kept in vacuum. She had no idea where anyone would be in relation to that room, and more worrisome, she had no idea if the girl she was chasing was still in there, hiding behind one of the boxes.

Anna carefully pulled herself from crate to crate to the other end of the long, narrow compartment. Bits of plastic and freeze-dried food drifted around her like a cloud of oddly shaped insects. The broken crates might have been relics of a fight or debris created by the speed change; she had no way to know. She reached into the small bag tethered to her EVA pack and pulled out the taser. She'd never fired one in microgravity or in vacuum. She hoped neither thing affected it. Another gamble no Belter would ever take.

To her great relief, she found an airlock at the other end of the room, and it opened at a touch of the panel. Cycling it took several minutes, while Anna pulled the heavy EVA pack off her back and played with the taser to make sure she knew how to turn the safety off. The military design was intuitive, but less clearly labeled than the civilian models she was accustomed to. The panel flashed green and the inner doors opened.

No one was in sight. Just a deck that looked like a machine shop with tool lockers and workbenches and a ladder set into one wall. Bookending the ladder were two hatches, one going toward the front of the ship, the other toward the back. Anna was thinking that she was most likely to run into crewmembers by going toward the front of the ship when there was a loud bang from the back and the lights went out.

Yellow LEDs set into the walls came on a moment later, and a genderless voice said, "Core dump, emergency power only," and repeated it several times. Her helmet muffled the sound, but there was clearly still air in the ship. She pulled the helmet off and hung it from her harness.

Anna was fairly certain you only ejected the core in emergencies related to the engine room, so she moved to that hatch instead. With the constant rumble of the ship gone and her helmet removed she could hear faint noises coming through the hatch. It took her several long moments to figure out how to access it, and when she finally did the hatch snapped open so suddenly it made her almost yelp with surprise.

Inside, Melba was murdering someone.

A Belter woman with long dark hair and a greasy coverall was having her throat crushed by the mechanical arms Melba wore. The woman—Anna could see now that it was James Holden's second-in-command, Naomi Nagata—looked like Melba had beaten her badly. Her arm and shoulder were covered in blood, and her face was a mass of scrapes and contusions.

Anna drifted down into the vaulted chamber. The reactor room's walls curving inward like a church, the cathedrals of the fusion age. She felt an almost overwhelming need to hurry, but she knew she'd only get one shot with the taser, and she didn't trust herself to fire on the move.

Naomi's face was turning a dark, bruised purple. Her breath the occasional wet rasp. Somehow, the Belter managed to raise one hand and flip Melba off. Anna's feet hit the decking, and her boots stuck. She was less than three meters behind Melba when her finger pressed the firing stud, aiming for the area of her back not covered by the skeletal frame of the mech, hoping the taser would work through a vacuum suit.

She missed, but the results were impressive anyway.

Instead of hitting the fabric of Melba's suit, the taser's two microdarts hit the mech dead center. The trailing wires immediately turned bright red and began to fall apart like burning string. The taser got so hot Anna could feel it through her glove, so she let go just before it melted into a glob of gooey gray plastic. The mech arced and popped and the arms snapped straight out. The room smelled like burning electrical cables. All of Melba's hair was standing straight up, and even after the taser had died her fingers and legs continued to twitch and jerk. A small screen on the mech's arm had a flashing red error code.

"Who are you?" Naomi Nagata asked, drifting in a way that told Anna she'd be slumping to the floor at the first hint of gravity.

"Anna. My name's Anna," she had said. "Are you all right?"

After the third injection, Naomi took a long, shuddering breath and said, "Who's Anna?"

"Anna is me," she said, then chuckled at herself. "You mean who am I? I'm a passenger on the *Thomas Prince*."

"UN? You don't look like navy."

"No, a passenger. I'm a member of the advisory group the secretary-general sent."

"The dog and pony show," Naomi said, then hissed with pain as Anna tightened the bandage and activated the charge that would keep it from unwinding.

"Everyone keeps calling it that," Anna said as she felt the bandage. She wished she'd paid more attention in the church first aid class. Clear the airway, stop the bleeding, immobilize the injury was about the limit of what she knew.

"That's because it is," Naomi said, then reached up with her good hand to grab a rung of the nearby ladder. "It's all political bullsh—"

She was cut off by a mechanical-sounding voice saying, "Reboot complete."

Anna turned around. Melba was staring at them both, her hair still standing straight out from her head, but her hands no longer twitching uncontrollably. She moved her arms experimentally, and the half mech whined, hesitated, and then moved with her.

"Fuck me," Naomi said. She sounded annoyed but unsurprised.

Anna reached for her taser before she remembered it had melted. Melba bared her teeth.

"This way," Naomi said as the hatch slid open above them. Anna darted through it, with Naomi close behind using her one good arm to pull herself along. Melba surged after them, reaching out with one foot to push off the reactor housing.

Naomi pulled her leg through just in time to avoid being grabbed by the mech's claw, then tapped the locking mechanism with her toe and the hatch slammed shut on the mech's wrist. The hatch whined as it tried to close, crushing the claw in a spray of sparks and broken parts. Anna waited for the scream of pain that didn't come, then realized that the gloves Melba used to control the machine were in the mech's forearms, several centimeters behind the point of damage. They hadn't hurt her, and she'd sacrificed the use of one of the mech's claws in order to keep the hatch open. The other claw appeared in the gap, gripping at the metal, bending it.

"Go," Naomi said, her voice tight with pain, her good hand pointing at the next hatch up the ladder. After they were both through, Anna took a moment to look around at the new deck they were on. It looked like crew areas. Small compartments with flimsy-looking doors. Not a good place to hole up. Naomi flew through the empty air and the dim shadows cast by the emergency lights, and Anna followed as best she could, the feeling of nightmare crawling up her throat.

After they'd passed through the hatch into the next level, Naomi stopped to tap on the small control screen for several seconds. The emergency lights shifted to red, and the panel on the hatch read SECURITY LOCKDOWN.

"She's not trapped down there," Anna said. "She can get out through the cargo bay. There's a hole in the doors."

"That's twice now someone has done that," Naomi replied, pulling herself up the ladder. "Anyway, she's wearing a salvage mech rig, and she's in the machine shop. Half the stuff in there is made to cut through ships. She's not trapped. We are."

This took Anna by surprise. They'd gotten away. They'd locked a door behind them. That was supposed to end it. The monster isn't allowed to open doors. It was fuzzy, juvenile thinking, and Anna became less sure that all the drugs had actually passed through her system. "So what do we do?"

"Medical bay," Naomi said, pointing down a short corridor. "That way."

That made sense. The frail-looking Belter woman was getting a gray tone to her dark skin that made Anna think of massive blood loss, and the bandage on her shoulder had already soaked through and was throwing off tiny crimson spheres. She took Naomi by the hand and pulled her down the corridor to the medical bay door. It was closed, and the panel next to it flashed the security lockdown message like the deck hatches had. Naomi started pressing it, and Anna waited for the door to slide open. Instead, another, heavier-looking door slid into place over the first, and the panel Naomi was working on went dark.

"Pressure doors," Naomi said. "Harder to get through."

"But we're on this side of them."

"Yeah."

"Is there another way in?" Anna asked.

"No. Let's go."

"Wait," Anna said. "We need to get you in there. You're very badly hurt."

Naomi turned to look at her, frowned as if she'd only really seen Anna for the first time. It was a speculative frown. Anna felt she was being sized up.

"I have two injured men in there. My crew. They're helpless," Naomi finally said. "Now they're as safe as I can make them. So you and I are going to go up to the next deck, get a gun, and make sure she follows us. When she shows up, we're going to kill her."

"I don't—" Anna started.

"Kill. Her. Can you do that?"

"Kill? No. I can't," Anna said. It was the truth.

Naomi stared at her for a second longer, then just shrugged with her good hand. "Okay, then, come with me."

They moved through the next hatch to the deck above. Most of the space was taken up by an airlock and storage lockers. Some of the lockers were large enough to hold vacuum suits and EVA packs. Others were smaller. Naomi opened one of the smaller lockers and pulled out a thick black handgun.

"I've never shot anyone either," she said, pulling the slide back and loading a round. To Anna's eye the bullet looked like a tiny rocket. "But those two in the med bay are my family, and this is my home."

"I understand," Anna said.

"Good, because I can't have you—" Naomi started, then her eyes rolled up in her head and her body went limp. The gun drifted away from her relaxed hand.

"No no no," Anna repeated in a sudden wash of panic. She floated over to Naomi and held her wrist. There was still a pulse, but it was faint. She dug through the first aid pack, looking for something to help. One ampule said it was for keeping people from going into shock, so Anna jabbed Naomi with it. She didn't wake up.

The air in the room began to smell different. Hot, and with the melted plastic odor her damaged taser had given off when it died. A spot of red appeared on the deck hatch, then shifted to yellow, then to white. The girl in the mech, coming for them.

The hatch above them, the one that led forward on the ship, was closed and flashing the lockdown message. Naomi hadn't told her what the override code was. The airlock was on their level, but it was locked down too.

The deck hatch began to open in lurching increments. Anna could hear Melba panting and cursing as she forced it. And Naomi's lockdown code hadn't kept the insane woman out, it had only locked them in.

Anna pulled Naomi's limp body over to one of the large vacuum suit storage lockers and put her inside, climbing in after her. There was no lock on the door. Between the unconscious woman and the suit, there was hardly enough room for her to close it. She set both of her feet at the corner where the door of the locker met the deck and set the magnets up to full. She felt the suit lock onto the metal, clamping her legs into place and pulling her up close against the locker door.

On the far side, metal shrieked. Something wet brushed against the back of Anna's neck. Naomi's hand, limp and bloody. Anna tried not to move, tried not to breathe loudly. The prayer she offered up was hardly more than a confusion of fear and hope.

A locker door slammed open off to her left. Then another one, closer. And then another. Anna wondered where Naomi's gun had gotten to. It was in the locker somewhere, but there was no light, and she'd have to unlock the magnets on her boots to look for it. She hoped they hadn't left it outside with the crazy woman. Another locker opened.

The door centimeters from Anna's face shifted, but didn't open. The vents and the cracks in the locker door flared the white of a cutting torch, then went dark. A mechanical voice said, "Backup power depleted." The curse from the other side was pure frustration. It was followed by a series of grunts and thumps: Melba taking the mech rig off. Anna felt a surge of hope.

"Open it," Melba said. Her voice was low, rough, and bestial.

"No."

"Open it."

"You... I can hear that you're feeling upset," Anna said, horrified by the words even as she spoke them. "I think we should talk about this if you—"

Melba's scream was unlike anything Anna had heard before, deep and vicious and wild. If the id had a throat, it would have sounded like that. If the devil spoke.

Something struck the metal door and Anna flinched back. Then another blow. And another. The metal began to bow in, and droplets of blood clung to the vent slits. *Her fists*, Anna thought. *She's doing this with her hands.*

The screaming was wild now, obscene where it wasn't wordless, and inhuman as a hurricane. The thick metal of the door bent in, the hinges starting to shudder and bend with each new assault. Anna closed her eyes.

The top hinge gave way, shattering.

And then, without warning, silence fell. Anna waited, sure she was being lulled into a trap. No sound came except a small animal gurgle. She could smell the stomach-turning acid stench of fresh vomit. After what felt like hours, she turned off the magnets and pushed the warped and abused door open.

Melba floated curled against the wall, her hands pressed to her belly and her body shuddering.

Chapter Twenty-Nine: Bull

The truth was, distance was always measured in time. It wasn't the sort of thing Bull usually thought about, but his enforced physical stillness was doing strange things with his awareness. Even in the middle of the constant press of events, the calls and coordination, the scolding from his doctor, he felt some part of his mind coming loose. And strange ideas kept floating in, like the way that distance got measured in time.

Centuries before, a trip across the Atlantic Ocean could take months. There was a town near New Mexico named Wheeless where the story was some ancient travelers of the dust and caliche had a wagon break down and decided that it was easier to put down roots than go on. Technologies had come, each building on the ones before, and months became weeks and then hours. And outside the gravity well, where machines were freed from the tyranny of air resistance and gravity, the effect was even more profound. When the orbits were right, the journey from Luna to Mars could take as little as twelve days. The trek from Saturn to Ceres, a few months. And because they were out there with their primate brains, evolved on the plains of prehistoric Africa, everyone had a sense of how far it was. Saturn to Ceres was a few months. Luna to Mars was a few days. Distance was time, and so they didn't get overwhelmed by it.

The slow zone had changed that. Looking at a readout, the ships from Earth and Mars were clustered together like a handful of dried peas thrown in the same bowl. They were drifting now, coming together and spreading apart, taking their places in the captured ring around the eerie station. Compared to the volume of ring-bordered sphere, they seemed huddled close. But the distance between them and the Ring was time, and time meant death.

From the farthest of the ships to the *Behemoth* was two days' travel in a shuttle, assuming that the maximum speed didn't ratchet down again. The closest, he could have jumped to. The human universe had contracted, and was contracting more. With every connection, every stark, frightened voice he heard in the long, frantic hours, Bull grew more convinced that his plan could work. The vastness and strangeness and unreasonable danger of the universe had traumatized everyone it hadn't killed. There was a hunger to go home, to huddle together, back in the village. The instinct was the opposite of war, and as long as he could see it cultivated, as long as the response to the tragedies of the lockdown were to get one another's backs and see that everyone who needed care got it, the grief and fear might not turn to more violence.

The feed went to green, then blue, and then Monica Stuart was smiling professionally into the camera. She looked tired, sober, but human. A face people knew. One they could recognize and feel comfortable with.

"Ladies and gentlemen," she said. "Welcome to the first broadcast of Radio Free Slow Zone, coming to you from our temporary offices here on board the OPA battleship *Behemoth*. I am a citizen of Earth and a civilian, but it's my hope that this program can be of some use to all of us in this time of crisis. In addition to bringing whatever unclassified news and information we can, we will also be conducting interviews with the command crews of the ships, civilian leaders on the *Thomas Prince*, and live musical performances.

"It's an honor to welcome our first guest, the Reverend Father Hector Cortez."

A graphic window opened, and the priest appeared. To Bull's eyes, the man looked pretty ragged. The too-bright teeth seemed false and the blazing white hair had a greasy look to it.

"Father Cortez," Monica Stuart said. "You have been helping with the relief effort on the *Thomas Prince*?"

For a moment, the man seemed not to have heard her. A smile jerked into place.

"I have," the old man said. "I have, and it has been...Monica, I'm humbled. I am...humbled."

Bull turned off the feed. It was something. It was better than nothing.

The Martian frigate *Cavalier*, now under the command of a second lieutenant named Scupski, was shutting down its reactors and transferring all its remaining crew and supplies to the *Behemoth*. The *Thomas Prince* had agreed to move its wounded, its medical team, and all the remaining civilians—poets, priests, and politicians. Including the dead-eyed Hector Cortez. It was a beginning, but it wasn't all he could do. If they were to keep coming, if the *Behemoth* was to become the symbol of calm and stability and certainty that he needed it to be, there had to be more. The broadcast channel could give a voice and a face to the growing consolidation. He'd need to talk to Monica Stuart about it some more. Maybe there could be some sort of organized mourning of the dead. A council with representatives from all sides that could make an evacuation plan and start getting people back through the Ring and home.

Except that when the lockdown came, they'd lost all their long-distance ships to it. And the Ring itself had retreated, because they had to move so slowly, and because distance was measured in time.

His hand terminal chirped, and he came back to wakefulness with a start. Outside his room a woman shouted and a man's tense voice replied. Bull recognized the sound of the crash team rushing to try and revive some poor bastard from collapsing into death. He felt for the team of medics. He was doing the same kind of work, just on a different scale. He shifted his arms, scooped up the terminal, and accepted the connection. Serge appeared on the screen.

"Bist?" he asked.

"I'm doing great," Bull said dryly. "What's up?"

"Mars. They got him. Hauling the cabron back alive."

Instinctively, uselessly, Bull tried to sit up. He couldn't sit and up was a polite abstraction.

"Holden?" he said.

"Who else, right? He's on a skiff puttering slow for the MCRN *Hammurabi*. Should be there in a few hours."

"No," Bull said. "They've got to bring him here."

Serge raised his hand in a Belter's nod, but his expression was skeptical.

"Asi dulcie si, but I don't see them doing it."

Somewhere far away down below Bull's chest, the compression sleeves hissed and chuffed and expanded, massaging the blood and lymph around his body now that movement wouldn't keep his fluids from pooling. He couldn't feel it. If they'd caught fire, he wouldn't feel it. Something deep and atavistic shifted in fear and disgust as his hindbrain rediscovered his injuries for the thousandth time. Bull ground the heel of his palm against the bridge of his nose.

"Okay," he said. "I'll see what I can do. What does Sam say about the project?"

"She got the rail guns off and they're working on cutting back the extra torpedo tubes, but the captain found out and he's throwing grand mal."

"Well, that had to happen sometime," Bull said. "Guess I'll take care of that too. Anything else?"

"Unless tu láve mis yannis, I think you got plenty. Take a breath, we'll take a turn, sa sa? You don't have to do it all yourself."

"I've got to do something," Bull said as the compression sleeves relaxed with a sigh. "I'll be in touch."

Tense, low voices drifted in with the burned-moth stink of cauterized flesh. Bull let his gaze focus on the blue-white ceiling above the bed he was strapped to.

Holden was back. They hadn't killed him. If there was one thing that had the potential to destroy the fragile cooperation he was building, it would be the fight over who got to hold James Holden's nuts to a Bunsen burner.

Bull scratched his shoulder more for the sensation than because it itched and considered the consequences. Protocol was that they'd question him, hold him in detention, and start negotiating extradition with whoever on the Earth side was investigating the *Seung Un*. Bull's guess was they'd beat him bloody and drop him outside. The man was in custody, but he was responsible for too many deaths to assume he'd be safe there.

It was time to try hailing the *Rocinante* again. Maybe this time they'd answer. Since the catastrophe, they'd been silent. Their communications array might have been damaged, they might be staying silent as some sort of political tactic, or they might all be dying or dead. He requested a connection again and waited with no particular hope of being answered.

Later, when they were outside the Ring, people could wrestle for jurisdiction as much as they wanted. Right now, Bull needed them to work together. Maybe if he—

Against all expectation, the connection to the *Rocinante* opened. A woman Bull didn't recognize appeared. Pale skin, unrestrained red hair haloing her face. The smudge on her cheek might have been grease or blood.

"Yes," the woman said. "Hello? Who is this? Can you help us?"

"My name's Carlos Baca," Bull said, swallowing shock and confusion before they could get to his voice. "I'm chief security officer on the *Behemoth*. And yes, I can help you."

"Oh, thank God," the woman said.

"So how about you tell me who you are and what the situation is over there."

"My name is Anna Volovodov, and I have a woman who tried to kill the crew of the *Rocinante* in...um...custody? I used all the sedatives in the emergency pack because I can't get into the actual medical bay. I taped her to a chair. Also, I think she may have blown up the *Seung Un*."

Bull folded his hands together.

"Why don't you tell me about that?" he said.

Captain Jakande was an older woman, silver-haired with a take-no-shit military attitude that Bull respected, even though he didn't like it.

"I still don't have orders to release the prisoner," Captain Jakande said. "I don't see that it's likely that I'll get them. So for the foreseeable future, no."

"I have a shuttle already going to collect his crew and the woman he accused of being the real saboteur," Bull said. "And last time I looked, I have two dozen of your people slated to come over once we have the drum spun up."

Jakande nodded once, confirming everything he'd said without being moved by any of it. Bull knotted his fingers together and squeezed until the knuckles were white, but he did it out of range of the communication deck's cameras.

"It's going to be better for all of us if we can get everyone together," Bull said. "Pool resources and plan the evacuation. If you don't have shuttles, I can arrange transportation for you and your crew. There's plenty of space here."

"I agree that it would be better to be under a single command," Jakande said. "If you are offering to turn over the *Behemoth*, I'm willing to accept control and responsibility."

"Not where I was taking that, no," Bull said.

"I didn't think so."

"Mister Baca," Ashford barked from the doorway. Bull held out a hand in a just-a-minute gesture.

"This is something we're going to have to revisit," he said. "I've got a lot of respect for you and your position, and I'm sure we can find a way to get this done right."

Her expression made it clear she didn't see anything wrong.

"I'll be in touch," Bull said, and dropped the connection. So much for the pleasant part of his day. Ashford pulled himself through the door, coming to rest against the wall nearest the foot of Bull's bed. He looked angry, but it was a different kind of angry. Bull was used to seeing Ashford cautious, even tentative. This man wasn't either. Everything about him spoke of barely restrained rage. *Grief makes people crazy*, Bull thought. Grief and guilt and embarrassment all together maybe did worse.

Maybe it broke people.

Pa floated in behind him, her eyes cast down. Her face had the odd waxy look that came from exhaustion. The doctor followed her, and then Serge and Macondo looking anyplace but at him. The crowd filled the little room past its capacity.

"Mister Baca," Ashford said, biting at each syllable. "I understand you gave the order to disarm the ship. Is that true?"

"Disarm the ship?" Bull said, and looked at Doctor Sterling. Her gaze was straight on and unreadable. "I had Sam take the rail guns off so we could spin up the drum."

"And you did this without my permission."

"Permission for what?"

Blood darkened Ashford's face, and rage roughened his voice.

"The rail guns are a central component of this ship's defensive capabilities."

"Not if they don't work," Bull said. "I had her take apart the thrust-gravity water reclamation system too. Rebuild it at ninety degrees so it'll use the spin. You want me to run through all the stuff I'm having her repurpose because it doesn't work anymore, or are we just caring about the guns?"

"I also understand that you have authorized non-OPA personnel to have access to the communications channels of the ship? Earthers. Martians. All the people we came out here to keep in line."

"Is that why we came out here?" Bull said. It wasn't a denial, and that seemed to be close enough to a confession for Ashford. Besides which, it wasn't like Bull had been hiding it.

"And enemy military personnel? You're bringing them aboard my ship as well?"

Pa had agreed to everything Ashford was listing off. But she stood behind the captain, not speaking up, expression unreadable. Bull wasn't sure what was going on between the captain and his XO, but if they were working out some internal power struggle, Bull knew which side he'd want to end up on. So he bit the bullet and didn't mention Pa's involvement. "Yes, I'm bringing in everyone I can get. Humanitarian outreach and consolidation of control. It's textbook. A second-year would know to do it." Pa winced at that.

"Mister Baca, you have exceeded your authority. You have ignored the chain of command. All orders given by you, all permissions granted by you, are hereby revoked. I am relieving you of duty and instructing that you be placed in a medical coma until such time as you can be evacuated."

"Like fuck you are," Bull said. He hadn't intended to, but the words came out like a reflex. They seemed to float in the air between them, and Bull discovered that he'd meant them.

"This isn't open for debate," Ashford said coldly.

"Damn right it's not," Bull said. "The reason you're in charge of this mission and not me is that Fred Johnson didn't think the crew would be comfortable with an Earther running a Belter ship. You got the job because you kissed all the right political asses. You know what? Good for you. Hope your career takes off like a fucking rocket. Pa's here for the same reason. She's got the right-sized head, though at least hers doesn't seem to be empty."

"That's a racist insult," Ashford said, trying to interrupt, "and I won't have—"

"I'm here because they needed someone who could get the

job done and they knew we were screwed. And you know what? We're still screwed. But I'm going to get us out of here, and I'm going to keep Fred from being embarrassed by what we did here, and you are going to stay out of my way while I do it, you pinche motherfucker."

"That's enough, Mister Baca. I will—"

"You know it's true," Bull said, shifting to face Pa. Her expression was closed, empty. "If he's in charge of this, he's going to get it wrong. You've seen it. You know—"

"You will stop addressing the XO, Mister Baca."

"—what kind of decisions he makes. He'll send them back to their ships, even if it means people die because—"

"You are *relieved*. You will be—"

"—he wasn't the one that invited them. It's going to—"

"—quiet. I do not give you permission—"

"—make all of this more dangerous, and if someone—"

"—to speak to my staff. You will be—"

"—else pisses that thing off, we could all—"

"—*quiet!*" Ashford shouted, and he pushed forward, his mouth in a square gape of rage. He hit the medical bed too hard, pressing into Bull, grabbing him by the shoulder and shaking him hard enough to snap his teeth shut. "I told you to *shut up*!"

The restraints opened under Ashford's attack, the Velcro ripping. Pain lanced through Bull's neck like someone was pushing a screwdriver into his back. He tried to push the captain away, but there was nothing to grab hold of. His knuckles cracked against something hard: the table, the wall, something else. He couldn't say what. People around him were shouting. His balance felt profoundly wrong, the dead weight of his body flowing limp and useless in the empty air, but tugged at by the tubes and the catheters.

When the world made sense again, he was at a forty-degree angle above the table, his head pointing down. Pa and Macondo were gripping Ashford's arms, the captain's hands bent into claws. Serge was bunched against the wall, ready to launch but not sure what direction he should go.

Doctor Sterling appeared at his side, gathering his legs and drawing him quickly and professionally back toward the bed.

"Could we please not assault the patient with the crushed spinal cord," she said as she did, "because this makes me very uncomfortable."

Another vicious flare of pain, hot and sharp and evil, ran through Bull's neck and upper back as she strapped him down. One of the tubes was floating free, blood and a bit of flesh adhering to its end. He didn't know what part of his body it had come out of. Pa was looking at him, and he kept his voice calm.

"We've already screwed up twice. We came through the Ring, and we let soldiers go on the station. We won't get a third. We can get everyone together, and we can get them out of here."

"That's dangerous talk, mister," Ashford spat.

"I can't be captain," Bull said. "Even if I wasn't stuck in this bed, I'm an Earther. There has to be a Belter in charge. Fred was right about that."

Ashford pulled his arms free of Pa and Macondo, plucked his sleeves back into trim, and steadied himself against the wall.

"Doctor, place Mister Baca in a medical coma. That is a direct order."

"Serge," Bull said. "I need you to take Captain Ashford into custody, and I need you to do it now."

No one moved. Serge scratched his neck, the sounds of fingernails against stubble louder than anything in the room. Pa's gaze locked in the middle distance, her face sour and angry. Ashford's eyes narrowed, cutting over toward her. When she spoke, her voice was dead and joyless.

"Serge. You heard what the chief said."

Ashford gathered himself to launch for Pa, but Serge already had a restraining hand on the captain's shoulder.

"This is mutiny," Ashford said. "There'll be a reckoning for this."

"You need to come with us now," Serge said. Macondo took Ashford's other arm and put it in an escort hold, and the three of them left together. Pa stayed against the wall, held steady by a strap, while the doctor, tutting and muttering under her breath, replaced the catheters and checked the monitors and tubes attached to his skin. For the most part, he didn't feel it.

When she was done, the doctor left the room. The door slid closed behind her. For almost a minute, neither of them spoke.

"Guess your opinion on mutiny changed," Bull said.

"Apparently," Pa said, and sighed. "He's not thinking straight. And he's drinking too much."

"He made the decision that brought us all here. He can sign his name to all the corpses on all those ships."

"I don't think he sees it that way," Pa said. And then, "But I think he's putting a *lot* of effort into not seeing it that way. And he's slipping. I don't think... I don't think he's well."

"It'd be easier if he had an accident," Bull said.

Pa managed a smile. "I haven't changed *that* much, Mister Baca."

"Didn't figure. But I had to say it," he said.

"Let's focus on getting everyone safe, and then getting everyone home," she said. "It was a nice career while it lasted. I'm sorry it's ending this way."

"Maybe it is," Bull said. "But did you come out here to win medals or to do the right thing?"

Pa's smile was thin.

"I'd hoped for both," she said.

"Nothing wrong with a little optimism, long as it doesn't set policy," he said. "I'm going to keep on getting everyone on the *Behemoth*."

"No weapons but ours," she said. "We keep taking all comers, but not if it means having an armed force on the ship."

"Already done," Bull said.

Pa closed her eyes. It was easy to forget how much younger than him she was. This wasn't her first tour, but it could have been her second. Bull tried to imagine what he'd have felt like, still half a kid, throwing his commanding officer into the brig. Scared as hell, probably.

"You did the right thing," he said.

"You'd have to say that. I backed your play."

Bull nodded. "I did the right thing. Thank you for supporting me, Captain. Please know that I'll be returning that favor as long as you sit in the big chair."

"We aren't friends," she said

"Don't have to be, so long as we get the job done."

Chapter Thirty: Holden

The marines weren't gentle, but they were professional. Holden had seen Martian powered armor used by a recon marine before. As they moved back through the caverns and tunnels of the station, Holden in thick foam restraints slung across one soldier's back like a piece of equipment, he was aware of how much danger he was in. The men and women in the suits had just watched one of their own be killed and eaten by an alien, they were deep within territory as threatening and unfamiliar as anything he could imagine, and the odds were better than even that they were all blaming him for it. That he wasn't dead already spoke to discipline, training, and a professionalism he would have respected even if his life hadn't depended on it.

Whatever frequencies they were speaking on he didn't have access to, so the furtive journey from the display chamber or whatever it had been back to the surface all happened in eerie silence as far as he was concerned. He kept hoping to catch a glimpse of Miller. Instead, they passed by the insectile machines, now as still as statues, and over the complex turf. He thought he could see something like a pattern in the waves and ripples that passed along the walls and floor, complicated and beautiful as raindrops falling on the surface of a lake, or music. It didn't comfort him.

He tried to get through to the *Rocinante*, to Naomi, but the marine he was strapped to had either disabled his suit radio when they were restraining him or something had jammed the signal. One way or another, he couldn't get anything. Not from the *Roci*, not from the marines, not from anywhere. There was only the gentle loping and an almost unbearable dread.

His suit gave him a low air warning.

He didn't have any sense of where they were or how far they'd gone. The surface of the station might be through the next tunnel or they might not have reached the halfway point. Or, for that matter, the station could be changing around them, and the way they'd come in might not exist. The suit said he had another twenty minutes.

"Hey!" he shouted. He tried to swing his legs against the armor of the person carrying him. "Hey! I'm going to need air!"

The marine didn't respond. No matter how hard Holden tried to thrash, his strength and leverage were a rounding error compared to the abilities of the powered armor. All he could do was hope that he wasn't about to die from an oversight. Worrying about that was actually better than wondering about Naomi and Alex and Amos.

The air gauge was down to three minutes and Holden had shouted himself hoarse when the marine carrying him crouched slightly, hopped up, and the station fell away beneath them. The luminescent surface irised closed behind them, automatic and unthinking. The skiff hung in the vacuum not more than five hundred meters away, its exterior lights making it the brightest thing in the eerie starless sky. They found their way into the mass airlock quickly. Holden's suit was blaring its emergency, the carbon dioxide levels crept up toward the critical level, and he had to fight to catch his breath.

The marine flipped him into a wall-mounted holding bar and strapped him in.

"I'm out of air!" Holden screamed. "Please!"

The marine reached out and cracked the seal on Holden's suit. The rush of air smelled like old plastic and poorly recycled urine. Holden sucked it in like it was roses. The marine popped off his own helmet. His real head looked perversely small in the bulk of the combat armor.

"Sergeant Verbinski!" a woman's voice snapped.

"Yes, sir," the marine who'd been carrying him said.

"There something wrong with the prisoner?"

"He ran out of air a few minutes back."

The woman grunted. Nothing more was said about it.

The acceleration burn, when it came, was almost subliminal. A tiny sensation of weight settling Holden into his suit, gone as soon as it came. The marines murmured among themselves and ignored him. It was all the confirmation he needed. What Miller had said was true. The slow zone's top speed had changed again. And from the expressions on their faces, he guessed that the casualties had been terrible.

"I need to check in with my ship," he said. "Can someone contact the *Rocinante*, please?" No one answered him. He pressed his luck. "My crew may be hurt. If we could just—"

"Someone shut the prisoner up," the woman who'd spoken before said. He still couldn't see her. The nearest marine, a thick-jawed man with skin so black it seemed blue turned toward him. Holden braced himself for a threat or violence.

"There's nothing you could do," the man said. "Please be quiet now."

His cell in the brig of the *Hammurabi* was a little over a meter and a half wide and three meters deep. The crash couch was a dirty blue and the walls and floor a uniform white that gleamed in the harsh light of the overhead LED. The jumpsuit he'd been issued felt like thick paper and crackled when he moved. When the guards came for him, they didn't bother putting the restraints back on his arms and legs.

The captain floated near a desk, her close-cropped silver hair making her look like an ancient Roman emperor. Holden was strapped into a crash couch that was canted slightly forward, so that he had to look up at her, even without the convenience of an up.

"I am Captain Jakande," she said. "You are a military prisoner. Do you understand what that means?"

"I was in the navy," Holden said. "I understand."

"Good. That'll cut about half an hour of legal bullshit."

"I'll happily tell you everything I know," Holden said. "No need for the rough stuff."

The captain smiled like winter.

"If you were anyone else, I'd think that was a figure of speech," she said. "What is your relationship to the structure at the center of the slow zone? What were you doing there?"

He had spent so many months trying not to talk about Miller, trying not to tell anyone anything. Except Naomi, and even then he'd felt guilty putting the burden of the mystery on her. On one hand, the chance to unburden himself pulled at him like gravity. On the other...

He took a deep breath.

"This is going to sound a little strange," he said.

"All right."

"Shortly after the protomolecule construct lifted off from Venus and headed out to start assembling the Ring? I was... contacted by Detective Josephus Miller. The one who rode Eros down onto Venus. Or at least something that looked and talked like him. He's shown up every few weeks since then, and I came to the conclusion that the protomolecule was using him. Well, him and Julie Mao, who was the first one to be infected, to drive me out through the Ring. I thought that they...it wanted me to come here."

The captain's expression didn't change. Holden felt a strange lump in his throat. He didn't want to be having this conversation here. He wanted to be talking with Naomi in their bedroom on the *Rocinante.* Or at a bar on Ceres. It didn't matter where. Only who.

Was she dead? Had the station killed her?

"Go on," the captain said.

"Apparently I was mistaken," Holden said.

He began with the journey out, with the protomolecule's vision of Miller waiting for him at the station. The attack by her marine, and the consequences as Miller explained them. The visions of the vast empire and the darkness that flowed over it, the death of suns. He relaxed as he went along, the words coming easier, faster. He sounded insane even to himself. Visions no one else could see. Vast secrets revealed only to him.

Except it had all been a mistake.

He'd thought he was important. That he was special and chosen, and that what had happened to him and his crew had been dictated by a vast and mysterious power. He'd misunderstood everything. *Doors and corners*, Miller had said, and because he hadn't puzzled out what the dead man meant by it, they'd all come through the Ring. And to the station. His relief and his growing self-disgust mingled with every phrase. He'd been a fool dancing at the edge of the cliff, because he'd been sure that he couldn't fall. Not him.

"And then I was here, talking to you," he said dryly. "I don't know what happens next."

"All right," she said. Her expression gave away nothing.

"You'll want a full medical workup to see if there's anything organically wrong with my brain," Holden said.

"Probably," the captain said. "My medical staff has its hands full at the moment. You will be kept in administrative detention for the time being."

"I understand," Holden said. "But I need to get in contact with my crew. You can monitor the connection. I don't care. I just need to know they're okay."

The angle of the captain's mouth asked why he thought they were.

"I'll try to get a report to you," she said. "Everyone's scrambling right now, and the situation could get worse quickly."

"Is it bad, then?"

"It is."

Time in his cell passed slowly. A guard brought tubes of rations: protein, oil, water, and vegetable paste. Sometimes it had a nearly homeopathic dose of curry. It was food meant to keep you alive. Everything after that was your own problem. Holden ate it because he had to stay alive. He had to find his crew, his ship. He had to get out of there.

He had seen a massive alien empire fall. He'd seen suns blown apart. He'd watched a man overwhelmed and slaughtered by nightmare mechanisms on a space station that human hands hadn't built. All he could think about was Naomi and Amos and Alex. How they were going to keep their ship. How they were going to get home. And home meant anyplace but here. Not for the first time, he wished they were all transporting sketchy boxes of unknown cargo to Titania. He floated in the coffin-sized cell and tried not to go crazy from the toxic combination of inaction and mind-bending fear.

Even if the whole crew was well, he was in custody of Mars now. He hadn't harmed the *Seung Un*, and everyone would know that. He hadn't made the false broadcast. All the things they were accusing him of could fall away, and there would still be the fact that Mars would take away his ship. He tried to focus on that despair, because as bad as it would be, if he kept the ship and lost his crew, that would feel worse.

"You've got lousy taste in friends," Miller said.

"Where the hell have you been?" Holden snapped.

The dead man shrugged. In the cramped quarters, Holden could smell the man's breath. A firefly flicker of blue sped around Miller's head like a low-slung halo and vanished.

"Time's hard," he said, as if the comment carried its own context. "Anyway, we were talking about something."

"The station. The lockdown."

"Right," Miller said, nodding. He plucked off his ridiculous hat and scratched his temple. "That. So the thing is, as long as there's a shitload of high energy floating around, the station's not going to get comfortable. You guys have, what? Twenty big ships?"

"About that, I guess."

"They've all got fusion reactions. They've all got massive internal power grids. Not a big deal by themselves, but the station's been spooked a couple times. It's jumpy. You're going to have to give it a little massage. Show that you're not a threat. Do that, and I'm pretty sure I can get you moving again. That or it'll break you all down to your component atoms."

"It'll what?"

Miller's smile was apologetic.

"Sorry," he said. "Joke. Just get the reactors off-line and the internal grids off. It'll get you below threshold, and I can take it from there. I mean, if that's what you decide you want to do."

"What do you mean, *if*?"

Holden shifted. The ceiling brushed against his shoulders. He couldn't stretch in here. There wasn't room for two people.

There wasn't room for two people.

For a fraction of a second, his brain tried to fit two images—Miller floating beside him and the too-small cell—together and failed. The flesh on his back felt like there were insects crawling all over it. The two things couldn't both be true, and his brain shuddered and recoiled from the fact that they were. Miller coughed.

"Don't do that," he said. "This is hard enough the way it is.

What I mean by *if* is that lockdown's lockdown. I don't get to pick what part of the trap gets unsprung. If I take off the dampening and you all start burning for home or shooting at each other or whatever, that means I also open the gates. All of them."

"Including the ones with the burned-up stars?"

"No," Miller said. "Those gates are gone. Only real star systems on the other side of the ones that are left."

"Is that a problem?"

"Depends on what comes through," Miller said. "That's a lot of doors to kick down all at once." The only sound was the hiss of the air recyclers. Miller nodded as if Holden had said something. "The other option is figure out a way to sneak back home with your tails between your legs and try and pretend this all never happened."

"You think we should do that?"

"I think there was an empire once that touched thousands of stars. The Eros bug? That's one of their tools. It's a wrench. And something was big enough to put a bullet in *them*. Whatever it is could be waiting behind one of those gates, waiting for someone to do something stupid. So maybe you'd rather set up shop here. Make little doomed babies. Live and die in the darkness. But at least whatever's out there stays out there."

Holden put his hand on the crash couch to steady himself. His heart was beating a mile a minute, and his hands were clammy and pale. He felt like he might throw up, and wondered whether he could get the vacuum commode working in time. In his memory, stars died.

"You think that's what we should do?" he asked. "Be quiet and get the hell out of here?"

"No, I want to open 'em. I've learned everything I can get from here, especially in lockdown. I want to figure out what happened, and that means going and taking a look at the scene."

"You're the machine that finds things."

"Yes," Miller said. "Consider the source, right? You might

want to talk about it with someone who's not dead. You people have more to lose than I do."

Holden thought for a moment, then smiled. Then laughed.

"I'm not sure it matters. I'm not in much of a position to set policy," he said.

"That's true," Miller said. "Nothing personal, but you've got lousy taste in friends."

Chapter Thirty-One: Melba

She was in her prison cell when they spun up the drum. In its previous life, the cell had been some sort of veterinary ward for large animals. Horses, maybe. Or cows. A dozen stalls, six to a side, with brushed steel walls and bars. Real bars, just like all the old videos, except with a little swinging door at the top where they could shovel in hay. Everything else was antiseptic white. Everything was locked. Her clothes were gone, replaced by a simple pale pink jumpsuit. Her hand terminal was gone. She didn't miss it. She floated in the center of the space, the walls just out of reach of her fingers and toes. It had taken a dozen attempts, reaching the wall and pushing back more and more gently, to find just the right thrust for the air resistance to stop her out where nothing could touch or be touched. Where she could float and be trapped by floating.

The man in the other cell bounced off his walls. He laughed

and he shouted, but mostly he sulked. She ignored him. He was easy to ignore. The air surrounding her had a slight breeze, the way everything did in a ship. She'd heard a story once on the way out about a ship whose circulation failed in the middle of a night shift. The whole crew had died from the zone of exhausted gas that bubbled around them, drowning in their own recycled air. She didn't think the story was true, because they would have woken up. They would have gasped and thrashed around and gotten up out of their couches, and so they would have lived. People who wanted to live did that. People who wanted to die, on the other hand, just floated.

The Klaxons sounded through the whole ship, the blatting tone resonating through the decks, taking on a voice like a vast trumpet. First, a warning. Then another. Then another. Then, silently, the bars retreated from her, falling away, and the back wall touched her shoulder like it wanted her attention but hesitated to ask. Inch by inch, her skin came to rest against the wall. For almost half a minute, the wall touched her, its energy and her inertia pressing them together like praying hands. The drum's acceleration was invisible to her. She only felt the spin sweeping her forward, and then because forward, down. Her body slid inch by inch, moving down the wall toward the deck. Her body began to take on weight; the joints in her knees and spine shifting, bearing load. She remembered reading somewhere that a woman coming back from a long time at null g could have grown almost two inches just from the disks in her spine never having the fluid pushed out of them. Between that and the muscle atrophy, coming back to weight—spin, thrust, or gravity—was the occasion for the most injury. Spinal disks were supposed to be pushed on, supposed to have the fluids go into them and back out. Without that, they turned into water balloons, and sometimes, they popped.

Her knee brushed the floor, then pressed into it. It had to have been an hour or more since the Klaxons. Up and down existed again, and she let down take her. She folded against herself, empty as damp paper. There was a drain in the floor, white ceramic unstained by any animal's blood or piss. The lights overhead flickered and grew steady again. The other prisoner was shouting for something. Food, maybe. Water. A guard to escort him to the head.

It was natural to think of it as the head now. Not the restroom. Not the water closet. She didn't call for anyone to help her, she just felt her body grow heavier, being pulled down. And because down, out. It wasn't real gravity, so it wasn't real weight. It was her mass trying to fly off into the dark and being restrained. Someone came for the other prisoner. She watched the thick plastic boots flicker across her line of sight. Then voices. Words like *loyal* and *mutiny*. Phrases like *When the time's right* and *Restore order*. They washed over her and she let them go. Her head hurt a little where her temple pushed against the floor. She wanted to sleep, but she was afraid to dream.

More footsteps, the same boots going the other way, passing her. More voices. The boots coming back. The deep metallic clank of the shackle being taken off the stall's door. Her body didn't move, but her attention focused. The guard was different. A woman with broad shoulders and a gun in her hand. She looked at Melba, shrugged, and put a hand terminal into her field of vision.

The man on the screen didn't look like a cop. His skin was pale brown, like cookie dough. There was something strange about the shape of his face—broad chin, dark eyes, wrinkles in his forehead and the corners of his mouth—that she couldn't place until he spoke and she saw him in motion. Then it was clear he was lying down and looking up at the camera.

"My name's Carlos Baca," the lying-down man said. "I'm in charge of security on the *Behemoth*. So this prison you're in? It's mine."

All right, Melba thought.

"You, now. I'm thinking you got a story to tell. The UN records of your DNA says you're Melba Koh. A bunch of people I've got no reason to disbelieve say you're Clarissa Mao. The XO of the *Rocinante* says you tried to kill her, and this Russian priest lady's backing her story. And then there's this sound engineer who says you hired him to place interruption electronics on the *Rocinante*." He went quiet for a moment. "Any of that ringing a bell?"

The case on the hand terminal was green ceramic. Or maybe enameled metal. Not plastic. A hairline scratch in the screen made an extra mark across the man's cheek, like a pirate's dueling scar in a kid's book.

"All right, how about this," he said. "Doctor says you've got a modified endocrine bundle. The kind of things terrorists use when they need to do something showy and hard to detect. And, you know, they don't give a shit if it turns their nervous system into soup in a few years. Not the kind of thing a maintenance tech could afford. Or have much reason to get."

It felt strange, the weight of her head pressing against the floor and looking down from the camera into the man's face both at the same time. Partly, she supposed that was from being weightless for so long. Her brain was still getting used to the spin gravity after relying on visual clues, and now here was this anomalous visual cue. She knew intellectually what it was, but the special analysis part of her brain still gnawed at it.

The man on the screen—he'd said his name, but she didn't remember it—pressed his lips together, then coughed once. It was a wet sound, like he was fighting off pneumonia.

"I don't think you understand how much trouble you're in," he said. "There's people accusing you of blowing up an Earth military vessel, and the case they're building is pretty goddamn good. You can take it from me, the UN has no sense of humor about that kind of thing. They will kill you. You understand that? They'll put you in front of a military tribunal, listen to a couple lawyers for maybe fifteen, twenty minutes. Then they'll blow your brains out. I can help you avoid that, but you have to talk to me.

"You know what I think? I don't think you're a professional. I think you're an amateur. You made a bunch of amateur mistakes, and things got away from you. You tell me if I'm right, and we'll go from there. But you keep playing this catatonia shit, and you're going to get killed. Do you understand what I'm saying?"

He had a good voice. It had what her singing coach would have called a thorough range. Deep as gravel, but with reedy overtones. It was the kind of voice she'd expect in a man who'd been well bruised by the world. Her singing voice had always been a little reedy too, like her father's. Petyr, poor thing, had never been able to hold a melody. The others—Michael, Anthea, Julie, Mother—had all had very pure voices. Like flutes. The problem with a flute was that it couldn't help being pure. Even sorrow sounded posed and over-lovely when the flute was expressing it. Reeds had that deeper buzz, that dirtiness, and it gave the sound authenticity. She and her father were reeds.

"Corin?" the man on the screen said. "Does she understand what I'm saying?"

The woman with the gun picked up the hand terminal, looked down at Melba, and then into the screen.

"I don't think so, chief."

"The doctor said there wasn't any brain damage."

"Did," the woman agreed. "That don't make her right, though."

The sigh carried.

"Okay," the man's voice said. "We're going to have to go from a different angle. I got an idea, but you should come back in first."

"Sa sa," the woman said. She stepped out of the cell. The bars closed again. They were narrow enough to keep a horse's hoof from passing through. She could imagine a horse trying to kick, getting its leg stuck, panicking. That would be bad. Better to avoid the problem. Wiser. Easier to stay out than to get out. Someone had said that to her once, but she didn't know who.

"Hey. Hey," the other prisoner said. He wasn't shouting, just talking loud enough that his voice carried. "Was that true? You have glandular implants? Can you break the door? I'm the captain of this ship. If you can get me out of here, I can help you."

Julie had been the best singer, except that she wouldn't do it. Didn't like performing. Father had been the performer. He'd always been the one to lead when there were songs to be sung. He was always the one to direct the poses when the family pictures were taken. He was a man who knew what he wanted and how to get it. Only he was in prison now. Not even a name, only a number. She wondered whether his cell was like hers. It would be nice if it was. Only his would be under a full g, of course. The spin gravity wasn't even up to a half g. Maybe a third, maybe even less. Like Mars or Ceres. Funny that of all the places humans lived, the Earth was always the highest gravity. It was like if you could escape from home, you could escape from anything.

"Are you there? Are you awake? I saw them bring you in. Help me, and I'll help you. Amnesty. I can get you amnesty. And protection. They can't extradite from Ceres."

That wasn't true, and she knew it. Annoyance almost moved her to speak. Moved her to *move*. But not quite. The floor was a single sheet of polymer plating, formed to slant down to the drain. With her head against the floor like this, the drain was hardly more than a black line in a field of white. A crow on a frozen lake.

"I have been taken prisoner in an illegal mutiny," the man said. "We can help each other."

She wasn't entirely sure that she could be helped. Or if she could, what she would be helped to do. She remembered wanting something once. Holden. That was right. She'd wanted him dead and worse than dead. Her fantasies of it were so strong, they were like memories. But no, she *had* done it. Everyone had hated him. They'd tried to kill him. But something else had gone wrong, and they'd thought that Julie did it.

She'd been so close. If she could have killed the *Rocinante*, they would never have found her. If she'd died on it, they'd never have been sure, and Holden would have gone down in history as the smug, self-righteous bastard that he was. But her father would have known. All that way away, he'd have heard what happened, and he would have guessed that she'd done it. His daughter. The one he could finally be proud of.

It occurred to her that the other prisoner had gone quiet. That was fine. He was annoying. Her knees ached. Her temple hurt where it pressed against the floor. They called bedsores pressure sores. She wondered how long it took for skin to macerate just from not moving. Probably a pretty long time, and she was basically healthy. She wondered how long it had been since she'd moved. It had been a long time. She found she was oddly proud of that.

The footsteps came again. More of them, this time. The plastic boots made a satisfying *clump-clump*, but there were other ones now. High, clicking footsteps, like a dog's claws on tile. She felt a tiny flicker of curiosity, like a candle in a cathedral. The boots came, and with them, little blue pumps. An older woman's ankles. The bars clanked and swung open. The pumps hesitated at the threshold, and then came in. Once they were in motion, the steps were confident. Sure.

The woman in the pumps sat, her back against the wall. Tilly Fagan looked down at her. Her hair was dyed, and her lipstick the same improbable red that made her lips look fuller than they were.

"Claire, honey?" The words were soft and uncomfortable. "It's me."

Tension crawled up her back and into her cheeks. Tension, and resentment at the tension. Aunt Tilly didn't have any right to be here. She shouldn't have been.

Tilly put a hand out, reaching down and stroking her head like it was a cat. The first human touch she could remember since she'd come to. The first gentle one she could remember at all. When Tilly spoke, her voice was low and soft and full of regret.

"They found your friend."

I don't have a friend, she thought, and then something deep under her sternum shifted and went hollow. Ren. They'd found Ren. She pulled her arm out from under her body, pressed the back of her hand against her mouth. The tears were warm and unwelcome and thick as a flood. They'd found Ren. They'd opened her tool chest and found his bones and now Soledad would know. And Bob and Stanni. They'd know what she'd done. The first sob was like a cough, and then the one after it and the one after, and Tilly's arms were around her. And God help her, she was screaming and crying into Tilly Fagan's thighs while the woman stroked her hair and made little hushing sounds.

"I'm *sorry*," she shrieked. The words ripped at her throat. They had hooks on them. "I'm *sorry*. I'm *sorry*."

"I know, honey. I know."

She had her arms around Tilly's waist now, burying her face against her side, holding on to her like Tilly's body could keep her from sinking down. From drowning. The guard said something, and she felt Tilly shaking her head no, the motion translated through their bodies.

"I did it," she said. "I killed him. I thought I had to. I told him to look at the readout so that he'd bend, so that he'd bend his neck, and he *did*. And I—and I—and I— Oh, God, I'm going to puke."

"Trashy people puke," Tilly said. "Ladies are *unwell*."

It made her laugh. Despite everything, Clarissa laughed, and then she put her head down again and cried. Her chest hurt so badly she was sure something really was breaking. Aortic aneurysm, pulmonary embolism, something. Sorrow couldn't really feel like a heart breaking, could it? That was just a phrase.

It went on forever. And then past that, and then it slowed. Her body was as limp as a rag. Tilly's blouse was soaked with tears and snot and saliva, but she was still sitting just as she'd been. Her hand still ran through Clarissa's hair. Her fingernails traced the curve of her ear.

"You put the bomb on the *Seung Un*," Tilly said, "and framed Jim Holden for it."

It wasn't a question or an accusation. She didn't want Clarissa to confess, just to confirm. Clarissa nodded against Tilly's lap. When she spoke, her voice clicked and her throat felt thick and raw.

"He hurt Daddy. Had to do something."

Tilly sighed.

"Your father is a first-class shit," she said, and because it was her saying it, it didn't hurt to hear.

"I've got to tell the chief," the guard said, apology in her voice. "I mean about what happened. He wants me to report in."

"I'm not stopping you," Tilly said.

"You need to come with me," the guard said. "I can't leave you there with her. It's not safe."

A flash of panic lit her mind. She couldn't be alone. Not now. They couldn't leave her locked up and alone.

"Don't be ridiculous," Tilly said. "You go do whatever it is you need to do. I'll be here with Claire."

"Ah. That girl killed a lot of people, ma'am."

The silence was just a beat, and without shifting her head, Clarissa knew what look was on Tilly's face. The guard cleared her throat.

"I'll have to lock the door, ma'am."

"Do what you need to, Officer," Tilly said.

The bars shifted and crashed. The lock clacked home. The footsteps retreated. Clarissa wept for Ren. Maybe the others would come later. The dead soldiers on the *Seung Un*. Holden's lover whom she'd beaten and brutalized. All the men and women who'd died because they'd followed Holden through the Ring. She might have tears for them, but now it was only Ren, and she didn't think she would stop in her lifetime.

"I deserve to die," she said. "I've become a very bad person."

Tilly didn't disagree, but she didn't stop cradling her either.

"There's someone I'd like you to talk to," she said.

Chapter Thirty-Two: Anna

The security force had come first, three soldiers in a shuttle with guns and restraints for Melba. Or Clarissa. Whoever she was. Then, much later, a medical evacuation had come, taking the *Rocinante*'s crew.

Anna's own ride arrived almost a day later, not an afterthought, but not a priority. The way things had all come about, she thought not being a priority was probably a sign things were going well for her.

When she arrived on the *Behemoth*, she had expected to see someone from that ship's security team. Or, if they were well enough, maybe Naomi and the other two crewmen from the *Rocinante*.

Hector Cortez stood in the shuttle bay. He smiled when he saw her and raised his hand in a little wave of greeting. The motion reminded her of her grandfather in his failing days: careful and a little awkward. She thought Cortez had aged a decade in a few days, then realized he must have been injured in the catastrophe.

"Anna," he said. "I am so glad to see you."

The *Behemoth*'s massive drum section was spinning now, creating a vertigo-inducing false gravity. Anna's feet told her that she was standing on solid ground. Her inner ear argued that she was falling over sideways, and kept trying to get her to tilt her body the other direction. It wasn't enough to make her steps unsteady, but it did make everything feel a little surreal. Having Hector Cortez, celebrity and minister to the powerful, kiss her cheek didn't make things any less dreamlike.

"It's good to see you too," she said. "I didn't know you were on the *Behemoth*."

"We've all come," he said. "They've left the smallest of crews on the *Thomas Prince*, and we've all come here. All of us that are left. We've lost so many. I attended services yesterday for the fallen. Father Michel. Rabbi Black. Paolo Sedon."

Anna felt a little twinge of dread.

"Alonzo Guzman?"

Cortez shook his head.

"Neither alive nor dead," he said. "They have him in a medical coma, but he's not expected to survive."

Anna remembered the man's pleading eyes. If she'd only found help for him sooner...

"I'm sorry to have missed that service," she said.

"I know," Cortez said. "It's why I wanted to meet you. May I walk with you?"

"Of course," Anna said. "But I don't know where I'm going."

"Then I will give you the basic orientation," the old man said, turning a degree and sweeping his hand toward the shuttle bay. "Come with me, and I will bring you to the glory of the lift system."

Anna chuckled and let him lead the way. He walked carefully too. Not mincing, but not striding. He seemed like a different person than the one who'd called the three factions of humanity together to pass through the Ring and into the unknown. It was more than just how he held his body too.

"I thought it was important that those of us who were part of the petition speak at the service," he said. "I wanted our regret to have a voice."

"Our regret?"

He nodded.

"Yours. Mine. All of us who advised that we come to this darkness. It was hubris, and the innocent have suffered because of it. Died for listening to our bad advice. God has humbled me."

His voice still had the richness of a lifetime's practice, but there was a new note in it. A high, childlike whine underneath the grandeur. Sympathy for his distress and an uncharitable annoyance sprang up in her.

"I don't know that I see it that way," she said. "We didn't come here to glorify ourselves. We did it to keep people from fighting. To remind ourselves and each other that we're all together in this. I can't think that's an evil impulse. And I can't see what happened to us as punishment. Time and chance—"

"Befall all men," Hector said. "Yes."

Behind them, a shuttle's attitude rocket roared for a moment, then cut off. A pair of Belters in gray jumpsuits sauntered toward it, toolboxes in their hands. Cortez was scowling.

"But even given what grew from that seed? You still don't think we were punished? The decision was not made out of arrogance?"

"History is made up of people recovering from the last disaster," Anna said. "What happened was terrible. *Is* terrible. But I still can't see God's punishment in it."

"I do," Cortez said. "I believe we have fallen into a realm of evil. And more, Doctor Volovodov, I fear we have been tainted by it."

"I don't see—"

"The devil is here," Cortez said. He shook his head at Anna's protesting frown. "Not some cartoon demon. I'm not a fool. But the devil has always lived in men when they reach too far, when they fail to ask if they *should* do something just because they *can* do it. We have— *I* have fallen into his trap. And worse, we have blazed the trail to him. History will not remember us kindly for what we have done."

Anna knew quite a few members of the Latter-day Saints church. They agreed with the Methodists on a few minor things like not drinking alcohol, which gave them a sense of solidarity at interfaith conventions. They disagreed on some important things, like the nature of God and His plan for the universe, which didn't seem to matter as much as Anna would have thought. They tended to be happy, family-oriented, and unassuming.

Standing in the belly of the *Behemoth*, Anna would never have guessed they would build something like the massive generation ship. It was so big, so extravagant. It was like a rebellious shout at the emptiness of space. *The universe is too big for our ship to move through it in a reasonable time? Fine, we'll stuff all the bits of the universe we need inside of our ship and then go at our own pace.* The inner walls of the rotating drum curved up in the distance, Coriolis effect masquerading as mass, metal ribbing and plates pretending to be substrate, just waiting for soil and plants and farm animals. Through the center of the drum, half a kilometer over Anna's head, a narrow thread of bright yellow light shone down on them all. The sun, stretched into a line in the sky. The entire idea of it was arrogant and defiant and grandiose.

Anna loved it.

As she walked across a wide empty plain of steel that should have been covered in topsoil and crops, she thought that this audaciousness was exactly what humanity had lost somewhere in the last couple of centuries. When ancient maritime explorers had climbed into their creaking wooden ships and tried to find ways to cross the great oceans of Earth, had their voyage been any less dangerous than the one the Mormons had been planning to attempt? The end point any less mysterious? But in both cases, they'd been driven to find out what was on the other side of the long trip. Driven by a need to see shores no one else had ever seen before. Show a human a closed door, and no matter how many open doors she finds, she'll be haunted by what might be behind it.

A few people liked to paint this drive as a weakness. A failing of the species. Humanity as the virus. The creature that never stops filling up its available living space. Hector seemed to be moving over to that view, based on their last conversation. But Anna rejected that idea. If humanity were capable of being satisfied, then they'd all still be living in trees and eating bugs out of one another's fur. Anna had walked on a moon of Jupiter. She'd looked up through a dome-covered sky at the great red spot, close enough to see the swirls and eddies of a storm larger than her home world. She'd tasted water thawed from ice as old as the solar system itself. And it was that human dissatisfaction, that human audacity, that had put her there.

Looking at the tiny world spinning around her, she knew one day it would give them the stars as well.

The refugee camp was a network of tents and prefabricated temporary structures set on the inner face of the drum, the long thin line of sun-bright light pressing down onto them all like a spring afternoon on Earth. It took her almost half an hour to find Chris Williams' tent. The liaison from the *Thomas Prince* let her know that the young naval officer had survived the catastrophe, but had suffered terrible injuries in the process. Anna wanted to find him, and maybe through him the rest of the little congregation she'd formed during the trip out.

A few questions of helpful refugees later, and she found his tent. There was no way to knock or buzz, so she just scratched at the tent flap and said, "Chris? You in there?"

"That you, Pastor? Come on in."

The liaison hadn't been specific in her descriptions of Chris' injuries, so Anna braced herself for the worst when she entered. The young lieutenant was lying in a military-style cot, propped up by a number of pillows. He had a small terminal on his lap that he set aside as she came in. His left arm and left leg both ended at the middle joint.

"Oh, Chris, I'm—"

"If your next word is 'sorry,' " he said, "I'm going to hop over there and kick your ass."

Anna started laughing even as the tears filled her eyes. "I am sorry, but now I'm sorry for being sorry." She sat by the edge of his cot and took his right hand. "How are you, Chris?"

"With a few obvious exceptions"—he waved his shortened left arm around—"I came through the disaster better than most. I didn't even have a bad bruise."

"I don't know how the navy health plan works," Anna started, but Chris waved her off.

"Full regrowth therapy. We ever get out of here and back to civilization, and a few painful and itchy months later I'll have bright pink replacements."

"Well, that's good," Anna said. She'd been about to offer to pay for his treatment, not knowing how she'd actually do that. She felt a moment of relief and shame. "Have you heard from anyone else who was in our group? I haven't had time to find them yet."

"Yeah," Chris said with a chuckle, "I heard. You've been doing commando raids while I've been laid up. If I'd known they trained you guys to take down souped-up terrorists, I'd have paid more attention in church as a kid."

"I ran away from her until she had a seizure, and then I taped her to a chair. Not very heroic."

"I'm getting a medal for falling into a pressure hatch, sacrificing an arm and a leg to keep seven sailors from being trapped in a compromised part of the ship. I was unconscious at the time, but that doesn't seem to matter. Heroism is a label most people get for doing shit they'd never do if they were really thinking about it."

Anna laughed at that. "I've been thinking a lot about that exact thing recently." Chris relaxed back into his pile of pillows and nodded for her to continue.

"Labels, I mean. People are calling the aliens evil, because they hurt us. And without context, how do we know?"

"Yeah," Chris said. "I lose a couple limbs getting drunk and falling into a harvesting combine, I'm an idiot. I lose the same limbs because I happened to be standing next to the right door when the ship was damaged, I'm a hero."

"Maybe it's as simple as that. I don't know. I feel like something really important is about to happen, and we're all making up our minds ahead of time what it will be."

Chris absentmindedly scratched at the stump of his left leg, then grimaced. "Like?"

"We came through the Ring to stop James Holden from talking to the aliens first. But this is the same man that helped send Eros to Venus instead of letting it destroy the Earth. Why did we assume he'd do a bad job of being the first human the aliens met? And now something has slapped us down, taken all our guns away, but not killed us. That should mean something. Certainly anything this powerful could kill us as easily as it declawed us. But it didn't. Instead of trying to figure out what it means, we're hurting so we call it evil. I feel like we're children who've been punished and we think it's because our parents are mean."

"They stopped our ships to... what? Pacify us?" Chris asked.

"Who knows?" Anna said, shrugging. "But I know we're not asking those questions. Humans do bad things when they're afraid, and we're all very afraid right now."

"Tara died," Chris said.

Anna racked her brain trying to remember who Tara was. Chris saw her confusion and added, "Short blond hair? She was a marine?"

"Oh no," Anna replied, feeling the tears well up again. Her angry marine had died. A whole future in which she'd worked with Tara to find out the source of her anger vanished. Conversations she'd already had in her head, lines of questioning, the anticipation of satisfaction she'd get from having the marine open up to her. Gone, as if someone had flicked a switch. It was hard not to sympathize with Cortez's view a little. After all, the aliens had killed one of her congregation now.

But maybe not on purpose, and intent mattered. The universe made no sense to her otherwise.

She managed to finish off her visit without, she hoped, seeming too distracted. Afterward, she went to find her own assigned tent and try to rest. She had no reason to think that sleep would come. After she found her place, Tilly Fagan appeared. Anna lifted her arm in greeting, but before she could get a word out, Tilly threw both arms around her and was squeezing until she could hear her ribs pop. Tilly was surprisingly strong for such a thin woman.

"I was furious with myself for letting you leave," Tilly said, squeezing even tighter and leaning her weight against Anna. She was heavy. They both were in the spinning drum. It took some getting used to.

When Tilly finally let up the pressure a bit, Anna said, "I think I was...altered."

"That was my fault, too," Tilly said, followed by more squeezing. Anna realized the only thing to do was ride it out, and patted Tilly on the lower back until her friend got it out of her system.

After a few moments, Tilly released Anna and stepped back, her eyes shiny but a smile on her face. "I'm glad you didn't die. Everyone else from the *Prince* is a pod." Anna decided not to ask what a pod was. "The *Behemoth* has become the place to be," Tilly continued. "If we never figure out how to escape this trap, it's the place it will take us the longest to die. That makes it the high-rent district of the slow zone."

"Well, that's...important."

Tilly laughed. She pulled a cigarette out and lit it as they walked. At Anna's shocked look she said, "They let you do it here. Lots of the Belters do. They obsess over air filters and then suck poisonous particulates into their lungs recreationally. It's a fabulous culture."

Anna smiled and waved the smoke away from her face.

"So," Tilly said, pretending not to notice. "I demanded they let me go on the first shuttle over. Did you manage to retrieve Holden?"

"I didn't find him," Anna said. "Just his crew. But I think I might have saved their lives."

At first, she thought Tilly's expression had cooled, but that wasn't quite right. It wasn't coldness. It was pain. Anna put her hand on Tilly's arm.

"I have someone I need you to talk to," Tilly said. "And you probably aren't going to like it, but you're going to do it for me. I'll never ask you for anything again, and you're buying a lifetime of expensive markers to trade in with this."

"Whatever I can do."

"You're going to help Claire."

Anna felt like the air had gone out of the room. For a moment, she heard the throat-scarring screams again and felt the blows transferred through the buckling locker door. She heard Chris tell her that Tara had died. She saw Cortez, and heard the buzzsaw despair in his voice. She took a breath.

"Yes," she said. "Of course I am."

Chapter Thirty-Three: Bull

"You need to get up," Doctor Sterling said. Spin changed the shape of her face, pulling down her cheeks and hair. She looked older and more familiar.

"I thought I wasn't supposed to move around," Bull said, and coughed.

"That was when I was worried about your spinal cord. Now I'm worried about your lungs. You're having enough trouble clearing secretions, I'm about ready to call it mild pneumonia."

"I'll be fine."

"Spin gravity's not going to do you much good if you're flat on your back," she said, tapping his shoulder for emphasis. "You have to sit up more."

Bull gritted his teeth.

"I can't sit up," he said. "I don't have abdominal muscles. I can't do *anything*."

"You have an adjustable bed," the doctor said, unfazed. "Adjust it. Stay upright as much as you can."

"Isn't that going to screw up my spine even worse?"

"We can brace you," she said. "Anyway, you can live without functioning legs. You can't live without functioning lungs."

The medical wards had changed. Spinning up the drum had meant stripping away as many of the alterations that had changed the generation ship into a weapon of war as they could. The medical stations and emergency showers had all been turned ninety degrees in the refit, prepared to use under thrust or not at all. What had been designed back in what seemed like ancient times to be floors had become walls, and now they were floors again. The whole thing was a hesitation. A stutter-step in industrial steel and ceramic. It was like something that had been broken and grew back wrong.

"I'll do what I can," Bull said, his teeth clenched against another cough. "If I've got to sit up, can I at least get something that travels a little? I'm getting pretty tired of being in the same room all the time."

"I don't recommend it."

"You gonna stop me?"

"I am not."

They paused. Frustration and animosity hung in the air between them. Neither one had slept enough. Both were pushing themselves too hard trying to keep people alive. And they weren't going to make each other happy.

"I'll do what I can, doc," Bull said. "How's it going out there?"

"People are dying. It's slowing down, though. At this point, almost all of the emergent cases are stabilized or dead. Right now it's pretty much the same for everyone. Wound care and support. Keep an eye out for people who had some sort of internal injury we didn't see at the time and try to catch them before they crash. Rest, fluid, light exercise, and prayer."

"All right," he said as his hand terminal chimed. Another connection request. From the *Hammurabi*, the Martian frigate where Captain Jim Holden was being held.

"And how's it going on your end?" Doctor Sterling said. Her lips were pressed thin. She knew the answer. Bull used the controls on his bed, shifting himself up to something approaching a seated position. He could feel a difference in his breath, but if anything it made it harder to keep from coughing.

"Let you know in a minute," he said and accepted the connection. Captain Jakande appeared on the screen.

"Captain," Bull said, making the title a greeting.

"Mister Baca," she said in return. "I got your last message."

"I don't suppose you're calling to arrange the transfer of the prisoner and your remaining crew?"

She didn't smile.

"I wanted to thank you for the staging area you've provided for our medical staff. We will not, however, be transferring any further personnel to your vessel or remanding the prisoner to your custody."

"You don't have a sufficient complement left on your ship to run it. Not even as a skeleton crew. Between the injured and the medics and the injured medics, I've got two-thirds of your people here right now."

"And I thank you for that."

"My point is you have a third or less of your crew left standing. You're pulling double, maybe triple shifts. Earth is still making noise about transferring Holden to them until he's answered charges for the *Seung Un*." He hadn't mentioned Clarissa Mao's confession. That was a card he could play another time. He lifted his hand. "All of us have watched someone we cared about die because of something we don't understand. All of us are grieving and scared. If we don't all come together, someone's going to do something we'll all regret."

"The Martian military code requires—"

"I've got an open investigation here. I'll share all the information we've gathered. Some of it's pretty damn interesting."

Something moved in his chest, and he was coughing so hard he couldn't speak or listen. Phlegm filled his mouth, and he leaned over, supporting himself with his arms, to spit it out. Maybe there was something to this sitting-up thing.

"The Martian military code prohibits the surrender of prisoners except in cases of trades authorized by the government. We can't talk to the MCR, so nothing's getting authorized."

"You could surrender to me."

She laughed that time. The façade of military propriety cracked.

"I wish. I'd be able get a full shift's sleep. But that tin can you're in couldn't take us, even if we *could* fight."

"Which we can't, so we're pretty much down to angry letters at twenty paces. I appreciate the call," he said. "I'll let the captain know it's no-go. But hey, lemme ask you. What are you guys gonna do when Earth sends a couple dozen marines with cutting torches and kitchen knives?"

"Fight with cutting torches and knives," she said. "This is the *Hammurabi* signing off."

Bull watched the dull standby screen for half a minute before he put it down. He'd have to tell Pa, but he wasn't looking forward to that. She had enough on her plate coordinating all the things he couldn't because he was trapped in the medical ward.

No matter what Holden's criminal status with Earth and Mars was, no matter how many people took the blame for the things he was accused of, it didn't matter. It was a pretext. He was the only person not covered by military treaty who could be debriefed about whatever was on the alien station. Earth wanted him. The OPA wanted him. Mars had him, and wouldn't give him up just for the joy of having something other people wanted.

And sooner or later some Martian with too much stress and not enough sleep who thought Holden was responsible for drawing them all through the Ring was going to take revenge for a lover or friend who'd died. Bull scratched at his neck, the stubble rough against his fingertips. His body, empty, splayed out before him in the one-third g.

"Bull?"

He looked up. The nurse seemed, if anything, more tired than the doctor had been.

"You've got a couple visitors, if you're up for it," he said.

"Depends. Who you got?"

"Priest," he said. It took a moment to realize it wasn't a name but a job description.

"The Russian from the *Rocinante*?"

The nurse shook his head. "The politician. Cortez."

"What does he want?"

"As far as I can tell? Save your soul. He's talking about protecting humanity from the devil. I think he wants you to help with that."

"Tell him to talk to Serge at the security office. Who else wants a piece of me?"

The nurse's expression changed. For a moment, Bull couldn't say what was strange about it, then he realized it was the first time in his memory he'd seen the nurse smile.

"Someone's got a little prezzie for you," the nurse said, then leaned back out into the corridor. "Okay. Come on in."

Bull coughed again, bringing up more phlegm. Sam appeared in the doorway, grinning. Behind her, two techs were carrying a blue plastic crate so big he could have put Sam inside it.

"Rosenberg? You been wasting time when you should be fixing my ship?"

"You've still got one more mutiny before it's your ship," Sam said. "And yeah, when the crew heard about what happened with you and Ashford, some of us wanted to put together a little present."

Bull shifted, then caught himself. He was so used to having the muscles in his trunk to hold himself up that every time he began to fall, it was a little surprising. It was one of the things he missed about null g. Sam didn't notice, or pretended not to. She shifted to the side and took hold of the crate's release bar like a stage magician about to reveal an illusion. Doctor Sterling appeared in the doorway, a sly smile haunting her lips. Bull had the uncomfortable feeling of walking in on his own surprise party.

"You're making me nervous," he said.

"You're getting smarter," she said. "Ready?"

"Yeah, I don't think so."

The crate slid open. The mech inside looked complicated, blocky, and thick. Bull laughed for lack of anything he could think to say.

"It's a standard lifting mech," Sam said, "but we carved a bunch of the reinforcing out of its tummy and put in a TLS orthosis the medics gave me. We swapped out the leg actuation with a simple joystick control. It won't take you dancing, and you're still going to need help going potty, but you're not stuck in bed. It's not as comfortable as a top-end wheelchair, but it will get you anywhere in the ship you want to go, whether it was built for accessibility or not."

Bull thought he was about to cough again until he felt the tears welling up in his eyes.

"Aw shit, Sam."

"None of that, you big baby. Let's just get you in and adjust the support plates."

Sam took one shoulder, the nurse the other. The sensation of being carried was strange. Bull didn't know the last time anyone had picked him up. The brace in the guts of the mech was like a girdle, and Sam had put straps along the mech's struts to keep his legs from flapping around. It was an inversion of the usual; instead of using his legs to move the mech, he was using the mech to move his legs. For the first time since the catastrophe, Bull walked down the short hall and into the general ward. Sam kept pace, her gaze on the mechanism like a mother duck taking her ducklings for their first swim. His sense of wrongness didn't leave, but it lessened.

The worst of the injured from all three sides were here, men and women, Belter and Earther and Martian. A bald man with skin an unhealthy yellow struggled to breathe; a woman so young-looking Bull could hardly believe she wasn't a child lay almost naked in a bed, her skin mostly burned away and a distant look in her eyes;

a thick-bodied man with an Old Testament prophet's beard and body hair like a chimp moaned and shifted through his sedation. In the disposable plastic medical gowns, there was nothing to show who belonged to what side. They were people, and they were on his ship, so they were his people.

At the end of the corridor, Corin stood in front of a doorway, a pistol on her hip. Her salute was on the edge between serious and mocking.

"Macht *sly*, chief," she said. "Suits."

"Thank you," Bull said.

"Here to see the prisoners?"

"Sure," Bull said. He hadn't meant to go anywhere in particular, but since he could, he could. The lockdown ward was smaller, but other than one of his security staff at the door, there weren't any signs that the patients here were different. *Prisoners* was a strong word. None of them were legally bound. They ranged from high-value civilians from Earth to the highest-ranking Martian wounded. Anyone whom Bull thought might be particularly useful, now or later. All of the dozen beds were full.

"How's it feeling?" Sam asked.

"Seems like it lists to the right a little," Bull said.

"Yeah, I was thinking maybe—"

The new voice came from the farthest bed, weak and confused but unmistakable:

"Sam?"

Sam's attention snapped to the back, and she took a couple tentative steps toward the woman who had spoken.

"Naomi? Oh holy crap, sweetie. What happened to you?"

"Got in a fight," the XO of the *Rocinante* said through bruised and broken lips. "Whipped her ass."

"You know Nagata?" Bull asked.

"From the bad old days," Sam said, taking her hand. "We were roommates for about six days while she and Jim Holden were having a fight."

"Where," Naomi said. "Where's my *crew*?"

"They're here," Bull said, maneuvering his mech closer to her. "All but Holden."

"They're all right?"

"I've felt better," a balding, slightly pudgy man with skin the color of toast said. He had the drawl of Mariner Valley on Mars or West Texas on Earth. It was hard to tell the difference.

"Alex," Naomi said. "Where's Amos?"

"Next bed over," Alex said. "He's been sleepin' a lot. What happened, anyway? We get arrested?"

"There was an accident," Bull said. "A lot of people got hurt."

"But we ain't arrested," Alex said.

"No."

"Well that's all right, then."

On her bed, Naomi Nagata had visibly relaxed. Knowing her crew were alive and with her carried a lot of weight. Bull filed the information away in case it was useful later.

"The woman who attacked you is under arrest," Bull said.

"She's the one. The bomb," Naomi said.

"We're looking into that," he said, trying to keep his tone reassuring. Another coughing fit spoiled the effect.

Naomi frowned, remembering something. Bull wished he could take her other hand. Build some rapport. The mech was a fine way to walk around, but there were other ways it was limiting.

"Jim?" she said.

"Captain Holden has been taken into custody by the Martian navy," Bull said. "I'm trying to negotiate his release into our custody, but it's not going very well so far."

Naomi smiled as if he'd given her good news and nodded. Her eyes closed.

"What 'bout Miller?"

"Who?" Bull asked, but she was already asleep. Sam shifted to Alex's bed and Bull stepped over to look down on the *Rocinante*'s sleeping mechanic. Amos Burton. They were a pretty sad bunch, and far too small a crew to run a ship like theirs safely. Maybe Jakande could get some pointers from them.

Until he got Holden, they were going to be at a disadvantage. The man was a professional symbol, and creating calm when there was no reason for it was all about symbols. Captain Jakande wouldn't bend, because if she did, she'd be court-martialed when they got back. If they got back. Bull didn't like it, but he understood it. If they'd been anywhere but the slow zone, they'd all have been rattling sabers and baring teeth. Instead, all they could do was talk...

Bull's mouth went dry. Sam was still looking at Naomi Nagata's bed, her face angry and despairing.

"Sam," Bull said. "Got a minute?"

She looked up and nodded. Bull flicked the little joystick, and the mech trod awkwardly around. He steered it back out through the door and back to his own private room. By the time they got there, Sam's expression had shifted to curious. Bull closed the door, coughing. He felt a little light-headed and his heart was racing. Fear, excitement, or being vertical for the first time since they'd passed through the Ring, he didn't know.

"What's up, boss?"

"The comm laser," Bull said. "Say I wanted to make it into a weapon. What's the most power we could put through it?"

Sam's frown was more than an engineer making mental calculations. The spin gravity made her seem older. Or maybe bathing in death and fear just did that to people.

"I can make it about as hot as the middle of a star for a fraction of a second," Sam said. "It'd burn that side of the ship down to a bad smell, though."

"What's the most we could do and get, say, three shots out of it? And not melt our ship?"

"It can already carve through a ship's hull if you've got time to spare. I can probably pare that time down a bit."

"Get that going, will you?"

Sam shook her head.

"What?" Bull asked.

"That big glowy ball out there can turn off inertia when it feels threatened. I don't feel comfortable making light into a weapon. Seriously, what if it decides to stop all the photons or something?"

"If we have it, we won't need to use it."

Sam shook her head again.

"I can't do that for you, Bull."

"What about the captain? Would you do it for a Belter?"

Sam's cheeks flushed. It might have been embarrassment or anger.

"Cheap shot."

"Sorry, but would you take a direct order from Captain Pa?"

"From her, yes. But not because she's a Belter. Because she's the captain and I trust her judgment."

"More than mine."

Sam held up her hands in a Belter shrug.

"Last time I just did whatever you told me to, I wound up under house arrest."

Bull had to give her the point. He fumbled to extricate his arm from the mech, scooped up his hand terminal, and put in a priority connection request to Pa. She took it almost immediately. She looked older too, worn, solid, certain. Crisis suited her.

"Mister Baca," she said. "Where do we stand?"

"Captain Jakande isn't going to bring her people over, even though they all know it would be better. And she won't give up Holden."

"All right," Pa said. "Well, we tried."

"But she might surrender to you," Bull said. "And seems to me it's going to be a lot easier being sheriff if we can get the only gun in the slow zone."

Pa tilted her head.

"Go on," she said.

Chapter Thirty-Four: Clarissa

The guards came, brought thinly rationed food-grade protein and measured bottles of water, led the prisoners to the head with pistols drawn, and then took them back. For the most part, Clarissa lay on the floor or stretched, hummed old songs to herself or drew on the skin of her arms—white fingernail scratches. The boredom would have been crushing if she'd felt it, but she seemed to have unconnected from time.

The only times she cried were when she thought of killing Ren and when she remembered her father. The only things she anticipated at all were another visit from Tilly or her mysterious friend, and death.

The woman came first, and when she did, Clarissa recognized her. With her red hair pulled down by spin, her face looked softer, but the eyes were unforgettable. The woman from the galley on the *Thomas Prince.* And then, later, from the *Rocinante.* Anna. She'd told Naomi that her name was Anna.

Just one more person Clarissa had tried to kill once.

"I have permission to speak with her," Anna said. The guard—a broad-faced man with a scarred arm that he wore like a decoration—crossed his arms.

"She's here, si no? Talk away."

"Absolutely not," Anna said. "This is a private conversation. I can't have it in front of the others."

"You can't have it anywhere else," the guard said. "You know how many people this coya killed? She's got implants. Dangerous."

"She knows," Clarissa said, and Anna flashed a smile at her like they'd shared a joke. A feeling of unease cooled Clarissa's gut. There was something threatening about a woman who could take being attacked and treat it like it was a shared intimacy. Clarissa wondered whether she wanted to talk with her after all.

"It's the risk I came here to take," Anna said. "You can find us a place. An...an interview room. You have those, don't you?"

The guard's stance settled deeper into his knees and hips, immovable.

"Can stay here until the sun burns out," he said. "That door's staying closed."

"It's all right," Clarissa said.

"No it isn't," Anna said. "I'm her priest, and the things we need to talk about are private. Please open the door and take us someplace we can talk."

"Jojo," the captain at the far end of the hall said. Ashford. That was his name. "It's all right. You can put them in the meat freezer. It's not in use and it locks from the outside."

"Then I get a dead preacher, ano sa?"

"I believe that you won't," Anna said.

"Then you believe in vacuum fairies," the guard said, but he unlocked the cell door. The bars swung open. Clarissa hesitated. Behind guard and priest, the disgraced Captain Ashford watched her, peering through his bars to get a look. He needed to shave and he looked like he'd been crying. For a moment, Clarissa gripped the cold steel bars of her door. The urge to pull them closed, to retreat, was almost overwhelming.

"It's all right," Anna said.

Clarissa let go of the door and stepped out. The guard drew his sidearm and pressed it against the back of her neck. Anna looked pained. Ashford's expression didn't shift a millimeter.

"Is that necessary?" Anna asked.

"Implants," the guard said and prodded Clarissa to move forward. She walked.

The freezer was warm and larger than the galley back on the *Cerisier.* Strips of metal ran along floor and ceiling and both walls with notches every few centimeters to allow the Mormon colonists who never were to lock walls and partitions into place. It made sense that the veterinary stalls that had been pressed into service as her prison would be near the slaughterhouse. Harsh white light spilled from LEDs set into the walls, unsoftened and directional, casting hard shadows.

"I'm back in fifteen minutes," the guard said as he pushed Clarissa through the doorway. "Anything looks funny, I'll shoot you."

"Thank you for giving us privacy," Anna said, stepping through after her. The door closed. The latch sounded like the gates of hell, closing. The lights flickered, and the first thought that flashed across Clarissa's mind, rich with disapproval, was, *Shouldn't tie the locking magnet to the same circuit as the control board.* It was like a relic from another life.

Anna gathered herself, smiled, and put out her hand.

"We've met before," she said, "but we haven't really been introduced. My name's Anna."

A lifetime's etiquette accepted the offered hand on Clarissa's behalf. The woman's fingers were very warm.

"My priest?" Clarissa said.

"Sorry about that," Anna said. "I didn't mean to presume. I was getting angry, and I tried to pull rank."

"I know people who do worse. When they're angry."

Clarissa released the woman's hand.

"I'm a friend of Tilly's. She helped me after the ship crashed. I was hurt and not thinking very straight, and she helped me," she said.

"She's good that way."

"She knew your sister too. Your father. The whole family," Anna said, then pressed her lips together impatiently. "I wish they'd given us chairs. I feel like we're standing around at a bus terminal."

Anna took a deep breath, sighing out her nose, then sat there in the middle of the room with her legs crossed. She patted the metal decking at her side. Clarissa hesitated, then lowered herself to sit. She had the overwhelming memory of being five years old, sitting on a rug in kindergarten.

"That's better," Anna said. "So, Tilly's told me a lot about you. She's worried."

Clarissa tilted her head. From just the form, it seemed like the place where she would reply. She felt the urge to speak, and she couldn't imagine what she would say. After a moment, Anna went on, trying again without seeming to.

"I'm worried about you too."

"Why?"

Anna's eyes clouded. For a moment, she seemed to be having some internal conversation. But only for a moment. She leaned forward, her hands clasped.

"I didn't help you before. I saw you just before the *Seung Un* blew up," she said. "Just before you set off the bomb."

"It was too late by then," Clarissa said. Ren had already been dead. "You couldn't have stopped it."

"You're right," Anna said. "That's not the only reason I'm here. I also... I lost someone. When all the ships stopped, I lost someone."

"Someone you cared about," Clarissa said. "Someone you loved."

"Someone I hardly knew, but it was a real loss. And also I was scared of you. I *am* scared of you. But Tilly told me a lot about you, and it's helped me to get past some of my fear."

"Not all of it?"

"No. Not all of it."

Something deep in the structure of the ship thumped, the whole structure around them ringing for a moment like a gigantic bell tolling far, far away.

"I could kill you," Clarissa said. "Before they got the door open."

"I know. I saw."

Clarissa put her hand out, her palm against the notched runner. The finish was smooth and the metal cool.

"You want a confession, then?" she said.

"If you want to offer one."

"I did it," Clarissa said. "I sabotaged the *Rocinante* and the *Seung Un*. I killed Ren. I killed some people back on Earth. I lied about who I was. All of it. I'm guilty."

"All right."

"Are we done, then?"

Anna scratched her nose and sighed. "I came out to the Ring even though it upset my wife. Even though it meant not seeing my baby for months. I told myself that I wanted to come see it. To help people make sense of it and, whatever it was, to not be afraid. You came out here to... save your father. To redeem him."

"Is that what Tilly says?"

"She's not as polite about it."

Clarissa coughed out a laugh. Everything she could say felt trite. Worse, it felt naive and stupid. *Jim Holden destroyed my family* and *I wanted my father to be proud of me* and *I was wrong.*

"I did what I did," Clarissa said. "You can tell them that. The security people. You can tell them I confessed to it all."

"If you'd like. I'll tell them."

"I would. I want that."

"Why did you try to kill Naomi?"

"I wanted to kill all of them," Clarissa said, and each word was hard to speak, as though they were too large to fit through her throat. "They were part of him, and I wanted him not to be. Just not to exist at all anymore. I wanted everyone to know he is a bad man."

"Do you still want that?"

"I don't care," Clarissa said. "You can tell them."

"And Naomi? I'm going to see her. Is there anything you'd want me to tell her in particular?"

Clarissa remembered the woman's face, bruised and bleeding. She flexed her hand, feeling the mech's glove against her fingers. It would have taken nothing to snap the woman's neck, a feather's weight of pressure. She wondered why she hadn't. The difference between savoring the moment and hesitating warred at the back of her mind, and her memory supported both. Or neither.

"Tell her I hope she gets well soon."

"Do you hope that?"

"Or am I just being polite, you mean?" Clarissa said. "Tell her whatever you want. I don't care."

"All right," Anna said. "Can I ask a question?"

"Can I stop you?"

"Yes."

The silence was no more than three long breaths together.

"You can ask me a question."

"Do you want to be redeemed?"

"I don't believe in God."

"Do you want to be redeemed by something other than God, then? If there was forgiveness for you, could you accept it?"

The sense of outrage began in Clarissa's stomach and bloomed out through her chest. It curled her lips and furrowed her brow. For the first time since she'd lost consciousness trying to beat her way through the locker on the *Rocinante*, she remembered what anger felt like. How large it was.

"Why should I be forgiven for anything? I did it. That's all."

"But if—"

"What kind of justice would that be? 'Oh, you killed Ren, but you're sorry now so it's okay'? *Fuck* that. And if that's how your God works, then fuck Him too."

The freezer door clanked. Clarissa looked up at it, resenting the accident of timing and then realizing they'd heard her yelling. They were coming to save the preacher. She balled her hands into fists and looked down at them. They were going to take her back to her cell. She felt in her gut and her throat how little she wanted that.

"It's all right," Anna said as the guard stepped into the freezer, his sidearm trained on Clarissa. "We're okay."

"Yeah, no," the guard said. His gaze was sharp and focused. Frightened. "Time's passed. Meeting's over."

Anna looked at Clarissa with something like frustration in her expression. Not with her, but with the situation. With not getting everything to be just the way she wanted it. Clarissa had some sympathy for that.

"I'd like to talk with you again," Anna said. "If it's all right."

"You know where I live," Clarissa said with a shrug. "I don't go out much."

Chapter Thirty-Five: Anna

Bull wasn't in his office when she arrived. A muscular young woman with a large gun on her hip shrugged when Anna asked if she could wait for him, then ignored her and continued working. A wall screen was set to the Radio Free Slow Zone feed, where a young Earther man was leaning in toward Monica Stuart and speaking earnestly. His skin was a bright pink that didn't seem to be his natural color. Anna thought he looked peeled.

"I haven't changed my commitment to autonomy for the Brazilian shared interest zones," he said. "If anything I feel like I've broadened it."

"Broadened it how?" Monica asked. She seemed genuinely interested. It was a gift. The peeled man tapped at the air with his fingertips. Anna felt sure she'd seen him on the *Thomas Prince*, but she couldn't for the life of her remember his name. She had the vague sense he was a painter. Some kind of artist, certainly.

"We've all changed," he said. "By coming here. By going through the trials that we're all going through, we've all *been* changed. When we go back, none of us will be the people we were before. The tragedy and the loss and the sense of *wonder* changes what it means to be human. Do you know what I mean?"

Oddly, Anna thought she did.

Being a minister meant being in the middle of people's lives. Anna had counseled dating congregation members, presided over their weddings, baptized their babies, and in one heartbreaking case presided over the infant's funeral a year later. Members of the congregation included her in most of the important events of their lives. She was used to it, and mostly enjoyed the deep connection to people it brought. Charting the course of a life was making a map of the ways each event changed the person, leaving someone different on the other side. Passing through the Ring and the tragedies it had brought wouldn't leave any of them the same.

The exodus from the rest of the fleet to the *Behemoth* was in full swing. The tent cities spread across the curved inner surface of the habitation drum like wildflowers on a field of flat, ceramic steel–colored earth. Anna saw tall gangly Belters helping offload wounded Earthers from emergency carts, plugging in IVs and other medical equipment, fluffing pillows and mopping brows. Inners and outers offloaded crates in mixed groups without comment. Anna couldn't help but be warmed by that, even in the face of their recent disaster. Maybe it took real tragedy to get them all working together, but it did. They did. There was hope in that.

Now if they could just figure out how to do it without the blood and screaming.

"Your work has been criticized," Monica Stuart said, "as advocating violence."

The peeled man nodded.

"I used to reject that," he said. "I've come to the conclusion that it may be valid, though. I think when we come home, there will be some readjustment."

"Because of the Ring?"

"And the slow zone. And what's happened here."

"Do you think you would encourage other political artists to come out here?"

"Absolutely."

Chris, her young officer, had asked about organizing mixed-group church services on the *Behemoth*. She'd assumed he meant mixed religions at first, but it turned out he meant a church group with Earthers and Martians and Belters. Mixed, as if God categorized people based on the gravity they'd grown up in. It had occurred to Anna then that there really wasn't any such thing as a "mixed" church group. No matter what they looked like, or what they chose to call Him, when a group of people called out to God together, they were one. Even if there was no God, or one God, or many gods, it didn't matter. *Faith, hope, and love*, Paul had written, *but the greatest of these is love*. Faith and hope were very important to Anna. But she could see Paul's point in a way she hadn't before. Love didn't need anything else. It didn't need a common belief, or a common identity. Anna thought of her child and felt a rush of longing and loneliness. She could almost feel Nami in her arms, almost smell the intoxicating new-baby scent on her head. Nono the Ugandan and Anna the Russian had blended themselves together and made Nami. Not a mix, nothing so crude as that. More than just the sum of her parts and origins. A new thing, individual and unique.

No mixed group, then. Just a group. A new thing, perfect and unique. She couldn't imagine God would see it any other way. Anna was pretty sure she had her first sermon too. She was about halfway through typing up an outline for her "no mixed groups in God's eyes" sermon on her handset when Bull came through the door, his mechanical legs whining and thumping with each step. Anna thought it gave Bull even more gravitas than he'd had before. He moved with a deliberateness caused by mechanical necessity, but easily mistaken for formality and stateliness. The electric whine of the machine and the heavy thump of his tread were a sort of herald calling out his arrival.

Anna imagined the annoyance Bull would feel if she told him this, and giggled a little to herself.

Bull was in the middle of speaking to a subordinate and didn't even notice her. "I don't care how they feel about it, Serge. The agreement was no armed military personnel on the ship. Even if there weren't a shitload of guns built in, those suits would still be weapons. Confiscate their gear or throw them off the damn ship."

"Si, jefe," the other man with him replied. "Take it how, sa sa? Can opener?"

"Charm the bastards. If we can't make them do anything now, while we're all friends, what do we do when they decide we aren't friends? Four marines in recon armor decide they own this ship, they fucking own it. So we take the armor away before they do. I don't even want that stuff in the drum. Lock it in the bridge armory."

Serge looked deeply unhappy at this task. "Some help, maybe?"

"Take as many as you want, but if you don't need them it's only gonna piss the marines off, and if you do, they won't actually help."

Serge paused, mouth open, then closed it with a snap and left. Bull noticed Anna for the first time and said, "What can I do for you, Preacher?"

"Anna, please. I came to talk about Clarissa Mao," she said.

"If you're not her lawyer or her union representative—"

"I'm her priest. What happens to her now?"

Bull sighed again. "She confessed to blowing up a ship. Nothing much good comes after that."

"People say you spaced a man for selling drugs. They say you're hard. Cold."

"Do they?" Bull said. Anna couldn't tell if the surprise in his voice was genuine or mocking.

"Please don't kill her," she said, leaning closer and looking him in the eye. "Don't you let anyone else kill her either."

"Why not?" The way he said it wasn't a challenge or a threat. It was as if he just didn't know that answer, and sort of wondered. Anna swallowed her dread.

"I can't help her if she's dead."

"No offense, but that's not really my concern."

"I thought you were the law and order here."

"I'm aiming for order, mostly."

"She deserves a trial, and if everyone knows what you know about her, she won't get one. They'll riot. They'll kill her. At least help me get her a trial."

The large man sighed. "So are you looking for a trial, or just a way to stall for time?"

"Stall for time," Anna said.

Bull nodded, weighing something in his mind, then gestured for her to precede him into his office. After she sat down next to his battered desk, he clumped around the small space making a pot of coffee. It seemed an extravagance considering the newly implemented water rationing, but then Anna remembered Bull was now the second most powerful person in the slow zone. The privileges of rank.

She didn't want coffee, but accepted the offered cup to allow Bull a moment of generosity. Generosity now might lead to more later, when she was asking for something she really wanted.

"When Holden starts telling people who actually sabotaged the *Seung Un*—and he's Jim Holden, so he will—the UN people are going to ask for Clarissa. And if they give me enough that I can get everyone here, together, and safe until we can get out of this trap, I'm going to give her to them. Not off the ship, but in here."

"What will they do?" Anna took a companionable sip of her coffee. It burned her tongue and tasted like acid.

"Probably, they'll put together a tribunal of flag officers, have a short trial, and throw her in a recycler. I'd say space her, normally, but that seems wasteful considering our predicament. Supplies sent from home will take as long to fly through the slow zone to us as they'll take to get to the Ring."

His voice was flat, emotionless. He was discussing logistics, not a young woman's life. Anna suppressed a shudder and said, "Mister Baca, do you believe in God?"

To his credit, he tried not to roll his eyes. He almost succeeded. "I believe in whatever gets you through the night."

"Don't be flip," Anna said, and was gratified when Bull straightened a little in his walker. In her experience, most strong-willed men had equally strong-willed mothers, and she knew how to hit some of the same buttons.

"Look," Bull said, trying to reclaim the initiative. Anna spoke over the top of him.

"Forget God for a moment," she said. "Do you believe in the concept of forgiveness? In the possibility of redemption? In the value of every human life, no matter how tainted or corrupted?"

"Fuck no," Bull said. "I think it is entirely possible to go so far into the red you can't ever balance the books."

"Sounds like the voice of experience. How far have you been?"

"Far enough to know there's a too damn far."

"And you're comfortable being the judge of where that line is?"

Bull pulled on the frame of his walker, shifting his weight in the straps that held him. He looked wistfully at the office chair he could no longer use. Anna felt bad for him, broken at the worst possible time. Trying to keep his tiny world in order, and burning through the last reserves of his strength with reckless abandon. The bruised eyes and yellow skin suddenly seemed like a flashing battery indicator, warning that the power was almost gone. Anna felt a pang of guilt for adding to his burden.

"I don't want to kill that girl," he said, taking another sip of the terrible coffee. "In fact, I don't give a shit about her one way or the other, as long as she's locked up and isn't a danger to my ship. The one you should talk to is Holden. He's the one who's gonna get the torches-and-pitchforks crowd wound up."

"But the Martians..."

"Surrendered twenty hours ago."

Anna blinked.

"They've been wanting to for days," Bull said. "We just had to find a way to let 'em save face."

"Save face?"

"They got a story they can tell where they don't look weak. That's all they needed. But if we didn't find something, they'd have stuck to their posts until they all died. Nothing ever killed more people than being afraid to look like a sissy."

"Holden's coming here, then?"

"Already be on a shuttle escorted by four recon marines, which is another fucking headache for me. But how about this? I won't talk about the girl until I have reason to. What Holden does, though, he just does."

"Fine, then I'll talk to him when he arrives," Anna said.

"Good luck with that," Bull said.

Chapter Thirty-Six: Holden

When the Martians came for him—two men and two women, all in uniform and all armed—Holden's isolation-drunk mind had spun out in a dozen directions at once. The captain had found room for him in the medical clinic and she wanted to grill him again about what happened on the station and they were going to throw him out an airlock and they'd had news that Naomi was dead and they'd had news that she wasn't. It felt like every neuron he had from his brain down to his toes was on the edge of firing. It was all he could do not to launch himself off the cell's wall and into the narrow corridor.

"The prisoner will please identify himself," one of the men said.

"James Holden. I mean, it's not like you have very many prisoners here, right? Because I've been trying to find someone to talk with for it feels like about a decade since I got here, and I'm pretty sure there isn't so much as a dust mite in this place besides me."

He bit his lips to stop talking. He'd been alone and scared for too long. He hadn't understood how much it was affecting him. Even if he hadn't been mentally ill when he came to the *Hammurabi*, he was going to be real soon now if nothing changed.

"Record shows prisoner identified himself as James Holden," the man said. "Come along."

The corridor outside the cells was so narrow that two guards ahead and two behind was effectively a wall. The low Martian gravity made their bodies more akin to Belters than to him, and all four of them hunched slightly, bending in over him. Holden had never felt so relieved to be in a tiny, cramped hallway in his life. But even the relief was pushed aside by his anxiety. The guards didn't actually push him so much as start to move with an authority that suggested that he really should match them. The hatch was only five meters away, but after being in his cell, it seemed like a huge distance.

"Was there any word from the *Roci*?"

No one spoke.

"What's...ah...what's going on?"

"You're being evacuated," the man said.

"Evacuated?"

"Part of the surrender agreement."

"Surrender agreement? You're surrendering? Why are you surrendering?"

"We lost the politics," one of the women behind him said.

If the skiff they loaded him onto wasn't the same one that had taken him back from the station, it was close enough that he couldn't tell the difference. There were only four soldiers this time, all of them in full combat armor. The rest of the spaces were taken up by men and women in standard naval uniform. Holden thought at first they were the wounded, but when he looked closer, none of them seemed to have anything worse than minor injuries. It was the exhaustion in their faces and bodies that made them seem broken. The acceleration burn wasn't even announced. The thrust barely shifted the crash couches. All around him, the Martians slept or brooded. Holden scratched at the hard, flexible plastic restraints on his wrists and ankles, and no one told him to stop. Maybe that was a good sign.

He tried to do the math in his head. If the new top speed was about as fast as a launched grenade, then every hour, they'd travel…As tired as he was, he couldn't make the numbers add up to anything. If he'd had his hand terminal, it would have been a few seconds' work. Still, he couldn't see asking to have it. And it didn't matter.

He slept and woke and slept again. The proximity Klaxon woke him from a dream about making bread with someone who was his father Caesar and also Fred Johnson and trying to find the salt. It took him a moment to remember where he was.

The skiff was small enough that when the other ship's crew banged against the airlock, Holden could hear it. From his seat, he couldn't see the airlock open. The first thing he knew was a slightly different scent in the air. Something rich and oddly humid. And then four new people stepped into his view. They were Belters. A broad-faced woman, a thick man with a startling white beard, and two shaven-headed men so similar they might have been twins. The twins had the split circle of the OPA tattooed on their arms. All four wore sidearms.

The *Behemoth*, Holden thought. They'd surrendered to the *Behemoth*. That was weird.

One of the marines, still in battle armor, floated over to them. The Belters didn't show any sign of fear. Holden gave them credit for that.

"I am Sergeant Alexander Verbinski," the Martian said. "I have been ordered to hand over this skiff and her crew and company in accordance with the agreement of surrender."

The woman and white-bearded man looked at each other. Holden thought he could see the question—*You gonna tell them they can't take their suits in?*—pass between them. The woman shrugged.

"Bien alles," she said. "Welcome aboard. Bring them through in sixpacks and we'll get you sorted, sa sa?"

"Yes, ma'am," Verbinski said.

"Corin," one of the twins said. The woman turned to see him gesture toward Holden with his chin. "Pa con esá parlan, si?"

The woman's nod was curt.

"We'll take Holden out now," she said.

"Your show," the marine said. Holden thought from his tone he'd have been as happy to shoot him. That might have been paranoia, though.

The Belters escorted him through the airlock and a long Mylar tube to the engineering deck of the *Behemoth*. A dozen people were waiting with hand terminals at the ready, prepared for the slow, slogging administrative work of dealing with a defeated enemy. Holden got to skip the line, and he wasn't sure it was an honor.

The woman floating near the massive doors at the transition point where the engineering section met the drum looked too young for her captain's insignia. Her hair, pulled back in a severe bun, reminded him of a teacher he'd had once when he'd still been on Earth.

"Captain Pa," the security woman—Corin, one of the twins had called her—said. "You wanted to talk with this one."

"Captain Holden," Captain Pa said with a nod. "Welcome aboard the *Behemoth*. I'm giving you liberty of the ship, but I want you to understand that there are some conditions."

Holden blinked. He'd expected another brig at least. Freedom of the ship was pretty much the same as freedom period. It wasn't like there were a lot of places he could go.

"Ah. All right," he said.

"You are to make yourself available for debriefing whenever you are called upon. No exceptions. You are not to discuss what happened or didn't happen on the station with anyone besides myself or the security chief."

"I know how to shut it off," Holden said.

The younger captain's expression shifted.

"You what?"

"I know how to get the protomolecule to take us all off of lockdown," he said, and went on to explain all of what he'd told Captain Jakande again—seeing Miller, the plan to lull the station into a lower alert level so that the dead man could shut it down—fighting to sound calm, rational, and sane as he did it. He didn't go so far as the massive civilization-destroying invasion that had wiped out the protomolecule's creators. It all sounded bad enough without that.

Pa listened carefully, her face a mask. She wasn't someone he'd want to play poker against. He had the powerful, painful memory of Naomi telling him that she'd teach him how to play poker, and his throat closed.

The security man with the white beard floated up, two angry-looking Martians matching vector behind him.

"Captain?" the Belter said, barely restrained rage in his voice.

"Just a minute, Mister Gutmansdottir," she said, then turned back to Holden. She had to be overwhelmed, but it was only a tightness in her jaw, if it was even that much. "I'll…take that under advisement, but for the immediate future—"

"My crew?"

"They're in the civilian medical bay," Pa said, and the white-bearded man cleared his throat in a way that meant he hadn't needed to. "There are directions posted. If you'll excuse me."

"Captain, there's a load of contraband among the new prisoners," Gutmansdottir said, hitting the last word hard. "Thought you'd want to address that before it got to Bull."

Pa took a deep breath and pushed off after her security man. A few seconds later, Holden realized he hadn't been dismissed so much as forgotten. Fallen down the list of things that the young captain had to do *right now*, and so fuck him. He moved out past the transition point and to the platforms where the axis of the little world spun. There was a long ramp for carts, and he shuffled down it, the spin slowly shifting from pure Coriolis to the sensation of weight. He could feel in his knees how long he'd been on the float and hoped that the medical bays weren't too far away.

If they'd been on the far side of the system, though, he'd have grabbed an EVA suit, as much spare air as he could haul, and started out, though. The idea that he was breathing the same air as Naomi and Alex and Amos was like a drug.

Only Captain Pa hadn't actually said that. All she'd said was that his crew was there. The "remaining" might have been implied. He tried to jog, but got winded after only a couple of minutes and had to pause to catch his breath.

The great body of the drum stretched out before him, a world wrapped into a tube. The long strip of the false sun glowed white above him, now that there was a clear "above," and reached out across two kilometers to a swirling ramp at the other end, the mirror of the one he was on. Thin clouds drifted in tori around the unbearable brightness. The air clung to him, the heat pressing at his skin, but he could imagine the bare metal of the drum's surface covered in green, the air sweet with the scent of apple blossoms, the cycle of evaporation and condensation cooling it all. Or if not, at least making it into a long, permanent summer afternoon.

It was a dream. Someone else's and doomed now to failure, but worthy. Beautiful, even in ruins.

"Captain Holden? Can I speak with you?"

It was a small woman with bright red hair pulled into tight braids, and wearing a plain brown suit. She was the sort of very comfortable middle-aged that always made him think of his mothers.

"My name is Annushka Volovodov," she said with a smile. "But you can call me Anna if you like."

"You can call me Jim," he said, holding out a hand. He almost had his wind back. Anna shook his hand without a hint of fear. His "most dangerous man in the solar system" reputation must not have reached her yet. "Eastern European?"

"Russian," she replied with a nod. "Born in Kimry. But a Muscovite for most of my adult life. North American?"

"Montana. Farming collective."

"I hear Montana is nice."

"Population density is good. Still more cows than people."

Anna nodded and plucked at her suit. Holden got the sense that she actually had something she wanted to say but was having a hard time getting to the point. "Kimry was like that. It's a tourist place you know, the lakes—" Anna started.

"Anna," Holden cut her off gently. "Do you need to say something to me?"

"I do," she said. "I need to ask you not to tell anyone about Clarissa, and what she did."

Holden nodded.

"Okay," he said. "Who's Clarissa and what did she do?"

The woman tilted her head.

"They didn't tell you?"

"I don't think they liked me much," Holden said. "Is there something I should know?"

"Well, this is awkward. Just after the catastrophe, a girl calling herself Melba attacked your ship," Anna said. "It's a long story, but I followed her and tried to help. Your first officer? Naomi? She was hurt in the attack. Badly."

Holden felt the universe contract. Naomi was hurt while he'd been dicking around with Miller on the station. His hands were shaking.

"Where is she?" he asked, not sure if he meant Naomi or the woman who'd hurt her.

"Naomi's here. They brought her over to the *Behemoth*," Anna said. "She's in the medical bay right now receiving treatment. They assure me she'll recover. The rest of your crew is here too. They were hurt earlier. When the speed limit changed."

"They're alive?"

"Yes," Anna said. "They are."

The mix of relief and sorrow and anger and guilt made the ship seem to spin a little beneath him. Anna put a hand on his arm to steady him.

"Who is this Melba and why did she attack my crew?"

"It's not her real name. My friend knows her, knows her family. Apparently she has something of an obsession with you. Her name is Clarissa Mao."

Mao.

The mysterious and powerful Julie. The Julie rebuilt by the protomolecule like his ghostly Miller. The Julie who had hired Cohen the soundman to hack their ship, the Julie he'd sculpted for them later who'd never looked *quite* right. The Julie who'd been manipulating every detail of his life for the last year just to get them through the gate and down to the station.

It wasn't Julie at all.

"She's not well," Anna was saying, "but I believe that she can be reached. If there's time. But if they kill her—"

"Where's Naomi? Do you know where she is?"

"I do," Anna said. And then, "I'm sorry. I may have been a little wrapped up in my own issue. Can I take you there?"

"Please," Holden said.

Fifteen minutes later, Holden stepped into a small room in the medical ward that his little family had to themselves. Naomi lay on a gurney, one arm in an inflatable cast. Her face was mottled with half-healed bruises. Tears stung his eyes, and for a moment he couldn't speak. A killing rage burned in him. This wasn't a disaster. It wasn't an accident. Someone had done this to her.

When she saw him, her smile was gentle and amused.

"Hey," she said. In a moment, he was at her side, holding her good hand, his throat too thick for speech. There were tears in Naomi's eyes too, but no anger. He was amazed how grateful he was for that.

"Anna," Naomi said. She looked genuinely pleased to see her, which was a good start. "Jim, you met Anna? She saved me from the psycho with the demolition mech."

"Saved us too, I guess," Amos said. "So thanks for that, Red. I guess I owe you one."

It took Holden a moment to realize that "Red" meant Anna. She seemed surprised by it too.

"I'm happy I was able to help. I'm afraid I was very stoned

on pain medication at the time. It could have easily gone the other way."

"Just take the marker," Alex said. "Soon as you figure out what Amos is good for, you can trade it in."

"Asshole," Amos said, and threw a pillow at him

"Thank you," Holden said. "If you saved them, I owe you everything."

"I'm happy I was able to help," she repeated. To Naomi she said, "You look better than the last time I saw you."

"Getting better," Naomi replied, then tested her injured arm with a grimace. "We'll see how mobile it is once the bones knit up."

Anna nodded and smiled at her, and then the smile faded.

"Jim? I'm sorry, but I still need to speak to you," she said to him. "Maybe privately?"

"No. I never thought I'd see these people again. I'm staying right here. If you want to talk to me, go ahead and do it."

The woman's eyes shifted between the crewmen. Her expression could have been hope or polite resignation.

"I need something," she finally said.

"Anything," Amos answered instantly, sitting up in bed a bit. Holden knew Anna wouldn't understand how literally Amos meant that. Hopefully a preacher didn't need anyone murdered.

"If we got it," Alex added, "it's yours." Amos nodded agreement.

Anna directed her answer at Holden. "I've talked to the head of security and he's agreed to keep quiet about Clarissa's confession. All that she's done. I need you to keep quiet too."

Holden frowned, but didn't reply. Naomi said, "Why?"

"Well," Anna said. "It's James Holden. He has a reputation for announcing things—"

"Not why ask us?" Naomi said. "Why don't you want people to know?"

Anna nodded. "If it gets out, given our current situation, they'll probably execute her."

"Good," Holden said.

"She does kind of have it coming," Amos added.

Anna held her hands tight in front of her and nodded. She didn't mean that she agreed, only that she heard them. That she understood.

"I need you to forgive her," she said. "If nothing else, as a favor to me. You said I could have anything. That's what I want."

In the pause, Amos let out a long breath. Alex's eyebrows were climbing up his forehead.

"Why?" Naomi said again, her voice calm.

Anna pressed her lips thin. "She's not evil. I believe that Clarissa did what she did out of a love. A sick love, but love. And if she's dead, there won't be any hope for her. And I have to hope."

Holden saw the words wash over Naomi, a sudden pain in her eyes that he didn't understand. She pulled back her lips, baring her teeth. Her whisper was obscene and so quiet that no one but him could hear it. He squeezed her hand, feeling the bones of her fingers against his own.

"Okay," Naomi said. "We'll keep quiet."

The rage flared in his breast. Speaking was suddenly easy.

"I won't," Holden said. "We're talking about an insane member of the Mao clan, the people who've *twice* tried to kill everyone in the solar system, who followed us all the way to the Ring, tried to kill us. To kill you. She blew up a spaceship full of innocent people just to try and make me look bad. Who knows how many other people she's killed? If the UN wants to space her, I'll push the damn button myself."

There was a long moment of silence. Holden watched Anna's face fall as he crushed her hopes. Alex started chuckling, and everyone turned to look at him.

"Yeah," Alex said in his drawling voice. "I mean, Naomi only got beat half to death. She can cut this Clarissa slack, it's no big deal. But the captain's *girlfriend* got hurt. He's the *real* victim here."

The room got quiet again as everyone stopped breathing. Blood flushed into Holden's face, rushing like a river in his ears. It was hatred and pain and outrage. His mind seemed to flicker, and the urge to strike out at Alex for the insult was almost too much to resist.

And then he understood Alex's words, saw Naomi's eyes on his, and it all drained away. *Why*, he wanted to ask, but it didn't matter. It was Naomi, and she'd made her decision. It wasn't his revenge to take.

He was spent. Exhausted. He wanted to curl up on the floor there with his people around him and sleep for days. He tried out a smile.

"Wow," he finally said. "Sometimes I am just a gigantic asshole."

"No," Amos said. "I'm right there with you. I'd kill this Clarissa myself for the shit she's pulled. But Red asked us to let it go, and Naomi's playing along, so I guess we gotta too."

"Don't get me wrong," Holden said to Anna, his voice cold. "I will never forgive this woman for what she's done. Never. But I won't turn her over to the UN, as a favor to you, and because if Naomi can let it go, I guess I have to."

"Thank you," Anna said.

"Things change, Red," Amos said, "you let us know. Because I'll still be happy to kill the shit out of her."

Chapter Thirty-Seven: Clarissa

She didn't know at first what the change was. It presented in little things. The decking she'd been able to sleep on like she was dead suddenly wasn't comfortable. She found herself wondering more what her father did in his cell, five billion kilometers away and, for all she knew, in another universe. She tapped her hands against the bars just to hear the subtle differences in tone that the different bars made when struck. And she hated.

Hatred was nothing new. She'd lived with it for long enough that the memories of the times before all carried the same colors of rage and righteousness. Only before, she'd hated Jim Holden, and now she hated Clarissa Mao. Hating herself had a kind of purity that she found appealing. Cathartic. Jim Holden had shifted out from under her thirst for vengeance, refusing to be consumed by it. She could live in the flames and know she deserved to burn. It was like playing a game on easy.

She tapped the bars. There wasn't enough variation between them to play a melody. If there had been she would have, just for something to distract her. She wondered whether her extra glands would be enough to bend the bars or lift the door off its hinges. Not that it would matter. At best, leaving her cell would have meant being gunned down by an OPA guard. At worst, it would have meant freedom.

The captain had stopped talking to her, at least. She watched the stream of visitors coming to him. She had a pretty clear idea which of the guards answered to him. And there were a couple of Martians in military uniforms who came, and a few UN officers too. They came and met with Captain Ashford, speaking in the low voices of people who took themselves and each other very seriously. She recognized the sound from eavesdropping on her father. She remembered that she had been impressed by it once. Now it made her want to laugh.

She paced her tiny world. She did push-ups and lunges and all the pointless exercises that the light gravity allowed. And she waited for punishment or for the end of the world. When she slept, Ren was there, so she tried not to sleep much.

And slowly, with a sense of growing horror, she understood that the change was her coming back to herself. Falling awake. After her failure on the *Rocinante*, there had been a kind of peace. A disconnection from everything. But even before that, she'd been in a sort of a dream. She couldn't tell if it had started with the day she'd killed Ren or when she'd taken the identification to become Melba Koh. Or earlier, even. When she'd heard her father had been arrested. Whenever she'd lost herself, she was coming back now, and it was like her whole consciousness was suffering pins and needles. It was worse than pain, and it drove her in circles.

The more she thought about it, the clearer the mind games that the red-haired priest had played on her were. The priest and, in her way, Tilly Fagan too. Maybe Anna had come thinking that the promise of forgiveness would need to be dangled in front of her in order to get the confession. If so, the woman was double stupid: first because she'd thought Clarissa wouldn't admit to what she'd done, and second because she'd thought forgiveness was something Clarissa wanted. Or would accept.

I'd like to speak with you again, she'd said, and at the time it had seemed so sincere. So real. Only she hadn't come back. A small rational part of Clarissa's mind knew that it hadn't really been that long. Being in the cell changed the experience of time and made her feel isolated. That was the point of cells. Still, Anna hadn't come back. And neither had Holden. Or Naomi, whom Clarissa hadn't quite killed. They were done with her, and why shouldn't they be? Clarissa didn't have anything else to offer them. Except maybe a warning that the power on the ship was about to change hands again, as if that would even matter. Who got to sit in the doomed ship's captain's chair seemed like a terribly petty thing to worry about. It was like arguing about who was the prettiest girl in the prison camp.

Still, it was the only show playing, so she watched.

The voices from the other cell had taken on a new tone. An urgency. Even before the well-dressed man came down toward her, she knew that their little drama was about to play out. He stood at her door, looking in. His white hair, brilliant and perfectly coiffed, just made him look old. There was a darkness in his professionally avuncular eyes. When he put his hands around the bars, it looked like he was the one imprisoned.

"I'm guessing that you don't remember me," he said. His voice was sad and sweet both.

"Father Cortez," she said. "I remember who you are. You used to play golf with my father."

He chuckled ruefully, stepping his feet back from the bars in a way that brought his forehead closer to them.

"I did, but that was a long time ago. You wouldn't have been more than…what? Seven?"

"I've seen you in the newsfeeds since."

"Ah," he said. His eyes focused on nothing. "That feels like it was a long time ago too. I was just now talking with the captain. He said he's been trying to convince you to join us, only he hasn't had much success."

Two guards came in, walking down the rows of stalls. She recognized them both as Ashford's allies. Cortez didn't take notice of them at all.

"No, he hasn't," she said. And then, "He lies a lot."

Cortez's eyebrows rose.

"Lies?"

"He said he could get me amnesty. When we get back home, he could take me to Ceres and put me under OPA protection. Only he can't do that."

Cortez took a long breath and let it out again. "No. No, he can't. May I be honest with you?"

"I don't see that I'm in a position to stop you," Clarissa said.

"I think that you and I have a great deal in common. You have blood on your hands. The blood of innocents."

She tried to sneer, tried to retreat into a dismissive pose, but it only left her feeling exposed and adolescent. Cortez went on as if he hadn't noticed. Maybe he hadn't.

"I was…instrumental in bringing us through the gate. The combined force, representing all three divisions of humanity, joined gloriously together." Bitterness darkened the words, but then he smiled and she thought maybe there was something as wounded in him as there was in her. "Vainglory is an occupational hazard for men in my profession. It's one I've battled with limited success, I'm afraid."

"I was the one who drove Holden through the Ring," Clarissa said, unsure whether she was confessing a crime or offering Cortez an out.

"Yes. And I led all the others in after him. And so when they died, it was because I had blinded them to the dangers they faced. I led my flock to the slaughterhouse. I thought I was putting my faith in providence, but…"

Tears filled his eyes, and his expression went empty.

"Father?" she said.

"When I was a child," Cortez said, "my cousin found a dead man. The body was in an arroyo out behind our land. She dared me to go and look at it. I was desperately afraid, but I went and I held my head high and I pretended that I wasn't in order not to be. When the medics arrived, we found out the man had died from one of the old hemorrhagic fevers. They put me on prophylactic antivirals for the rest of the summer. So perhaps I've always done this. I thought I was putting my faith in providence, but perhaps I was only covering my own fears. And my own fears led a great many people to die."

"It's not your fault."

"But it is my problem. And perhaps my failings were in the service of a greater good. You were right, my dear. There will be no amnesty for you or for me either. But not for the reason you imagine."

Clarissa stood. Cortez's gaze was on her like a weight. The intimacy of the old man's confession and the fear and grief carried with such dignity made her respect him even though she'd never particularly liked him.

"The dangers that the aliens pose are too great. To think that we could harness them or treat them as equals was hubris, and the deaths we have seen already will be like a raindrop in the ocean. We've delivered ourselves into the hands of the devil. Not everyone understands that, but I think perhaps you do."

To her surprise, she felt dread welling up in her throat. At the far end of the hall, metal clanked. Ashford's stall door swung open. One of the guards said something, but Cortez's full attention was on her and it felt like pouring cool water on a burn.

"I think I do," she said softly.

"Captain Ashford's freedom is my doing because he and I have come to a meeting of the minds that I could not manage with the present captain. When they began to bring the crews of the various ships together here, they did it in part by creating a weapon."

"Weapons don't work here."

"Light does, and they have made a weapon out of it. The communications laser has been made strong enough to cut through hulls. And it can be made stronger. Enough so, we believe, that it will destroy the Ring and close the gate."

"We'll be on the wrong side of it," Clarissa said.

"Yes. But if we wait, others will come. They'll be tempted. 'If we can manipulate the gates,' they'll say, 'what glories would come to us.' I can already hear them."

"You were saying that. You *were* one of them."

"I was, and I've learned a terrible lesson. And you were driven here by hatred. Have you?"

Ashford laughed. One of the guards said, "Welcome back, Captain." Clarissa tapped her fingertips against the bars, and they chimed.

"We were wrong," Cortez said. "But now we have a chance to make it right. We can protect all of humanity from making the mistakes we've made. We can protect them. But there will be a sacrifice."

"Us. All of us."

"Yes. We will die here in the darkness, cut off from all of those we have preserved. And among those who are with us here, we will be reviled. We may be punished. Even put to death." He shifted his hand to touch hers. The contact, skin to skin, was electric. "I'm not lying to you, Clarissa. The things I am asking of you will have no reward in this life."

"What are you asking?" she said. "What do you want me to do about any of this?"

"People will try to stop us. They may try to kill the captain. I understand that the modifications made to your body have the potential to elevate your natural abilities to something exceptional. Come with us. See to it that the captain isn't hurt, and that he isn't stopped. It may be you need do nothing but stand witness. Or you may be the difference between success and failure."

"Either way, I'm dead."

"Yes. But one will only be a death. The other will have meaning."

Captain Ashford and his guards began walking toward them. The click of their heels against the deck was like the soft sounds of a mechanical clock. The moment drew toward its end, and resentment burned a little. She didn't want Ashford to come. She wanted to stay here, talking with the reverend about sacrifice and death. About the burden of having done something so wrong the scales couldn't be balanced while she lived.

Even though his mouth was set, Cortez's pale blue eyes smiled at her. He didn't look like her father at all. His face was too doughy, his jaw was too wide. He was all sincerity where her father always had a sense of laughing at the world from behind a mask. But at that moment, she saw Jules-Pierre Mao in him.

"The people we killed," she said. "If we do this, all of them will have died for a reason too."

"For the noblest of reasons," Cortez agreed.

"We have to get going," Ashford said, and Cortez stepped back from the doorway, folding his hands together. Ashford turned to her. His too-large head and thin Belter's frame made him seem like something from a bad dream. "Last chance," he said.

"I'll go," Clarissa said.

Ashford's eyebrows rose and he glanced from her to Cortez and back. A slow smile stretched his lips.

"You're sure?" he asked, but the pleasure in his voice made it clear he wasn't really looking for her thoughts or justifications.

"I'll make sure no one stops you," she said.

Ashford looked at Cortez for a moment, and his expression showed that he was impressed. He saluted her, and—awkwardly—she saluted back.

She felt a moment's disorientation stepping out of her cell that didn't come from a change in gravity or Coriolis. It was the first free step she'd taken since the *Rocinante*. Ashford walked ahead of her, his two guards talking about action groups and locking down the *Behemoth*. Engineering and command weren't in the rotating drum, and so they would take control of the transfer points at the far north and south of the drum and the exterior elevator that passed between them. How to maintain calm in the drum until they could lock it all down, who was tracking the enemy, who was already a loyalist and who would need persuasion. Clarissa didn't pay much attention. She was more aware of Cortez walking at her side and the sense of having left some kind of burden behind in the cell. She was going to die, and it was going to make all the things she'd done wrong before make sense. Every child born on Earth or Mars or the stations of the Belt would be safe from the protomolecule because of what they were about to do. And Soledad and Bob and Stanni, her father and her mother and her siblings, they would all know she was dead. Everyone who'd known and loved Ren would be able to sleep a little better knowing that his killer had come to justice. Even she'd sleep better, if she got any sleep.

"And she has combat implants," Ashford was saying as he pointed his fist back toward her. One of the guards looked back toward her. The one with off-colored eyes and the scar on his chin. Jojo.

"You sure she's one of us, Captain?"

"The enemy of my enemy, Jojo," Ashford said.

"I will vouch for her," Cortez said.

You shouldn't, Clarissa thought, but didn't say.

"Claro," Jojo said with a Belter gesture equivalent to a shrug. "She's on command deck with tu alles tu."

"That'll be fine," Ashford said.

The hall opened into a larger corridor. White LEDs left the walls looking pale and antiseptic. A dozen people armed with slug throwers, men and women both, sat in electric carts or stood beside them. Clarissa wanted the air itself to smell different, but it didn't. It was all just plastic and heat. Captain Ashford and three armed men jostled in the cart just ahead.

"It will take some time before the ship is fully secured," Cortez said. "We'll have to gather what allies we can. Suppress the resistance. Once we assemble everything we need and get off the drum, they won't be able to stop us." He sounded like he was trying to talk himself into believing something. "Don't be afraid. This has all happened for a reason. If we have faith, there is nothing to fear."

"I'm not afraid," Clarissa said. Cortez looked over at her, a smile in his eyes. When he met her gaze the smile faltered a little. He looked away.

Chapter Thirty-Eight: Bull

Bull tried not to cough. The doctor listened to his breath, moved the stethoscope a few inches, listened some more. He couldn't tell if the little silver disk was cold. He couldn't feel it. He coughed up a hard knob of mucus and accepted a bit of tissue from the doctor to spit it into. She tapped a few notes into her hand terminal. The light from its screen showed how tired she looked.

"Well, you're clearing a little," the doctor said. "Your white count is still through the roof, though."

"And the spine?"

"Your spine is a mess, and it's getting worse. By which I mean it's getting harder to make it better."

"That's a sacrifice."

"When's it going to be enough?" she asked.

"Depends on what you mean by 'it,' " Bull said.

"You wanted to get everyone together. They're together."

"Still got crews on half the ships."

"Skeleton crews," the doctor said. "I know how many people you have on this ship. I treat them. You wanted to bring everyone together. They're together. Is that enough?"

"Be nice to make sure everyone doesn't just start shooting at each other," Bull said.

The doctor lifted her hands, exasperated. "So as soon as humans aren't humans anymore, then you'll let me do my job."

Bull laughed, which was a mistake. His cough was deeper now, rattling in the caverns of his chest, but it wasn't violent. Before he could really work up a good gut-wrencher, he'd need abdominal muscles that fired. The doctor handed him another tissue. He used it.

"We get everything under control," he said, "you can knock me out, all right?"

"Is that going to happen?" she asked. It was the thing everyone wanted to know, whether they came right out and said it or not. The truth was, he didn't like the plan. Part of that was because it came from Jim Holden, part was that it came from the protomolecule, and part was that he badly wanted it to be true. The fallback was that he'd start evacuating who he could with the shuttles he had, except that shuttles weren't built for long-haul work. It wasn't viable.

They had to start making food. Generating soil to fill the interior of the drum. Growing crops under the false strip of sun that ran along the *Behemoth*'s axis. And getting the goddamned heat under control. He had to see to it that they made it, whatever that meant. Medical comas could last a pretty long time when ships slower than a decent fastball made a voyage across emptiness wider than Earth's oceans.

All of the reasons they'd come out—Earth, Mars, the OPA; all of them—seemed almost impossibly distant. Worrying about the OPA's place in the political calculus of the system was like trying to remember whether he'd paid back a guy who bought him a beer when he was twenty. After a certain point, the past becomes irrelevant. Nothing that happened outside the slow zone mattered. All that counted now was keeping things civilized until they found out if Holden's mad plan was more than a pipe dream.

And in order to do that, he had to keep breathing.

"Might pull it off. Captain Pa's got a plan she's looking at might get us burning again. Maybe," he said. "While we're waiting, though, you think you could hook me up?"

She scowled, but she got an inhaler from the pack beside the bed and tossed it to him. His arms still worked. He shook the thing twice, then put the formed ceramics to his lips and breathed. The steroids smelled like the ocean, and they burned a little. He tried not to cough.

"That's not going to fix anything," she said. "All we're doing is masking the symptoms."

"It's just got to get me through," Bull said, trying out a smile. The truth was he felt like crap. He didn't hurt, he just felt tired. And sick. And desperate.

With the inhaler stowed, he angled the walker back out toward the corridor. The medical bays were still full. The growing heat gave everything the sick, close feeling of a tropical summer. The smell of bodies and illness, blood and corruption and fake floral antiseptics made the rooms feel smaller than they were. Practice had made him more graceful with the mechanism. He used the two joysticks to shift out of the way of the nurses and therapists, making himself as unobtrusive as the rig allowed as he made his way back toward the security office.

His hand terminal chimed. He drove to a turn in the corridor, snugging himself into the corner to stay out of the way, then dropped the joysticks and took up the terminal. Corin requesting a connection. He thumbed to accept.

"Corin," he said. "What you got?"

"Boss?" she said. The tension in her voice brought his head up a degree. "You running a drill?"

"What's going on?"

"Jojo and Gutmansdottir just came by and said they were taking over the security office. When I told them they could have it when my shift was up, they drew down on me."

Bull felt a black dread descending upon him. He gripped the terminal and kept his voice low.

"They *what*?"

He pulled up his security interface, but the red border refused him. He was locked out of the command systems. They'd been moving fast.

"Was hoping it was some kind of test. Way they were talking, I got the feeling they were looking to find you there. I'm heading over to Serge's. He's trying to figure out what the hell's going on," she said. "If it was the wrong call—"

"It wasn't. You walked away, you did the right thing. Where were they supposed to be?"

"Sir?"

"They were on shift. Where were they supposed to be?"

For a moment, Corin's wide face was a mask of confusion. He watched her understand, a calm and deadly focus coming into her eyes. She didn't need to say it. Jojo and Gutmansdottir had been guarding the prisoners. Meaning Ashford.

Pa should have let him kill the bastard.

"Okay. Find Serge and anyone you trust. We've got to get this shit contained."

"Bien."

They'd be going for the armory. If they had security, the guns and gear were already theirs. Bull let a thin trickle of conversational obscenities fall from his lips while he tried to think. If he knew how many of his people had turned back to Ashford, he'd know what he had to work with.

"We can't let him get to Monica and the broadcast center," Bull said. "It gets out that we've got fighting in the drum, we'll get a dozen half-assed rescue missions trying to get their people out."

"You want us to concentrate there?" Corin asked.

"Don't concentrate anywhere," Bull said. "Not until we know what we're looking at. Just get as many people and guns as you can and stay in touch."

He had to get a plan. He had to have one now, only his brain wasn't working the way it should. He was sick. Hell, he was dying. It seemed deeply unfair that he should have to improvise at the same time.

"Get to Serge," he said. "We'll worry about it from there. I've got some people I've got to talk to."

"Bien, boss," Corin repeated, and dropped the connection.

A nurse pushed a rolling table around the corner, and Bull had to put his terminal away in order to step out of the man's path. He wished like hell he could walk and hold his terminal at the same damn time. He requested a priority connection to Pa. For a long moment, he was sure she wouldn't pick up, that Ashford had gotten to her already. The screen flickered, and she was there. He couldn't see what room she was in, but there were voices speaking in the background.

"Mister Baca," Pa said.

"Ashford's loose," he said. "I don't know how many people he's got or what he's doing, but a couple of my people just drew weapons and took over the security station."

Pa blinked. To her credit, she didn't show even a moment's fear, only the mental shifting of gears.

"Thank you, Mister Baca," Pa said. He could tell from the movement of her image on the screen that she was already walking away from wherever she'd been. Getting someplace unpredictable. That was what he needed to be doing too.

"I'll try to get in touch when I have a better idea what I'm looking at," he said.

"I appreciate that," she said. "I have a few people nearby that I trust. I'm going there now."

"I figure he's going to try to take over the broadcast station."

"Then we'll try to reinforce them," Pa said.

"Maybe it's just a few assholes," Bull said. "Ashford may be trying to keep his head low too."

"Or he may be getting ready to throw us both into a soil recycler," Pa said. "Which way do you want to bet?"

Bull smiled. He almost meant it.

"Take care of yourself, Captain."

"You too, Mister Baca."

"And hey," he said. "I'm sorry I got you into this."

Now it was Pa's turn to smile. She looked tired. She looked old.

"You didn't make any decisions for me," she said. "If I'm paying for my sins, at least give me that they're mine."

Her gaze jumped up from the terminal's camera toward something off the screen. Her lips pressed thin and the connection dropped. Bull had to fight not to request another connection, just so he could know what happened. But there wasn't time. He had to hurry. He tried connections to Ruiz in infrastructure and Chen without getting replies. He wondered how many supporters Ashford had gotten from the upper ranks of the staff. He cursed himself for having let Ashford pass under his radar. But he'd been so busy…

He tried Sam, and almost as soon as he put in the request, she was there.

"We got a problem," he said. "Ashford's trying to take back the ship. He's got security already."

"And engineering," Sam said.

Bull licked his lips.

"Where are you, Sam?"

"Right now? Funny you should ask. Engineering. Ashford left about five minutes ago. Had a little wish list of things he'd like me to do and about two dozen fellas with guns and scowls. That man's lost his shit, Bull. Seriously. He used to be a prick, but… He wants me to take out the Ring. Your comm laser trick? He wants it overclocked."

"You got to be kidding me."

"Not."

"He's looking to nuke the way *home*?"

"Calls it saving humanity from the alien threat," Sam said sweetly. Her eyes were hard.

"All right," Bull said, even though nothing about this was all right.

"And he's not at all happy with you. Are you someplace safe?"

Bull looked up and down the corridor. There wasn't cover. And even if there was, he was one man in a modified lifting mech and no spinal cord past the middle of his back.

"No," he said. "I don't think I am."

"Might want to get moving."

"I've got no place safe to go," Bull said.

Someone on the other end of the connection shouted and Sam looked up at them.

"I'm trying to scramble up all the technicians I can," she shouted back. "Things have been a tiny bit disorganized. Had a little trouble with the rules of physics changing on us. Maybe you noticed."

The first voice shouted again. Bull couldn't hear the words, but he knew the timbre of the voice. Garza. The guy who'd always gotten bulbs of coffee for whoever was stuck in the security office. Garza was one of theirs. Bull wished he'd gotten to know the man better. Especially after the catastrophe, he should have been checking in with his staff more. He should have seen this all coming.

This was his fault. All of this was his fault.

Sam looked back down at the screen. At him.

"Okay, sweetie," she said. "You should get scarce. Head for the second level, section M. There's a bunch of empty storage there. The door codes are all on default. Straight zeros."

"Why are they on default?"

"Because there's nothing in them, bossypants, and changing the locks on all the empties never made the top of my to-do list. Is this really the time?"

"Sorry," Bull said.

"Don't worry," she said. "Both of us under a little stress right now. Just get your head down before someone knocks it off. And Pa—"

"Pa knows. She's heading for safety too."

"All right, then. I'll try to get you some help."

"No," Bull said. "You don't know who you can trust."

"Yes, I do," Sam said. "Let's don't argue in front of the children."

A voice brought him back to the corridor, the medical center. Not the groans of the wounded, not the professional calm of the nurses. Someone was excited and aggressive. Angry. Someone answered in a lower voice, and the first one came back with *Do I look like I care?* It was trouble, and despite everything, his first impulse was to turn toward it. His job was to get in the middle of things, to make sure that no one got hurt, and if anyone did, it was him. Him first, then the bad guys.

"I got to go," he said, and dropped the connection. It only took a second to stow his hand terminal and get his palms back on the mech's controls. Long enough for him to fight back his instincts. He shifted the mech to head down the corridor, away from the voices. They were Ashford's people. Ashford and whoever was backing him. If he got caught now, he wouldn't be any use to anybody. Chances were they'd just kill him. Might not even get as far as the airlock first. The mech's legs moved slowly. Even full-out, it didn't go more than a modest walk. The voices behind him shifted. Something crashed. He heard his doctor shouting now and waited for the report of gunfire. If they started shooting, he'd have to go back. The mech inched toward the farther door, toward the exit and what passed for safety. Bull pressed the joystick forward so hard his fingers ached, as if the force would make the machine understand the danger.

The voices got louder, coming close. Bull shifted the mech so that it was walking along the wall. If someone came around the corner behind him, it would give him an extra fraction of a second before he was seen. The thick metal legs slid forward, shifted weight, shifted again.

The doorway was six feet away. Four. Three. He let go of the controls and reached out for the door a little too soon and had to inch the mech forward before he tried again. He was sweating, and he hoped it was only fear. If something in his guts had given way, he wouldn't have known. Probably it was just fear.

The door opened, and he slammed the little joystick forward again. The mech took him through, and he closed the door behind him. He didn't have time to wait or think. He angled the mech down another hall toward the internal lifts and the long trip to second level, section M.

The great interior halls and passageways of the *Behemoth* had never seemed less like home. As he descended, the spin gravity grew almost imperceptibly stronger. His numb flesh sat a little heavier in its harness. He was going to have to get someone to change out his piss bag soon unless he could figure out some way to get his arms inside the mech's frame, but his elbows only bent one direction, so that seemed unlikely. And if his spine didn't grow back, if they didn't get the *Behemoth* and everyone else back out of the trap the protomolecule had caught them in, he'd live like this until he died.

Don't think about it, he told himself. *Too far ahead. Don't think about it. Just do your job.*

He didn't take one of the main internal lifts. Chances were too good that Ashford's men would be watching for that. Instead, he found one of the long, spiraling maintenance passages and set the mech to walking on its own. If it drifted too near one wall or the other, he could correct it, but it gave him a few seconds. He pulled out the hand terminal. He was shaking and his skin looked gray under the brown.

Serge answered almost immediately.

"Ganne nacht, boss," the tattooed Belter said. "Was wondering when you were going to check in."

"Ashford," Bull said.

"On top of it," Serge said. "Looks like he's got about a third of our boys and a bunch of crazy-ass coyos from other ships.

Right now they got the transition points off the drum north to command and south to engineering, the security office and the armory, y some little wolf packs going through the drum stirring up trouble."

"How well armed?"

"Nicht so bien sa moi," Serge said, grinning. "They savvy they got us locked out of the communications too, but I got back door open."

"You what?"

"Always ready for merde mal, me. Bust me down later," Serge said. "I'm putting together squads, clean up the drum. We'll get this all smashed flat by bedtime."

"You have to be careful with these guys, Serge."

"Will, boss. Know what we're doing. Know the ship better than anyone. You get safe, let us take care."

Bull swallowed. Giving over control ached.

"Okay."

"We been trying to get the captain, us," Serge said.

"I warned her. She may be refusing connections until she knows more who she can trust," Bull said. He didn't add, *Or they may have found her.*

"Check," Serge said, and Bull heard in the man's voice that he'd had the same thought. "When we track Ashford?"

"We don't have permission to kill him," Bull said.

"A finger slips, think we can get forgiveness?"

"Probably."

Serge grinned. "Got to go, boss. Just when es se cerrado, and they make you XO, keep me in mind for your chair, no?"

"Screw that," Bull said. "When this shit's done, you can be XO."

"Hold you to, boss," Serge said, and the connection went dead.

Chapter Thirty-Nine: Anna

The first sermon Anna had delivered in front of a congregation, fresh out of seminary and filled with zeal, was seventeen pages of single-spaced notes. It had been a lengthy dissection of the first chapter of Malachi, focusing on the prophet's exhortation not to deliver substandard sacrifices to God, and how that related to modern worship. It had been detailed, backed by all of the evidence and argument Anna's studious nature and seven years of graduate school could bring to bear. By the end of it, Anna was pretty sure not one member of the audience was still awake.

She'd learned some important lessons from that. There was a place for detailed Bible scholarship. There was even a place for it in front of the congregation. But it wasn't what people came to church *for.* Learning a bit more about God was part of feeling closer and more connected to Him, and the closeness was what mattered. So Anna's sermons now tended to be just a page or two of notes, and a lot more speaking from the heart. She'd delivered her message on "mixed" churches in God's eyes without looking at the notes once, and it seemed to go over very well. After she concluded with a short prayer and began the sacrament, Belters and Martians and Earthers got into line together in companionable silence. A few shook hands or clapped each other on the back. Anna felt like it might be the most important message she'd ever delivered.

"Well, it wasn't the worst thing I've ever heard," Tilly said once the service was over. She had the twitchy look she got when she wanted a cigarette, but Anna had asked her not to smoke in the meeting tent and she'd agreed. "Though, admittedly, my tolerance for lovey togetherness is low."

"That's very flattering," Anna whispered, then paused to shake hands with a Belter woman who tearfully thanked her for organizing the meeting. Tilly gave the woman her most insincere smile but managed not to roll her eyes.

"I need a drink," Tilly said once the woman had left. "Come with. I'll buy you a lemonade."

"They closed the bar. Rationing."

Tilly laughed. "I have a supplier. The guy running the rationing sold me a bottle of their best Ganymede hooch for the low price of a thousand dollars. He tossed in the lemonade for free."

"A thousand—"

"One of two things will happen," Tilly said, taking out a cigarette and putting it in her mouth but leaving it unlit. "We'll get out of here, back into the solar system where I'm rich and a thousand bucks doesn't matter, or we won't get out and nothing will matter."

Anna nodded because she didn't know what else to say. As much as she'd come to enjoy and rely on Tilly's friendship, she was occasionally reminded how utterly different their worlds were. If she and Nono had an extra thousand UN dollars lying around, it would have immediately gone into Nami's college fund. Tilly had never in her life had to sacrifice a luxury to get a necessity. If there was any actual mixing in the congregation, it was that. The one thing the Belters and inner planet naval people had in common was that none of them would be drinking thousand-dollar alcohol that night, but Tilly would.

God might not care about financial standing, but He was the only one.

"I admit, lemonade sounds nice," Anna said, fanning her face with her hand terminal. The *Behemoth*'s big habitat drum was built to house a lot more people than it currently held, but they'd stripped a lot of the environmental systems out of it when they converted it to a warship. It was starting to seem like they were reaching the atmosphere processing limits. Or maybe just the air conditioning. The temperature was generally higher now than a girl raised in Russia and most recently living on one of Jupiter's icy moons enjoyed.

After one more tour of the tent to say goodbye to the last lingering remnants of her congregation, Anna followed Tilly out. It wasn't much cooler outside the tent, but the spin of the drum and the air recycling system did combine to create a gentle breeze. Tilly looked over her flushed red face and sweat-plastered hair with a critical eye and said, "Don't worry, everyone who's coming over is here. I heard Cortez talking to some OPA bigwig a couple days ago. This is as hot as it's going to be. And as soon as they find a way to cool us down that doesn't involve venting our atmosphere into space, they'll do it."

Anna couldn't help but laugh. When Tilly raised an eyebrow, Anna explained, "We flew across the entire solar system, almost to the orbit of Neptune, a world so cold and distant from the sun we didn't even know it was there until Bouvard noticed that something was bumping Uranus around."

Tilly's eyebrow crept higher. "Okay."

"And when we get here, who knows how far from the sun and with billions of kilometers of empty space in every direction? We somehow manage to be hot and crowded."

"Thank God the Belters thought to bring this rattletrap with them," Tilly said, ducking to enter her tent. She flopped down into a folding chair and started rummaging in a plastic cooler next to it. "Can you imagine trying to stuff everyone onto the *Prince*? We'd be twelve to a bunk there. Lovely culture, these Belters."

Anna pulled her cassock off and laid it over the edge of Tilly's cot. Underneath she was wearing a white blouse and a knee-length skirt that was much less stifling. Tilly pulled a plastic bulb of lemonade out of the cooler and handed it to her, then poured herself a glass of something as clear as water that smelled like hospital cleanser. When Anna took the bulb she was surprised to find it cold. Small drops of condensation were already forming on its surface. She put the cool bottle against the back of her neck and felt a delightful chill run down her spine.

"How did you manage ice?"

"Dry ice," Tilly said around a lit cigarette, then paused to down her first shot. "Apparently it's easy for the people in atmosphere processing to make. Lots of carbon dioxide just lying around."

If Tilly was spending a thousand dollars a bottle for the antiseptic she was drinking, Anna didn't want to know what a steady supply of ice was costing her. They drank in companionable silence for a while, the cool lemonade doing wonders for Anna's heat exhaustion. Tilly brought up the idea of finding something to eat, and they wandered out of her tent in search of a supply kiosk.

There were people walking through the crowded tent city carrying guns.

"This looks bad," Tilly said. It did. These weren't bored security officers with holstered sidearms. These were grim-faced Belter men and women with assault rifles and shotguns carried in white-knuckled grips. The group moving between the tents was at least a dozen strong, and they were looking for something. Or someone.

Anna tugged at Tilly's sleeve. "Maybe we should try to get people to go back to the church tent to wait this out."

"Annie, if the bullets start flying in here, even God can't make that tent a safe place to hide. I want to know what's going on."

Anna reluctantly followed her in a path that paralleled the

armed group, which moved with purpose, occasionally stopping to look in tents or quietly question people. Anna began to feel very frightened without being sure why.

"Oh," Tilly said. "Here we go."

Bull's second-in-command—Serge was his name, Anna thought—rounded one of the larger tents trailing half a dozen security people behind him. They were all armed as well, though only with handguns. Even to Anna's untrained eye, the difference between six people with pistols and twelve people with rifles was dramatic. Serge had a faint smile on his face as though he hadn't noticed. Anna saw the muscular young woman from the security office standing behind him, though her face was a worried scowl. Oddly enough, seeing someone else look worried made Anna feel better.

"No guns in the drum, sa sa?" Serge said to the armed Belter group, though the volume of his voice made it clear he was speaking to the onlookers as well. "Drop 'em."

"You have guns," a Belter woman said with a sneer. She held a rifle at the ready.

"We're the cops," Serge said, placing one hand on the butt of his gun and grinning back at her.

"Not anymore," she replied and in one quick movement shifted her rifle and shot him in the head. A tiny hole appeared in his forehead, and a cloud of pink mist sprayed into the air behind him. He sank slowly to the floor, an expression of vague puzzlement on his face.

Anna felt her gorge rise, and had to double over and pant to keep from vomiting. "Jesus Christ," Tilly said in a strangled whisper. The speed with which the situation had gone from unsettling to terrifying took Anna's breath away. *I've just seen a man have his brains blown out.* Even after the horrors of the slow zone catastrophe, it was the worst thing she'd ever seen. The security man hadn't thought the woman would shoot him, hadn't suspected the true nature of the threat, and the price he'd paid for it was everything.

At that thought, Anna threw up all over her shoes and then sank to her knees, gagging. Tilly dropped down next to her, not even noticing that the knees of her pants were in a pool of vomit. Tilly hugged her for a second then whispered, "We need to go." Anna nodded back because she couldn't open her mouth without fear of losing control again. A few dozen meters away, the Belters were disarming the security team and tying their arms behind their backs with plastic strips.

At least they weren't shooting anyone else.

Tilly pulled her to her feet, and they hurried back to her tent, all thought of food forgotten. "Something very bad is happening on this ship," Tilly said. Anna had to suppress a manic giggle. Given their current circumstances, things would have to be very bad indeed for Tilly to think the situation had gotten worse. Sure, they were all trapped in orbit around an alien space station that periodically changed the rules of physics and had killed a bunch of them, but now they'd decided to start shooting each other too.

Yes, *very bad.*

Hector Cortez came to Tilly's tent about an hour after the shooting. Anna and Tilly had spent the time staying as close to the floor of the tent as possible, arranging Tilly's few bits of furniture into barricades around them. It had the feeling of performing ritual magic. Nothing in the room would actually stop a bullet, but they arranged it anyway. A blanket fort to keep the monsters at bay.

Mercifully, there hadn't been any further sounds of gunfire.

The few times they peeked out of the tent, they saw smaller groups of no more than two or three armed Belters patrolling the civilian spaces. Anna avoided meeting their eyes, and they ignored her.

When Cortez arrived, he cleared his throat loudly outside the tent, then asked if he could enter. They were both afraid to answer, but he came in anyway. Several people waited for him outside, though Anna couldn't see who.

He glanced once around the inside of the gloomy space, looking over their flimsy barricade, then pulled a chair away from it and sat down without commenting on it.

"The shooting is over. It's safe to sit," he said, gesturing at the other chairs. He looked better than he had in a while. His suit had been cleaned and somehow he'd found a way to wash his thick white hair. But that wasn't all of it. Some of his self-assurance had returned. He seemed confident and in charge again. Anna climbed up off the floor and took a chair. After a moment, Tilly did the same.

"I'm sorry you were frightened," Cortez said with a smile that didn't seem sorry at all.

"What's going on, Hank?" Tilly asked, her eyes narrowing. She took out a cigarette and began playing with it without lighting it. "What are you up to?"

"I'm not *up to* anything, Matilda," Cortez said. "What's happening is that the rightful authority on this ship has been restored, and Captain Ashford is once more in command."

"Okay, *Hector*," Tilly replied, "but how are you involved? Seems like internal OPA politics to me. What's your play?"

Cortez ignored her and said to Anna, "Doctor Volovodov, may we speak privately?"

"Tilly can hear anything—" Anna started, but Tilly waved her off.

"I think I'll go outside for a smoke."

When she'd left the tent, Cortez pulled his chair close enough that his knees were almost touching Anna's. He leaned forward, taking her hands in his own. Anna had never had the sense that Hector was interested in her sexually, and still didn't, but somehow the closeness felt uncomfortably intimate. Invasive.

"Anna," he said, giving her hands a squeeze. "Things are about to change dramatically on this ship, and in our calling here. I've been fortunate in that Captain Ashford trusts me and has sought my counsel, so I've had some input on the direction these changes take."

The forced intimacy, combined with the bitter taste still in her mouth from having seen a man murdered, brought up an anger she hadn't expected. She pulled her hands away from him with more violence than she intended, then couldn't help but feel a twinge of satisfaction at the hurt and surprise on his face.

"How nice for you," she said, carefully keeping her tone neutral.

"Doctor Volovodov...*Anna*, I would like your support." Anna couldn't stop the snort of disbelief in time, but he pressed on. "You have a way with people. I'm fine in front of a camera, but I'm not as good one-on-one, and that's where you shine. That's your gift. And we are about to face terrible personal challenges. Things people will have a hard time understanding. I would like your voice there with me to reassure them."

"What are you talking about?" Anna said, barely squeezing the words past a growing lump in her throat. She had the sense of a terrible secret about to be revealed. Cortez shone with the invincible certainty of the true believer.

"We are going to close the gate," he said. "We have a weapon in our possession that we believe will work."

"No," Anna said more in disbelief than in denying his claims.

"Yes. Even now engineers work to refit this vessel's communications laser to make it powerful enough to destroy the Ring."

"I don't mean that," Anna started, but Cortez just continued speaking.

"We are lost, but we can protect those we've left behind. We can end the greatest threat the human race has ever known. All it requires is that we sacrifice any hope of return. A small price to pay for—"

"No," Anna said again, more forcefully. "No, you don't get to decide that for all of these people." *For me*, she thought. *You don't get to take my wife and daughter away like that. Just because you're afraid.*

"In times of great danger and sacrifice such as this, some will step forward to make the difficult decisions. Ashford has done that, and I support him. Now it is our role to make sure the people understand and cooperate. They need to know that their sacrifice will protect the billions of people we've left behind."

"We don't know that," Anna said.

"This station has already claimed hundreds of lives, maybe thousands."

"Because we keep making decisions without knowing what the consequences are. We chased Holden's ship through the Ring, we sent soldiers to the station to hunt him, we keep acting without information and then being angry when it hurts us."

"It didn't hurt us. It killed us. A lot of us."

"We're like children," Anna said, pushing herself to her feet and lecturing down at him. "Who burn their hands on a hot stove and then think the solution is to blow up all the stoves."

"Eros," Cortez started.

"*We* did that! And Ganymede, and Phoebe, all the rest! We did it. We keep acting without thinking and you think the solution is to do it one more time. You have allied yourself with stupid, violent men, and you are trying to convince yourself that being stupid and violent will work. That makes you stupid too. I will never help you. I'll fight you now."

Cortez stood up and called to the people waiting outside. A Belter with protective chest armor and a rifle came into the tent.

"Will you shoot me too?" Anna said, putting as much contempt into the words as she could.

Cortez turned his back on her and left with the gunman.

Anna sank down into her chair, her legs suddenly too shaky to support her. She doubled over, rocking back and forth and taking long shuddering breaths to calm herself. Somehow, she didn't black out.

"Did he hurt you?" Tilly said from behind her. Her friend put a gentle hand on the back of her neck as she rocked.

"No," Anna said. It wasn't technically a lie.

"Oh, Annie. They have Claire. They wouldn't let me talk to her. I don't know if she's a hostage or—"

Before she knew she was going to do it, Anna had jumped to her feet and run out of the tent. They'd be going to the elevator that ran up the side of the drum and connected with the passages to the command decks and engineering. They'd be going to the bridge. Men like Cortez and Ashford, men who wanted to be in charge, they'd be on the bridge. She ran toward the elevator as fast as her legs would carry her. She hadn't actually run in years. Living in a small station tunneled into the ice of Europa, it just hadn't come up. She was out of breath in moments, but pushed on, ignoring the nausea and the stitch in her ribs.

She reached the elevator just as Cortez and his small band of gun-toting thugs climbed inside. Clarissa was standing at the back of the group, looking small and frail surrounded by soldiers in armor. As the doors slid closed, she smiled at Anna and raised one hand in a wave.

Then she was gone.

Chapter Forty: Holden

Hey, Cap?" Amos said from his bed. "That was the third armed patrol that's gone past this room in about three hours. Some shit is going down."

"I know," Holden said quietly. It was obvious that the situation on the *Behemoth* had changed. People with guns were moving through the corridors with hard expressions. Some of them had pulled a doctor aside, had a short but loud argument with her, then taken a patient away in restraints. It felt like a coup in progress, but according to Naomi the security chief Bull had already mutinied and taken the ship from the original Belter captain. And nothing had happened that would explain why he'd suddenly need to put a lot more boots on the ground or begin making arrests.

It felt like a civil war was brewing, or being squashed.

"Should we do something?" Amos asked.

Yes, Holden thought. *We should do something. We should get back to the* Rocinante *and hide until Miller gets done doing whatever he was doing and releases the ships in the slow zone.* Then they should burn like hell out of this place and never look back. Unfortunately, his crew was still laid up and he didn't exactly have a ride waiting to take him to his ship.

"No," he said instead. "Not until we understand what's happening. I just got *out* of jail. Not in a hurry to go back."

Alex sat up in bed, and then moaned at the effort. The top of his head was swathed in bloodstained bandages, and the left side of his face had a mushy, pulpy look to it. The speed limit change had thrown him face first into one of the cockpit's viewscreens. If he hadn't been at least partially belted into his chair, he'd probably be dead.

"Maybe we should find a quieter place than this to hole up," he said. "They don't seem opposed to arresting patients so far."

Holden nodded with his fist. He was starting to pick up Naomi's Belter-style gestures, but whenever he caught himself using one he felt awkward, like a kid pretending to be an adult. "My time on this ship has been limited to the docking bay and this room. I don't have any idea where a quieter place would be."

"Well," Naomi said. "That puts you one up on us. None of us were conscious when they brought us here."

Holden hopped off the edge of her bed and moved to the door, closing it as quietly as possible. He looked around for something to jam it shut with, but quickly decided it was hopeless. The habitation spaces in the *Behemoth*'s drum were built for low weight, not durability. The walls and door of the hospital room were paper-thin layers of epoxy and woven carbon fiber. A good kick would probably bring the entire structure down. Barricading the door would only signal patrols that something was wrong, and then delay them half a second while they broke it.

"Maybe that preacher can help us," Alex said.

"Yeah." Amos nodded. "Red seems like good people."

"No hitting on the preacher," Holden said, pointing at Amos with an accusing finger.

"I just—"

"But it doesn't matter, because if she has even half a brain—and I suspect she has a lot more than that—she'll be busily hiding herself. And she's not from here. We need an insider."

"Sam," Naomi said, just as Holden was thinking the same name. "She's chief engineer on this boat. No one will know it like she does."

"Does she owe you any favors?" Holden asked.

Naomi gave him a sour look and pulled his hand terminal off his belt. "No. I owe her about a thousand," she said as she opened a connection request to Sam. "But she's a friend. Favors don't matter."

She laid the terminal on the bed with the speaker on. The triple beep of an unanswered voice request sounding once a second. Alex and Amos were staring at it intensely, eyes wide. As though it were a bomb that might go off at any moment. In a way, Holden thought, it was. They were about as helpless right now as he could ever remember them being. Holden found himself wishing that Miller would appear and fix everything with alien magic.

"Yo," a voice said from the terminal. "Knuckles."

At some point over the last year, Sam had given Naomi the nickname Knuckles. Holden had never been able to figure out why, and Naomi had never offered to explain.

"Sammy," Naomi replied, the relief in her voice obvious. "We really, really need your help."

"Funny," Sam said. "I was just thinking of coming by to ask for *your* help. Coincidence? Or something more?"

"We were calling you to find a hiding spot," Amos yelled out. "If you were calling us for the same thing, you're fucked."

"No, that's a good idea. I've got a spot you can hole up for a while, and I'll come meet you there. Knuckles, you'll have the layout in just a second. Just follow the map. I'll be there as soon as I can. You kids take care of yourselves."

"You do the same, Sammy," Naomi said, then killed the connection. She worked the terminal for a few seconds. "Okay, I see it. Looks like unused storage just a couple hundred meters aft and spinward."

"You get to navigate," Holden said to her, then added, "Can everyone walk?"

Amos and Alex both nodded, but Naomi said, "Alex's skull is being held together with glue right now. If he gets dizzy and falls, he's not getting up again."

"Now XO," Alex objected. "I can—"

"Naomi can't walk," Amos said. "So you put her on a rolling bed with Alex and push them. I'll take point. Gimme that map."

Holden didn't argue. He picked Naomi up from her bed, trying to jostle her as little as possible, then set her next to Alex on his. "Why am I pushing instead of walking point?"

"He broke his left arm," Naomi said, scooting as close to Alex as possible and then securing the lap restraint across them both. When Amos began to protest she added, "And all the ribs on his left side."

"Right," Holden said, grabbing the push bars at the head of the bed and kicking off the wheel locks. "Lead the way."

Amos led them through the makeshift hospital corridors, smiling at everyone he passed, moving with an easy stride that made him look like a man with a destination but no hurry to get there. Even the armed patrol they passed barely gave him a glance. When they looked curiously at Holden, pushing two injured people on the same bed, he said, "Two to a bed now. That's how crowded we're getting." They just nodded him past, their expressions both sullen and bored.

Holden hadn't had much chance to look around the rest of the hospital. After leaving the docks he'd hurried straight to his crew's room and hadn't left since. But now, as he moved through the halls and intersections toward the exit, he had a chance to look over the full extent of the damage the catastrophic speed limit change had caused.

Every bed in every room was filled with injured people, and sometimes the benches and chairs in the waiting areas. Most of the injuries were contusions or broken bones, but some were more severe. He saw more than one amputation, and quite a few people hanging in traction with serious spinal injuries. But more than the physical damage, there was the stunned look of shock on every face. The sort of expression Holden associated with the recent victims or witnesses of violent crime. The *Rocinante* had tracked and disabled a pirate slaver ship a few months back, and the beaten and starving prisoners pulled from her hold had looked like this. Not just hurt, but robbed of hope.

Someone with a doctor's uniform watched Holden push the bed past, his eyes following their progress, but exhaustion robbing him of curiosity. From a small room to his right, Holden heard the electric popping sound of a cauterizing gun, and the smell of cooking meat filled the air.

"This is horrifying," he whispered to Naomi. She nodded but said nothing.

"None of us shoulda come here," Alex said.

Doors and corners, Miller had warned him. The places where you got killed if you weren't paying attention. Where the ambushes happened. *Could have been a little more explicit*, Holden thought, and then imagined Miller shrugging apologetically and bursting into a cloud of blue gnats.

Amos, half a dozen meters ahead, came to a four-way junction in the corridor and turned right. Before Holden could cross half the distance to the turn, a pair of OPA goons walked into the intersection from the left.

They paused, looking over Naomi and Alex snuggled up in the rolling bed. One of them smirked and half turned to his companion. Holden could almost hear the joke he was about to make about two people to a bed. In preparation, he smiled and readied a laugh. But before the jokester could speak, his companion said, "That's James Holden."

Everything after that happened quickly.

The pair of OPA thugs scrambled to get at the shotguns slung over their shoulders. Holden shoved the rolling gurney into their thighs, knocking them back, and gave the corridor a frantic glance looking for a weapon. One of the thugs managed to fumble his shotgun down off his shoulder and rack it, but Naomi scooted forward on the bed and drove her heel into his groin. His partner stepped back, finished getting his hands on his shotgun, and pointed it at her. Holden started to run forward, knowing he was too slow, knowing he'd watch Naomi blown apart long before he could reach the gunman.

Then both gunmen turned toward each other and slammed their faces together. They slumped to the floor, guns falling from nerveless fingers. Amos stood behind them, grimacing and massaging his left shoulder.

"Sorry, Cap," he said. "Got a little too far ahead there."

Holden leaned against the corridor wall, legs barely able to support him even in the light gravity. "No apologies. Nice save." He nodded toward the shoulder that Amos continued to rub with a pained look. "Thought that was broken."

Amos snorted. "It didn't fall off. Plenty left in here for a couple of idiots like this." He bent down and stripped the two fallen men of their weapons and ammunition. A nurse walked up behind Holden, a plastic case in her hands and a question on her face.

"Nothing to see here," Holden said. "We'll be gone in a minute."

She pointed at a nearby door. "Supply closet. No one will notice them in there for a while." Then she turned and went back the way she came.

"You have a fan," Naomi said from the bed.

"Not everyone in the OPA hates us," Holden replied, moving around the gurney to help Amos drag the unconscious men into the closet. "We did good work for them for over a year. People know that."

Amos handed Holden a compact black pistol and a pair of extra magazines. Holden tucked the gun into the waistband of his pants and pulled his shirt down over it. Amos did the same with a second gun, then put the two shotguns onto the gurney next to Naomi and covered them with the sheet.

"We don't want to get in a gunfight," Holden warned Amos as they began moving again.

"Yeah," Amos said. "But if we're in one anyway, it'll be nice to have guns."

The hospital exit was a short distance down the right-hand hallway, and suddenly they were outside. Or as outside as you could get in the *Behemoth*'s massive habitation drum. From outside, the hospital structure looked cheap and hastily assembled. A football-field-sized shanty made of epoxied carbon and fiberglass. A few hundred meters away, the edge of a city of tents spread out like acne on the drum's smooth skin.

"That way," Naomi said, pointing toward a more permanent-looking steel structure. Holden pushed the gurney, and Amos walked a few meters ahead, smiling and nodding at anyone who looked at them. Something in Amos' face making them scurry away and not look back.

As they approached the squat metal structure, a door opened in the side and Sam's pixie face appeared, waving a hand at them impatiently. A few minutes and some twisty corridors later, they were in a small, empty metal-walled room. Amos immediately dropped to the floor, laying his left arm and back flat against it.

"Ow," he said.

"You hurt?" Sam asked, locking the door behind them with a small metal keycard, and then tossing the card to Naomi.

"Everyone's hurt," Holden said. "So what the hell is going on?"

Sam blew her lips out and ran one greasy hand through her red hair. The streaks of black already in it told Holden she'd been doing a lot of that. "Ashford retook the ship. He's got some sort of coalition of bigwigs from the UN Navy, the Martians, and some of the important civilians."

"Okay," Holden said, realizing that his lack of context made most of that sentence pretty meaningless, but not wanting to waste time with explanations. "So the people roaming the halls with guns are Ashford's?"

"Yep. He's taking out anyone who helped Bull or Pa with the original mutiny, or, y'know, anyone he thinks is a threat."

"From the way they tried to shoot us, we're on that list," Naomi said.

"Definitely." Sam nodded. "I haven't been able to track down Pa, but Bull called me, so I know he's okay."

"Sam," Holden said, patting the air in a calming gesture. "Keep in mind I have no idea who these people are or why they are important, and we don't have time for a who's who. Just tell us the important bits."

Sam started to object, then shrugged and briefly explained the plan to use the comm laser. "If I do what he's asking me to do, we'll be able to get a pulse out of it that'll be hotter than a star for about three-quarters of a second. It will melt that entire side of the ship in the process."

"Does he know that?" Naomi asked, incredulity in her voice.

"He doesn't care. Whether it works on the Ring or not, we have to stop him. There are thousands of people on this ship right now, and they'll all die if he gets his way."

Holden sank down onto the edge of the gurney with a long exhale. "Oh, we're the least of the problem," he said. "This is suddenly much, much bigger than that."

Sam cocked her head at him, frowning a question.

"I've seen what this station does to threats," Holden said. "Miller showed me, when I was there. All this slow zone stuff is non-lethal deterrent as far as it's concerned. If that big blue ball out there decides us monkeys are an actual threat, it will autoclave our solar system."

"Who's Miller?" Sam asked.

"Dead guy," Amos said.

"And he was on the station?"

"Apparently," Amos said with a lopsided shrug.

"Jim?" Naomi said, putting her hand on his arm. This was the first she'd heard him speak of his experiences on the station, and he felt a pang of guilt for not telling her before.

"Something was attacking them, the protomolecule masters or whatever they were. Their defense was causing the star in any... *infected* solar system to go supernova. That station has the power to blow up stars, Naomi.

"If Ashford does this, it will kill every human there is. Everyone."

There was a long silence. Amos had stopped rubbing his arm and grunting. Naomi stared up at him from the bed, eyes wide, the fear on her face mirroring his own.

"Well," Sam finally said. "Good thing I'm not gonna let him, then, isn't it?"

"Say again?" Amos said from the floor.

"I didn't know about this other thing with ghosts and aliens," Sam said in a tone of voice that made it clear she wasn't totally buying Holden's story. "But I've been sabotaging the laser upgrades. Delaying the process while I build in short points. Weaknesses that will blow every time he tries to fire it. It should be easy enough to explain away because of course the system was never designed for this, and the ship is a flying hunk of cobbled-together junk at this point anyway."

"How long can you get us?"

"Day. Maybe a day and a half."

"I think I love you," Alex said, the words coming out in a pain- and medication-induced mumble.

"We all do, Sam," Holden said to cover for him. "That's brilliant, but there aren't very many of us, and it's a big, complicated ship. The question is how we get control of it."

"Bull," she replied. "That's why I called you. Bull's kind of messed up right now and he needs help and I don't know anyone else on this ship I trust." This last part she directed at Naomi.

"We'll do whatever we can," Naomi replied, holding up her hand. Sam crossed the room and took it. "Anything you need, Sammy. Tell us where Bull is, and I'll send my boys to go collect him."

Amos pushed himself up off the floor with a grunt and moved

to the gurney. "Yeah, whatever you need, Sam. We owe you about a million at this point, and this Ashford guy sounds like an asshole."

Sam gave a relieved smile and squeezed Naomi's fingers. "I really appreciate it. But be careful. Ashford loyalists are everywhere, and they've already killed some people. If you run into any more of them, there'll be trouble."

Amos pulled one of the shotguns out from under the sheet and laid it casually across his shoulder.

"Man can hope."

Chapter Forty-One: Bull

The storage cells were too large to be a prison. They were warehouses for the supplies to start again after a hundred ecological collapses. Seed vaults and soil and enough compressed hydrogen and oxygen to recreate the shallow ocean of a generation ship. Bull drove his mech across the vast open space, as wide and tall and airy as a cathedral, but without a single image of God. It was a temple dedicated to utility and engineering, the beauty of function and the grandeur of the experiment that would have launched humanity at the distant stars.

Everything was falling to shit around him. All the information he could put together, hunched close to his hand terminal like he was trying to crawl into it, showed that Ashford had taken over engineering and the reactor at the far south of the drum and command at the north. His squads were moving through the drum with impunity. Pa was missing and might be dead. She still had a lot of people loyal to her, including Bull, to his surprise, but if they found her body in a recycler someplace that would fade quickly. He'd done everything he could. He hadn't had the power, so he'd tried for finesse, and when that didn't work, he'd grabbed the power. He'd taken the massacre of thousands by the protomolecule's station and gone at least halfway to building a city out of it. A little civilization in the mouth of the void. If he'd been a little more ruthless, maybe he could have made it work. Clanking softly through the massive space, that was the thing that haunted him. Not his sins, not even the people he'd killed, but the thought that if he'd killed just one or two more it might have been enough.

And even with that darkness in his heart, he couldn't keep from feeling moved by the scale of the steel and ceramic. The industrial beauty of design. He wished they'd gone to the stars instead of flying it into the mouth of hell. He wished he'd been able to make it all work out.

He tried to connect with Serge, but got nothing. He tried Corin. He wanted to reach out to Sam again, but he couldn't risk Ashford finding out they were in contact. He checked the broadcast feed or Radio Free Slow Zone, but Monica Stuart and her crew hadn't made any announcements. He let himself hope that Ashford's plan would collapse in on itself the way that all of his own plans had. Not much chance of that, though. Ashford just wanted to blow shit up. That was always easier than making something.

He thought about recording a last message to Fred Johnson, but he didn't know if he wanted to apologize, commiserate, or make the man feel guilty for putting a petulant little boy like Ashford in charge, so instead he waited and hoped for something unexpected. And maybe good for a change.

He heard the footsteps coming from the aftmost access corridor. More than one person. Two. Maybe three. If it was Ashford's men coming for him, he wasn't going to have to worry much about what to say to Fred. He took the pistol out of his holster and checked the magazine. The soft metallic sounds echoed. The footsteps faltered.

"Bull?" a familiar voice called out. "Are you in there?"

"Who's asking?" Bull said, then coughed. He spat on the deck.

"Jim Holden," the voice said. "You aren't planning to shoot me, are you? Because Sam sort of gave us the impression that we were on the same side."

Holden stepped into the storage area. This was who she'd meant when she said she knew who she could trust. And she had a point. Holden was outside every command. His reputation was built on being a man without subtexts. The man behind him with the shotgun was Amos Burton. For a moment, Bull was surprised to see the wounded Earther on his feet, then remembered his own condition and smiled. He lowered his gun, but he didn't put it away.

"And why would she think that?" he asked.

"Same enemies," Holden said. "We have to stop Ashford. If he does what he's planning, we're all trapped in here until we die. And I'm pretty sure the Ring kills everybody on the other side. Earth, Mars. The Belt. Everyone."

Bull felt something deep in his chest settle. He didn't know if it was only the weight of his worst fears coming true or if something unpleasant was happening in his lungs. He put the pistol in his holster, took the joysticks, and angled himself toward the two men. The mech's movements seemed louder now that there were other people to hear them.

"Okay," Bull said. "How about you start at the beginning and tell me what the hell you're going on about."

Bull had been around charisma before. The sense that some people had of moving through their lives in a cloud of likability or power. Fred Johnson had that, and there were glimmers of it in Holden too. In fact, there was something about Holden's open-faced honesty that reminded Bull of the young Fred Johnson's candor. He said things in a simple, matter-of-fact way—the station wouldn't come off lockdown until they turned off all the reactors and enough of the electronics on the ships; the makers of the protomolecule had been devoured by some mysterious force even badder-ass than they were; the station would destroy the solar system if it decided humans and their weapons constituted a real threat—that made them all seem plausible. Maybe it was the depth of his own belief. Maybe it was just a talent some people were born with. Bull felt a growing respect for Jim Holden, the same way he'd respect a rattlesnake. The man was dangerous just by being what he was.

When Holden ran out of steam, repeating himself that they had to stop Ashford, that Sam was buying them time, that the skeleton crews on the other ships had to shut down their reactors and power down their backup systems, Bull scratched his chin.

"What if Ashford's right?" he said.

"I don't understand," Holden said.

"All this stuff you got from the alien? What if it's bullshitting you?"

Holden's jaw went hard, but a moment later he nodded.

"He might be," he said. "I don't have any way of making sure. But Sam says Ashford's going to sacrifice the *Behemoth* when he shoots at the Ring, and if Miller wasn't lying, he's sacrificing everything else along with it. Is that a chance you're willing to take?"

"Taking it either way," Bull said. "Maybe we stop him, and we save the system. Maybe we leave the Ring open for an invasion by things that are going eat our brains on toast. Flip a coin, ese. And we got no time to test it out. No way to make sure. Either way, it's a risk."

"It is," Holden said. "So. What are you going to do?"

Bull's sigh started him coughing again. The mucus that came up into his mouth tasted like steroid spray. He spat. That was what it came down to. It wasn't really a question.

"Figure we got to retake engineering," Bull said. "Probably going to be a bitch of a fight, but we got to do it. With the drum spinning, the only path between engineering and command is the external lift or in through the command transition point, and then all the way through the drum to the engineering transition point with a shitload of people and spin gravity to slow them down. Any reinforcements he's got up top won't make it before the fight's done one way or the other."

"Sammy's already in engineering," Amos said. "Might be she could soften up the terrain for us before we go in."

"That'd be good," Bull said.

"And once we take it?" Holden said.

"Pump an assload of nitrogen into command, and pull 'em all out after they've gone to sleep, I figure," Bull said. "If Captain Pa's still alive, they're her problem."

"What if she ain't?" Amos said.

"Then they're mine," Bull said. Amos' smile meant the man had unpacked Bull's words just the way he'd meant them.

"And the reactor?" Holden said. "Are you going to shut it down?"

"That's the backup plan," Bull said with a grin. "We shut it down. We get everyone else to shut down."

"Can I ask why?"

"Might be that we can get this thing off of lockdown and it won't kill off the sun, even if Ashford does get a shot off," Bull said.

"Fair enough," Holden said. "I've got my crew. We're a little banged up."

"Pure of heart, though," Amos said.

"I don't know how many people I still got," Bull said. "If I can get through to a couple of them, I can find out."

"So where do we set up shop?"

Bull paused. If they were going to try an assault on engineering, a distraction would help. Something that would pull Ashford's attention away from what actually mattered to something else. If there was a way to slap him down. Hurt his pride. Ashford hadn't been the kind of man who thought things through well before the catastrophe, but he had been cautious. If there was a way to make him angry, to overcome that caution. But doing that and getting the word to the other ships that they needed to shut down would be more time than he had, unless…

"Yeah," he said sourly. "I know where we're going. May be a little dangerous getting there. Ashford's people are all through the drum."

"Not as many as there were when we started," Amos said. Bull didn't ask what he meant.

"Lead on," Holden said. "We'll follow you."

Bull tapped his fingers on the joysticks. Embarrassment and shame clawed their way up his guts. A shadow of confusion crossed Holden's face. Bull felt a stab of disgust with himself. He was about to put a bunch of civilians in danger in order to draw Ashford's attention, he was going to do it of his own free will, and he was ashamed of the things that he didn't actually have any control over. He didn't know what that said about him, but he figured it couldn't be good.

Radio Free Slow Zone was in what had once been the colonial administrative offices. The narrow office spaces had been designed into the walls and bulkheads of the original ship, back when it had been the *Nauvoo*, and the amount of work it would have taken to strip the cubicles back until the space could be used for something else had never been worth the effort. Bull had given it to Monica Stuart and her crew because it was a cheap favor. Something he didn't need—the old offices—for something he did: a familiar face and reassuring voice to help make the *Behemoth* into the gathering place for the full and fractured fleet.

The broadcast studio was a sheet of formed green plastic that someone had pried off the floor and set on edge. The lights were jerry-rigged and stuck to whatever surfaces came to hand. Bull recognized most of the faces, though he didn't know many of them. Monica Stuart, of course. Her production team was down to an Earther woman named Okju and a dark-skinned Martian called Clip. Holden had called his crew there, but they hadn't arrived yet.

Bull considered the space from a tactical point of view. It wouldn't be hard to block off accessways. The little half walls provided a lot of cover, and they were solid enough to stop most slug throwers. An hour or two with some structural steel and a couple welders and the place could be almost defensible. He hoped it wouldn't need to be. Except that he hoped it would.

"We went black as soon as the fighting started," Monica said. "Thought it would be better not to go off half-cocked."

"Good plan," Bull said, and his hand terminal chimed. He held up a finger and fumbled to accept the connection. Corin's face flickered to life. She looked pale. Shell-shocked. He knew the expression.

"How bad?"

"I've got about thirty people, sir," Corin said. "Armed and armored. We control the commissary and most of the civilians. Once Ashford got control of the transition points, he mostly fell back."

"Pa?"

"Alive," Corin said. "Pretty beat up, but alive."

"We'll call that a win."

"We lost Serge," Corin said, her voice flat and calm. That was it, then. Bull felt *I'm sorry* coming by reflex and pushed it back. Later. He could offer sympathy later. Right now, he only had room for strong.

"All right," he said. "Bring whoever you can spare to the colonial administrative offices. And weapons. All the weapons we've got, bring them here."

"New headquarters?"

"Security station in exile," Bull said, and Corin almost smiled. There was no joy in it, but maybe a little amusement. Good enough for now. She saluted, and he returned the gesture as best he could before dropping the connection.

"So this is a coup," Monica said.

"Counter-countercoup, technically," Bull said. "Here's what I need you to do. I want you reporting on what's going on here. Broadcast. The *Behemoth*, the other ships in the fleet. Hell, tell the station if you think it'll listen. Captain Ashford was relieved for mental health reasons. The trauma was too much for him. He and a few people who are still personally loyal to him have holed up in command, and the security team of the *Behemoth* is going to extract him."

"And is any of that true?"

"Maybe half," Bull said.

Behind Monica's back, the wide-set Earther woman named Okju looked up and then away.

"I'm not a propagandist," Monica said.

"Ashford's going to get us all killed," Bull said. "Maybe everyone back home too, if he does what he's thinking. The catastrophe? Everything we've been through here? These were the kid gloves. He's trying to start a real fight."

It was strange how saying the words himself made them seem real in a way that hearing from Holden hadn't. He still wasn't sure whether he believed it was true, even. But right now, it needed to be, and so it was. Monica's eyes went a little rounder and bright red splotches appeared on her cheeks.

"When this is over," she said, "I want the full story. Exclusive. Everything that's really going on. Why it came down the way it did. In-depth interviews with all the players."

"Can't speak for anyone but myself right now," Bull said. "But that's a fair deal by me. Also, I need you to talk the other ships in the fleet into shutting down their reactors and power grids, pulling the batteries out of every device they can find that's got them."

"Because?"

"We're trying to get the lockdown on the ships taken off," he said. "Let us go home. And if we can't stop Ashford, getting off lockdown is the only chance we've got to keep the station from retaliating against the folks on the other side of the Ring."

And because if the insults and provocations, the false threats and misdirections all failed, that would be enough. If Ashford could see the other plan coming together, if he could see *his* heroic gesture, *his* grand sacrifice being taken away, he would come. He'd do whatever he could to shut down the studio, and every gun that came here was one less that would be at engineering or command.

Monica looked nonplussed.

"And how am I going to convince them to do that, exactly?"

"I have an idea about that," Bull said. "I know this priest lady who's got people from damn near every ship out here coming to her services. I'm thinking we recruit her."

Even, he didn't say, *if it puts her in the firing line.*

Chapter Forty-Two: Clarissa

The end came. All the running around stopped, and a kind of calm descended on Ashford. On Cortez. All of them. The order went out to secure the transition points. No one was passing into or out of the drum. Not now. Not ever again.

It felt almost like relief.

"I've been thinking about your father," Cortez said as the lift rose toward the transition point, spin gravity ebbing away and the growing Coriolis making everything feel a little bit off. Like a dream or the beginning of an unexpected illness. "He was a very clever man. Brilliant, some would say, and very private in his way."

He tried to turn the protomolecule into a weapon and sell it to the highest bidder, Clarissa thought. The thought should have stung, but it didn't. It was just a fact. Iron atoms formed in stars; a Daimo-Koch power relay had one fewer input than the standard models; her father had tried to militarize the protomolecule. He hadn't known what it was. No one had. That didn't keep them from playing with it. Seeing what they could do. She had the sudden visual memory of a video she'd seen of a drunken soldier handing his assault rifle to a chimp. What had happened next was either hilarious or tragic, depending on her mood. Her father hadn't been that different from the chimp. Just on a bigger scale.

"I'm sorry I didn't have the chance to know him better," Cortez said.

Ashford and seven of his men were on the lift with them. The captain stood at the front, hands clasped behind his back. Most of his men were Belters too. Long frames, large heads. Ren had had that look too. Like they were all part of the same family. Ashford's soldiers had sidearms and bulletproof vests. She didn't. And yet she kept catching them glancing over at her. They still thought of her as Melba. She was the terrorist and murderer with the combat modifications. That she looked like a normal young woman only added to the sense that she was eerie. This was why Ashford had wanted her so badly. She was an adornment. A trophy to show how strong he was and paper over his failure to hold his own ship before.

She wished that one of them would smile at her. The more they acted like she was Melba, the more she felt that version of herself coming back, seeping up into her cognition like ink soaking through paper.

"There was one time your brother Petyr came to the United Nations buildings when I was visiting there."

"That would have been Michael," she said. "Petyr hates the UN."

"Does he?" Cortez said with a gentle laugh. "My mistake."

The lift reached the axis of the drum, slowing gently so that they could all steady themselves with the handrails and not be launched up into the ceiling. Behind them, a series of vast conduits and transformers powered the long, linear sun of the drum. Before she'd come out to the Ring, she'd never seriously thought about balancing power loads and environmental control systems.

That kind of thing had been for other people. Lesser people. Now, with all she'd learned, the scale of the *Behemoth*'s design was awing. She wished the others could have seen it. Soledad and Bob and Stanni. And Ren.

The doors slid open, and the Belters launched themselves into the transition with the grace of men and women who'd spent their childhoods in low or null g. She and Cortez didn't embarrass themselves, but they would never have the autonomic grace of a Belter on the float.

The command decks were beautiful. The soft indirect lighting took everyone's shadows away. Melba launched herself after Ashford and the Belters, swimming through the air like a dolphin in the sea.

The command center itself was beautifully designed. A long, lozenge-shaped room with control boards set into ceramic desks. On one end of the lozenge, a door opened into the captain's office, on the other, to the security station. The gimbaled crash couches looked less like functional necessities than the natural, beautiful outgrowth of the ship. Like an orchid. The walls were painted with angels and pastoral scenes. The effect was only slightly spoiled by the half dozen access panels that stood open, repairs from the sudden stop still uncompleted. Even the guts of the command center were beautiful in their way. Clarissa found herself wanting to go over and just look in to see if she could make sense of the design.

Three men floated at the control boards, all of them Belters. "Welcome back, Captain," one of them said.

Ashford sailed through the empty air to the captain's station. Three of the soldiers drifted out to take positions in the corridor, the others arraying themselves around the room, all with sightlines on the doors leading in. Anyone who tried to take the command center would have to walk through a hailstorm of bullets. Clarissa pulled herself over to the door of the security station, as much to get out of the way as anything, and Cortez followed her, his expression focused, serious, and a little agitated.

Ashford keyed in a series of commands, and his control panel shifted, growing brighter. His eyes tracked over the readouts and screens. Lit from below, he looked less like the man set to save all of humanity at the sacrifice of himself and his crew and more like a lower university science teacher trying to get his simulations to work they way they were meant to.

"Jojo?" he said, and the voice of the prison guard came from the control deck like the man was standing beside them.

"Here, Captain. We've got the engineering transition point locked down. Anyone wants to get in here, we'll give 'em eight kinds of hell."

"Good man," Ashford said. "Do we have Chief Engineer Rosenberg?"

"Yes, sir. She's making the modifications to the comm array now."

"Still?"

"Still, sir."

"Thank you," he said, then tapped the display, his fingertips popping against the screen. "Sam. How long before the modifications are done?"

"Two hours," she said.

"Why so long?"

"I'm going to have to override every safety device in the control path," she said. "This thing we're doing? There's a lot of built-in design that was meant to keep it from happening."

Ashford scowled.

"Two hours," he said, and stabbed the connection closed.

The waiting began. Two hours later, the same woman explained that the targeting system had been shaken out of round by the catastrophe. It just meant a delay getting lock for most purposes, but since this was a one-shot application, she was realigning it. Three more hours. Then she was getting a short loop error that he had to track down. Two more hours.

Clarissa saw Ashford's mood darken with every excuse, every hour that stretched past. She found the toilets tucked at the back of the security station and started wondering about getting a few tubes of food. If the only working commissary was in the drum, that might actually be a problem. Cortez had strapped himself into a crash couch and slept. The guards slowly became more and more restless. Clarissa spent an hour going from access panel to access panel, looking at the control boards and power relays that fed the bridge. It was surprising how many of them were the same as the ones she'd worked with on the Earth ships coming out. Cut an Earther or a Belter, they both bled the same blood. Crack an access panel on the *Behemoth* and the *Prince*, and both ships had the same crappy brownout buffers.

She wondered how the *Behemoth* felt about being the *Behemoth* and not the *Nauvoo*. She wondered how she felt about being Clarissa Mao and not Melba Koh. Would the ship feel the nobility of its sacrifice? Lost forever in the abyss, but with everyone else redeemed by her sacrifice. The symmetry seemed meaningful, but it might only have been the grinding combination of fear and uncertainty that made it seem that way.

Seven hours after they'd taken the bridge, Ashford stabbed at the control console again, waited a few seconds, and punched the console hard enough that the blow pushed him back into his couch. The sound of the violence startled Cortez awake and stopped the muttered conversation between the guards. Ashford ignored them all and tapped at the screen again. His fingertips sounded like hailstones striking rock.

The light from the screen flickered.

"Sir?"

"Where's Sam Rosenberg?" Ashford snapped.

"Last I saw her, she was checking the backup power supply for the reactor bottle, sir. Should I find her?"

"Who's acting as her second?"

"Anamarie Ruiz."

"Get Sam and Anamarie up to command, please. If you have to take them under guard, that's fine."

"Yes, sir."

Ashford closed the connection and pushed away from the console, his crash couch shushing on its bearings.

"Is there a problem, Captain?" Cortez asked. His voice was thick and a little bleary.

"Nothing I can't handle," Ashford replied.

It was almost another hour before Clarissa heard the doors from the external elevator shaft open. New voices came down the hall. The gabble of conversation tried to hide some deeper strain. Ashford tugged at his uniform.

Two women floated in the room. The first was a pretty woman with a heart-shaped face and grease-streaked red hair pulled back in a bun. It made her think of Anna. The second was thin, even for a Belter, with skin the color of dry soil and brown eyes so dark they were black. Three men with pistols followed them in.

"Chief Rosenberg," Ashford said.

"Sir," the red-haired woman said. She didn't sound like Anna.

"We are on our fourth last-minute delay now. The more time we waste, the more likely it is that the rogue elements in the drum will cause trouble."

"I'm doing my best, Captain. This isn't the kind of thing we get to take a second shot at, though. We need to be thorough."

"Two hours ago, you said we'd be ready to fire in two hours. Are we ready to fire now?"

"No, sir," she said. "I looked up the specs, and the reactor's safeties won't allow an output the size we need. I'm fabricating some new breakers that won't screw us up. And then we have to replace some cabling as well."

"How long will that take?" Ashford asked. His voice was dry. Clarissa thought she heard danger in it, but the engineer didn't react to it.

"Six hours, six and a half hours," she said. "The fab printers only go so fast."

Ashford nodded and turned to the second woman. Ruiz.

"Do you agree with that assessment?"

"All respect to Chief Rosenberg, I don't," Ruiz said. "I don't see why we can't use conductive foam instead."

"How long would that take?"

"Two hours," Ruiz said.

Ashford drew a pistol. Almost before the chief engineer's eyes could widen, the gun fired. In the tight quarters, the sound itself was an assault. Sam's head snapped back and her feet kicked forward. A bright red globe shivered in the air, smaller droplets flying out from it. Violent moons around a dead planet.

"Mister Ruiz," Ashford said. "Please be ready to fire in two hours."

For a moment, the woman was silent. She shook her head like she was trying to come back from a dream.

"Sir," she said.

Ashford smiled. He was enjoying the effect he'd just had.

"You can go," he said. "Tick-tock. Tick-tock."

Ruiz and the three guards pulled themselves back out. Ashford put his pistol away.

"Would someone please clean this mess away," he said.

"My God," Cortez said, his voice somewhere between a prayer and blasphemy. "Oh my God. What have you done?"

Ashford craned his neck. Two of the guards moved forward. One of them had a utility vacuum. When he thumbed it on, the little motor whined. When he put it in the blood, the tone of it dropped half a tone from E to D-sharp.

"I shot a saboteur," Ashford said, "and cleared the way to saving humanity from the alien threat."

"You killed her," Cortez said. "She had no trial. No defense."

"Father Cortez," Ashford said, "these are extreme circumstances."

"But—"

Ashford turned, bending his just-too-large Belter head forward. "With all respect, this is my command. These are my people. And if you think I am prepared to accept another mutiny, you are very much mistaken." There was a buzz in the captain's voice like a drunk man on the edge of a fight. Clarissa put a hand on Cortez's shoulder and shook her head.

The older man frowned, ran a hand across his white hair, and put on a professionally compassionate expression.

"I understand the need for discipline, Captain," Cortez said. "And even some violence, if it is called for, but—"

"Don't make me put you back in the drum," Ashford said. Cortez closed his mouth, his head bowed as if being humbled was old territory for him. Even though she knew that wasn't true, Clarissa felt a warm sympathy for him. He'd seen dead people. He'd seen people die. Seeing someone killed was different. And killing someone was different than that, so in some ways, she was ahead of him.

"Come on," she said. Cortez blinked at her. There were tears in his eyes, floating more or less evenly across his sclera, unable to fall. "The head's this way. I'll get you there."

"Thank you," he said.

Two of the guards were wrapping the dead engineer with tape. The bullet had struck just above her right eye, and a hemisphere of blood adhered to it, shuddering but not growing larger. The woman wasn't bleeding anymore. *She was the enemy*, Clarissa thought, but the idea had a tentative quality about it. Like she was trying on a vest to see how it fit. *She was the enemy and so she deserved to die even though she had red hair like Anna.* It wasn't as comforting as she'd hoped.

In the head, Cortez washed his face and hands with the towelettes and then fed them into the recycler. Clarissa mentally followed them down to the churn and through the guts of the ship. She knew how it would work on the *Cerisier* or the *Prince*. Here, she could only speculate.

You're trying to distract yourself, a small part of herself said. The thought came in words, just like that. Not from outside, not from someone else. A part of her talking to the rest. *You're trying to distract yourself.*

From what? she wondered.

"Thank you," Cortez said. His smile looked more familiar now. More like the man she saw on screens. "I knew that there would be some resistance to doing the right thing here. But I wasn't ready for it. Spiritually, I wasn't ready for it. Surprised me."

"It'll do that," Clarissa said.

Cortez nodded. He was about her father's age. She tried to imagine Jules-Pierre Mao floating in the little space, weeping over a dead engineer. She couldn't. She couldn't imagine him here at all, couldn't picture what he looked like exactly. All of her impressions were of his power, his wit, his overwhelming importance. The physical details were beside the point. Cortez looked at himself in the mirror, set his own expression.

He's about to die, she thought. *He's about to condemn himself and everyone on this ship to dying beyond help, here in the darkness, because he thinks it is the right and noble thing to do.* Was that what Ashford was doing too? She wished now that she'd talked to him more when they'd been prisoners together. Gotten to understand him and who he was. Why he was willing to die for this. And more than that, why he was willing to kill. Maybe it was altruism and nobility. Maybe it was fear. Or grief. As long as he did what needed doing, it didn't matter why, but she found she was curious. She knew why she was here, at least. To redeem herself. To die for a reason, and make amends.

You're trying to distract yourself.

"—don't you think?" Cortez said. His smile was gentle and rueful, and she didn't have any idea what he'd been saying.

"I guess," she said and pushed back from the doorframe to give him room. Cortez pulled himself by handholds, trying to keep his body oriented with head toward the ceiling and feet toward the floor, even though crawling along the walls was probably safer and more efficient. It was something people who lived with weight did by instinct. Clarissa only noticed it because she wasn't doing it. The room was just the room, no up or down, anything a floor or a wall or a ceiling. She expected a wave of vertigo that didn't come.

"You know it doesn't matter," she said.

Cortez smiled at her, tilting his head in a question.

"If we're all sacrifices, it doesn't matter when we go," Clarissa said. "She went a little before us. We'll go a little later. It doesn't even matter if we all go willingly to the altar, right? All that matters is that we break the Ring so everyone on the other side is safe."

"Yes, that's right," Cortez said. "Thank you for reminding me."

An alert sounded in the next room, and Clarissa turned toward it. Ashford had undone his straps and was floating above his control panel, his face stony with rage.

"What's going on, Jojo?"

"I think we've got a problem, sir..."

Chapter Forty-Three: Holden

Everything about the former colonial administrative offices made Holden sad. The drab, institutional green walls, the cluster of cubicles in the central workspace, the lack of windows or architectural flourishes. The Mormons had been planning to run the human race's first extrasolar colony from a place that would have been equally at home as an accounting office. It felt anticlimactic. *Hello, welcome to your centuries-long voyage to build a human settlement around another star! Here's your cubicle.*

The space had been repurposed in a way that at least gave it a lived-in feel. A cobbled-together radio occupied one entire closet, just off the main broadcasting set. The size saying more about the slapdash construction than about the broadcasting power. The current fleet was in a small enough space to pick up a decent handheld set. A touch screen on one wall acted as a whiteboard for the office, lists of potential interviews and news stories listed along with contact names and potential public interest. Holden was oddly flattered to see his name next to the note *Hot, find a way to get this.*

Now the room buzzed with activity. Bull's people were trickling in a few at a time. Most of them brought duffel bags full of weapons or ammunition. A few brought tools in formed plastic cases with wheels on the bottom. They were preparing to armor the former office space into a mini-fortress. Holden leaned against an unused desk and tried to stay out of everyone's way.

"Hey," Monica said, appearing at his side out of nowhere. She nodded her head at the board. "When I heard you were back from the station, I was hoping I could get an interview from you. Guess I missed my chance, though."

"Why?"

"Next to this end-of-the-world shit, you've slipped a couple notches in the broadcast schedule."

Holden nodded, then shrugged. "I've been famous before. It's not so great."

Monica sat on the desk next to him and handed him a drinking bulb. When Holden tasted it, it turned out to be excellent coffee. He closed his eyes for a moment, sighing with pleasure. "Okay, now I'm just a little in love with you."

"Don't tease a girl," she replied. "Will this work? This plan of Bull's?"

"Am I on the record?"

Someone started welding a sheet of metal to the wall, forcing them both to throw up their hands to block the light. The air smelled like sulfur and hot steel.

"Always," Monica said. "Will it?"

"Maybe. There's a reason military ships are scuttled the second someone takes engineering. If you don't own that ground, you don't own the ship."

Monica smiled as if that all made sense to her. Holden wondered how much actually did. She wasn't a wartime reporter. She was a documentary producer who'd wound up in the wrong place at the right time. He finished off the last of his coffee with a pang of regret and waited to see if she had anything else to ask. If he was nice, maybe she'd find him a refill.

"And this Sam person can do that?" she said.

"Sam's been keeping the *Roci* in the air for almost three years now. She was one of Tycho's best and brightest. Yeah, if she's got your engine room and she doesn't like you, you're screwed."

"Want more coffee?"

"Good God, yes," Holden said, holding out his bulb like a street beggar.

Before Monica could take it, Bull came clumping over to them in his mechanical walker. He started to speak and then began a wet, phlegmy cough that lasted several seconds. Holden thought he looked like a man who was dying by centimeters.

"Sorry," Bull said, spitting into a wadded-up rag. "That's disgusting."

"If you die," Monica said, "I won't get my exclusive."

Bull nodded and began another coughing fit.

"If you die," Holden said, "can I have all your stuff?"

Bull gave a grand, sweeping gesture at the office around them. "Someday, my boy, this will all be yours."

"What's the word?" Holden asked, raising the bulb to his lips and being disappointed at its emptiness all over again.

"Corin found the preacher, huddled up with half her congregation in their church tent."

"Great," Holden said. "Things are starting to come together."

"Better than you think. Half the people in that room were UN and Martian military. They're coming with her. She says they'll back her story when she asks the other ships to shut down. It also won't hurt to have a few dozen more able bodies to man the defenses when Ashford comes after us."

As Bull spoke, Holden saw Amos enter the offices pushing the bed Alex and Naomi were on. A knot he hadn't even realized he had relaxed in his shoulders. Bull was still talking about utilizing the new troops for their defensive plans, but Holden wasn't listening. He watched Amos move the gurney to a safe corner at the back of the room and then wander over to stand next to them.

"Nothing new outside," Amos said when Bull stopped talking. "Same small patrols of Ashford goons walking the drum, but they don't act like they know anything's up."

"They'll know as soon as we do our first broadcast," Monica said.

"How's that shoulder?" Holden asked.

"Sore."

"I've been thinking I want you to take command of the defense here once the shit hits the intake."

"Yeah, okay," Amos said. He knew Holden was asking him to protect Naomi and Alex. "I guess that means you're going down to—"

He was interrupted by a loud buzzing coming from Bull's pocket. Bull pulled a beat-up hand terminal out and stared at it like it might explode.

"Is that an alarm?" Holden asked.

"Emergency alert on my private security channel," Bull said, still not answering it. "Only the senior staff can use that channel."

"Ashford, trying to track you down?" Holden asked, but Bull ignored him and answered the call.

"Bull here. Ruiz, I—" Bull started, then stopped and just listened. He grunted a few times, though Holden couldn't tell if they were assents or negations. When he finished the call, he dropped the hand terminal on the desk behind him without looking at it. His brown skin, recently gray with sickness, had turned almost white. He reached up with both hands to wipe away what Holden realized with shock were tears. Holden would not have guessed the man was capable of weeping.

"Ashford," Bull started, then began a long coughing fit that looked suspiciously like sobbing. When he'd finally stopped, his eyes and mouth were covered with mucus. He pulled a rag out of his pocket and wiped most of it off, then said, "Ashford killed Sam."

"What?" Holden asked. His brain refused to believe this could be true. He'd heard the words clearly, but those words could not be, so he must have heard them wrong. "What?"

Bull took a long breath, gave his face one last wipe with the rag, then said, "He brought her up to the bridge to ask about the laser mods, and then he shot her. He made Anamarie Ruiz the chief engineer."

"How do you know?" Monica asked.

"Because that was Ruiz on the line just now. She wants us to get her the hell out of there," Bull said. Almost all traces of his grief were gone from his face. He took another long, shuddering breath. "She knows Ashford has completely gone around the bend, but what can she do?"

Holden shook his head, still refusing to believe it. Brilliant little Sam, who fixed his ship, who was Naomi's best friend, whom Alex and Amos shared a good-natured crush on. *That* Sam couldn't be dead.

Amos was staring at him. The big man's hands were curled into fists, his knuckles a bloodless white.

"We have to hold this ground," Holden said, hoping to head off Amos' next words. "I need you to hold it or this whole thing falls apart."

"Then you kill him," Amos said, his words terrifyingly flat and emotionless. "None of this trial bullshit. No righteous man among the savages bullshit. You fucking kill him, or so help me God…"

Holden felt a sudden nausea almost drive him to his knees. He took a few deep breaths to push it back. This was what they had to offer to Sam's memory. After all she'd done for them. All she'd meant to them. They had violence, arguments about the best way to get revenge. Sam, who as far as he knew had never hurt another person in her life. Would she want this? He could picture her there, telling Amos and Bull to put their testosterone away and act like adults. The thought almost made him vomit.

Monica put a hand on his back. "Are you okay?"

"I have to tell Naomi," was all he could say, then he pushed her hand away and walked across a floor that moved under his feet like the rolling deck of an oceangoing ship.

Naomi reacted only with sorrow, not with anger. She cried, but didn't demand revenge. She repeated Sam's name through her tears, but didn't say Ashford's once. It seemed like the right reaction. It seemed like love.

He was holding Naomi while she gently wept when Bull clumped up behind him. He felt a flash of anger, but swallowed it.

"What?"

"Look," Bull said, rubbing his buzz cut with both hands. "I know this is a shitty time, but we have to talk about where we go from here."

Holden shrugged.

"Sam's gone, and she was pretty central to our plans..."

"I understand," Naomi said. "I'll go."

"What?" Holden said, feeling like they were having a conversation in some kind of code he didn't understand. "Go where?"

"With Sam gone, Naomi is the best engineer we've got," Bull said.

"What about this Ruiz person? I thought she was the chief engineer now."

"She was in charge of infrastructure," Bull said. "And I've seen Nagata's background. She's got the training and the experience. And we trust her. If someone's going to take Sam's place—"

"No," Holden said without thinking about it. Naomi was hurt. She couldn't fight her way into the engine room now. And Sam had been killed.

"I'll go," Naomi repeated. "My arm is for shit, but I can walk. If someone can help me once we get there, I can take out the bridge and shut down the reactor."

"No," Holden said again.

"Yeah, me too," Alex added. He was sitting on the edge of the gurney facing away from them. He'd been shaking like he was crying, but hadn't made a sound. His voice sounded dry, like fallen leaves rustling in the wind. Brittle and empty. "I guess I have to go too."

"Alex, you don't—" Naomi started, but he kept talking over the top of her.

"Nobody pulled the *Roci*'s batteries off-line when we left, so if we're shutting everything down, she'll need someone to do it."

Bull nodded. Holden wanted to smack him for agreeing with any of this.

"And that'll be me," Alex said. "I can tag along as far as engineering, grab an EVA pack there, and use the aft airlock to get out."

Amos moved over behind Bull, his face still flat, emotionless, but his hands in fists. "Alex is going?"

"New plan," Bull said loud enough for everyone to hear. People stopped whatever they were doing and moved over to listen. More must have arrived, because there were almost fifty in the office now. At the back of the room stood a small knot of people in military uniforms. Anna the redheaded preacher was with them. She was holding hands with an aggressively thin woman who alternated smoking and tapping her front teeth with her pinky fingernail. Bull spotted them at the same time Holden did, and waved them forward.

"Anna, come on up here," he said. "Most everyone is here now, so this is how it's going to go down."

The room got quiet. Anna made her way up to Bull and waited. Her skinny friend came with her, staring at the crowd around the preacher with the suspicious eyes of a bodyguard.

"In"—Bull stopped to look at a nearby wall panel with a clock on it—"thirty minutes, I will take a team made up of security personnel and the crew of the *Rocinante* to the southern drum access point. We will retake that access point and gain entrance into the engineering level. Once we control engineering, Monica and her team will begin a broadcast explaining to the rest of the fleet about the need to kill the power. Preacher, that's where you and your people come in."

Anna turned and smiled at her group, a motley collection of people in the uniforms of a variety of services and planetary allegiances. Most of them injured in one way or another. Some quite badly.

"The target for the shutdown is 1900 hours local, about two and a half hours from now. We need them to keep it down for two hours. That's our window. We need the *Behemoth* down during that two hours."

"We'll make it happen," Naomi said.

"But when our broadcast starts, Ashford will probably try to take this location. Amos and the remainder of my team, along with any volunteers from among the rest of you, will hold this position as long as possible. The more bad guys you can tie up here, the fewer we'll have trying to take engineering back from us. But I need you to hold. If we can't keep Anna and her people on the air long enough to get everyone on board with our shutdown plan, this thing ends before it starts."

"We'll hold," Amos said. No one disagreed.

"Once we control engineering, we'll send a team forward to put restraints on the hopefully unconscious people on the bridge and we'll own the ship. The lights go out, the aliens let us go, and we get the fuck out of this miserable stretch of space once and for all. How's that sound?"

Bull raised his voice with the final question, looking for a cheer from the group, and the group obliged. People began to drift back toward their various tasks. Holden squeezed Naomi's uninjured shoulder and moved over to Anna. She looked lost. Along the way he grabbed Amos by the arm.

"Anna," Holden said. "Do you remember Amos?"

She smiled and nodded. "Hello, Amos."

"How you doing, Red?"

"Amos will be here to protect you and the others," Holden continued. "If you need anything, you let him know. I feel safe in saying nothing will get in here to stop you from doing your job as long as he's alive."

"That's the truth," Amos said. "Ma'am."

"Hey, guys," someone called out from the doorway. "Look what followed me home. Can I keep them?"

Holden patted Anna on the arm and gave Amos a meaningful look. *Protect this one with your life.* Amos nodded back. He looked vaguely offended.

He left them together and caught up with Bull heading for the door. The security officer Corin, Bull's new second-in-command, was leaning next to the door with a shit-eating grin.

"Come on in, boys," she said, and four Martians with military haircuts came into the room. They stood on the balls of their feet, slowly looking over every inch of the room. Holden had known someone who always entered a room that way. Bobbie. He found himself wishing she were here. The man in the lead was powerfully familiar.

"Sergeant Verbinski," Bull said to one of them. "This is a surprise."

Holden hadn't recognized the man without his armor. He looked big.

"Sir," Verbinski said. "I heard you're about to start a fight to get us all out of here."

"Yeah," Bull said. "I am."

"Sounds like a noble cause," Verbinski replied. "Need four grunts with nothing else to do?"

"Yeah," Bull said with a growing smile. "I really do."

Chapter Forty-Four: Anna

They'd failed.

Anna watched the busy men and women in the radio offices as they strapped on body armor, loaded weapons, hung grenades from their belts, and she felt only sadness and despair.

A history professor at university had once told her, *Violence is what people do when they run out of good ideas. It's attractive because it's simple, it's direct, it's almost always available as an option. When you can't think of a good rebuttal for your opponent's argument, you can always punch them in the face.*

They'd run out of ideas. And now they were reaching for the simple, direct, always available option of shooting everyone they disagreed with. She hated it.

Monica caught her eye from across the room and held up a small thermos of coffee in invitation. Anna waved her off with a smile.

"Are you insane?" Tilly asked. She was sitting on the floor next to her in a back corner of the offices, trying to stay out of everyone's way. "That woman has the only decent coffee on this entire ship." She waved at Monica, pointing at herself.

"I should have spent more time talking to Cortez," Anna said. "The OPA captain might be intractable, but I could have reached Cortez with enough time."

"Life is finite, dear, and Cortez is an asshole. We'll all be better off if someone puts a bullet in him before this is over." Tilly accepted a pour of Monica's coffee with a grateful smile. Monica set the thermos down and sat on the floor next to them.

"Hey, we—" she started, but Anna didn't notice.

"You don't mean that," Anna said to Tilly, annoyance creeping into her voice. "Cortez isn't a bad person. He's frightened and unsure, and has made some bad choices, but at worst he's misguided, not evil."

"He doesn't deserve your sympathy," Tilly said, then tossed back the last of her coffee like she was angry with it.

"Who are we—" Monica started again.

"He does. He does deserve it," Anna said. Watching the young men and women prepare for war, preparing to kill and be killed right in front of her, made her more angry with Tilly than she probably would have been otherwise. But she found herself very angry now. "That's exactly the point. They *all* deserve our sympathy. If Bull's right about Ashford, and he's gone crazy with fear and humiliation and the trauma of seeing his crew killed, then he deserves our sympathy. That's a terrible place to be. Cortez deserves our understanding, because he's doing exactly the same thing we are. Trying to find the right thing to do in an impossible situation."

"Oh," Monica said. "Cortez. He's the—"

"That's a load of crap, Annie. That's exactly how you know who the good guys and the bad guys are: by what they do when the chips are down."

"This isn't about good guys and bad guys," Anna said. "Yes, we've picked sides now, because some of the actions they are about to take will have serious consequences for us, and we're going to try to stop them. But what you're doing is demonizing them, making them the enemy. The problem with that is that once we've stopped them and they can't hurt us anymore, they're still demons. Still the enemy."

"Believe me," Tilly said, "when I get out of here, it will be my mission in life to burn Cortez to the ground for this."

"Why?"

"What do you mean, why?"

"He won't be on a ship trying to destroy the Ring anymore. He won't be supporting Ashford anymore. All of the circumstances that made him your enemy will be gone. What's the value in clinging to the hate?"

Tilly turned away and fumbled around in her pocket for her cigarettes. She smoked one aggressively, pointedly not looking at Anna.

"What's the answer, then?" Monica asked after a few tense moments of silence.

"I don't know," Anna said, pulling her legs close and resting her chin on her knees. She tucked her back as far into the corner of the room as it would go, her body looking for a safe place with a small child's insistence. But the hard green walls offered no comfort.

"So it's all just academic, then," Monica said. Tilly snorted in agreement, still not looking at Anna.

Anna pointed at the people getting ready in the room around them. "How many will be dead by the end of today?"

"There's no way to know," Monica said.

"We owe it to them to look for other answers. We've failed this time. We've run out of ideas, and now we're reaching for the gun. But maybe next time, if we've thought about what led us here, maybe next time we find a different answer. Certainty doesn't have a place in violence."

For a while, they were silent. Tilly angrily chain-smoked. Monica typed furiously on her terminal. Anna watched the others get ready for war, and tried to match faces with names. Even if they won out today, there was a very good chance she'd be presiding over more than one funeral tomorrow.

Bull clunked over to them, his walking machine whining to a stop. He had deteriorated during the few hours they'd spent in the office. He was coughing less, but he'd begun using his inhaler a lot more often. Even the machine seemed ill now, its sounds harsher, its movements jerkier. As though the walker and Bull had merged into one being, and it was dying along with him.

"Everything okay?" he asked.

"Fine," Anna said. She considered telling him he needed rest, then abandoned the idea. She didn't need to lose another argument just then.

"So we're getting pretty close to zero hour here," Bull said, then stifled a wet-sounding cough. "You have everything you need?"

No, Anna thought. *I need an answer that doesn't include what you're about to do.*

"Yes," she said instead. "Monica has been making notes for the broadcast. I've compiled a list of all the ships we have representatives from. We're missing a few, but I'm hoping planetary allegiance will be enough to get their cooperation. Chris Williams, a junior officer from the *Prince*, has been a big help on that."

"You?" Bull asked, jabbing a thick hand toward Monica.

"My team is ready to go," she said. "I'm a bit worried about getting the full broadcast out before Ashford's people stop us."

Bull laughed. It was a wet, unpleasant sound. "Hold on." He called out to Jim Holden, who was busy reassembling a stripped-down rifle of some sort and chatting with one of the Martian marines. Holden put the partly assembled rifle on a table and walked over.

"What's up?"

"These people need reassurance that they'll be protected long enough to finish their broadcast," Bull said.

Holden blinked twice, once at Bull, once at the three women sitting cross-legged on the floor. Anna had to suppress a giggle. Holden was so comically earnest, she just wanted to give him a hug and pat him on the head.

"Amos will make sure you're not interrupted," he finally said.

"Right," Bull said. "Tell them why that's reassuring."

"Oh. Well, when Amos is angry he's the meanest, scariest person I've ever met, and he'd walk across a sea of corpses he personally created to help a friend. And one of his good friends just got murdered by the people who are going to be trying to take this office."

"I heard about that," Anna said. "I'm sorry."

"Yes," Holden said. "And the last people in the galaxy I'd want to be are the ones that are going to try and break in here to stop you. Amos doesn't process grief well. It usually turns into anger or violence for him. I have a feeling he's about to process the shit out of it on some Ashford loyalists."

"Killing people won't make him feel better," Anna said, regretting the words the second they left her mouth. These people were going to be risking their lives to protect her. They didn't need her moralizing at them.

"Actually," Holden said with a half smile, "I think it might for him, but Amos is a special case. You'd be right about most anyone else."

Anna looked across the room at Amos. He was sitting quietly by the front door to the broadcast office, some sort of very large rifle laid across his knees. He was a large man, tall and thick across the shoulders and chest. But with his round shaved head and broad face, he didn't look like a killer to Anna. He looked like a friendly repairman. The kind who showed up to fix broken plumbing or swap out the air recycling filters. According to Holden, he would kill without remorse to protect her.

She imagined trying to explain their current situation to Nono. *I've fallen in with killers, you see, but it's okay because they are the right killers. The good guy killers. They don't shoot innocent chief engineers. They shoot the people who do.*

Monica was asking Holden something. When he started to answer, Anna got up and left with an apology to everyone and no one. She dodged through the crowded office, smiling and patting people on the arm as she passed, distributing gentle reassurance to everyone around her. It was all she had to offer them.

She pulled an unused chair over next to Amos and sat down. "Red," he said, giving her a tiny nod.

"I'm sorry." She put her hand on his arm. He stared down at it as though he couldn't figure out what it was.

"Okay," he said, not asking the obvious question. Not pretending not to understand. Anna found herself liking him immediately.

"Thank you for doing this."

Amos shifted in his chair to face her. "You don't need to—"

"In a few hours, we might all be dead," she said. "I want you to know that I know what you're doing, and I know why, and I don't care about any of that. Thank you for helping us."

"God damn, Red," Amos said, putting his hand on hers. "You must be hell on wheels as a preacher. You're making me feel the best and worst I've felt in a while at the same time."

"That's all I wanted to say," Anna said, then patted his hand once and stood up.

Before she could leave, Amos grabbed her hand in an almost painfully tight grip. "No one's gonna hurt you today."

There was no boast in it. It was a simple statement of fact. She gave him a smile and pulled her hand away. Good-hearted unrepentant killers were not something she'd had to fit into her worldview before this, and she wasn't sure how it would work. But now she'd have to try.

"All right, people, listen up," Bull yelled out over the noise. The room fell silent. "It's zero hour. Let's get the action teams divided up and ready to go."

A shadow fell across Anna. Amos was standing behind her, clutching his large gun. "Defense," he called out. "To me."

A group of maybe two dozen extricated themselves from the general crowd and moved over to Amos. Anna found herself surrounded by heavily armed and armored Belters with a few inner planet types mixed in. She was not a tall woman, and it felt like being at the bottom of a well. "Excuse me," she said, but no one heard her. A strong hand gripped her arm, pulled her through the knot of people, and deposited her outside of it. Amos gave her a smile and said, "Might want to find a quiet corner, Red."

Anna thought about trying to cross the room back to Tilly and Monica, but there were too many people in the way. Amos had a sort of personal field that kept anyone from standing too close to him, so Anna just stayed inside it to keep from getting trampled on. Amos didn't appear to mind.

"Assault team," Holden called out, "to me."

Soon he had a group of two dozen around him, including Naomi and Alex from the *Rocinante*, the four Martian marines, a bunch of Bull's security people, and Bull himself. The only people in the group without obvious physical injuries were the four marines. Alex and Naomi looked especially bad. Naomi's shoulder was bound tight in a harness that immobilized it and her arm, and she winced every time she took a step. Alex's face was swollen so badly that his left eye was almost completely closed. Blood spotted the bandages around his head.

These are the people who helped stop Protogen, who fought the monsters around Ganymede, she told herself. *They're tough, they'll make it.* It sounded thin even in her own head.

"Well," Bull said. The crowd seemed to be waiting for last words from him. "I guess this is it. Good hunting, everyone."

A few people clapped or called out to him. Most didn't. Across the room Monica was talking to her camera people. Anna knew she should join them, but found herself not wanting to. All these people would be risking their lives to buy her time. *Her.* So it was all on her whether the whole plan succeeded or failed. If she couldn't convince an entire flotilla of ships from three separate governments that turning off their power for a couple hours was the right thing to do, then it would all be for nothing. She found herself wanting to delay that moment as long as possible. To keep it from being her responsibility as long as she could.

"Better go, Red," Amos whispered to her.

"What if they're all too scared to shut down their ships?" she replied. "We're in the haunted house, and I'm about to tell everyone that the way to escape is to turn out all the lights. I would find that unconvincing in their shoes."

Amos nodded thoughtfully. Anna waited for the words of encouragement.

"Yeah," he finally said. "That'll be a bitch. My job's a lot easier. Good luck."

Somehow, the honesty in not even trying to sugarcoat it cracked the last of Anna's fear, and she found herself laughing. Before she could reconsider, she grabbed Amos around the middle and gave him a squeeze.

"Again," she said, letting him go after a few seconds, "thank you. I was being a big scaredy-cat. You're a good person, Amos."

"Nah, I'm not. I just hang with good company. Get going, Red. I gotta get my game face on."

The assault team was heading for the door, and Anna moved to the wall to let them by. Holden stopped next to Amos and said, "Be here when I get back, big man."

Amos shook his hand and slapped him on the back once. Holden's face was filled with worry. Anna had a sudden vision of her future, sending Nami off to school one day, being terrified that she wouldn't be there to look after her and having to let her go anyway.

"Keep Naomi and Alex safe," Amos said, pushing Holden toward the door. From Anna's position, she could see the worry lines on Holden's face only deepen at that. He was going to have to let them go too. Even if they all survived the assault on engineering, Alex would be leaving the ship to fly to the *Rocinante*, and Naomi would be left behind to keep the power shut down while Holden continued on toward the bridge. Anna knew the little crew had been together for several years now. She wondered if they'd ever had to split up and fight like this before.

Holden's face seemed to be saying they hadn't.

Anna was watching them file out the door, again trying to memorize faces and names, trying not to think about why. Monica grabbed her and started pulling her toward the makeshift film studio.

"Time to start working," she said. She deposited Anna just outside the camera view and stepped in front of the unadorned green wall they used as a backdrop.

"Welcome," she said, her face and voice shifting into cheery video host mode. "I'm Monica Stuart in the offices of Radio Free Slow Zone. I've got some exciting guests today, including Doctor Anna Volovodov, and a number of UN and Martian military officers. But even more exciting, today we're bringing you the most important broadcast we've ever done.

"Today, we'll tell you how to go home."

Chapter Forty-Five: Bull

Bull felt the time moving past like it was something physical, like he was falling through it and couldn't catch himself. Anamarie Ruiz had an hour left before she had to decide whether to do what Ashford wanted or get killed. If she didn't have to choose, she wouldn't choose wrong, and every minute that he wasn't in the engineering deck took them closer to where they couldn't get back.

They'd left the colonial administration offices in a small convoy. Six electric carts with twenty-five people, including Jim Holden and three-quarters of his crew, the four Martian marines, an even dozen of the *Behemoth*'s crew who'd stayed loyal to Pa, and five Earth soldiers whom Corin had found in the drum and brought along. They had some riot armor that hadn't been taken out of the armory before Ashford's forces occupied it. They had an ugly collection of slug-throwing pistols and shotguns loaded with ballistic gel rounds; a mix of weapons designed to subdue without permanent injury and those meant to assure the enemy's death. The four Martian marines had the four best guns they'd been able to scrounge up, but there were too few of both. The whole thing stank of improvisation.

He couldn't sit down, so he'd taken the canopy off the electric cart and wedged his mech in the back. He sailed through the hot, close air of the drum like a figurehead on the prow of some doomed pirate ship. Corin was at the wheel, hunched over it like she could make it go faster by the raw act of will. The Martian sergeant Verbinski who'd brought Jim Holden to the *Behemoth* in restraints sat at her side looking focused and bemused at the same time.

They passed through the main corridors heading south. The tires made a loud ripping sound against the decking. High above, the long, thin strip of blinding white illuminated the curve of the drum. The southern transfer point loomed ahead of them like a ceramic steel cliff face.

People parted before them, making a path. Bull watched them as he passed. Anger and fear and curiosity. These were his people. They hadn't all been to start with, but he'd brought them here to the *Behemoth*. He'd made the ship important and the OPA's role in the exploration beyond the Ring central. Earthers and Martians and Belters. The ones who'd lived. As the faces turned toward him, watching the convoy pass like flowers back on Earth tracking the arc of the sun, he wondered what Fred Johnson would have thought of all this. It was a clusterfuck from start to finish, no question about that. He hoped that when it came time to settle up accounts, he'd done more good than harm.

"We're a pretty compromised force," Verbinski said, craning his neck back and up to look at Bull. "How many people you think we're going up against?"

"Not sure," Bull said. "Probably a little more than we got, but they're divided between engineering and command."

"They as banged up as we are?"

Bull glanced over his shoulder. The truth was at least half of the people he was about to take into battle were already injured. There were people with pressure casts holding their arms together, with sutures keeping their skin closed. In normal circumstances, half his force would still be in the infirmary. Hell, he didn't have any damn business going into a fire zone either, except that he wasn't going to stay back and send people into a meat grinder he wouldn't step into himself.

"Just about," Bull said.

"You know, if I still had that recon armor you took off of us, I could just go get this done. Not even me and my squad. Just me."

"Yeah. I know that."

"Kind of makes you wish you'd trusted me a little bit, doesn't it?"

"Kind of does," Bull said.

There were two ways to reach the transfer point. The elevator was big enough to fit half the force into a box small enough that when the doors opened at the top, a single grenade would incapacitate nearly all of them. The alternative was a wide, sloping ramp that rose from the floor of the drum and spun up in a tight spiral to the axis. Its curve was going into the drum's spin, so the faster they drove up it, the more the cart tires would push down into the floor. That wouldn't matter down here, but when they reached the top where the fighting would essentially be in free fall, every bit of stability and control they could glean would matter.

The first shots came down from the axis, spraying bits of the ceramic roadway up in front of the lead cart. Bull tried to bend his head back far enough to see whether the attack was coming from the transfer point itself or a barricade closer in.

"Juarez!" Verbinski shouted. "Cover us."

"Yes, sir," a voice called from one of the back carts. Bull swiveled the mech enough to look over his shoulder. On the third cart back, one of the Martian marines was lying on his back, a long scoped rifle pointing up. He looked like he was napping until the rifle fired once. Bull tried to look up again, but the mech prevented him. He took out his hand terminal and used its camera like a mirror. High above them, a body was floating in the null-g zone, a pink cloud of blood forming around its waist.

"One less," Verbinski said.

The firing continued as they took the ramp at speed. The semi-adhesive ripping of the tires against the deck changed its tone as less and less weight pressed against them. Bull felt his body growing lighter in its brace. The edge of the ramp was a cliff now, looking down almost a third of a kilometer to the floor of the drum below. Ashford's men were above them, but not so far now that Bull couldn't see the metal barricades they'd welded to the walls and deck. He was painfully aware of being the highest target. His neck itched.

Two heads popped up from behind the barricades. The muzzle flashes were like sparks. The Martian's rifle barked behind him, and one of the attackers slumped down, the other retreating.

"Okay," Bull said. "This is as close as we get without cover."

Corin spun the cart nose in to the wall and slipped out, taking cover with Verbinski behind it while the next cart came ahead mirroring her. They were in microgravity here. Maybe a tenth of a g. Maybe less. Bull had to turn the magnets on in his mech's feet to keep from floating away. By the time he'd gotten off the cart, the fighting was already far ahead of him. He drove the mech forward, marching up past the improvised barricades of the carts. The closest of them was less than ten meters from the first of Ashford's barricades, and Jim Holden, Corin, and one of the Earthers were already pressed against the enemy's cover, ducking to the side, firing, and falling back. The smell of spent gunpowder soured the air.

"Where's Naomi?" Bull shouted. He didn't have a clear idea whether any of the technical staff in there besides Ruiz were still loyal to Pa, and if they got their only real engineer killed before they made it into engineering, he was going to be pissed. Something detonated behind the barrier and two bodies pinwheeled out into the empty air. The light was behind them, and he couldn't tell if they were his people or Ashford's. At the last of the carts, he stopped. The battle was well ahead of him now, almost at the transfer point itself. That was good. It meant they were winning.

A thin man was still at the cart's wheel. At a guess, he was in his early twenties, brown skin and close-cropped hair. The hole in his chest had already stopped bleeding and his eyes were empty. Bull felt a moment's regret and pushed it away. He'd known. They'd all known. Not just coming to this fight, but when they'd put their boots on the *Behemoth* and headed out past the farthest human habitation, they'd known they might not make it back. Maybe they'd even known that the thing that killed them might not be the Ring, but the people who'd gone out alongside them. People like Ashford. People like him.

"Sorry, ese," Bull said, and drove the joysticks forward.

Ashford's forces were pulling back. There was no question about it now. Verbinski and his team were laying down a withering and professional spray of gunfire. The sniper, Juarez, didn't fire often, but when he did it was always a kill shot. The combination of constant automatic weapons fire and the occasional but lethal bark of Juarez's rifle kept moving the enemy back in toward the transfer point like they were boxing in the queen on a chessboard. Even the most powerful of Ashford's guns couldn't find a safe angle on them, and Verbinski kept the pressure on, pushing back and back and back until Ashford's people broke, running.

The transfer point itself was a short hallway with emergency decompression doors at each end. As Bull watched, the vast red-painted circular hatches groaned and began rolling into place. They wouldn't be enough to stop Bull and his people, but they'd slow things down. Maybe too much.

"Charge!" Bull shouted, then fell into a fit of coughing that was hard to stop. When he could, he croaked, "Come on, you bastards! Get in there before they lock us out!"

They launched through the air, guns blazing. The noise was deafening, and Bull could only imagine what it would sound like from farther away. Distant thunder in a land that had never known rain. He pushed his mech forward, magnetic boots clamping and releasing, as the doors rolled their way nearer to closed. He was the last one into the corridor. At the far end, the air was a cloud of smoke and blood. The farther door was almost closed, but at the side, Naomi Nagata was elbow deep in an access panel, Holden at her back with assault rifle in hand. As Bull approached, the woman pulled something free. A stream of black droplets geysered out into the empty space of the corridor, and the sharp smell of hydraulic fluid cut through the air. The door stopped closing.

In the chaos it was hard to say, but at a guess, Bull thought he still had between fifteen and twenty people standing. It wasn't great, but it could have been worse. Once they got into engineering, things would open up again. There would be cover. The few meters beyond the second door, though, would be a kill zone. It was the space all his people had to go through to get anyplace else. If Ashford's people had any tactical sense at all, they'd be there, waiting for the first sign of movement.

It was a standoff, and he was going to have to be the one to break it. Verbinski skimmed by, as comfortable weightless as a fish in water. He turned, tapped his feet against the wall, and came to something close to a dead stop.

"Going to be a bear making it through there," the Martian said.

"I was just thinking that," Bull said.

Verbinski looked at the half-closed door like a carpenter sizing up a board.

"Be nice if we had some explosives," he said. "Something to clear the area a little. Give us some breathing room."

"You trying to tell me something, Sergeant?"

Verbinski shrugged and took a thin black cassette out of his pocket. Bull hoisted his eyebrows.

"Concussion?" he said.

"Two thousand kilojoules. We call them spine crackers."

"You smuggled arms onto my ship, Sergeant?"

"Just felt a little naked without 'em."

"I'll overlook it this time," Bull said and raised his hands, rallying the troops to him. They took cover behind the half-closed door. Verbinski crawled out onto the surface and peeked over the side, out and back fast as a lizard's tongue. Half a dozen bullets split the air where his head had been. The Martian floated in the air, his legs in lotus position, as he armed the little black grenade. Bull waited, Holden and Corin at his side.

"Just to check," Holden said. "We're throwing grenades into the place that controls the reactor?"

"We are," Bull said.

"So the worst-case scenario?"

"Worst-case scenario is we lose and Ashford kills the solar system," Bull said. "Losing containment on the reactor and we all die is actually second worst."

"Never a sign things have gone well," Holden said.

Verbinski held up a fist, and everyone in the group put their hands over their ears. Verbinski did something sharp with his fingers and flicked the black cassette through the gap between the door and its frame. The detonation came almost at once. Bull felt like he'd been dropped into the bottom of a swimming pool. His vision pulsed in time with his heart, but he pushed the joysticks forward. His ears rang and he felt his consciousness starting to slip a little. As he maneuvered his mech through the space into engineering, it occurred to him that he was going to be lucky if he didn't pass out during the fight. He had a broken spine and his lungs were half full of crap. No one would have thought less of him if he'd stayed behind. Except he didn't care what people thought about him. It was Ashford who cared about that.

The fight on the other side was short. The grenade had been much worse for the defenders. Half of the soldiers had dropped their weapons before all of Bull's people made it in. Only Garza had held out, holding the long corridor between main engineering and the communications array board until Corin had stepped into the space and shot him in the bridge of the nose, doing with a pistol what would have been a difficult shot with a scoped rifle. They took half a dozen of Ashford's men alive, the prisoners zip-tied to handholds in the bulkheads. None of them had been Bull's.

They found Ruiz under a machining table, curled with her arms around her knees. When she came out, her skin had a gray cast to it, and her hands were trembling. Naomi moved around her, shifting from a display panel to the readouts on the different bits of equipment, checking what was being reported in one place against what it said elsewhere. Holden hovered behind her like the tail of a kite.

"Anamarie," Bull said. "You all right?"

Ruiz nodded.

"Thank you," she said, and then before she could say anything else, Naomi sloped in, stopping herself against the desk.

"Was this where Sam was working?" she asked.

Ruiz looked at her for a moment, uncomprehending. When she nodded, it seemed almost tentative.

"What are you seeing?" Bull said. "Can you shut it down?"

"If you just want to drop the core, I can probably do that," Naomi said. "But I don't know if I can get her started again, and there are some folks on the ship who might want to keep breathing. Controlled shutdown would be better."

Bull smiled.

"We need to shut everything down," Holden said. "The reactor. The power grid. Everything."

"I know, honey," Naomi said, and Holden looked chagrined.

"Sorry."

In one of the far corners of the deck, someone yelped. Corin came gliding across the open space, serenely holding in a choke an Earther Bull didn't recognize. It occurred to him that she might be having too much fun with this part. Might not be healthy.

"I don't know what Sam put in place to sabotage the comm laser," Naomi said. "I have to do an audit before I can undo any of it. And without—" Naomi stopped. Her jaw slid forward. She cleared her throat, swallowed. "Without Sam, it's going to be harder. This was her ship."

"Can you just take the laser off-line?" Bull asked.

"Sure," Naomi said. "As long as no one's shooting at me while I'm doing it."

"And how about turning up the nitrogen in the command enough that everyone up there takes a little nap?"

"I can help with that," Ruiz said. Her voice sounded a little stronger.

"All right," Bull said. "Here's what we're doing. Nagata's in charge of engineering. Anything she says, you do." Ruiz nodded, too numb to protest. "Your first priority is get the laser off-line so none of those pendejos in control can fire it. Your second priority is to tweak the environmental controls on the command deck. Your third priority is to shut down the ship so we can bring it back up, see if Mister Holden's ghost is going to keep its promises."

"Sir," Naomi said.

"Corin!" Bull shouted. The coughing stopped him for a moment. It still wasn't violent, and it didn't bring anything up. He didn't know if that was a good sign or a bad one. Corin launched herself to the control board. "You and Holden head up the external elevator shaft with a handful of zip ties. When everyone up there's asleep, you two make sure they don't get confused and hurt themselves."

Corin's smile was cold. Might be that Ashford wasn't a problem he'd have to solve. Bull tried to bring himself to care one way or the other, but his body felt like he'd been awake for a week.

"Why am I doing that?" Holden asked.

"To keep you out of her way," Bull said. "We'll keep your XO safe. We need her."

He could see Holden's objections gathering like a storm, but Naomi stopped them. "It's okay." And that seemed to be that.

"Alex is going to the *Roci* to shut down whatever we left on," Holden said, shrugging. "I'll help him with the EVA suit before I go."

"Okay," Bull said gravely. He was willing to pretend they'd struck some kind of compromise, if that helped. He heard the sound of men laughing and recognized the timbre of Sergeant Verbinski's voice. "Excuse me."

The mech clanked across the deck, magnetic locks clinging and releasing. The others all floated freely in the air, but with three-quarters of his body dead and numb, Bull knew he wouldn't be able to maneuver. It was like he was the only one still constrained by gravity.

Verbinski and his squad were in an alcove near the supply shop. One of the marines had been shot in the elbow. His forearm was a complication of bone and meat, but he was laughing and talking while the others dressed the wound. Bull wondered how much they'd doped him. He caught Verbinski's gaze and nodded him closer.

"You and your people," Bull said when they were out of earshot. "You did good work back there."

"Thank you," Verbinski said. The pride showed right through the humble. "We do what we can. If we'd had our suits, now—"

"Thing is," Bull said. "Those grenades? How many of them you still have on you?"

"Half a dozen," Verbinski said.

"Yeah." Bull sighed. "Nothing personal, but I'm going to need to confiscate those."

Verbinski looked shocked for a moment. Then he laughed.

"Always the hardass," he said.

Chapter Forty-Six: Clarissa

What's going on, Jojo?"

"I think we've got a problem, sir. Take a look."

Monica Stuart appeared on the monitors, her professionally calm face like a being from a different reality.

"Today," she said, her hands folded in her lap and a twinkle in her eye, "we'll tell you how to go home."

"What. The. *Fuck!*" Ashford shouted, dashing his hand across the display. "What is this?"

"They're making a new broadcast, sir," the security man said. Clarissa watched Ashford turn and stare at him, watched the man shrivel under the weight of his gaze.

"Exclusive to Radio Free Slow Zone," Monica said, "we have reason to believe that if we in the united human fleet can reduce our energy output low enough to no longer appear threatening—"

"Shut her down," Ashford said. "Call everyone that's still in the drum and shut that feed off. Get me Ruiz. I want power cut to that whole section if we have to."

"Is this something we need to concern ourselves with?" Cortez asked. His voice had an overtone of whining. "What they do or say can't matter now, can it?"

"This is my ship!" Ashford shouted. "I'm in control."

"Once we've destroyed the Ring, though—"

Clarissa put a hand on Cortez's shoulder and shook her head once.

"He's the father," she said. "The ship is his house."

"Thank you," Ashford said to her, but with his eyes still on Cortez. "I'm glad that someone here understands how this works."

"Suppression team is dispatched," Jojo said. "You want me to pull from the guard units too?"

"Whatever it takes," Ashford said. "I want you to get it done."

On the screen, the view shifted, and Anna's face filled the screen. Her hair was pulled back, and someone had given her makeup in a way that made her look like everyone else in broadcast. Clarissa felt a strange tug in her chest, resentment and alarm. *Get out of there*, she thought at the screen. *God's not going to stop bullets for you.*

"The idea," Anna said, "is that the station has identified us as an ongoing threat. Its actions toward us have been based in a kind of fear. Or, that's wrong. A caution. We are as unknown and unpredictable to it as it is to us. And so we have reason to believe that if we appear to be less threatening, it may relax its constraints."

The camera cut back to Monica Stuart, nodding and looking sober. All the physical cues that would indicate Anna was a serious woman with important opinions.

"And what is your plan, exactly?" Monica asked.

Anna's laughter bubbled. "I wouldn't call the plan mine. What we're thinking is that if we power down the reactors in all the ships and reduce energy being used, the station can be induced to . . . well, to see us less as a threat and more as a curiosity. I mean, see this all from its perspective. A gate opened, and whatever it had been expecting to come through, instead there came a ship running ballistic at tremendous speed. Then a flotilla of new ships behind that, and armed soldiers who went aboard the station itself with weapons firing. If something came to us that way, we'd call it an invasion."

"And so by giving some indication that we aren't escalating the attack...?"

"We give whatever we're dealing with here the opportunity to not escalate against us," Anna said. "We've been thinking of the protomolecule and all the things that came from it as—"

The screen went dark. Ashford scowled at his control boards, calling up and dismissing information with hard, percussive taps. Cortez floated beside Clarissa, frowning. Humiliated. He had engineered Ashford's escape and reconquest of the *Behemoth*, and she could see in the older man's eyes that it wasn't what he'd expected it to be. She wondered if her own father had that same expression in his cell back on Earth, or wherever it was they'd put him.

"Ruiz," Ashford snapped. "Report. What's our status?"

"I still have half an hour, sir," the woman said through the connection.

"I didn't ask how much time you had left," the captain said. "I asked for a report."

"The conductant is in place and curing," the woman said. "It looks like it'll be done on time. I've found a place in the breaker system that Sam...that Sam put in a power cutout."

"You've replaced that?"

"I did, but I don't know if there are others. She could have sabotaged the whole circuit."

"Well," Ashford said. "You have half an hour to check it."

"That's what I'm doing. Sir."

Ashford tapped the control panel again. Clarissa found herself wishing he'd put the newsfeed back on. She wanted to know what Anna was saying, even if it was only as a way to pass the time.

The air on the bridge wasn't as hot and close as it had been in the drum, but the coolness wasn't comforting. If anything, it seemed to underscore the time they'd been waiting. Her belly was beginning to complain with hunger, and she had to imagine that the others were feeling the same. They were holding the bridge of the largest spacecraft humanity had ever built, trapped in the starless dark by an alien power they barely began to comprehend, but they were still constrained by the petty needs of flesh, and their collective blood sugar was getting pretty low. She wondered what it said about her that she'd watched a women shot to death not two hours before and all she could think about now was lunch. She wondered what Anna would have thought.

"Have we shut those bitches up yet?" Ashford snapped.

"The suppression teams are arriving at the colonial administrative offices, sir," Jojo said. And then, a moment later, "They're encountering some resistance."

Ashford smiled.

"Do we have targeting?" he asked.

"Sir?" one of the other guards said.

"Are the comm laser's targeting systems online?"

"Um. Yes. They're responsive."

"Well, while they mop up downstairs, let's line up our shot, shall we?"

"Yes, sir."

Clarissa kept hold of a handle on the wall absently, watching the captain and his men coordinating. It was hard for her to remember how small the Ring was, and how vast the distances they'd traveled to be here. She had to admire the precision and care that they would need to destroy it. The beauty of it was almost surgical. Behind her, the security station popped and clicked. Among the alerts, she heard the murmur of a familiar voice, lifted in fear. She looked around. No one was paying any attention to her, so she pushed herself gently back.

The security station monitor was still on the newsfeed. Monica Stuart looked ashen under her makeup, her jaw set and her lips thin. Anna, beside her, was squeezing the tip of one thumb over and over anxiously. Another man was propped between them in a medical gurney.

"—anything we can to cooperate," the earnest man was saying into the camera.

"Thank you, Lieutenant Williams," Monica Stuart said. "I hate to add a complicating note to all this, but I've just been informed that armed men have arrive outside the studio and we are apparently under attack at the moment." She laughed nervously, which Clarissa thought was probably newsfeed anchor code for, *Oh my God, I'm going to die on the air.* Anna's voice came in a moment before the cameras cut to her.

"This is an extreme situation," Anna said, "but I think something like this is probably going on in every ship that's listening to us right now. We're at the point where we, as a community, have to make a choice. And we're scared and grieving and traumatized. None of us is sure what the right thing to do would be. And—"

In the background, the unmistakable popping of slug throwers interrupted Anna for a moment. Her face paled, but she only cleared her throat and went on.

"And violence is a response to that fear. I hope very much that we can come together, though, and—"

"She'll go down talking," Cortez said. Clarissa hadn't heard him come in behind her, hadn't sensed him approaching. "I have a tremendous respect for that woman."

"But you think she's wrong."

"I think her optimism is misplaced," Cortez said.

"—if we do escalate our attacks on the station and the Ring," Anna said, "we have to expect that the cycle will go on, getting bigger and more dangerous until one side or the other is destroyed, and I wish—"

"What do you think she'd say about your pessimism?" Clarissa asked.

Cortez looked up at her, his eyes wide with surprise and amusement. "My pessimism?"

Clarissa fought the sudden, powerful urge to apologize. "What else would you call it?"

"We've looked the devil in the eyes out here," Cortez said. "I would call it realism."

You didn't look into the devil's eyes, she thought. *You saw a bunch of people die. You have no idea what real evil is.* Her memory seemed to stutter, and for a moment, she was back on the *Cerisier*, Ren's skull giving way under her palm. *There's a difference between tragedy and evil, and I am that difference.*

"Captain! They're taking fire at engineering!"

Cortez turned back toward the bridge and launched himself awkwardly through the air. Clarissa took a last look at Anna on the screen, leaning forward and pressing the air with her hands as if she could push calm and sanity through the camera and into the eyes of anyone watching. Then she followed Cortez.

"How many down?" Ashford demanded.

"No information, sir," Jojo said. "I have a video feed."

The monitor blinked to life. The engineering deck flickered, pixelated, and came back. A dozen of Ashford's men were training guns at a pressure door that was stuck almost a third of the way closed. Ashford strained against his belts, trying to get closer to the image. Something—a tiny object or a video feed artifact—floated across the screen, and everything went white. When the image came back, Ashford said something obscene.

Armed people poured through the opening like sand falling through an hourglass. Clarissa recognized Jim Holden by the way he moved, the intimacy of long obsession making him as obvious as her own family would have been. And so the tall figure beside him had to be Naomi, whom Melba had almost killed. And then, near the end, the only one walking in the null-g environment, Carlos Baca. Bull. The head of security, and Ashford's nemesis. He walked slowly across the deck, his real legs strapped together and his mechanical ones lumbering step by painful step. One of Ashford's people tried to fire and was shot, his body twisting in the air in a way that reminded her of seeing a caterpillar cut in half. She realized that the sound she was hearing was Ashford cursing under his breath. He didn't seem to stop for breath.

"Lock down the perimeter," Ashford yelled. "Ruiz! Ruiz! We have to fire. We have to fire now!"

"I can't," the woman's voice said. "We don't have a connection."

"I don't care if it's stable, I have to fire now."

"It's not unstable, sir," the woman said. "It's not *there*."

Ashford slammed his fist against the control panel and grimaced. She didn't know if he'd broken his knuckles, but she wouldn't have been surprised. For the next fifteen minutes, they watched the battle play out, the invading force sweeping through the engineering deck. Clarissa tried to keep tabs on where Holden and Naomi were, the way she might watch a dramatic show for one or two favorite minor actors.

"Redirect the suppression teams," Ashford said.

"Yes...ah..."

Ashford turned toward Jojo. The guard's face was pale. "I'm having trouble getting responses from the controls. I think...I think they're locking us out."

Ashford's rage crested and then sank into a kind of deathly calm. He floated in his couch, his hands pressed together, the tips of both index fingers against his lower lip.

"Environmental controls aren't responding," Jojo said, his voice taking on the timbre of near panic. "They're changing the atmosphere, sir."

"Environmental suits," Ashford said. "We'll need environmental suits."

Clarissa sighed and launched herself across the cabin to the open access panels.

"What are you doing?" Ashford shouted at her. She didn't answer.

The internal structure of the *Behemoth* wasn't that different from any other bridge, though it did have more redundancy than she'd expected. If it had been left in its original form, it would have been robust, but the requirements of a battleship were more rigorous than the elegant generation ship had been, and some of the duplicate systems had been repurposed to accommodate the PDCs, gauss guns, and torpedoes. She turned a monitor on, watching the nitrogen levels rise in the bridge. Without the buildup of carbon dioxide, they wouldn't even feel short of breath. Just a little light-headed, and then out. She wondered whether Holden would let them die that way. Probably Holden wouldn't have. Bull, she wouldn't bet on.

It didn't matter. Ren had trained her well. She disabled remote access to their environmental systems with the deactivation of a single circuit.

"Sir! I have atmo control back!" Jojo shouted.

"Well, get us some goddamn air, then!" Ashford shouted.

Clarissa looked at her work with a sense of calm pride. It wasn't pretty, and she wouldn't have wanted to leave it that way for long, but she'd done what needed doing and it hadn't shut down the system. That was pretty good, given the circumstances.

"How much have you got?" Ashford snapped.

"I've got mechanical, atmosphere...everything local to command, sir."

Like a thank-you would kill you, Clarissa thought as she floated back toward the door to the security station.

"Can we do it to them?" Ashford asked. "Can we shut off their air?"

"No," Jojo said. "We're just local. But at least we don't need those suits."

Ashford's scowl changed its character without ever becoming a smile.

"Suits," he said. "Jojo. Do we have access to the powered armor Pa took from those Martian marines?"

Jojo blinked, then nodded sharply. "Yes, sir."

"I want you to find four people who'll fit in them. Then I want you to go down to engineering and get me control of my ship."

Jojo saluted, grinning. "Yes, sir."

"And Jojo? *Anyone* gets in your way, you kill them. Understand?"

"Five by five."

The guard unstrapped and launched himself toward the hallway. She heard voices in the hall, people preparing for battle. *We have to expect the cycle will go on, getting bigger and more dangerous until one side or the other is destroyed.* Who said that? It seemed like something she'd just heard. Under local control the ventilation system had a slightly different rhythm, the exhalations from recyclers coming a few seconds closer together and lasting half as long. She wondered why that would be. It was the sort of thing Ren would have known. It was the sort of thing she only noticed now.

Ren. She tried to imagine him now. Tried to see herself the way he would see her. She was going to die. She was going to die and make everyone else safe by doing it. It wouldn't bring him back to life, but it would make his dying mean something. And it would avenge him. In her mind's eye, she still couldn't see him smiling about it.

Half an hour later, the four people Jojo had selected came into the room awkwardly. The power of the suits made moving without crashing into things difficult. The cowling shone black and red, catching the light and diffusing it. She thought of massive beetles.

"We've got no ammunition, sir," one of them said. Jojo. His voice was made artificially flat and crisp by the suit's speakers.

"Then beat them to death," Ashford said. "Your main objective is the reactor. If all you can get is enough for us to fire the laser, we still win. After that, I want Bull and his allies killed. Anyone who's there that isn't actively fighting alongside you, count as an enemy. If they aren't for us, they're against us."

"Yes, sir."

"Sir!" one of the men at the controls said.

"What?"

"I think we have someone in the external elevator shaft, sir."

"Assault force?"

"No, but they may be trapping it."

Clarissa turned away.

In the security station, the newsfeed was still spooling. Women's voices punctuated by occasional gunfire. Ashford's men hadn't taken the station yet. She wondered whether he'd let his men gun down Monica Stuart and Anna on a live feed where everyone could see it. Then she wondered how he'd prevent it from happening even if he wanted to. It wasn't like there would be any consequences. If they won and blew the Ring, they'd all die here one way or another. A few premature deaths along the way should be neither here nor there. When what came next didn't matter, anybody could do anything. Nothing had consequences.

Except that everyone always dies. You're distracting yourself from something.

Cortez floated in the security booth itself. His face lit from below by the monitor. He looked over as she approached, his smile gentle and calm.

"Ashford's sending men down to retake engineering," she said.

"Good. That's very good."

"—on the *Corvusier*," a brown-skinned woman was saying. "You know me. You can trust me. All we're asking is that you shut down the reactor for a few hours and pull the batteries from the emergency backups. Power down the systems, so we can get out of here."

"They value their own lives so much," Cortez said. "They don't think about the price their survival brings with it. The price for everybody."

"They don't," Clarissa agreed, but something sat poorly with the words. Something itched. "Do you believe in redemption?"

"Of course I do," Cortez said. "Everything in my life has taught me that there is nothing that fully removes us from the possibility of God's grace, though sometimes the sacrifices we must make are painfully high."

"—if we can just come together," Anna said on the screen, leaning in toward the camera. A lock of red hair had come out of place and fell over her left eye. "Together, we can solve this."

"What about you?" Cortez asked. He put his hand against her back. "Do you believe in redemption?"

"No," she said. "Just sacrifice."

"Mao," Ashford barked from the other room. "Get out here."

Clarissa floated to the doorway. The captain looked grayer than he had before. There was swelling around his eyes that would have been dark circles if they'd had any gravity.

"Captain?"

"You understand how all this crap is wired up."

"A little," she said.

"I've got something I need you to do."

Chapter Forty-Seven: Holden

The elevator shaft that ran outside the entire two-kilometer length of the *Behemoth*'s drum section stretched out ahead of him. With Naomi consolidating control over the ship, most of the ancillary systems were down or unsafe to use. The primary elevator was locked at the shaft's midway point. There was a secondary elevator in storage near the top of the shaft, but it could only be activated if the first elevator was removed from the tracks and locked down. So instead of a comfortable four-minute ride, the trip to the bridge was a two-kilometer-long zero-g float through hard vacuum with a big steel-and-ceramic box blocking the midpoint.

It could be worse. From the security camera streams Naomi had been able to dig into, it didn't look like Ashford expected anyone to come at the bridge that way. He'd fortified his position at the command-level transition point once word had gone out about the attack on engineering. But so far they hadn't reinforced the elevator shaft at all. They'd been expecting to hold both ends, and apparently it hadn't occurred to them yet that they didn't.

Bull had warned him that Ashford might be losing his mind under the stress of the situation, but he wasn't a stupid man. He'd had a notably mistake-free career as an OPA captain up to that point, which was why he'd seemed the safe choice to Fred Johnson. Holden couldn't count on him to make mistakes that would make things easy. But if Naomi won out in engineering it wouldn't matter. By the time they reached the bridge everyone there would be blissfully asleep.

Holden had the broadcast from Radio Free Slow Zone playing at low volume in his helmet. Anna and Monica were still explaining to the flotilla about the need to shut down all the power in a back-and-forth sort of interview format while occasional volleys of gunfire popped in the background. Somehow it made the crazy things Anna was saying seem sane. Holden gave Monica points for knowing it would work that way. And, so far, the sounds of fighting seemed light. Amos was probably bored.

They'd made a plan, and so far everything was more or less going the way they'd hoped. The thought left Holden increasingly terrified.

Without warning the wall-mounted LEDs in the shaft went out. Holden turned on his suit lights but didn't slow his climb. He threw a strange double shadow on the bulkhead when Corin's suit lights came on.

"I'm not sure if that means we're winning or losing," he said, just to have something to say.

Corin grunted at him noncommittally. "I see the lift."

Holden tilted his torso back to shine the suit lights farther up the shaft. The bottom of the elevator was visible a hundred meters ahead as a wall of metal and composite.

"There's supposed to be a maintenance hatch we can open."

Corin held up a fist in assent, and while still drifting up the elevator shaft began rummaging around in the duffel she'd brought from engineering. She pulled out a handheld plasma torch.

Holden rotated his body to hit the bottom of the elevator feet first, then kicked on his boot magnets. He walked over to the hatch and tried to open it, but as they suspected it was locked from the inside. Without waiting to be asked Corin started cutting it open with her torch.

"Bull, you there?" Holden asked, switching to the agreed-upon channel.

"Trouble?"

"Just cutting the elevator right now, wanted to check in."

"Well," Bull said, drawing the word out. "We're hitting either home runs or strikes here. We own the essential systems, we've got the laser down, and we're working on killing the reactor."

"What are we missing?" Holden asked. Corin's torch sputtered and went out, and she began a quiet profanity-laced conversation with herself as she replaced the power pack with another from her duffel.

"Naomi can't get into the bridge systems. They've got her totally locked out, which means no knockout gas for the entry."

Which meant, by last count, him and Corin fighting their way past at least fifteen of Ashford's people, and possibly more. Through a narrow doorway, down a long corridor with no cover. It would make the entry into engineering look like a walk in the park.

"We can't do that with two people," Holden said. "There's no chance."

Corin, who'd been listening in on her radio, looked up. She hit the elevator hatch with one gauntleted fist and the cut piece fell inside, edges glowing dull red. She made no move to enter, waiting for the outcome of his conversation with Bull. Her expression was blank; it could have meant anything.

"We're sending some help, so sit tight at the command deck entry hatch and wait for—" He stopped, and Holden could hear someone speaking to him, though the words were too low to make out. It sounded like Naomi.

"What's up?" Holden asked, but Bull didn't answer. An increasingly animated conversation happened on Bull's end for several minutes. Bull's replies were fragments that without context meant nothing to Holden. He waited impatiently.

"Okay, new problem," Bull finally said.

"Bigger than the 'we can't get into the bridge without dying' problem?"

"Yeah," Bull said. Holden felt his stomach drop. "Naomi caught something on a security cam they missed in the corridor outside the bridge. Four people in power armor just left the command deck. It's the armor we took from the Martians. No way to track them, but I can guess where they're headed."

There was only one place Ashford would be sending that much firepower. Engineering.

"Get out," Holden said, more panic in his voice than he'd hoped to hear. "Get out now."

Bull chuckled. It was not a reassuring sound. "Oh, my friend, this will be a problem for you before it is for us."

Holden waited. Corin shrugged with her hands and climbed inside the elevator to open the upper hatch. No need to cut it. The locks were on the inside.

"There are only three ways to get to us," Bull continued. "They can go down through the drum, but that's messy. The maintenance corridor on the other side of the drum can't be accessed when the drum is rotating. That leaves one good way to head south on this beast."

"Right through us," Holden said.

"Yup. So guess what? Your mission just changed."

"Delaying action," Corin said.

"Give the lady a prize. We still might be able to win this thing if we can buy Naomi a little more time. You get to buy it for her."

"Bull," Holden said. "There are two of us with light assault rifles and sidearms here. Those people have force recon armor. I've watched someone work in that gear up close. We won't be a delay. We'll be a cloud of pink mist they fly through at full speed."

"Not quite that fast. I'm not an idiot, I pulled all the ammo from the suits, and as an added precaution I went ahead and yanked the firing contacts in the guns."

"That's good news, actually, but can't they just tear us limb from limb?"

"Yeah," Bull said. "So don't let them grab you if you can avoid it. Buy us as much time as you can. Bull out."

Holden looked at Corin, who was looking back at him, the same blank expression on her broad face. His heart was beating triple time. Everything took on a sense of almost painful reality. It was like he'd just woken up.

He was about to die.

"Last stand time," he said, trying to keep his voice steady.

"This is as good a place as any." She pointed at the boxy and solid-looking elevator. "Use the upper hatch for cover, they'll have to come at us without any cover of their own, and without guns they'll have to close and engage at point blank. We can dump a lot of fire into them as they approach."

"Corin," Holden said. "Have you ever seen one of those suits at work?"

"Nope. Does it change what we need to do here?"

He hesitated.

"No," he said. "I guess it really doesn't." He pulled the assault rifle off his back and left it floating next to him. He checked his ammo. Still the same six magazines it had been when he stuffed them in the bandolier.

Nothing to do but wait.

Corin found a spot by the hatch where she could hook one foot under a handhold set into what would be the wall under thrust. She settled in, staring up the elevator shaft through her sights. Holden tried doing the same, but got antsy and had to start moving around.

"Naomi?" he said, switching to their private channel and hoping she was still on the radio.

"I'm here," she said after a few seconds.

Holden started to reply, then stopped. Everything that came

into his head to say seemed trite. He'd been about to say that he'd loved her since the moment he met her, but that was ludicrous. He'd barely even noticed Naomi when they first met. She'd been a tall, skinny engineer. When he got to know her better, she'd become a tall, skinny, and brilliant engineer, but that was it. He felt like they'd eventually became friends, but the truth was he could barely remember the person he'd been back on the *Canterbury* now.

Everyone had lost something in the wake of the protomolecule. The species as a whole had lost its sense of its own importance. Its primacy in the universal plan.

Holden had lost his certainty.

When he thought back to the man he'd been before the death of the *Cant*, he remembered a man filled with righteous certainty. Right was right, wrong was wrong, you drew the lines thus and so. His time with Miller had stripped him of some of that. His time working for Fred Johnson had, if not removed, then filed down what remained. A sort of creeping nihilism had taken its place. A sense that the protomolecule had broken the human race in ways that could never be repaired. Humanity had gotten a two-billion-year reprieve on a death sentence it hadn't known it had, but time was up. All that was left was the kicking and screaming.

Oddly enough, it was Miller who had given him his sense of purpose back. Or whatever the Miller construct was. He couldn't really remember that version of himself who'd known exactly where all the lines were drawn. He wasn't sure of much of anything anymore. But whatever had climbed up off of Venus and built the Ring, it had built Miller too.

And it had wanted to talk. To him.

A small thing, maybe. The new Miller didn't make much sense. It had an agenda that it wasn't explaining. The protomolecule didn't seem particularly sorry for all the chaos and death it had caused.

But it wanted to talk. And it wanted to talk to him. Holden realized he'd found a lifeline there. Maybe there was a way out of all of the chaos. Maybe he could help find it. He recognized that latching on to the idea that the protomolecule, or at least their agent Miller, had picked him as their contact fed all of his worst inclinations to arrogance and self-importance. But it was better than despair.

And now, only starting to see that murky path out of the hole the protomolecule had dug and humanity had hurled itself into with self-destructive gusto, now he was about to be killed because of yet another petty human with more power than sense. It didn't seem fair. He wanted to live to see how humanity bounced back. He wanted to be part of it. For the first time in a long time he felt like he might be able to turn into the kind of man who could make a difference.

And he wanted to explain this to Naomi. To tell her that he was turning into a better person. The kind of person who would have seen her as more than just a good engineer all those years ago. As if he could, by being a different person now, retroactively fix the shallow, vain man he'd been then. Maybe even make himself worthy of her.

"I like you," he said instead.

"Jim," she replied after a moment. Her voice was thick.

"I've enjoyed your company ever since we met. Even when you were just an engineer and shipmate, you were a very likable one."

There was only a faint static hiss on the radio. Holden pictured Naomi retreating into herself, letting her hair fall across her eyes to hide them in that way she did when she was in an uncomfortable emotional situation. Of course, that was silly. With no gravity her hair wouldn't do that. But the image made him smile.

"Thank you," he said, letting her off the hook. "Thank you for everything."

"I love you, Jim," she finally said. Holden felt his body relax. He saw his coming death, and wasn't afraid of it anymore. He'd miss all the good stuff to follow, but he'd help make it happen. And a very good person loved him. It was more than most people got in a lifetime.

A low screech started, which cycled up into a howl. For a second, Holden thought Naomi was screaming into her headset. He almost started comforting her before he realized he could feel the vibration in his feet. The sound wasn't coming across the radio. It was transmitting through his boots on the elevator wall. The entire ship was vibrating.

Holden placed his helmet against the wall to get a better sound, and the scream of the ship was almost deafening. It stopped after an endless minute with an ear-shattering bang. Silence followed.

"What the fuck?" Corin said under her breath.

"Naomi? Bull? Anyone still on the line?" Holden yelled, thinking that whatever had happened had torn the ship apart.

"Yeah," Bull said. "We're here."

"What—" Holden started.

"Mission change," Bull continued. "That sound was them slamming the brakes on the habitat drum. Catastrophic inertia change 2.0. There are a lot of people in that drum getting thrown around right now."

"Why would they do that? Just to stop the broadcast?"

"Nope," Bull said with a tired sigh. He sounded like a man who'd just been informed he was going to have to pull a double shift. "It means they think we fortified the elevator shaft and they're coming the other way."

"We're on our way back," Holden said, gesturing at Corin to follow him.

"Negative," Bull said. "If they get the laser back online here while Ashford's still sitting at that control panel, we lose."

"So what? We're supposed to get up there, break into the bridge, and shoot everyone while their guys are down there breaking into engineering and shooting all of you?"

Bull's sigh sounded tired.

"Yeah."

Chapter Forty-Eight: Bull

They came out of the maintenance shaft like an explosion. Four black-and-red monsters in roughly human shape. Bull and the people he'd managed to gather opened fire as soon as they saw them. A dozen guns against a maelstrom.

"Don't let them get to the reactor controls," Bull shouted.

"Roger that," one of the Earthers said. "Any idea how we stop them, sir?"

He didn't have one. He unloaded his pistol's clip with one hand, driving the mech backward across the deck with the other. One of the Martian marines cut across overhead, rifle blazing. Small white marks appeared on the breastplate of the nearest attacker, like a child's thumbprints on a window. The man in powered armor reached the nearest workstation, ripped the crash couch out of the decking with one hand, and threw it like a massive baseball.

The couch sang through the air and shattered against the bulkhead where it hit. If there had been anyone in its path, it would have been worse than a bullet.

Bull kept backing up. When his clip ran out, he gave his full attention to driving the mech. The last of the attackers out of the shaft tried to leap across the room, but the armor's amplification made it more like a launch. The red-and-black blur careened off the far wall with a sound like a car wreck.

"And that," Sergeant Verbinski said across the radio, "is why we spend six months training before they put us in those things." He sounded amused. Good thing somebody was.

Fighting in null g complicated the tactics of a firefight, but the basic rule stayed the same. Hold territory, stay behind cover, have someone there to keep the other side busy when you had to move. The problem, Bull saw almost at once, was that they didn't have anything that would damage their opponents. The best they could do was make loud noises and trust the people in the battle armor to give in to their reflexive caution. It wouldn't win the war. Hell, it would barely postpone losing the battle.

"Naomi," Bull said. "How're you doing back there?"

"I can dump the core, power this whole bastard down. Just give me three more minutes," she said. He could hear the focus and drive in her voice. The determination. It didn't count for shit.

"That's not going to happen," he said.

"Just... just hold on."

"They're coming back that way now," Bull said. "And there's not a goddamn thing we can do to stop them."

The four attackers bounced through engineering like grasshoppers, massive bodies crashing into walls and consoles, shearing off bits of the bulkhead where they scraped against it. At this point, their best hope was that the enemy force would beat itself to death against the walls. Bull pulled back toward the entryway to the drum, then took a position behind a crate and started firing at the enemy, trying to draw them toward him. If he could get the enemy out into the habitation drum, he might be able to close down the transition point and make the bastards dig back through. It might even give Naomi the minutes she needed.

The people in power armor didn't seem to notice he was there. One caught a desk, the steel bending in the suit's glove, and started pulling hand over hand toward the reactor controls.

"Can anybody stop that guy?" Bull asked. No one on the frequency answered. He sighed. "Naomi. You got to leave now."

"Core's out. I can drop the grid too. Just a few more minutes."

"You don't have them. Come out now, and I'll try to get you back in when things cool down."

"But—"

"You're no good to anyone dead," he said. The channel went quiet, and for a long moment he thought the Belter had been caught, been killed. Then she came sailing out of the hallway, leading with her chin, her good arm and hair streaming behind her like stabilizing fins. The nearest of the people in power suits grabbed at her, but she was already gone, and they were too timid to try jumping after her.

Bull saw another of the enemy struggling with something. A gun. The massive glove was too thick to fit through the weapon's trigger guard. As Bull watched, the enemy snapped the guard off and settled the gun in its fist, like a child's toy carried by a large man. Bull fired at it a few more times without much hope of doing damage.

Four Earthers shouted with one voice and launched themselves at the one with the gun. The attacker didn't fire. Just swept one big metal arm through the air, scattering Bull's people like they were sparrows.

His people were going to get killed—were *getting* killed—and there was nothing he could do to stop it.

"Okay kids," he said. "Let's pack up and go home. It's getting too hot in here."

"Bull!" Verbinski shouted. "Watch your six!"

Bull tried to swivel in the mech, but something hit him hard in the back. The magnetic feet creaked and lost their grip, and he was floating. The world all around began to shimmer gold and blue as his consciousness slipped away. He was aware distantly of a hand on his shoulder, slowing his fall, and he saw Naomi's face. Something had scraped her cheek, and she had a long bubble of blood clinging to her skin. He tried to turn and failed. That was right. No spine. He should have remembered that.

"What?" he said.

"They cut us off from the drum," Naomi said and turned him so that his mech's feet could touch deck. The air was a debris field. Twists of metal and shattered ceramic, sprays of blood slowly coalescing and growing larger like planets forming out of dust. Electricity arced from the ruins of a control panel, and the shattered glass floated in the tiny play of lightning. Two of the people in power armor stood rooted by the passage to the transition point. One held a rifle by the barrel as a club, the other had pistols with the trigger guard snapped off in either hand. A third was flailing in the air just above the maintenance shaft that they'd arrived through, struggling to get purchase on something. The fourth was shuffling across the deck toward them, its movements deliberate and controlled to keep from kicking off into the air.

"Elevator shaft airlock," Bull said. "Fall back."

"Everyone," Naomi said into her hand terminal. "We're falling back to the elevator shaft on my go. Go!"

Naomi pulled him around, then attached herself to his back in rescue hold and jumped. The enemy's guns opened fire. Bull caught a glimpse of a woman just as a bullet passed through her leg. Saw the grimace on her face and the blood fountaining out of her. *I'm sorry,* he thought.

The wall of the elevator shaft airlock loomed up, and Naomi pushed off from him, landing on the bulkhead with the grace of a woman born to zero g. Two more bodies came through the space, Martian marines, both of them. He recognized the man called Juarez and the woman named Cass. Naomi slapped the controls and the airlock doors began to collapse. Just as the opening seemed too narrow for a human form, two more came through. Sergeant Verbinski and a man from Bull's side of the security force schism.

Bull's head was swimming. He felt like he'd just run twenty miles in the hot New Mexican sun. He clapped his hands together less to command the attention of the people in the lock and more to bring himself back to awareness.

"That shaft's in vacuum," he said. "If that's the way we're going, we need to get suited up. Lockers are over there. Let's see what we've got to work with." A massive blow rang against the airlock door. Then another. "Might want to hurry," he said.

"You aren't going to fit," Verbinski said. "Not with that contraption."

"Yeah," Bull said. "Okay."

"Come on, big boy," the sergeant said. "Let's get you out of that."

No, Bull wanted to say. *I'm all right*. But Juarez and the other marine were already shucking him out of his brace, then out of the mech that Sam had made for him. He was a cripple again. That wasn't true. He'd been crippled ever since the catastrophe. Now he just had one fewer tool.

He'd worked with less.

The banging on the airlock door was getting louder, more intense. Along with the impact, there was something that sounded like tearing. He imagined the powered armor picking up handfuls of steel between massive fingers and pulling back, ripping at the skin of the ship. He clambered over to his mech, his body flowing out behind him, useless as a kite. He popped open the storage and took what was left of his pistol's ammunition and his hand terminal. For a moment, he didn't recognize the flat black package that he took out next. And then he did.

"If we're not staying, we'd best leave," Verbinski said.

"Let's go," Bull said, pushing the grenades into the pouch on the EVA suit's thigh.

Naomi cycled the door to the shaft. The sounds of the attack grew fainter and farther away as the air leaked out, and then the shaft was open below them. A full kilometer's fall to the trapped elevator, and then another past that to...what? Ashford? Certain death? Bull didn't know anymore what he was running from. Or to.

One by one, they pushed off, pulling themselves through the vacuum. Verbinski and the security man, Naomi and the marine, then Bull and Juarez. Without discussing it, they'd all paired off with someone who wasn't theirs. In Bull's sagging mind, that seemed important.

"Juarez?" Verbinski said on the radio, and Bull was surprised to hear his voice.

"Sir."

"If you get a good shot, you think you could crack the visors on those suits?"

"Your suit, maybe," Juarez said. "I keep mine in pretty good condition."

"Do your best," Verbinski said.

Bull felt it when the enemy force breached the airlock. He couldn't even say what it was exactly. Some little press of a shock wave, a whisper-thin breath of atmosphere. He looked down past his dead feet, and there was light at the bottom of the shaft where there shouldn't have been. There were probably about a thousand safety measures slamming down in engineering right now. He hoped so. Far below, he saw a muzzle flash, but they were so far ahead, the bullet almost certainly hit the sides of the shaft and spent itself before it could reach them.

Juarez turned, his rifle steadied between his feet. The man's face went calm and soft and the rifle flashed silently.

"Got one, Verb," he said. And then, "Sergeant?"

Verbinski didn't answer. He was still floating, skimming along the steel tracks that would guide the elevator, but his eyes were closed. His face was slack, and foam flecked his lips and nostrils. Bull hadn't even known the man was injured.

"Sergeant!" Juarez yelled.

"He's gone," Cass said.

The rest of the trip to the elevator was a thing carved from nightmares. Bull's body kept drifting wildly behind him, and his lungs felt full and wet. He'd stopped coughing, though. He didn't know if that was a good thing. Just as they reached the elevator, a lucky shot from their pursuers took the security man in the back, blowing out his air supply. Bull watched the man die, but he didn't hear it. The hatchway Corin had burned through the elevator's base seemed too small to fit through, but he got one arm in and Naomi pulled him the rest of the way.

In the body of the elevator car, Juarez took a position firing down the hole at the pursuers. Bull didn't know how much ammunition the marine had, but it had to be getting close to the end of his supply. Bull would have slouched against the wall if there had been any gravity. Instead he shifted his suit radio to the channel for Naomi.

"Give me a gun," she said before he could speak. "Give me something."

"You keep going," he said. "Get to the top of the shaft."

"But—"

"Maybe you can get the hatch open for them. Get into command."

"You can't access the controls from inside the shaft."

"In this piece-of-shit boat, you never know," Bull said. "Someone might have put a self-destruct button there. Wouldn't surprise me."

"That's your plan B?"

"I think we're pretty much on plan Z at this point," Bull said. "Anyway, you're the engineer. There's fuck-all you can do here. And I heard you with Holden before. You might as well get to see him again. Not like it costs us anything."

He watched her face as she decided. Fear, despair, regret, calm, in that order. Impressive woman. He wished he'd had a chance to know her better. And if she was able to ship with Jim Holden and love him, maybe he wasn't as bad as Bull thought either.

"Thank you," she said, then turned and launched herself along the elevator shaft toward command and her lover. *That was sweet*, Bull thought. Juarez's rifle flashed again and Bull shifted his radio frequencies to include the two marines.

"You two should go too. Head up top. See if you can storm the command."

"You sure?" Cass said, her voice calm and professional. "We've got cover here. There won't be a better place farther up."

"Yeah, pretty sure," Bull said.

"What about you?" Juarez asked.

"I'm staying here," Bull said.

"Okay, bro," Juarez said, then he and Cass were gone too. Bull thought about looking down through the shaft to see how close the enemy had come, but he didn't. Too much energy, and if he got shot in the eye at this point... well, that would just be sad. The little box of the elevator was a monochrome non-color, lit only by the backsplash from his own suit light. He took as deep a breath as he could. It was pretty shallow. He drew the grenades out from his pocket, one in either hand, and carefully dialed them down to the shortest fuse.

So he was going to die here. Not what he would have picked, but what the hell. It probably beat going back and having his spine grown back wrong. He'd seen guys who lived their whole lives in a drug haze fighting the pain of a bad regrowth. He hadn't really let himself think about that before. Now it was safe to.

He tried to decide whether he regretted dying, but the truth was he was too fucking tired to care. And he couldn't breathe for crap. He was sorry he hadn't killed Ashford, but that wasn't new. He was sorry he couldn't avenge Sam or find out if Pa was alive. Or whether Ashford would actually be able to destroy the Ring. If he was sad about anything, it was that everything that was in motion now would keep on being in motion without him, and he'd never know how it went. Never know if anything he'd done had made a difference.

His hand terminal blinked. A connection request from Monica Stuart. He wondered for a moment what she wanted with him, and then remembered that Ashford had stopped the drum. Things had to be for shit in there. He routed the request to his suit. No pictures, but the voice connection would be enough.

"Bull," the woman said. "We're being attacked up here. I think Anna's dead. What the hell's going on down there? How much longer?"

"Well, we lost engineering," he said. He felt a pang about Anna, but it was just one of many at that point. "Pretty much everyone in the attack party's dead now. Maybe five folks holed up in the elevator shaft, but the bad guys got the top and the bottom of that, so we're kind of screwed there. Managed to dump the core, but the grid's still up. It'll be enough to fire the laser. Ashford's guys are probably in engineering putting that back online, and I don't see we've got any damn way to stop him."

"Oh my God," Monica breathed.

"Yeah, it kind of sucks."

"What...what are you going to do about it?"

A beam of light shone through the hatch in the floor. Tiny bits of dust and particulate metal glimmered in it like it was swirling in water. He watched it with a half smile on his face. It meant the bad guys were almost there, but it was pretty to look at. He remembered that Monica was on the line. She'd asked him something.

"Yeah," Bull said. "So that thing where we power down the ship and save everyone? We're probably not going to do that."

"You can't give up," she said. "Please. There has to be a way."

Doesn't have to be, he thought, but didn't say. Anna thought there was a way. Where did that get her? *But if there is, I hope one of you folks finds it.*

"How bad is it in there?" he asked.

"It's...it's terrible. It's like the catastrophe happened all over again."

"Yeah, I can see that," Bull said.

"We can't go on," Monica said. "Oh God, what are we going to do?"

The light got stronger. Brighter. He couldn't see the dust motes anymore from the shine of the light.

"Monica?" Bull said. "Look, I'm sorry, but I kind of got to go now, okay? You folks just do your best. Hold it together in there, all right? And hey, if it all works out?"

"Yes?"

"Tell Fred Johnson he fucking owes me one."

He dropped the connection, unplugged his hand terminal. He took a grenade in each hand, his thumbs on the release bars. A head poked up through the hatch, then back down fast. When no one shot at it, the head came back more slowly. Bull smiled and nodded at it, welcoming. The opaque cowling went clear, and he saw Casimir staring at him. Bull grinned. Well, that was a pleasure, at least. A little treat on the way out.

"Hey," Bull said, even though the man couldn't hear him. "Hold this for me."

He tossed the two grenades, and watched the man's expression as he understood what they were.

Chapter Forty-Nine: Anna

Anna returned to consciousness floating in a tangled knot with Okju the camera operator, two office chairs, and a potted ficus plant. Someone was setting off firecrackers in long strings. Someone else was shouting. Anna's vision was blurry, and she blinked and shook her head to clear it. Which turned out to be a mistake, as shaking her head sent a spike of pain up her spine that nearly knocked her unconscious again.

"What?" she tried to say, but it came out as a slushy "bluh" sound.

"Christ, Red, I thought you were cooked there," a familiar voice replied. Rough but friendly. Amos. "I hated to think I broke my promise."

Anna opened her eyes again, careful not to move her head. She was floating in the center of what had been the studio space. Okju floated next to her, her foot tucked into Anna's armpit. Anna extricated her legs from the two office chairs they were twisted up in, and pushed the ficus away from her face.

More firecrackers went off in long, staccato bursts. It took Anna's muddled brain a few seconds to realize the sound was gunfire. Across the room, Amos was leaning against the wall next to the front door, taking a magazine out of his gun and replacing it with the smooth motion of long practice. On the other side of the door one of the UN soldiers they'd picked up was firing at someone outside. Answering gunfire blew chunks of molded fiberglass out of the back wall just a few meters from where Anna floated.

"If you aren't dead," Amos said, then paused to lean around the corner and fire off a short burst. "Then you'll probably want to get out of the middle of the room."

"Okju," Anna said, tugging on the woman's arm. "Wake up. We need to move."

Okju's arm flopped bonelessly when she pulled it, and the woman started slowly rotating in the air. Anna saw that her head was tilted at an acute angle to her shoulders, and her face was slack and her eyes stared at nothing. Anna recoiled involuntarily, the lizard living at the base of her spine telling her to get away from the dead person as quickly as possible. She yelped and pushed against Okju's body with her feet, sending it and herself floating away in opposite directions. When she hit the wall she grabbed on to an LED sconce and held on with all her strength. The pain in her neck and head was a constant percussive throb.

The sounds of gunfire didn't stop. Amos and his small, mixed band of defenders were firing out through every opening in the office space, several of which had been cut as gun ports.

They were under attack. Ashford had sent his people to stop them. Anna's memories of the last few moments came back in a rush. The terrible screeching sound, being hurled sideways at the wall.

Ashford must have shut down the drum to stop them so that his gunmen could finish them off. But if Okju had been killed as a result of the sudden stoppage, then that same effect would have been repeated dozens, maybe hundreds of times throughout the makeshift community on the *Behemoth*. Ashford was willing to kill them all to get his own way. Anna felt a growing rage, and was glad that no one had thought to give her a gun.

"Are we still broadcasting?" she yelled at Amos over the gunfire.

"Dunno, Red. Monica's in the radio room."

Anna pulled herself across the wall to the closet where they'd placed their broadcasting gear. The door was ajar, and she could see Monica floating inside, checking the equipment. The space wasn't large enough for both of them, so Anna just pushed the door open a little farther and said, "Are we still broadcasting? Can we get back on the air?"

Monica gave a humorless laugh but didn't turn around. "I thought you were dead."

"No, but Okju is. I think she broke her neck. I'll take the camera if you need me to. Where's Clip?"

"Clip was helping Amos, and he was shot in the hip. He's bleeding out in a side office. Tilly is helping him."

Anna pushed her way into the small room and put a hand on Monica's shoulder. "We have to get back on the air. We have to keep up the broadcast or this is all for nothing. Tell me what to do."

Monica laughed again, then turned around and swatted Anna's hand off of her arm. "What do you think is happening here? Ashford has men outside trying to break in and kill us. Bull and his people have lost the engine room, and Juarez says Bull's been killed. Who knows how many people he—"

Anna planted her feet against the doorjamb, grabbed Monica by the shoulders, and slammed the reporter up against the wall. "Does the broadcasting equipment still work?" She was amazed at how steady her voice sounded.

"It got banged around some, but—"

"Does. It. Work."

"Yes," Monica said. It came out as a frightened squeak.

"Get me on the channel the assault team was using, and give me a headset," Anna said, then let go of Monica's shoulders. Monica did as she asked, moving quickly and only occasionally giving her a frightened look. *I've become frightening*, Anna thought. Tasting the idea, and finding it less unpleasant than she'd expect. These were frightening times.

"Fuck!" Amos yelled from the other room. When Anna looked out, she saw one of the young Martian officers floating in the middle of the room spraying small globes of red blood into the air around him. Her friend Chris launched across the room by pushing off with his one good leg and grabbed the injured man with his one arm, then pulled him into cover.

"We're running out of time," Anna said to Monica. "Work faster."

Monica's reply was to hand her a headset with a microphone.

"Hello? This is Anna Volovodov at Radio Free Slow Zone. Is anyone left on this channel?"

Someone replied, but they were impossible to hear over the nearby gunfire. Anna turned the volume up to the maximum and said, "Repeat that, please."

"We're here," James Holden said at deafening levels.

"How many are left, and what's the situation?"

"Well," Holden said, then paused and grunted as though exerting himself for several seconds. He sounded out of breath when he continued. "We're holed up in the port elevator shaft just outside the command deck airlock. There are three of us at this position. Bull and the remaining marines are fighting the counterassault team at a position further down the shaft. I have no idea how that's going. We've run out of room to retreat, so unless someone decides to open the hatch and let us onto the bridge, we're sort of out of options."

The last part of his sentence was almost drowned out by a massive wave of incoming gunfire in her office. Amos and his group were hunkered down, leaning against the reinforced armor they'd attached to the walls. The reports of the shots and the sound of bullets hitting metal was deafening. When the fire lessened, a pair of men in *Behemoth* security armor rushed the room, spraying automatic weapons fire as they came. Two of Amos' team were hit, and more globes of red flew into the air. Amos grabbed the second man through the door and yanked him up off his magnetic hold to the floor, then threw him at his partner. They tumbled off across the room together and then Amos fired a long burst from his weapon into both as they spun. The air was filled with so many floating red orbs of various sizes that it became difficult to see. The rest of Amos' team opened fire, and whatever attack Ashford's people had launched was apparently driven back, as no more soldiers charged through the door.

"Is there anything we can do?" Anna yelled at Holden.

"Sounds to me like you're in some shit there yourself, Preacher," Holden replied. His voice was weary. Sad. "Unless you've got the bridge access controls nearby, I'd say you should concentrate on your own problems."

More fire came through the offices, but it was sporadic. Amos had driven off their big attack, and now they were taking petulant potshots. Monica was staring at her, waiting for her to issue another order. Somehow, she'd become the person in charge.

"Set me to broadcast on the Radio Free Slow Zone feed," Anna said. In the end, talking was all she had to offer. Monica nodded at her and pointed a small camera at her face.

"This is Anna Volovodov broadcasting from the offices of Radio Free Slow Zone to anyone on the *Behemoth* that's still listening. We've failed to hold engineering, so our plan to shut down the reactor and get everyone back home is failing as well. We have people trapped in the external elevator shaft, and they can't get onto the bridge.

"So, please, if anyone listening to this can help, we need you. Everyone on this flotilla needs you. The people dying right outside your door need you. Most of all, the people we left behind on Earth and Mars and the Belt need you. If the captain does what he's planning, if he fires the laser at the Ring, everyone back home will die too. Please, if you can hear me, help us."

She stopped, and Monica put down the camera.

"Think that will work?" Monica asked.

Anna was about to say no when the wall comm panel buzzed at her. A voice said, "How do you know that?" A young voice, female, sad. Clarissa. "What you said about destroying Earth if we attack the Ring, how do you know that?"

"Clarissa," Anna said. "Where are you?"

"I'm here, on the bridge. I'm in the security station. I was watching your broadcast."

"Can you open the door and let our people in?"

"Yes."

"Will you do that?"

"How," Clarissa repeated, her tone not changing at all, "do you know what you said?"

A man generally regarded as the instigator of two solar system–wide wars got all this information from a protomolecule-created ghost that no one else can see. It wasn't a particularly compelling argument.

"James Holden got it while he was on the station."

"So *he* told you that this would happen," Clarissa said, her tone doubtful.

"Yes."

"So how do you *know*?"

"I don't, Claire," Anna said, appropriating Tilly's pet name to try and create a connection. "I don't know. But Holden believes it's true, and the consequences if he's right are too extreme to risk. So I'm taking it on faith."

There was a long moment of silence. Then a male voice said, "Clarissa, who are you talking to in here?"

It took Anna a moment to recognize it as Hector Cortez. She'd known he was on the bridge with Ashford, but somehow the reminder that he'd sided with the men who killed Bull was too much. She had to restrain herself from cursing at him.

"Anna wants me to open the elevator airlock and let the other side into the bridge. She wants me to help stop Ashford from destroying the Ring. She says it will kill everyone on Earth if we do."

"Don't listen to her," Cortez said. "She's just afraid."

"Afraid?" Anna yelled. "Do you hear those sounds, Hector? That's gunfire. Bullets are flying by even as we speak. You're locked away safe and snug on the command deck planning to destroy something you don't understand, while I am risking gunshot wounds to stop you. Who's afraid here?"

"You're afraid to make the necessary sacrifices to protect the people we've left behind. You're only thinking of yourself," he yelled back. Anna heard the sound of a door closing in the background. Someone had shut the door to the security station to keep the argument from being overheard. If it was Clarissa, that was a good sign.

"Clarissa," Anna said, keeping her voice as calm as she could with the ongoing sounds of a gunfight behind her. "Claire, the people waiting outside the airlock door are going to be killed if you don't open it. They are trapped there. People are coming to kill them."

"Don't change the subject," Cortez started.

"It's Holden and Naomi out there," Anna continued, ignoring him. "And Bull is there too. Ashford will have them all killed."

"They wouldn't be in danger if they hadn't attacked Ashford's rightful command," Cortez said.

"That's three people who all made the choice to give you a second chance," Anna said. "Bull chose to protect you from the UN fleet's vengeance when he had no reason to. When I asked her to, Naomi forgave you for almost killing her. Holden agreed not to hurt you, in spite of the many provocations you gave him."

"Those people are *criminals*—" Cortez tried to say over the top of her, but she kept her voice level and continued.

"These people, the people who forgive, who try to help others. The people who give their lives to save strangers, they're on the other side of that door, dying. I don't have to take that on faith. That's fact. That's happening right now."

Anna paused, waiting for any sign Clarissa was listening. There was none. Even Cortez had stopped speaking. The comm station hissed faintly, the only sign it was still on.

"Those are the people I'm asking you to help," Anna said. "The person I'm asking you to betray is a man who kills innocent people for expedience's sake. Forget Earth, and the Ring, and everything else you'd have to take on faith. Ask yourself this: Do you want to let Ashford kill Holden and Naomi? No faith. Just that simple question, Claire. Can you let them die? What choice did they make when the same question was asked of them about you?"

Anna knew she was rambling. Knew she was repeating herself. But she had to force herself to stop speaking anyway. She wasn't used to trying to save a person's soul without being able to see them, to measure the effect her words were having by their reaction. She kept trying to fill that empty space with more talking.

"I don't like the idea of those people being killed any more than you do," Cortez said. He sounded sad, but committed to his position. "But there is the necessity for sacrifice. To sacrifice is literally to be made sacred."

"Seriously?" Anna gave a humorless laugh. "We're going to do dueling etymology?"

"What we are facing here is more than humanity is ready for," Cortez said.

"You don't get to decide that, Hank," Anna said, stabbing at the radio as if it were the man. "Think about the people you're killing. Look at who you're working with, and tell me that in clear conscience you know you're doing the right thing."

"Argument by association?" Cortez said. "Really? God's tools have always been flawed. We are a fallen people, but that we have the strength of will to do what we must, even in the face of mortal punishment, is what makes us moral beings. And you of all people—"

The feed went silent for a moment.

"Cortez?" Anna said. But when Cortez's voice came, he wasn't speaking to her.

"Clarissa, what are you doing?"

Clarissa sounded calm, almost half asleep. "I opened the doors."

Chapter Fifty: Holden

Naomi had taken an access panel off the wall next to the command deck airlock. She'd crawled halfway inside, and only her belly and legs were visible. Holden had planted his mag boots next to the airlock's outer door and was awaiting instructions from her. Occasionally she'd ask him to try opening the door again, but every attempt so far had failed. Corin floated next to him, watching down the elevator shaft through her gunsights. They'd seen a quick flash of light down there a few minutes back that had set the bulkheads to vibrating. Something violent and explosive had happened.

Holden, having now moved on to his second last stand of the day, had come to view the whole thing with a weary sense of humor. As far as places to die went, the small platform between the elevator shaft and the airlock was about as good as any other. It was a niche in the wall of the shaft about ten feet on a side. The floor, ceiling, and bulkheads were all the same ceramic steel of the ship's outer hull. The back wall was the airlock door. The front was empty space where the elevator would normally sit. At the very least, when Ashford's people came swarming up the shaft at them, the floor of the niche would offer some cover.

Naomi scooted sideways a bit and kicked one leg. Holden could hear her over the radio as she grunted with the effort of grabbing something just out of reach.

"Gotcha," she said in triumph. "Okay, try it now!"

Holden hit the button to open the outer airlock doors. Nothing happened.

"Are you trying it?" Naomi asked.

He hit the button two more times. "Yeah. Nothing."

"Dammit. I could've sworn..."

Corin shifted enough to give him a sardonic look, but said nothing.

The truth was, Holden was out of emotional gas. He'd gone through his existential moment of truth back when he thought he was making a last stand at the elevator to buy Naomi time. Then he'd been given a reprieve when the attackers chose another path, but Naomi had been put in the firing line, which was actually worse. And then she'd shown up a few minutes ago saying Bull had sent her on ahead to get the door open while he acted as rearguard.

Every plan they'd made had failed spectacularly, with more casualties piling up at every step. And now they were at yet another last stand, with a locked door behind them and Ashford's goons ahead of them and nowhere to go. It should have been terrifying, but at this point Holden just felt sleepy.

"Try it now," Naomi said. Holden jabbed the button a few times without looking at it.

"Nope."

"Maybe..." she said and moved around, kicking her legs again.

"Two incoming," Corin said, her voice harsh and buzzing over the radio. He'd never heard her voice when it wasn't on a suit radio. He wondered whether it would have that same quality naturally. He walked over to the edge of the platform and looked down, magnetic boots having tricked his brain into thinking there was an up and down again.

Looking through his gunsight's magnification, he saw two of the Martian marines hurtling up the shaft as fast as their cheap environment suits would let them. He didn't recognize them yet. Bull wasn't with them.

"Try it now," Naomi said.

"Busy," Holden replied, scanning the space behind the marines for pursuers. He didn't see any.

Naomi climbed out of her access panel and floated over next to him to see what was going on. The marines shot up the shaft toward them at high speed, flipped at the last minute, and hit the ceiling feet first to come to a rapid stop. They pushed off and landed next to Holden, sticking to the floor with magnetic boots.

Holden could see through their faceplates now, and recognized the sniper, Juarez, and a dark-skinned woman whose name he'd never gotten.

"We've lost the hold point," Juarez said. He clutched his long rifle in one hand and a fresh magazine in the other. He loaded the gun and said, "Last mag," to his partner.

She checked her harness and said, "Three."

"Report," Holden said, slipping into military command mode without even meaning to. He'd been a lieutenant in the navy. Juarez was enlisted. The training they'd received about who gave orders and who followed them in combat died hard.

"I took out one hostile with a headshot, I believe a second was neutralized with our remaining explosives. No intel on the other two. They may have been injured or killed by the explosion, but we can't count on that."

"Bull?" Corin asked.

"He was holding the explosives. That second kill was his."

"Bull," Corin said again, choking up. Holden was surprised to see her eyes filling with tears. "We have to go get him."

"Negative," Juarez said. "The elevator has become a barrier. He's inside it. Anything we do to remove his body actively degrades our defensive position."

"Fuck you," Corin said, taking an aggressive step toward Juarez, her hands closing into fists. "We don't *leave* him—"

Before she could take another step, Holden grabbed her by her weapon harness and yanked her off the floor, then spun around to slam her against the closest bulkhead. He heard the air go out of her in a whoosh over the radio.

"Mourn later," he said, not letting her go. "When we're done. Then we mourn for all of them."

She grabbed his wrists in her hands, and for one heartstopping moment Holden thought she might fight him. He seriously questioned his ability to win a zero-g grappling match with the stocky security officer. But she just pulled his hands off her harness, then pushed herself back down to the floor.

"Understood, sir," she said.

"Back on watch," Holden said, keeping his voice as gentle as possible.

She walked back to the edge of the platform. Juarez watched without comment. After a respectful moment he said, "Plan, sir?"

"Naomi is trying to get the door open, but without any success. Blowing the elevator may have bought you two a couple more minutes, but maybe that's all it bought you."

"We'll try to make the most of them," the other marine said with a half smile. Juarez chuckled and slapped her on the back.

"So this is our final defensive position, then. Good cover and field of fire. If I get lucky maybe I can crack another mask. Cass, why don't you take that right corner, Corin can keep the left, and I'll set up here in the center. Holden can rove and back up whichever side is taking the most heat."

He paused, nodding at Holden. "If you agree, sir."

"I agree," Holden said. "In fact, I'm giving you full tactical command of this position. I'm going to be trying to help Naomi with the door. Yell if you get in trouble."

Juarez kicked off his mags, then jumped up to plant his feet on the ceiling. He straightened out, his long rifle pointed over his head, straight down the shaft. From Holden's perspective he looked like a particularly well-armed bat hanging from the roof.

"Movement," he said almost immediately.

"Shit," the marine named Cass said. "They got through the barrier fast."

"Looks like they're not quite through, but the wall is bulging like they're beating their way through it."

"I have an idea," Naomi said and walked over to the edge of the platform, then out onto the wall and over to the opposite side of the elevator shaft.

"Where are you going?" Holden asked.

"Panel," was her only answer before she popped an access hatch off the elevator shaft bulkhead and climbed inside. It was large enough that she completely disappeared. Holden didn't think there would be anything in there that could help them get the airlock door open, but he didn't care. Naomi was hidden while she stayed in there. Ashford's people might not bother to look for her. They probably didn't have good intel on who had engaged in the assault on engineering.

"Here they come," Juarez said, looking down the shaft through his telescopic sight. "Two left." His muzzle flashed once. "Shit, no hit." It flashed twice more. Cass started firing with her assault rifle on single fire, carefully aiming each shot. The bad guys were just under a kilometer away. Holden didn't think he'd be able to hit a stationary transport shuttle at that range, much less a rapidly moving man-sized target. But after having spent some time with Bobbie Draper, Holden knew that if Cass was taking the shots, it was because she thought she had a chance to score hits. He wasn't about to argue with her.

"Eight hundred meters," Juarez said, his voice no different than if he'd been giving a stranger the time. "Seven-fifty." He fired again.

Cass fired off the last of her magazine, then replaced it in one smooth motion. She had one extra left. Holden took three magazines off his own bandolier and left them floating next to her left elbow. She nodded her thanks without pausing in her firing. Juarez fired twice more, then said, "Out." He continued sighting down the scope, calling out ranges for Cass. When he hit five hundred meters, Corin started firing as well.

It was all very brave, Holden thought. None of them were the kind of people who gave up, no matter the odds. But it was also sort of pointless. Juarez had the only gun that was even remotely a threat to troops in state-of-the-art recon armor, and he'd fired it dry and only scored one kill. So they'd throw a lot of bullets at the approaching enemy because that's what people like them did, even when there was no chance. But in the end, Ashford would win. If he wasn't so emotionally drained, Holden would have been pissed.

The LEDs in the elevator shaft came back on, bathing them all with white light. The two soldiers wearing their stolen power armor were flying up the corridor toward them. Before he'd had time to wonder why the power was back on, there was a thud that Holden could feel through his feet. A large section of the elevator bulkhead slid open. The backup elevator slowly moved out into the shaft on hydraulic arms, then locked into place on the wall-mounted tracks. Lights flashed on the elevator's control panel as its systems cycled through warm-up. Then a light on the panel flashed red three times and the elevator launched down the tracks at high speed.

"Huh," Juarez said.

The impact when the hurtling backup elevator slammed into the stationary main elevator shook the bulkheads hard enough to make Holden's helmet ring like a bell.

"Well," Cass said.

Corin leaned out over the edge of the platform, looking down, and yelled, "Fuck you!" through the vacuum.

A few seconds later, Naomi's head popped back out of the open access panel. She looked up at them and waved. "Did that work?"

Holden found that he wasn't too drained to feel relief. "I think so."

"The armor is pretty tough," Juarez said. "It might be okay. But at that speed, whatever's inside it is probably a liquid now."

Naomi walked across the elevator bulkhead and then stepped over and down onto their platform. "I'm not good with guns," she said in an almost apologetic voice.

"No," Juarez said, waving his hands in a gesture of surrender. "You just keep doing your thing. Warn me if I'm in the way."

"Doesn't solve our door problem," Naomi added, still with a tone of apology.

Because he couldn't kiss her in an environment suit, Holden put an arm around her shoulder and hugged her to his side. "I'm happy with you solving the 'about to be ripped to pieces' problem."

Corin, who'd turned to look at the airlock when Naomi mentioned it, said, "Open sesame," and the outer airlock door slid open.

"Holy shit," Holden said. "Did you just magic that door open?"

"The green cycle light was blinking," Corin replied.

"Did you do that?" Holden said, turning to Naomi.

"Nope."

"Then we should be careful." Holden handed his rifle and his remaining magazines to Juarez, then drew his sidearm. "Juarez, when the inner door opens, you have the point."

Cass nodded, and Naomi punched the cycle button. The outer door closed, and for two tense minutes the air pressure equalized. Everyone other than Naomi was pointing a gun at the inner door when it finally opened.

There was nothing on the other side but a short corridor that ended at another elevator, and a second hallway going left at the midway point.

"That's the one that leads to the bridge," Corin said. "Five meters long, a meter and a half or so wide. There's a hatch, but it only closes and locks in the event of emergency decomp. Or if someone in the security station hits the override."

"Then that's our first target," Holden said. "Cass, when we go in you break right and control the security station. Juarez, you go left and try to draw any return fire away from Cass. Corin and I will go right up the gut and try to get our hands on Ashford. If we put a gun to him, I think this ends immediately. Naomi, you stay here but be ready to come running when we call. Taking control of the ship will be your bit."

"Pretty shitty plan, El Tee," Juarez said with a grin.

"You have a better one?"

"Nope, so let's get it done." Juarez pulled the rifle to his shoulder and moved off down the corridor at a quick magnetic boot shuffle. Cass followed close behind, her hand on his back. Holden took third, with Corin bringing up the rear. Naomi waited by the elevator doors, clutching her tool case nervously.

When they reached the junction, Juarez signaled the stop, then leaned around the corner. He pulled back and said, "Looks clear to the bridge entry point. When we go, go fast. Stop for nothing. Maximum aggression wins the day here."

After a round of assents from everyone, he counted down from three, yelled, "Go go go," darted around the corner, and was immediately shot.

It was so unexpected, Cass actually took a step back into Holden. Juarez screamed in pain and launched himself back into their hallway. Bullets slammed into the bulkheads and deck around him. After the long silence of vacuum in the elevator shaft, the sound of gunfire and bullet impacts was disorienting. Deafening.

Cass and Holden grabbed Juarez by his arms and pulled him around the corner out of the gunfire. With Cass covering the intersection, Holden checked Juarez over for injuries. He had gunshot wounds in his hip, upper arm, and foot. None looked instantly lethal, but together they'd bleed him out in short order. Holden pulled him back down the corridor to the airlock. He pointed at the emergency locker until Naomi followed his gesture and nodded.

"Do what you can," he said, and moved back down the hallway to Cass.

When he put his hand on her back to let her know he was there, she said, "Based on volume of fire, I'd guess ten to twelve shooters. Mostly light assault rifles and sidearms. One shotgun. That corridor is a kill box. No way through that."

"Fuck!" Holden yelled in frustration. The universe kept waiting until he was thoroughly beaten, then tossing him a nibble of hope only to yank it away again.

"New plan?" Corin asked.

"Shoot back, I guess," he said, then leaned partway around the corner and fired off three quick shots. He ducked back in time to avoid a fusillade that tore up the bulkhead behind him. When the shooting slowed, Cass launched herself across the opening to the other side. A risky move, but she made it without taking a hit, and started leaning out to lay down fire with her assault rifle. When they drove her back with return fire, Corin leaned around Holden and fired off a few shots.

Before she could pull back out of the line of fire, a round went through the arm of her environment suit, blowing white padding and black sealing gel into the air.

"Not hit, not hit," she yelled, and Cass leaned out to fire again to keep the defenders off balance.

Holden looked back down the corridor, and Naomi was stripping Juarez out of his suit, spraying bandages on his open wounds as she went.

Another wave of fire drove Cass and Corin into cover. When it let up for a second, Holden leaned out and fired a few more shots.

It was what people like them did, even when there was no chance.

Chapter Fifty-One: Clarissa

What the hell did you do?" Ashford shouted. His face was thick and purple. The rage pulled his lips back like a dog baring his teeth. Clarissa knew she should feel fear. Should feel something. Instead, she shrugged the way she had when she was fourteen, and said it again.

"I opened the doors."

A man appeared in the hallway for a fraction of a second, and Ashford's men opened fire, driving him back.

"I've got five in the corridor," one of Ashford's people said. He was looking at the security camera feed. "Three women, two men. One of them's Corin. I think Jim Holden's one of them."

Ashford shook his head in disgust.

"Why the fuck did you let them in here?" he said. His tone dripped acid.

"I didn't kill them," Clarissa said. "So you don't get to."

"She was in distress," Cortez said, moving himself between her and Ashford. Shielding her with his body. "She misunderstood something I said. It wasn't an act of malice, Captain. The girl only—"

"Someone shoot her," Ashford said.

"No!" Cortez cried out. He sounded like someone was about to shoot him.

The guard nearest them turned. The barrel of his gun seemed suddenly enormous, but when the sound of gunfire came, it wasn't from him. A shape—maybe a woman, maybe a man—flickered at the edge of the corridor to the bridge, and the staccato sound of gunfire filled the room. Clarissa, forgotten, pushed herself back through the doorway into the security office. Cortez followed her, his hands up around his ears to block the noise or a bullet or both. He put his hand on her shoulder as if to comfort her, but it only pushed her a little lower to the floor, him a little nearer the ceiling.

"Oh," Cortez murmured, "I wish you hadn't done that. I wish you hadn't done that."

Anna was still speaking on the security station monitor. Radio Free Slow Zone, soldiering on. There was a fresh crackle of gunfire from the bridge. Ashford shouted, "Take them out! Take them all out!" But as far as she could tell, the guards hadn't rushed the corridor. They didn't need to. Sooner or later, Holden and Naomi and whoever they had with them would run out of bullets, and then they'd die. Or Ashford and all his men would, and then Holden would kill them. Either way, she didn't see how it looked good for her. And that was fine. That was what she'd come here for.

Except.

"You heard what she said? What Anna said?"

"Anna Volovodov is seriously mistaken about what is happening here," Cortez said. "It was a mistake letting her into the project in the first place. I knew I should have asked for Muhammed al Mubi instead."

"Did you hear what she *said*?"

"What are you talking about, child?"

"She said if we attack the Ring, it'll take action against the people on the other side. Against everyone."

"She can't know that," Cortez said. "It's just the sort of thing the enemy would say to trick us."

"It wasn't her," Clarissa said. "Holden told her."

"The same James Holden who started a war by 'telling' people things?"

Clarissa nodded. He'd started at least one war. He'd destroyed Protogen, and by doing so set up the dominoes that would eventually topple Mao-Kwik and her father. He'd done all of that.

But.

"He didn't lie. All those other things he did. He never lied once."

Cortez opened his mouth to reply, his face already in a sneer. Before he could, the gunfire boomed again. She could feel Cortez flinch from it. The air was filling with the smell of spent gunpowder, and the air recyclers were moving into high-particulate mode. She could hear the difference in the fans. Probably no one else on the bridge would have any idea what that meant. It would just be a slightly higher whirring to them. If it was anything.

Cortez ran his fingers through his hair.

"Stay out the way," he said. "When it's over, when he's done this, I can speak with Ashford. Explain that you didn't mean to undermine him. It was a mistake. He'll forgive you."

Clarissa bowed her head. Her mind was a mass of confusion, and the hunger and gunfire weren't doing anything to help. Jim Holden was out there in the corridor. The man she'd come so far to disgrace and destroy, and now she didn't want him dead. Her father was back on Earth and she was about to save him and everyone else or possibly destroy them all. She'd killed Ren, and there was nothing she could ever do that would make that right. Not even die for him.

She had been so certain. She'd given so much of herself. She'd given everything, and in the end all she'd felt was empty. And soiled. The money and the time and all of the people she could have been if she hadn't been worshiping at the altar of her family name had already been sacrificed. Now she had offered her life, except that after speaking to Anna, she wasn't sure that wouldn't be an empty sacrifice too.

Her confusion and despair were like a buzzing in her ears and the voice that rose out of it was peculiarly her own: contempt and rage and the one certainty she could hold to.

"Who is *Ashford* to forgive me for anything?" she said.

Cortez blinked at her, as if seeing her for the first time.

"For that matter," she said, "who the hell are *you*?"

She turned and kicked gently for the doorframe, leaving Cortez behind. Ashford and his men were all armed, all waiting for the next round of gunfire. Ashford, stretched out behind his control panel, pistol before him, slammed his palm against the controls.

"Ruiz!" he shouted. His voice was hoarse. How many hours had they been waiting for this apocalypse to come? She could hear the strain in him. "Are we ready to fire? Tell me we're ready to fire!"

The woman's voice came, shrill with fear.

"Ready, sir. The grid is back online. The diagnostics are all green. It should work. Please don't kill me. *Please.*"

This was it, then. And with an almost physical click, she knew how to fix it, if there was time.

She put her tongue to the roof of her mouth and pressed, swirling in two gentle counterclockwise circles. The extra glands in her body leapt into life as if they'd been waiting for her, and the world went white for a moment. She thought that she might have cried out in the first rush, but when she was back to herself—to better than herself—no one had reacted to her. They were all pointing their guns at the corridor. All drawn to the threat of James Holden the way she had been herself. All except Ashford. He was letting go of his weapon, leaving the pistol to hang in the air while he keyed in the firing instructions. That was how long she had. It wasn't enough. Even high as a kite on battle drugs, she couldn't do what needed to be done before Ashford fired the laser.

So he became step one.

She pulled both feet up to the doorframe and pushed out into the open air of the bridge. The air seemed viscous and thick, like water without the buoyancy. A woman ducked out of cover, firing toward Ashford, and Ashford's people returned fire, muzzles blooming flame that faded away to smoke and then bloomed again. She couldn't see the bullets, but the paths they made through the air persisted for a fraction of a second. Tunnels of nothing in nothing. She tucked her knees into her chest. She had almost reached Ashford. His finger was moving down, ready to touch the control screen, ready, perhaps, to fire the comm laser. She kicked out as hard as she could.

The sensation of her muscles straining, ligaments and tendons pushed past their maximum working specifications, was a bright pain, but not entirely without joy. Her timing was only a little off. She didn't hit Ashford in the center of his body, but his shoulder and head. She felt the impact through her whole body, felt her jaw clicking shut from the blow. He slid back through the air away from the control panel, his eyes growing wider. Two of the guards began to swing toward her, but she bent her body against the base of the crash couch and then unfolded, moving away. The guns flashed, one then another, then two together, like watching lightning in a thunderstorm. Bullets flew, and she spun through the air, pulling her arms tight against her to make her spin faster. Rifling herself.

One of the women in the corridor leaned in, spraying gunfire through the room. A bullet caught one of the guards, and Clarissa watched as she moved toward the farthest wall. It was like seeing frames from an old movie. The woman in the corridor, the muzzle of her weapon alive with fire, then Clarissa turned. The guard, unmoved, but blood already splashing out from his neck, the little wave radiating through his skin out from the impact like the ripple of a stone dropped in a pond, then she turned. The guard falling back, blood blooming out of him like a rose blossom. The same would happen to her, she knew. The drugs flowing through her blood, lighting her brain like a seizure, couldn't change the abilities of her flesh. She couldn't dodge a bullet if one found her. So instead she hoped that none would and did what needed to be done.

The access panel was open, the guts of the ship exposed. She grabbed the edge of the panel gently, slowing herself. Blood welled up from her palm where the metal cut into her. She didn't feel it as pain. Just a kind of warmth. A message from her body that she could ignore. The brownout buffer sat behind an array control board. She slid her hand down to it, her fingers caressing the pale formed ceramic. The fault indicator glowed green. She took a breath, gripped the buffer, pushed it down, turned and then pulled. The unit came loose in her hand.

A gun went off. A scar appeared on the wall before her, bits of metal spinning out from it. They were shooting at her. Or near her. It didn't matter. She flipped the unit end for end and reseated it. The buffer's indicator blinked red for a moment, then green. Just the way Ren had showed her. *Terrible design*, she thought with a grin and held down the buffer's reset. Two more guns fired, the sound pushing against her eardrums like a blow. Time stuttered. She didn't know how long she'd been holding the reset, if she'd slipped it off and back on. She thought it should have gone by now, but time was so unreliable. The world stuttered again. She was crashing.

The buffer's readout went red. Clarissa smiled and relaxed. She saw the cascading failure as if she were the ship itself. One bad readout causing the next causing the next, the levels of failure rapid and incremental. The nervous system of the *Behemoth* sensing a danger it couldn't define. Doing what it could to be safe, or at least to be sure it didn't get worse.

Failing closed.

She turned. Ashford stood on his couch, holding the restraint straps in one hand and pressing his feet into the gel. His mouth was a square gape of rage. Two of his people had shifted to face her as well, their guns trained on her, their faces almost blank.

Behind them all, far across the bridge, Cortez was framed by the security office doorway. His face was a mask of distress and surprise. He wasn't, she thought, a man who dealt well with the unexpected. Must be hard for him. She hadn't noticed before how much he looked like her own father. Something about the shape of their jaws, maybe. Or in their eyes.

The lights flickered. She felt her body starting to shudder. It was over. For her, for all of them. The first twitch of the collapse pulled at her back like a cramp. A rising nausea came to her. She didn't care.

I did it, Ren, she thought. *You showed me how, and I did it. I think I just saved everyone.* We *did.*

Ashford caught his pistol out of the air and swung toward her. She heard his screaming like it was meat ripping. Behind him, Cortez was shouting, launching himself through the space. There was a contact taser in the old man's hand, and the grief on the old man's face was gratifying. It was good to know that on some level, he cared what happened to her. The lights flared once and went out as Ashford brought the barrel to bear on her. The emergency lighting didn't kick in.

Everything was darkness, and then, for a moment, light.

And then darkness.

Chapter Fifty-Two: Holden

Holden ejected his spent magazine and reached for a new one. His fingers hit only an empty space where he expected it to be. He hadn't been managing his ammo well. He'd wanted to keep at least one magazine in reserve. Corin was firing around him with her rifle. She had spare pistol ammo on her belt. Without asking, he started pulling magazines off her belt and putting them in his. She fired off a few more shots and waited for him to finish. It was that sort of fight.

Cass was leaning around the corner firing. Answering bullets hit everyplace on her side of the corridor except where she was. Holden was about to shout at her to get back into cover when the lights went out.

It wasn't just the lights. So many things about his physical situation changed all at once that his hindbrain couldn't keep up. It told him to be nauseated just in case he'd been poisoned. It was working with fifty-million-year-old response algorithms.

Holden collapsed to his knees with the nausea, the sudden appearance of gravity being one of the many changes. His knees banged against the floor because he was no longer wearing a heavy environment suit. Which also meant he could smell the air. It had a vaguely swampy, sulfurous odor. His inner ear didn't report any Coriolis, so they weren't spinning. There were no engine sounds, so the *Behemoth* wasn't under thrust.

Holden fumbled at the ground around him. It felt like dirt. Damp soil, small rocks. Something that felt like ground-cover plants.

"Oh, hey, sorry," a voice said. Miller's. The light level came up with no visible source. Holden was kneeling naked on a wide plain of something that looked like a mix of moss and grass. It was as dark as a moonlit night, but no moons or stars shone overhead. In the distance, something like a forest was visible. Beyond that, mountains. Miller stood a few meters away, looking up at the sky, still wearing his old gray suit and goofy hat. His hands were in his pockets, his jacket rumpling around them.

"Where?" Holden started.

"This planet was in the catalog. Most Earth-like one I could find. Thought it'd be calming."

"Am I here?"

Miller laughed. Something in the timbre of his voice had changed since the last time Holden had spoken to him. He sounded serene, whole. Vast. "Kid, *I'm* not even here. But we needed a place to talk, and this seemed nicer than a white void. I've got processing power to spare now."

Holden stood up, embarrassed to be naked even in a simulation, but without any way of changing it. But if this *was* a simulation, then that brought up other issues.

"Am I still in a gunfight?"

Miller turned, not quite facing him. "Hmmm?"

"I was in a gunfight before you grabbed me. If this is just a sim running in my brain, then does that mean I'm still in that gunfight? Am I floating in the air with my eyes rolled back or something?"

Miller looked chagrined.

"Maybe."

"Maybe?"

"Maybe. Look. Don't worry about it. This won't take long."

Holden walked over to stand next to him, to look him in the eyes. Miller gave him his sad basset hound smile. His eyes glowed a bright electric blue.

"We did it, though? We got under the power threshold?"

"Did. And I talked the station into thinking you were essentially dirt and rocks."

"Does that mean we saved the Earth?"

"Well," Miller replied with a small Belter shrug of the hands. "We *also* saved the Earth. Never was the big plan, but it's a nice bonus."

"Good that you care."

"Oh," Miller said with that same vaguely frightening laugh. "I really don't. I mean, I remember being human. The simulation is good. But I remember caring without really caring, if you know what I mean."

"Okay."

"Oh, hey, look at this," Miller said, pointing at the black sky. Instantly the sky was filled with glowing blue Rings. The thousand-plus gates of the slow zone, orbiting around them like Alex's dandelion seeds, seen from the center of the flower. "Shazam!" Miller said. As one, the gates shifted in color and became mirrors reflecting thousands of other solar systems. Holden could actually see the alien stars, and the worlds whirring in orbit around them. He assumed that meant Miller was taking a little artistic license with his simulation.

There was a croaking sound at his feet, and Holden looked down to see something that looked like a long-limbed frog, with grayish skin and no visible eyes. Its mouth was full of sharp-looking little teeth, and Holden became very aware of his bare toes just a few dozen centimeters from it. Without looking down, Miller kicked the frog thing away with his shoe. It blurred away across the field on its too-long limbs.

"The gates are all open out there?"

Miller gave him a quizzical look.

"You know," Holden continued. "In reality?"

"What's reality?" Miller said, looking back up at the swirling gates and the night sky.

"The place where I live?"

"Yeah, fine. The gates are all open."

"And are there invading fleets of monsters pouring through to kill us all?"

"Not yet," Miller said. "Which is kind of interesting in its own way."

"I was joking."

"I wasn't," Miller said. "It was a calculated risk. But it looks clear for now."

"We can go through those gates, though. We can go there."

"Can," Miller said. "And knowing you, you will."

For a moment, Holden forgot about Ashford, the *Behemoth*, the deaths and the violence and the thousand other things that had distracted him from where they really were. What they were really doing.

What it all meant.

He would live to see humanity's spread to the stars. He and Naomi, their children, their children's children. Thousands of worlds, no procreation restrictions. A new golden age for the species. And the *Nauvoo* had made it happen, in a way. Fred could tell the Mormons. Maybe they'd stop suing him now.

"Wow," he said.

"Yeah, well let's not get too happy," Miller said. "I keep warning you. Doors and corners, kid. That's where they get you. Humans are too fucking stupid to listen. Well, you'll learn your lessons soon enough, and it's not my job to nursemaid the species through the next steps."

Holden scuffed at the ground cover with his toe. When it was scraped, a clear fluid that smelled like honey seeped out. This world was in the station's catalog, Miller had said. *I could live here someday.* The thought was astounding.

The sky shifted, and now all the ships that had been trapped around the station were visible. They drifted slowly away from each other. "You let them go?"

"I didn't. Station's off lockdown," Miller said. "And I've killed the security system permanently. No need for it. Just an accident waiting to happen when one of you monkeys sticks a finger where it doesn't belong. Is this Ashford cocksucker really thinking he can hurt the gates?"

"And there are worlds like this on the other side of all those gates?"

"Some of them, maybe. Who knows?" Miller turned to face Holden again, his blue eyes eerie and full of secrets. "Someone fought a war here, kid. One that spanned this galaxy and maybe more. My team lost, and they're all gone now. A couple billion years gone. Who knows what's waiting on the other side of those doors?"

"We'll find out, I guess," Holden replied, putting on a bold front but frightened in spite of himself.

"Doors and corners," Miller said again. Something in his voice told Holden it was the last warning.

They looked up at the sky, watching the ships slowly drift away from them. Holden waited to see the first missiles fly, but it didn't happen. Everyone was playing nice. Maybe what had happened on the *Behemoth* had changed people. Maybe they'd take that change back to where they came from, infect others with it. It was a lot to hope for, but Holden was an unapologetic optimist. Give people the information they need. Trust them to do the right thing. He didn't know any other way to play it.

Or maybe the ships moving was just Miller playing with his simulation, and humanity hadn't learned a thing.

"So," Holden said after a few minutes of quiet sky watching. "Thanks for the visit. I guess I'd better be getting back to my gunfight."

"Not done with you," Miller said. The tone was light, but the words were ominous.

"Okay."

"I wasn't built to fix shit humanity broke," Miller said. "I didn't come here to open gates for you and get the lockdown to let you go. That's incidental. The thing that made me just builds roads. And now it's using me to find out what happened to the galaxy-spanning civilization that wanted the road."

"Why does that matter now, if they're all gone?"

"It doesn't," Miller said with a weary shrug. "Not a bit. If you set the nav computer on the *Roci* to take you somewhere, and then fall over dead a second later, can the *Roci* decide it doesn't matter anymore and just not go?"

"No," Holden said, understanding and finding a sadness for this Miller construct he wouldn't have guessed was possible.

"We were supposed to connect with the network. We're just trying to do that, doesn't matter that the network's gone. What came up off of Venus is dumb, kid. Just knows how to do one thing. It doesn't know how to investigate. But I do. And it had me. So I'm going to investigate even though none of the answers will mean fuck-all to the universe at large."

"I understand," Holden said. "Good luck, Miller, I—"

"I said I'm not done with you."

Holden took a step back, suddenly very frightened about where this might be going. "What does that mean?"

"It means, kid, that I'll need a ride."

Holden was floating in free fall in an environment suit in absolute darkness. People were yelling. There was the sound of a gunshot, then silence, then an electric pop and a groan.

"Stop!" someone yelled. Holden couldn't place the voice. "Everyone stop shooting!"

Because someone was saying it with authority in their voice, people did. Holden fumbled with the controls on his wrist, and his suit's light came on. The rest of his team quickly followed his example. Corin and Cass were still unhurt. Holden wondered how long in actual time his jaunt into the simulation had taken.

"My name is Hector Cortez," the stop-firing voice said. "What's happening out there? Does anyone know?"

"It's over," Holden yelled back, then let his body relax into a dead man's float in the corridor. He was so tired that it was a struggle to not just go to sleep right where he was. "It's all over. You can turn everything back on."

Lights started coming on in the bridge as people took out hand terminals or emergency flashlights.

"Call Ruiz," Cortez said. "Have her send a team up here to fix whatever Clarissa did. We need to get the ship's power back. People will be panicking in the habitation drum right now. And get a medical team up here."

Holden wondered where Ashford was and why this Cortez guy was in charge. But he was saying all the right things, so Holden let it go. He pushed his way into the bridge, ready to help where he could, but keeping his hand near his pistol. Cass and Naomi traded places with Juarez, so Naomi could help with the repairs.

Clarissa, formerly Melba, was floating near an open access panel, blood seeping out of a gunshot wound. Cortez was pressing an emergency bandage to it. Ashford floated across the room, his mouth slack and his muscles twitching. Holden wondered if the captain was dead and then didn't care.

"Naomi. Call down to the radio offices. See if they've got working comms. Find out about Anna and Monica and Amos. Try to raise the *Roci* next. I really really want to get the hell out of here."

She nodded and started trying to make connections.

"Will she live?" Holden asked the white-haired man tending to her.

"I think so," he replied. "She did this," he added, waving a hand around to indicate the lack of lights and power.

"Huh," Holden said. "I guess I'm glad we didn't space her."

Chapter Fifty-Three: Clarissa

She woke up in stages, aware of the discomfort before she knew what hurt. Aware that something was wrong before she could even begin to put together some kind of story, some frame that gave the loose, rattling toolbox of sensations any kind of meaning. Even when the most abstract parts of herself returned—her name, where she was—Clarissa was mostly aware that she was compromised. That something was wrong with her.

The room was dirty, the air a few degrees too hot. She lay in the thin, sweat-stinking bed, an IV drip hanging above her. The significance of that took a long time to come to her. The bag hung there. She wasn't floating. There was gravity. She didn't know if it was spin or thrust, or even the calm pull of mass against mass that being on a planet brought. She didn't have the context to know. Only that it was nice to have weight again. It meant that something had gone right. Something was working.

When she closed her eyes, she dreamed that she had killed Ren, that she'd hidden him inside her own body and so she had to keep anyone from taking an imaging scan for fear they'd find him in her. It was a pleasure to wake up and remember that everyone already knew.

Sometimes Tilly came, sat by her bed. She looked like she'd been crying. Clarissa wanted to ask what was wrong, but she didn't have the strength. Sometimes Anna was there. The doctor who checked on her was a beautiful old woman with eyes that had seen everything. Cortez never came. Sleeping and waking lost their edges. Healing and being ill too. It was difficult if not impossible to draw a line between them.

She woke once to voices, to the hated voice, to Holden. He was standing at the foot of her bed, his arms crossed on his chest. Naomi was next to him, and then the others. The pale one who looked like a truck driver, the brown one who looked like a schoolteacher. Amos and Alex. The crew of the *Rocinante*. The people she hadn't managed to kill. She was glad to see them.

"There is absolutely no way," Holden said.

"Look at her," Anna said. Clarissa craned her neck to see the woman standing behind her. The priest looked older. Worn out. Or maybe distilled. Cooked down to something like her essence. She was beautiful too. Beautiful and terrible and uncompromising in her compassion. It was in her face. It made her hard to look at. "She'll be killed."

Alex, the schoolteacher, raised his hand.

"You mean she'll be tried in a court of law, with a lawyer, for killin' a bunch of folks that we all pretty much know she killed."

I did, Clarissa thought. *It's true*. Above her, Anna pressed her hands together.

"I mean that's what I want to happen," Anna said. "A trial. Lawyers. Justice. But I need someone to get her safely from here to the courts on Luna. With the evacuation starting, you have the only independent ship in the slow zone. You are the only crew that I trust to get her out safely."

Naomi looked over at Holden. Clarissa couldn't read the woman's expression.

"I'm not taking her on my ship," Holden said. "She tried to kill us. She almost *did* kill Naomi."

"She also saved you both," Anna said. "And everybody else."

"I'm not sure being a decent human that one time means I owe her something," Holden said.

"I'm not saying it does," Anna said. "But if we don't treat her with the same sense of justice that we'd ask for ourselves—"

"Look, Red," Amos said. "Everybody in this room except maybe you and the captain has a flexible sense of morality. None of us got clean hands. That's not the point."

"This is a tactical thing," Alex agreed.

"It is?" Holden said.

"It is," Naomi said. "Pretend that she's not a danger in and of herself. Taking her on board, even just to transport her to a safe place, puts us at risk from three different legal systems, and our situation is already... 'tenuous' is a nice word."

Clarissa reached up, took Anna's shirt between her fingers, tugging like a child at her mother.

"It's okay," she croaked. "I understand. It's all right."

"How much?" Anna asked. And then, off their blank looks, "If it's just risk versus return, how much would it take to be worth it to you?"

"More than you have," Holden said, but there was an apology in his tone. He didn't want to disappoint Anna and he didn't want to do what she said. No way for him to win.

"What if I bought the *Rocinante*?" Anna said.

"It's not for sale," Holden said.

"Not from you. I know about your legal troubles. What if I bought the *Rocinante* from Mars. Gave you the rights to it, free and clear."

"You're going to buy a warship?" Alex said. "Do churches get to do that?"

"Sure," Holden said, "do that, and I'll smuggle her out."

Anna held up a finger, then pulled her hand terminal out of her pocket. Clarissa could see her hands were trembling. She tapped at the screen, and a few seconds later a familiar voice came from the box.

"Annie," Tilly Fagan said. "Where are you? I'm having cocktails with half a dozen very important people and they're boring me to tears. The least you can do is come up and let them fawn over you for a while."

"Tilly," Anna said. "You remember that really expensive favor you owe me? I know what it is."

"I'm all ears," Tilly said.

"I need you to buy the *Rocinante* from Mars and give it to Captain Holden." Tilly was silent. Clarissa could practically see the woman's eyebrows rising. "It's the only way to take care of Clarissa."

Tilly's exhalation could have been a sigh or laughter.

"Sure, what the hell. I'll tell Robert to do it. He will. It'll be less than I'd get in a divorce. Anything else, dear? Shall I change the Earth's orbit for you while I'm at it?"

"No," Anna said. "That's plenty."

"You're damn right it is. Get up here soon. Really, everyone's swooning over you, and it'll be much more amusing for me to watch them try to squeeze up next to you in person."

"I will," Anna said. She put her hand terminal back in her pocket and took Clarissa's hand in her own. Her fingers were warm. "Well?"

Holden's face had gone pale. He looked from Clarissa to Anna and back and blew out a long breath.

"Um," he said. "Wow. Okay. We may not be going home right away, though. Is that cool?"

Clarissa held out her hand, astounded by its weight. It took them all a moment to understand what she was doing. Then Holden—the man she'd moved heaven and earth to humiliate and murder—took her hand.

"Pleased to meet you," she croaked.

They installed a medical restraint cuff to her ankle set to sedate her on a signal from any of the crew, or if it detected any of the products of her artificial glands, or if she left the crew decks of the ship. It was three kilos of formed yellow plastic that clung to her leg like a barnacle. The transfer came during the memorial service. Captain Michio Pa, her face still bandaged from the fighting, spoke in glowing terms about Carlos Baca and Samantha Rosenberg and a dozen other names and commended their ashes to the void. Then each of the commanders of the other ships in the flotilla took their turns, standing before the cameras on the decks of their own ships, speaking a few words, moving on. No one mentioned Ashford, locked away and sedated. No one mentioned her.

It was the last ceremony before the exodus. Before the return. Clarissa watched it on her hand terminal when she wasn't looking at the screen that showed the shuttle's exterior view. The alien station was inert now. It didn't glow, didn't react, didn't read to the sensors as anything more than a huge slug of mixed metals and carbonate structures floating in a starless void.

"They're not all going back, you know," Alex said. "The Martian team is plannin' to stay here, run surveys on all the gates. See what's on the other side."

"I didn't know that," Clarissa said.

"Yeah. This right now," the pilot said, gesturing toward the screen where a UN captain was speaking earnestly into the camera, her eyes hard as marbles and her jaw set against the sorrow of listing the names of the dead. "This is the still point. Before, this was all fear. After this, it'll all be greed. But this..." He sighed. "Well, it's a nice moment, anyway."

"It is," Clarissa said.

"So, just to check, are you still plannin' to kill the captain? Because, you know, if you are it seems like you at least owe us a warning."

"I'm not," she said.

"And if you were?"

"I'd still say I wasn't. But I'm not."

"Fair enough."

"Okay, Alex," Holden said from the back. "Are we there yet?"

"Just about to knock," Alex said. He tapped on the control panel, and on the screen the *Rocinante*'s exterior lights came on. The ship glowed gold and silver in the blackness, like seeing a whole city from above. "Okay, folks. We're home."

Clarissa's bunk was larger than her quarters in the *Cerisier*, smaller than the one from the *Prince*. She wasn't sharing it with anyone, though. It was hers as much as anything was.

All she had for clothing was a jumpsuit with the name *Tachi* imprinted in the weave. All her toiletries were the standard ship issue. Nothing was hers. Nothing was her. She kept to her room, going out to the galley and the head when she needed to. It wasn't fear, exactly, so much as the sense of wanting to stay out of the way. It wasn't her ship, it was theirs. She wasn't one of them, and she didn't deserve to be. She was a paid passenger, and not a fare they'd even wanted. The awareness of that weighed on her.

Over time, the bunk began to feel more like her cell on the *Behemoth* than anything else. That was enough to drive her out a little. Only a little, though. She'd seen the galley before in simulations, when she'd been planning how to destroy it, where to place her override. It looked different in person. Not smaller or larger, exactly, but different. The crew moved through the space going from one place to another, passing through in the way she couldn't. They ate their meals and had their meetings, ignoring her like she was a ghost. Like she'd already lost her place in the world.

"Well," Holden said, his voice grim, "we have a major problem. We're out of coffee."

"We still got beer," Amos said.

"Yes," Holden said. "But beer is not coffee. I've put in a request with the *Behemoth*, but I haven't heard back, and I can't see going into the vast and unknown void without coffee."

Alex looked over at Clarissa and grinned.

"The captain doesn't like the fake coffee the *Roci* makes," he said. "Gives him gas."

Clarissa didn't answer. She wasn't sure she was supposed to.

"It does not," Holden said. "That was one time."

"More than once, Cap'n," Amos said. "And no offense, but it does smell like a squirrel crawled up your ass and died there."

"Okay," Holden said, "you've got no room to complain. As I recall, I was the one who cleaned your bunk after that experiment with vodka goulash."

"He's got a point," Alex said. "That was damn nasty."

"I just about shat out my intestinal lining, that's true," Amos said, his expression philosophical, "but I'd still put that against the captain's coffee farts."

Alex made a fake gagging noise, and Amos buzzed his lips against his palm, making a rude sound. Naomi looked from one to the other like she didn't know whether to laugh or smack them.

"I don't get gas," Holden said. "I just like the taste of real coffee better."

Naomi put her hand on Clarissa's forearm and leaned close. Her smile was gentle and unexpected.

"Have I mentioned how nice it is to have another woman on the ship?" she asked.

It was a joke. Clarissa understood that. But it was a joke that included her, and her tears surprised her.

"I appreciate your saying all that about Bull," a man's voice said. Clarissa, moving through the ship, didn't recognize it. An unfamiliar voice in a spaceship caught the attention like a strange sound in her bedroom. She paused. "He was a friend for a lot of years, and...and I'll miss him."

She shifted, angled back toward the other crew cabins. Holden's door was open, and he sat in his crash couch, looking up at his monitor. Instead of the tactical display of the ships, the stations, the Rings, a man's face dominated the screen. She recognized Fred Johnson, traitor to Earth and head of the Outer Planets Alliance. The Butcher of Anderson Station. He looked old, his hair almost all gone to white, and his eyes the yellow color of old ivory.

"I asked a lot from him," the recording went on. "He gave a lot back to me. It…it got me thinking. I have a bad habit, Captain, of asking more than people can give sometimes. Of demanding more than I can fairly expect. I'm wondering if I might have done something like that with you."

"Gee, you think?" Holden said to the screen, though as far as she could see he wasn't recording.

"If I did, I apologize. Just between us. One commander to another. I regret some of the decisions I've made. I figure you can relate to that in your own way.

"I've decided to keep the *Behemoth* in place. We're sending out soil and supplies to start farming on the drum. It does mean the OPA's military fleet just lost its big kahuna. But it looks like we've got a thousand planets opening up for exploration, and having the only gas station on the turnpike is too sweet a position to walk away from. If you and your crew want to help out with the effort, escort some ships from Ganymede out to the Ring, there might be a few contracts in it for you. So that's the official part. Talk about it with the others, and let me know what decisions you come to."

Fred Johnson nodded once to the camera, and the screen fell to the blue emptiness and split circle of the OPA's default. Holden looked over his shoulder. She saw him see her.

"Hey," she said.

"Hey."

They were silent for a moment. She didn't know what to say. She wanted to apologize too, to walk down the path Fred Johnson had just showed her, but she couldn't quite.

She waited to see whether Holden would reach out to her. When he didn't she pulled herself back down toward the crew quarters. Her stomach felt tight and uncomfortable.

They weren't friends. They wouldn't be, because some things couldn't be made right.

She'd have to be okay with that.

Amos smelled of solvent and sweat. Of all the crew, he was the one most like the people she knew. Soladad and Stanni. And Ren. He came into the galley with a welding rig on, the mask pushed up over his forehead. He smiled when he saw her.

"You did a number on the place," Amos said. She knew that if the occasion arose, he would be perfectly willing to kill her. But until that moment, he'd be jovial and casual. That counted for more than she'd expected. "I mean, you had a salvage mech. Those are pretty much built for peeling steel."

"I didn't at the end," she said. "It ran out of power. The locker in the airlock was all me."

"Really?" he said

"Yeah."

"Well," he said, pulling a bulb of the fake coffee from the machine and drifting over to the table. "That was pretty impressive, then."

She imagined him working, the mask down to hide his face, the sparks, the flickering of his great hunched shadow. Hephaestus, the smith of the Gods, laboring in his underworld. It was the kind of association Clarissa Mao would make. Melba Koh would only have thought about the temperature of the arc, the composition of the plates he was fusing together. She could have both of those thoughts, but neither were really hers.

She was on the float now. Later, when the ship was under way and thrust gravity pinned her to the deck, she'd still be on the float. Her world had been constructed around stories about who she was. Jules-Pierre's daughter, Julie Mao's sister, the crew lead on the *Cerisier*, instrument of her father's vengeance. Now she was no one. She was a piece of baggage on her old enemy's ship going from one prison to another, and she didn't even resent it. The last time she'd felt this nameless, she'd probably been in an amniotic sac.

"What was the problem?"

"Hmm?"

"You said I really did a number on something. What's the problem?"

"Deck hatch between the machine shop and here gets stuck. Ever since you crumpled it up. Binds about half open."

"Did you check the retracting arm?"

Amos turned to her, frowning. She shrugged.

"Sometimes these door actuators put on an uneven load when they start to burn out. We probably swapped out four or five of them on the trip out here."

"Yeah?"

"Just a thought," she said. And then a moment later, "When we get back to Luna, they're going to kill me, aren't they?"

"If you're lucky, yeah. UN still has the death penalty on the books, but they don't use it much. I figure you'll be living in a tiny cell for the rest of your life. If it was me, I'd prefer a bullet."

"How long until we get there?"

"About five weeks."

They were silent for a moment.

"I'll miss this place," she said.

Amos shrugged.

"Actuator arm, huh? Worth checking. You want to help me take a look?"

"I can't," she said, gesturing at the clamp on her leg.

"Shit, I can reprogram that. Least enough to get you down to the machine shop. We'll grab you a tool belt, Peaches. Let's crack that thing open."

An hour later, she was running her hand over the frame of the door, looking for the telltale scrape of binding sites. *This was me*, she thought. *I broke it.*

"What'cha think, Peaches?" Amos asked from behind her.

"Feels good to fix something," she said.

Epilogue: Anna

Anna sat in the observation lounge of the *Thomas Prince* and looked out at the stars.

The lounge was a dome-shaped room where every flat surface was a high-definition screen displaying a 360-degree view of the outside. To Anna, sitting in it felt like flying through space on a park bench. It had become her favorite place on the ship, with the stars burning in their bright steady colors, no atmosphere to make them twinkle. They felt so close now. Like she could reach out and touch them.

Her hand terminal beeped at her to remind her that she was in the middle of recording a video message. She deleted the time she'd spent looking at the stars and started the recording again.

"So, that letter from the conference bishop turned out to be a request for a formal meeting. Apparently some people have complained about me. Probably Ashford. Neck deep in his own legal problems with the OPA and still finding time to make trouble for everyone else. But don't worry about it. They'll ask, I'll answer, I've got pretty good reasons for everything I did. I have lots of offers of support from people I worked with on the fleet. I probably won't need them. Speaking of which, I've invited my friend Tilly Fagan to come visit us in Moscow. She's abrasive and cranky and has no social filters at all. You'll love her. She can't wait to meet Nami."

Anna paused to attach a picture she'd taken of Tilly to the message. Tilly was looking at the camera through narrowed eyes, just seconds from telling Anna to "get that fucking thing out of my face." She held a cigarette in one hand; her other was pointing accusingly. It was not the nicest picture of Tilly she had, but it was the most accurate.

"Speaking of Nami, thank you so much for the videos you sent. I can't believe how enormous she's gotten. And crawling around in full gravity like she was born to it. She'll be walking again in no time. Thank you for taking her home. Sometimes I wish I'd just gone with you. Most of the time, actually. But then I think about all the things I did inside the Ring, and I wonder if any of it would have turned out as well if I hadn't helped. It seems arrogant to think that way, but I also believe that God nudges people toward the places they need to be. Maybe I was needed. I still plan on being very contrite when I get back. You, the bishop, Nami, my family, I have a lot of apologizing to do."

As clear as if she'd been in the room, Anna heard Nono say, *You never ask for permission, you just apologize later.* She laughed until her eyes watered. She wiped them and said to the camera, "You're still here, Nono. Still in my head. But I'd trade anything to have you hold me. The *Prince* will take another month to get back. It's an eternity. I love you."

She picked up the pillow she'd brought with her and held it tight to her chest. "This is you and Nami. This is both of you. I love you both so much."

She killed the recording and sent it off, winging ahead of the

Prince to Nono at the speed of light. Still too slow. She wiped away the tears that had accumulated at the corners of her eyes.

Outside, a flare of white light lit the sky, a line of fire a few centimeters long. Another ship in the flotilla, returning home. One of the *Prince*'s escort ships, to be so close. Finally going back, but without many of the sailors she'd brought to the Ring. Families would be waiting for her to bring their loved ones home, only to receive flags, posthumous medals, letters of sympathy. It wouldn't be enough to fill the holes those lost people left in their lives. It was never enough.

But the ships from Earth, Mars, and the various stations of the outer planets *were* going home. And they were bringing news of the greatest opportunity humanity had ever been offered. In the midst of all the sadness and tragedy, hope.

Would Nami spend her life at one of those points of light she could see right now? It was possible. Her baby had been born into a world where her parents couldn't afford to give her a sibling, where she'd have to work two years just to prove to the government she was worth receiving an education. Where resources were rapidly diminishing, and the battle to keep the waste from piling up used more and more of what was left.

But she'd grow up in a world without limits. Where a short trip took you to one of the stars, and the bounty of worlds circling them. Where what job you did or what education you pursued or how many children you had was your choice, not a government mandate.

It was dizzying to think of.

Someone walked into the lounge behind her, their footsteps clicking. "Tilly, I just sent—" Anna started, but stopped when she turned around and saw Hector Cortez.

"Doctor Volovodov," he said, his tone a mild apology.

"Doctor Cortez," she replied. The renewed formality between them seemed silly to Anna, but Hector insisted on it. "Please, sit." She patted the bench next to her.

"I hope I'm not disturbing you," he said, sitting and staring out at the stars. Not looking at her. He didn't look her in the eye anymore.

"Not at all. Just recording a message home and enjoying the view."

They sat silently for a few moments, watching the stars.

"Esteban lost," Cortez said, as if they'd been talking about that all along.

"I don't— Oh, the secretary-general. He did?"

"Nancy Gao is the new SG. You can see Chrisjen Avasarala's fingerprints all over that one."

"Who?"

Cortez laughed. It sounded genuine, a nice loud rumble coming up from his belly. "Oh, she would love to hear you say that."

"Who is she?"

"She's the politician no one has ever voted for, that runs the UN like her own personal fiefdom and keeps her name out of the press. The fact that she controls your home government and you've never heard of her means she's very, very good."

"Oh," Anna said. She was not a political creature. She felt that politics was the second most evil thing humanity had ever invented, just after lutefisk.

There was another long silence. Anna wondered where Tilly was, and if she'd show up and rescue her from the awkwardness of the moment.

"You backed the right horse," Cortez finally said. "I picked a bad one. I hope you won't hold that against me. I've grown to respect you a great deal, in spite of our differences. I wouldn't like it if you hated me."

"I don't, Hector," Anna said, taking his hand in both of hers and squeezing it. "Not at all. It was terrible, what we all went through. We all made bad decisions because we were afraid. But you're a good man. I believe that."

Cortez gave her a grateful smile and patted her hand. Anna nodded her head at the star field splashed across the wall.

"So many stars," she said. "Some of them might be ours someday."

"I wonder," Hector replied, his voice low and sad. "I wonder if we should have them. God gave man the Earth. He never promised him the stars. I wonder if He'll follow us out there."

Anna squeezed his hand again, and then let it go. "The God I believe in is bigger than all of this. Nothing we ever learn can be an attack on Him as long as that's true."

Cortez gave a noncommittal grunt.

"I want her to have them," she said, pointing at the spray of light around her. "My little Nami, I want her to have all of that someday."

"Whatever she finds out there," Cortez said, "just remember it's the future *you* chose for her."

His words were full of hope and threat.

Like the stars.

Acknowledgments

Once again, we have more people to thank than space to thank them in. This book and this series wouldn't exist without the hard work of our agent Danny Baror and the support and dedication of Tom Bouman, Susan Barnes, Ellen Wright, Tim Holman, Alex Lencicki, and the whole crew at Orbit. Thanks to the amazing Daniel Dociu for giving us the art that people can't help but pick up off the shelf, and to Kirk Benshoff for creating that wonderful design that ties the whole series together. We'll never be able to adequately express our gratitude to Carrie, Kat, and Jayné for feedback and support, and to Scarlet for allowing us to distract her with *Mythbusters* while we work. Thanks to the *Mythbusters* crew for being so entertaining to scientifically curious six-year-olds. Thanks again to the whole Sake River gang. Much of the cool in the book belongs to them. As always, the errors and infelicities and egregious fudging was all us.

About the author

James S. A. Corey is the pen name of fantasy author Daniel Abraham and Ty Franck, George R. R. Martin's assistant. They both live in Albuquerque, New Mexico. Find out more about this series at www.the-expanse.com